Praise for Christophe

Before and Afterlives

ঞ

"Barzak's sympathy and humor, his awareness, his easeful vernacular storytelling, are extraordinary."
—JONATHAN LETHEM, author of *Motherless Brooklyn*

"Throughout this collection, Barzak effectively writes people contending with their fears and doubts but most especially he writes about loneliness, and it is this writerly radar for alienation that perhaps makes him so perceptive when it comes to his teen characters. ...Barzak makes it all seem so easy, these gentle glimpses into his characters' lives, and even though these lives might include mermaids or ghostly parents or talking fireflies, the extraordinary aspects are not what make his tales so magical. It's the way he sees plain ordinary people that gives his stories such power; the way he sees us and yet loves us anyway. Bravo."
—*Bookslut*

"Masterfully crafted...each one packs a punch."
—*Publishers Weekly*

"[Barzak] treads a delicate line between the paranormal ghost romance and the more nuanced literary tradition that includes Shirley Jackson, Peter S. Beagle, and Robert Nathan... *Before and Afterlives* is a fine introduction to the short fiction of an author who, in a fairly short career, has established himself as one of the most distinctive voices and lyrically effective prose stylists in recent fantasy."
—GARY K. WOLFE for *Locus Magazine*

Before and Afterlives

Also by Christopher Barzak

One for Sorrow 2007
The Love We Share Without Knowing 2008
Interfictions 2 (co-edited with Delia Sherman) 2009
Birds and Birthdays 2012

Before and

Stories

Afterlives

Christopher Barzak

Lethe Press
Maple Shade, New Jersey

Published in 2013 by Lethe Press, Inc.
118 Heritage Avenue, Maple Shade, NJ 08052 USA
lethepressbooks.com / lethepress@aol.com
ISBN: 978-1-59021-369-8 / 1-59021-369-6
e-ISBN: 978-1-59021-285-1 / 1-59021-285-1

Set in Warnock, Sedona, and Snell Roundhand.
Interior design: Alex Jeffers.
Cover art and design: Steven Andrew.

LIBRARY OF CONGRESS CATALOGING-IN-PUBLICATION DATA
Barzak, Christopher.
  [Short stories. Selections]
  Before and afterlives : stories / Christopher Barzak.
      pages cm
  ISBN 978-1-59021-369-8 (pbk. : alk. paper) -- ISBN 978-1-59021-285-1
(e-book)
  1. Ghost stories, American. 2. Paranormal fiction. 3. Magic--Fiction. I.
Title.
  PS3602.A844B44 2013
  813'.6--dc23
                    2012038020

Before and

For Tony Romandetti
Before, After, Always

Christopher Barzak   **Before and**

Contents

Christopher Barzak

Before and

What We Know About the Lost Families of —— House

But is the house truly haunted?

OF COURSE THE HOUSE IS haunted. If a door is closed on the first floor, another on the second floor will squeal open out of contrariness. If wine is spilled on the living room carpet and scrubbed at furiously and quickly so that a stain does not set, another stain, possibly darker, will appear somewhere else in the house. A favorite room in which malevolence quietly happens is the bathroom. Many speculate as to why this room draws so much attention. One might think that in a bathroom things would be more carefree, in a room where the most private of acts are committed, that any damned inhabitants could let down their hair or allow a tired sigh to pass through their doomed lips.

Perhaps this is exactly what they are doing in the bathroom, and we have misunderstood them. They turn on the shower and write names in the steam gathered on the mirror (never their own names, of course). They tip perfume bottles over, squeeze the last of the toothpaste out of its tube, they leave curls of red hair in the sink. And no one who lives in the house—no one living, that is—has red hair, or even auburn. What's worse is when they leave the toilet seat up. They'll flush the toilet over and over, entranced by the sound of the water being sucked out. This is what these restless inhabitants are endlessly committing: private acts.

The latest victims

ALWAYS THERE HAS BEEN A family subject to the house's torture. For sixty-five years it was the Addlesons. Before that it was owned by the Oliver family. No one in town can remember who lived in the house before the Olivers, not even our oldest residents. We have stories, of course, re-countings of the family who built — House, but their name has been lost to history. If anyone is curious, of course there is the library with town records ready to be opened. No one has opened those records in over fifty years, though. Oral history, gossip, is best for this sort of situation.

Rose Addleson believed the house was trying to communicate some-thing. She told her husband women know houses better than men, and this is one thing Rose said that we agree with. There is, after all, what is called "Women's Intuition". What exactly the house was saying eluded Rose, though, as it eludes the rest of us. Where Rose wanted to figure out its motivations, the rest of us would rather have seen it burn to cinders.

"All these years?" Jonas told her. It was not Rose Addleson who grew up in the house after all, who experienced the years of closeness to these events, these fits that her husband had suffered since childhood. "If it's trying to communicate," he said, "it has a sad idea of conversation."

Rose and Jonas have no children. Well, to be precise, no living children. Once there had been a beautiful little girl, with cheeks that blushed a red to match her mother's, but she did not take to this world. She died when she was only a year old. On a cold winter's night she stopped breathing, when the house was frosted with ice. It wasn't until the next morning that they found her, already off and soaring to the afterlife. "A hole in her heart," the doctor said, pinching his forefinger and thumb together. "A tiny hole." They had never known it was there.

After their first few months of marriage, Rose and Jonas had become a bit reclusive. Out of shame? Out of guilt? Fear? Delusion? No one is able to supply a satisfactory reason for their self-imposed isolation. After all, we don't live in that house. If walls could talk, though, and some believe the walls of — House do talk, perhaps we'd understand that Jonas and Rose Addleson have good reason not to go out or talk to neighbors. Why even Rose's mother Mary Kay Billings didn't hear from her daughter but when she called on the phone herself, or showed up on the front porch of — House, which was something she rarely did. "That house gives me the creeps," she told us. "All those stories, I believe them. Why Rose ever wanted to marry into that family is beyond me."

Mary Kay has told us this in her own home, in her own kitchen. She sat on a chair by the telephone, and we sat across the table from her. She said, "Just you see," and dialed her daughter's number. A few rings later and they were talking. "Yes, well, I understand, Rose. Yes, you're busy, of course. Well, I wanted to ask how you and Jonas are getting along. Good. Mm-hmm. Good. All right, then. I'll talk to you later. Bye now."

She put the phone down on the cradle and smirked. "As predicted," she told us. "Rose has no time to talk. 'The house, Mother, I'm so busy. Can you call back later?' Of course I'll call back later, but it'll be the same conversation, let me tell you. I know my daughter, and Rose can't be pried away from that house."

We all feel a bit sad for Mary Kay Billings. She did not gain a son through marriage, but lost a daughter. This is not the way it's supposed to happen. Marriage should bring people together. We all believe this to be true.

Rose heard a voice calling

SHE HAS HEARD VOICES SINCE she was a little girl. Rose Addleson, formerly Rose Billings, was always a dear girl in our hearts, but touched with something otherworldly. If her mother doesn't understand her daughter's gravitation to — House, the rest of us see it all too clear. Our Rose was the first child to speak in tongues at church. Once, Jesus spoke through her. The voice that came through her mouth never named itself, but it did sound an awful lot like Jesus. It was definitely a male voice, and he kept saying how much he loved us and how we needed to love each other better. It was Jesus all over, and from our own sweet Rose.

We do not understand why, at the age of twelve, she stopped attending services.

But Rose also heard voices other than the Lord's. Several of us have overheard her speaking to nothing, or nothing any of us could see. She's hung her head, chin tucked into breastbone, at the grocery store, near the ketchup and mustard and pickles, murmuring, "Yes. Of course. Yes, I understand. Please don't be angry."

Rose heard the voices in — House, too. This is why she married Jonas: The house called for her to come to it.

It was winter when it happened. Rose was eighteen then, just half a year out of high school. She worked in Hettie's Flower Shop. She could arrange flowers better than anyone in town. We all always requested Rose to make our bouquets instead of Hettie, but Hettie never minded. She owned the place, after all.

On her way home from work one evening, Rose's car stalled a half mile from — House. She walked there to get out of the cold, and to call her mother. At the front door she rapped the lion-headed knocker three times. Then the door opened and wind rushed past her like a sigh. She smelled dust and medicine and old people. Something musty and sweet and earthy. Jonas stood in front of her, a frown on his sad young face. He was already an orphan at the age of thirty. "Yes?" he asked in a tone of voice that implied that he couldn't possibly be interested in any reason why our Rose was appearing before him. "Can I help you?"

Rose was about to ask if she could use his phone when she heard a voice calling from inside. "Rose," it whispered. Its voice rustled like leaves in a breeze. "Please help us," the house pleaded. And then she thought she heard it say, "Need, need, need." Or perhaps it had said something altogether different. The walls swelled behind Jonas's shoulder, inhaling, exhaling, and the sound of a heartbeat suddenly could be heard.

"Are you all right?" Jonas asked, cocking his head to the side. "Rose Billings, right? I haven't seen you since you were a little girl."

"Yes," said Rose, but she didn't know if she was saying yes to his question or to the house's question. She shook her head, winced, then looked up at Jonas again. Light cocooned his body, silvery and stringy as webs.

"Come in," he offered, moving aside for her to enter, and Rose went in, looking around for the source of the voice as she cautiously moved forward.

Mary Kay Billings didn't hear from her daughter for three days after that. That night she called the police and spoke to Sheriff Dawson. He'd found Rose's car stuck in the snow. They called all over town, to Hettie's Flower Shop, to the pharmacy, because Rose was supposed to pick up cold medicine for Mary Kay. Eventually Rose called Mary Kay and said, "I'm okay. I'm not coming home. Pack my things and send them to me."

"Where are you?" Mary Kay demanded.

"Have someone bring my things to — House," Rose said.

"— House?!" shouted Mary Kay Billings.

"I'm a married woman now, Mother," Rose explained, and that was the beginning of the end of her.

Jonas in his cups

HE HAD MANY OF THEM. Cups, that is. Most of them filled with tea and whiskey. Jonas Addleson had been a drinker since the age of eight, as if he were the son of a famous movie star. They are all a sad lot, the children of movie stars and rich folk. Too often they grow up unhappy, unaccustomed to living in a world in which money and fame fade as fast as they are heaped upon them.

Jonas Addleson was not famous beyond our town, but his family left him wealthy. His father's father had made money during the Second

World War in buttons. He had a button factory over in Pittsburgh, Pennsylvania. It's long gone by now, of course. They made all sorts of buttons, the women who worked in the factory while the men were in Europe. Throughout — House you will still find a great many buttons. In the attic, on the pantry shelves, in the old playroom for the children, littered in out-of-the-way places: under beds, in the basement, among the ashes in the fireplace (unburned, as if fire cannot touch them).

This is not to say Rose Addleson was a bad housekeeper. In fact, Rose Addleson should have got an award for keeping house. She rarely found time for anything but cleaning and keeping. It was the house that did this eternal parlor trick. No matter how many buttons Rose removed, they returned in a matter of weeks.

When Rose first arrived at — House, Jonas showed her into the living room, then disappeared into the kitchen to make tea. The living room was filled with Victorian furniture with carved armrests, covered in glossy chintz. A large mirror hung on the wall over the fireplace, framed in gold leaf. The fire in the fireplace crackled, filling the room with warmth. On the mantel over the fire, what appeared to be coins sat in neat stacks, row upon row of them. Rose went to them immediately, wondering what they were. They were the first buttons she'd find. When Jonas returned, carrying a silver tray with the tea service on it, he said, "Good, get warm. It's awfully cold outside."

He handed Rose a cup of tea and she sipped it. It was whiskey-laced and her skin began to flush, but she thanked him for his hospitality and sipped at the tea until the room felt a little more like home.

"The least I can do," he said, shrugging. Then remembering what she'd come for, he said, "The phone. One second. I'll bring it to you."

He turned the corner, but as soon as he was gone, the house had her ear again. "Another soul gone to ruin," it sighed with the weight of worry behind it. "Unless you do something."

"But what can I do?" said Rose. "It's nothing to do with me. Is it?"

The house shivered. The stacks of buttons on the mantel toppled, the piles scattering, a few falling into the fire below. "You have what every home needs," said the house.

"I'm no one," said Rose. "Really."

"I wouldn't say that," Jonas said in the frame of the doorway. He had a portable phone in his hand, held out for her to take. "I mean, we're all someone. A son or daughter, a wife or husband, a parent. Maybe you're right, though," he said a moment later. "Maybe we're all no one in the end."

Afterlives   *What We Know About the Lost Families of — House*

"What do you mean?" asked Rose. She put the teacup down to take the phone.

"I'm thinking of my family. All gone now. So I guess by my own definition that makes me nothing."

Rose batted her eyelashes instead of replying. Then she put the phone down on the mantel next to the toppled towers of buttons. She sat down in one of the chintz armchairs and said, "Tell me more."

The first lost family

BEFORE THE ADDLESONS, THE OLIVER family lived in — House. Before the Olivers lived in — House, the family that built the house lived there. But the name of that family has been lost to the dark of history. What we know about that family is that they were from the moors of Yorkshire. That they had come with money to build the house. That the house was one of the first built in this part of Ohio. That our town hadn't even been a town at that point. We shall call them the Blanks, as we do in town, for the sake of easiness in conversation.

The Blanks lived in — House for ten years before it took them. One by one the Blanks died or disappeared, which is the same thing as dying if you think about it, for as long as no one you love can see or hear you, you might as well be a ghost.

The Blanks consisted of Mr. Blank, Mrs. Blank, and their two children, twin boys with ruddy cheeks and dark eyes. The photos we have of them are black and white, but you can tell from the pictures that their eyes are dark and that their cheeks are ruddy by the serious looks on their faces. No smiles, no hint of happiness. They stand outside the front porch of — House, all together, the parents behind the boys, their arms straight at their sides, wearing dark suits.

The father, we know, was a farmer. The land he farmed has changed hands over the years, but it was once the Blank family apple orchard. Full of pinkish-white blossoms in the spring, full of shiny fat globes of fruit in autumn. It was a sight, let us tell you. It was a beautiful sight.

The first to disappear was one of the boys. Let's call him Ephraim. He was the ruddier of the two, and often on his own, even though his parents taught him not to wander. One afternoon he and his brother went into the orchard to pick apples, but in the evening, when the sun began to set, only Ephraim's brother returned to — House, tears streaming down his face.

"What's the matter?" asked Mrs. Blank. "Where's your brother?"

But the boy (William, we'll call him) could only shake his head. Finally he was able to choke out this one sentence:

"The orchard took him."

Then he burst into tears again.

This, of course, sparked a heated debate around town. We who live here have always been a spirited group of people, ready to speculate about anything that might affect us. The general consensus arrived at was that the boy had been taken. Someone must have stolen him, like the fairies did in the old country. A stranger passing through, who perhaps saw the perfect round ruddy globes of Ephraim's cheeks and mistook them for apples. It is a dark thought, this possible narrative. But dark thoughts move through this world whether we like it or not.

Mr. Blank died soon after his son's disappearance. He died, as they say, of a broken heart. Mrs. Blank found him in the kitchen, slumped over in his chair, his head on the table. She thought he was crying again, as he often did after his son's vanishing. But when she stroked his hair and then his cheek, she found him cold, his heart stopped up with sorrow.

They buried Mr. Blank in the orchard, beneath the tree where William last saw Ephraim. And only two years later Mrs. Blank woke one night to find that she was alone in — House. She searched every room twice, but could not find her last remaining family member, her young William.

It was the middle of winter, in the middle of the night, and when Mrs. Blank stepped outside onto the front porch, she found a set of footprints in the snow that gathered on the steps. She followed them down and out the front gate, around back of the house and through the orchard, where they came to a stop at her husband's grave, at the tree where William last saw Ephraim. Mrs. Blank called out for William, but she only got her own voice back. That and the screech of an owl crossing the face of the moon above her.

Suddenly a rumbling came from inside — House. Mrs. Blank looked at the dark backside of the house, at its gingerbread eaves and its square roof, at its dark windows tinseled with starlight, and shuddered at the thought of going back in without anyone waiting for her, without her son beside her. The house rumbled again, though, louder this time, and she went without further hesitation. Some women marry a house, and this bond neither man nor God can break.

William's body was never found, poor child. Like his brother, he vanished into nothing.

But we say the orchard took him.

Everything you need

IT TOOK ROSE AND JONAS Addleson less than a year to make their doomed daughter. Full of passion for one another, they made love as often as possible, trying to bring her into this world, trying to make life worth living. This was perhaps not what Rose felt she needed, but Jonas wanted children, and what Jonas wanted, Rose wanted too. That's the thing about marriage. Suddenly you want together. You no longer live in desire alone.

What Rose wanted was for Jonas to be happy. She would marry him within a day of meeting him on the front porch of — House during that fateful blizzard, knowing this was to be her home. The house had told her. And soon it had become apparent that Jonas didn't want her to leave either. When she went to call her mother, he had interrupted to say, "Would you like more tea?" When she had moved toward the front door, he'd stood up and said, "Would you like to lie down and rest?"

They shared more whiskey-laced tea, and before the night was over Rose found herself sitting next to Jonas on the sofa, holding his hand while he told her his family's story. How his grandfather had owned the button factory during the war, how his father had killed himself twenty years ago by placing a gun in his mouth and pulling the trigger. How his mother had worked her fingers to the bones taking care of everything: the house, Jonas, his father's bloody mess in the bathroom. "I found him," Jonas said. "I was ten. On the mirror in the bathroom. There was blood all over it. He was lying in a pool of blood on the floor. Mama scrubbed and scrubbed, but it wouldn't come out. Not until she asked the house to help her."

He paused, gulping the story down again. Rose watched the way the column of his throat moved as he swallowed. She wanted to kiss him right there, where the Adam's apple wriggled under the skin. Instead she asked, "What did the house do?"

He looked at her, his eyes full of fear. "She told me to leave the bathroom. So I left, closing the door behind me. I waited outside with my ear against the door, but I couldn't hear anything. After a few minutes passed, I knocked. Then a few more minutes passed. I was going to knock again, but before my knuckles hit, the door swung open, and there was Mama, wringing her hands in a damp rag. There was no blood on her, not even a speck. And when I looked behind her, the carpet was as clean as ever, as if no dead body had bled to death on it."

"The house loves you," Rose said.

Jonas looked at her curiously. "What do you mean?"

"It loves you. Can't you feel it? It's trying to tell you something."

Before and

"If it's trying to communicate," said Jonas. "It has a sad idea of conversation."

She held those words close as soon as he said them, she pressed them to her chest like a bouquet. This was why she had been brought there, she realized. In this instant she knew she would translate for him. She would bring back all that he had lost. She'd be his mother, she'd be his father, she'd be his wife, she'd have his children. A family, she thought. With a family, he'd never be alone.

She leaned into him, still holding his hand, and kissed him. Without moving back again, she looked up through her eyelashes and said, "I have everything you need."

A child bride

THE STORY OF THE OLIVER family is a sad one. No, let us revise that statement: It is not sad, it is disturbing. We don't like to talk about it around town anymore. We are all glad that — House took the Olivers, for they were a bad lot, given to drinking and gambling, as well as other unwholesome activities.

The Olivers moved into — House just past the turn of the century, after Mrs. Blank died. Our grandparents found Mrs. Blank several weeks after her passing, due to the smell that began to spread down Buckeye Street. It was one of the only times they'd gone into — House, and we remember it to this day: the hardwood floors, the chintz furniture, the stone mantel over the fireplace, the stairs that creaked as you stepped up into the long hallway of the second floor, the second floor itself, the lower half of the hall paneled with dark polished wood. And the bathroom, of course, where all of the trouble eventually focused its energy. It was a fine house, really, with wide windows to let light in, though even with all of that light the house held too many shadows. Our grandparents did not linger. They took Mrs. Blank's body to the county coroner's office in Warren and left the doctor to his business.

Less than a year later, Mr. and Mrs. Oliver came to — House with their three children: two boys, one nearly a man, one still muddling through adolescence, and a girl about to bloom. At first our grandparents didn't think badly of the Olivers. It takes a certain amount of time for a family to reveal its secrets. So for the first few years, they welcomed the Olivers as if they had always lived among us. The Olivers began attending the Methodist church on Fisher-Corinth Road. They sent the younger boy and girl to school with our children. The oldest boy worked as a field hand for local farmers. His work was good, according to Miles Willard, who paid the boy to clear fields those first few years, before all of the madness started to happen again.

How to tell about that madness. We suppose we might as well start with Mrs. Oliver's murder. Two of our children found her body in Sugar Creek. They had been going to catch crayfish, but found Mrs. Oliver's body tangled in the roots of a tree that grew out of the bank instead. She had been severely beaten: her face covered in yellow-brown bruises, her skull cracked on the crown. Dark fingerprints lingered on her throat, so we knew she had been strangled. We still do not forgive her murderer for leaving her for us to find. People should take care of their own dirty work.

Since they had a murder on their hands, our grandparents called on the sheriff to deal with the matter. They marched him right up to — House expecting trouble. But what they found was the front door open and, inside, Mr. Oliver's body spread out on the dining room table, a butcher knife sticking straight up out of his throat. The sheriff asked several of our grandfathers to back him up as he explored the rest of the house. And so they did, each carrying a rifle as they descended into the basement, then up to the second floor, finding nothing suspicious. It was when the ceiling creaked above them that they knew someone was in the attic.

They tried opening the attic door, but it had been locked from the inside. So they busted it down, only to be met with a blast from the rifle of Mr. and Mrs. Oliver's middle child. The sheriff took the shot in his shoulder. He fell backwards, but our grandfathers caught him. Several of them returned fire at the boy. He left a smear of blood on the wall as he collapsed against it.

They found the oldest boy and the girl bound and gagged in the attic. They were wild with fear. Their brother had killed their parents and was going to kill them, too, they said. This was all over a fight the boy had had with his parents about a debt he'd run up over in Meadville, playing poker with older men who knew how to outwit him. He wanted his parents to pay his debt, but they wouldn't. They insisted he work to pay for his debts and his drinking, just as their oldest son did. After he killed his parents, he wasn't sure what to do with his siblings, so he tied them up, and there they still were, alive and none the worse for wear, and we thought perhaps we had salvaged something from that house's evil.

The oldest Oliver boy and his sister stayed on at — House. They had nowhere to go, no people. Just each other. The boy kept working as a field hand, the girl continued her schooling. But soon her attendance dropped off, and then she stopped coming altogether. She started working to help with the keeping of the house and the paying of her brother's debts. She

Christopher Barzak

Before and

took in wash if people gave it to her. She mended stockings. She raised chickens, selling eggs at the general store to make extra money. Anything she could get her hands on she turned into cash.

At first she seemed awfully hard-working and a good girl, but we soon discovered not only was she working to pay off her brother's debts, but to prepare for the child growing inside her. When her stomach began to round out the fronts of her dresses, we knew what was going on up at — House. This was something our grandparents could not abide, so they stopped giving the girl work. They stopped buying her eggs, and the farmers released her brother from his duties. In no time at all, the brother and the child bride packed up their things and left. Without the aid of our grandparents, they could not live among us. This is the way all of the families that lived in — House should have been dealt with all these years maybe. Without mercy. But Lord knows we are a merciful lot.

Word came several months after the siblings left that they had been seen in Cleveland, living together, posing as a married couple.

The baby's room

HERE IT IS, IN THE same condition as when the baby was living. The crib with the mobile of brass stars still spinning in space above it, the rocking chair near the eastern window, where sunlight falls in the morning, the walls painted to look like the apple orchard in summer, the ceiling sky blue, as if the baby girl had lived outdoors forever, never inside the confines of — House.

We know the room is still like this because Mary Kay Billings has seen it. Twice since the baby died she has gone to visit her daughter, and both times the baby's room was as it was during her last visit. Two years after the child's death it begins to seem a bit odd, really. She suggested changing it into a sewing room maybe, but Rose shook her head. "No, Mother," she said. "That's not allowed to happen."

Mary Kay Billings has no patience with her daughter. We all understand this. If our daughters had married into a family that lived in — House without our permission, we'd have no patience either. Poor Mary Kay is one of the pillars of our community. She is one of our trustees, she sings in the church choir. At the elementary school, she volunteers her time three days a week, three hours each of those days, to aid in the tutoring of our children. Mary Kay Billings has raised her daughter, has lived through the death of her husband, God rest his soul (for he would roll in his grave to know what happened to his child), and yet Mary Kay still gives to others for the good of her community. This is the way a town works, not how Rose would have it. We all think Rose is a bit selfish, really, leaving her mother to struggle alone, leaving Hettie without any warning (we liked her flower arrangements better than Hettie's and better than the replacement girl's, so it's even more selfish of her to have done this). Leaving the community altogether, to go live in that place.

We must mention that not all of us think she is selfish, but only has the appearance of selfishness. Some of us (the minority) believe Rose is noble. A bit too noble, but noble nonetheless. Who else but a self-sacrificing person would take on — House and its curse? We say a crazy person, but some of us say Rose is doing us a favor. If it weren't Rose, who would the house have brought to its front door when it needed another soul to torment?

But the baby's room is a bit too much really. We asked Mary Kay Billings what the rest of the house was like and she said, "Buttons! Buttons everywhere, I tell you! I said to Rose, 'Rose! What's the matter with you? Why are all these buttons lying about?' and she says to me, 'Mother, I can't keep up with them. I try, but they keep coming.' And in the baby's room, too, I noticed. Right in the crib! I said to Rose, 'Rose! In the crib even?' and she says to me, can you believe this, she says to *me*, her own mother, 'Mother, I think it's best if you go.'"

"And Jonas?" we asked, leaning in closer. Mary Kay narrowed her eyes and sucked her teeth. "Drunk," she told us. "Drunk as usual."

Life during wartime

IN THE NINETEEN-FORTIES, MOST OF our men had been taken overseas to fight against the devil, and our women stayed behind, keeping things about town running smoothly. All over America, women came out of their houses and went into men's work places. We still argue about who was made for what sort of work, but in the end we know it's all a made up sort of decision. Nothing fell apart, nothing broke while the men were off fighting. In fact, things maybe went a bit smoother (this of course being an opinion of a certain sector of our population and must be qualified). In any case, the factories were full of women, and in Pittsburgh, just across the state border, James Addleson, the grandfather of our own Jonas, had his ladies making buttons for the uniforms of soldiers.

The Addlesons had bought — House several years before the war had broken out, but we rarely saw them. They were a Pennsylvania family and only spent part of their summers with us. Occasionally we'd see them in autumn for the apple festival. The Addlesons had money, and — House was one of their luxuries. They had passed through our town during their travels and Mrs. Addleson had seen the house and wanted it immediately. James Addleson didn't argue with her. Why on earth she would want to buy a house in the country, no matter how stately and beautiful, was beyond him. But he had gotten used to giving the woman what she wanted. It was easier. And it soothed any guilt he might have felt for other, less attractive activities in which he participated. Especially later, after the war started.

Now Mrs. Addleson was a beautiful woman. She had a smooth complexion, high cheekbones, and a smile that knocked men over like a high wind had hit them. She wore fire engine red lipstick, which we must say is a bit racy but something to look at. Occasionally she'd come to town without Mr. Addleson. She'd bring their children, a girl in her teens and the little boy who would later grow up to be Jonas Addleson's father. During the war, we started seeing her and the kids more often. We'd find her shopping in the grocery store, or coming to church on Sundays, sitting in the last pew as if she didn't want to intrude on our services. Eventually we got used to her being around, and some of the women even got to be something like friends with her.

Mr. Addleson often stayed in Pittsburgh to look after his factory. We felt bad for the Addlesons. Even though James Addleson didn't go to war since he had a business to manage, his family suffered like anyone's. Whenever we asked Mrs. Addleson how her husband faired, she'd say, "Buttons! Buttons everywhere!" and throw her hands in the air. She was a strange lady, now that we think about it. Never had a straight answer for anyone.

For a while we thought perhaps — House had settled into a restful sleep, or that even the spirit that inhabited the place had moved on to better climates. We hoped, we prayed, and during the war, it seemed our prayers had been answered. Finally a family lived in — House without murdering one another or disappearing altogether. We thought perhaps we'd been foolish all those years to think the house haunted. We shook our heads, laughing a little, thinking ourselves to be exactly what everyone who makes their homes in cities considers us: backwoods, superstitious, ignorant.

But then our peaceful period of welcome embarrassment broke. Like a cloud that's been gathering a storm, holding inside the rain and lightning and thunder until it bursts forth, flooding the lives of those who live below it, so — House released its evil upon our town once more.

This time, though, we realized its hand reached further than we had previously thought possible. This time we knew something was wrong when detectives from Pittsburgh began to appear on our doorsteps, asking questions about the Addlesons. How long had they been living in our town? How often did we see them? Did they go to church? Did they send their children to school with our children? What were they like? What did we know about their doings? In the end, we realized we knew little about the Addlesons. As we have said already, it takes time for families to reveal their secrets.

They found the first body in the basement, the second in the attic, the third buried in the orchard, and the fourth stuffed in a defunct well on the property. All women. All girls from Pittsburgh, the detectives told us. All pregnant with James Addleson's babies.

We were disgusted. Oh, but we were disgusted. Never had the house erupted with such evil before. Never! We thought the Oliver family massacre and the decline of its surviving children to be the worst, the worst possible manipulation the house could imagine. And here we were faced with something even more despicable. While Mrs. Addleson raised her children in the quiet of our country town, James Addleson had been manipulating his women workers into sleeping with him. At first we assumed the women were a bad sort, and possibly their lust had gotten them into this trouble (as any of the great sins will surely do) but then we heard the news that seven other girls in the button factory had come forward. He had threatened to take their jobs away from them, they said, if they wouldn't give him what he wanted. They had been lucky, they said. They hadn't gotten pregnant. "It could have been us," one of the girls said in an anonymous interview. "It could have been any one of us."

It took the police a week to find the bodies of all four girls. The one in the well was the hardest to locate. We all prayed for their poor families back in Pittsburgh, for their poor husbands at war, off fighting that devil while another devil pursued their wives at home.

We had a notion to burn down — House then, and were going to do that. We were gathering, the old and the young and the women left behind by their husbands. We were gathering to destroy the place when word came that Mrs. Addleson would not be leaving. She was going to stay and raise her children here among us. Her husband's factory would be closing; he'd be going to prison. She needed a place for her children. The children, we thought, oh what sacrifices we make for our children! This we understood all too well.

So we left the house alone, and her in it. And even after her daughter grew up to be a fine, respectable woman, graduating from our very own high school, and went off to college to marry a doctor, even after Mrs. Addleson died and left her son, the heir of James Addleson, alone in — House, we allowed him to live there without any interference as well.

He was smart enough not to court our daughters. He went to college like his sister and came back a married man, his wife already expecting. This was in the nineteen-seventies, mind you, and such things happened among our children, it seemed, without them thinking much about it. We said nothing. We scolded ourselves and told ourselves it was not our business, and to stop caring.

But if it is not the business of one's community, whose business is it?

If we'd have intervened, if we'd have tried to get the Addlesons some other living arrangement, perhaps poor Jonas would not have walked into the bathroom at the age of ten to find his father's dead body, the blood spilling out of his shattered skull.

Why did the son of James Addleson kill himself? You are probably wondering. The answer is simple. It was those girls his daddy murdered. We have seen and heard them ourselves on occasion, wandering through the orchards, climbing out of the well, beating on the windows of the cellar and attic. We have seen and heard them, and continued on our way, ignoring them.

James Addleson's son was not so lucky. He lived with them. He heard them day and night, talking about his father's evil. In the end, they convinced him to join them.

A visit

BUT NOT OUR OWN SWEET Rose! How could this have happened? We often wondered where we went wrong. Through all the years of that house's torments, never did our own children go near it. We taught them well, or so we thought. But that house would get what it wanted. Our own sweet Rose. How we have fretted these past three years she has been gone from us. How we pray for her and for Mary Kay Billings nightly. And how Mary Kay suffers. How she holds herself together, never mentioning her daughter unless we ask after her. Never wanting to burden us. And how we all have our crosses. Which is why we did what we have done.

We had let the Addleson family linger under the spell of the house's evil, and because of that Jonas's father took his own life, and Jonas himself became the wreck he is today. We thought we were doing best by them, leaving them to their own choices, trying not to interfere with the lives of others. But we saw how wrong we were when — House took our Rose, when it took our Rose's little girl. And then, recently, when Mary Kay Billings mentioned to one of us that Rose had been asking after her cousin, Marla Jean Simmons. "Could you send her on up here, Mother? I'm sort of lonesome. And I could use some help around the house."

It was then we decided to take action. Not one more of our children would we let that house ravage.

We approached Mary Kay Billings with our plans, and tears, buckets full of them, were shed that day. Poor Mary Kay, always trying to be the tough woman, the one who will not be disturbed, yet when we came to her and said, "We shall make that house a visit," she burst, she broke like a dam.

"Thank you," she told us. "Oh thank you, I can't do it alone any longer. Maybe with all of us there she'll let us talk some sense into her."

So we selected representatives. Mr. Adams, the town lawyer. He inspired fear in his opposition, so we chose him hoping the house would fear his authority. Mrs. Baker, the principal of our elementary school, who Rose once respected as a child. Pastor Merritt, since a man of God in cases such as this is necessary. Tom Morrissey, the undertaker, who has dealt with death long enough not to fear it. And Shell Richards, one of our school bus drivers, because she is simply a force to be reckoned with, and we all of us stay out of her way, especially when she's been drinking.

Together, led by Mary Kay Billings, we trudged up the road to — House on a cool spring evening when the buds were on the trees, the sap rising. At the gate, we hesitated for only a moment to look at each other and confirm our convictions by nodding. Then Mary Kay swung the gate open and up the path we went.

As soon as our feet touched those porch steps, though, we felt the life of whatever lived there coursing beneath us. We shuddered, but continued. Since it was not a social visit, we didn't bother knocking, just opened the door and went straight on in. "Rose!" we called loudly. "Rose!" And soon enough, she appeared on the landing above us, looking down at us with a peculiar glare, icy and distant.

"What are you all doing here?" she asked. Her voice sounded far away, as if she were speaking through her body, as if her body were this *thing* that came between her and the rest of the world. Her hand rested on the newel post of the landing, massaging it as she waited.

"We've come to help you, darling," Mary Kay said. We all thought it best that she spoke first.

"I don't need any help now," said Rose. "What help would I be needing, Mother? Why didn't you send Marla Jean like I asked?"

We immediately saw Mary Kay's resolve fading, so Mr. Adams spoke up. "Dear," he said. "Come down to us. We're taking you out of this place. We're taking you home this very instant."

Before and

Rose cocked her head to the side, though, and slowly shook it. "I don't think so," she told us. "I'm a grown woman. I can make my own decisions. And my home is here, thank you very much."

"Where's your husband?" asked Mrs. Baker. But Rose didn't answer. She only looked at Mrs. Baker suspiciously, as if a trap were being set.

"We're going to help him, too, dear," said Pastor Merritt. "But we need to get you both to safety. We must ask God to help us now."

"God?" said Rose, and we shivered. We'd never heard a word so full of goodness said in such a way that it sent chills up and down our spines. "God?" she said again, then started down the stairs toward us. "I haven't heard Him in a long time," said Rose. We nodded. We remembered. She hadn't come to church since she was twelve.

"He is always listening," said Pastor Merritt. "All you have to do is ask for His help, and He will provide."

"I don't talk," said Rose. "I'm the one who listens."

We didn't nod this time. We weren't sure what to make of what she was saying.

"Enough of this," said Shell Richards suddenly, and we all, even Rose, looked at her, puzzled by her outburst. "Enough dilly dallying," said Shell. She stepped right up to Rose, grabbed her arm and said, "You're coming with us, little girl."

Mary Kay ran up the stairs to gather a few things for her daughter while Rose fought to free herself from Shell's grip. "Stop struggling," Shell warned, but Rose struggled. She slipped, and as she fell buttons poured out of her sweater pockets, scattering across the floor.

Then a scream spilled down the staircase and we knew Mary Kay Billings was in trouble. We abandoned Rose on the floor and rushed up the stairs, one after the other, the steps creaking beneath us, until we came to the baby's room with the mural of the orchard painted on the walls and the sky on the ceiling. Mary Kay stood in the center of the room, near the crib, staring apparently at nothing. We followed her stare, and in the mural we saw the Blank boy, Ephraim, sitting in an apple tree, looking out at us. You could tell it was him by the dark eyes and the ruddy cheeks.

We took Mary Kay Billings by the arm and led her back down the stairs then, only to find that Rose had disappeared on us. "Who saw her last?" we asked each other, but no one had stayed with her. We had all gone running to Mary Kay when she called.

We searched the house from top to bottom, shouting for either of them to come to us. "Rose!" we called. "Jonas!" But all we found were buttons, and all we heard were the screams of dead mothers, and all we smelled was the house's evil circling us like a dark cloud.

 Afterlives

What We Know About the Lost Families of — House

We were too late. Our chance had come and we had failed her. The house had taken her and Jonas before we could free them, and so we left, defeated, not bothering to close the door behind us. Let the wind have it, we thought, let the rain flood it, let it all fall down in ruin. For that was the last family that — House would take, we decided at that very moment. Never again would we allow anyone to go near it.

If walls could talk

AND THEY DO TALK, IF you know how to listen. If you know how to pay attention to the way a roof sighs, or a window slides open with relief, or a step creaks its complaints out. If you know how to hear what those walls are saying, you will hear unbearable stories, stories you would never imagine possible, stories we would rather turn away from. But we cannot turn away, for they will only follow us. They will find us, one by one, alone and frightened, and tear us apart if we try to stop our ears up.

The Blank family is still with us. The Olivers too. And those poor dead girls from Pittsburgh still linger, howling through the night as we try to sleep. And Jonas's father, the gun cracking his life open like a pocket watch, to let all of the time spill out of him. And now Jonas, too. Wherever he is, we hope he's restful. And Rose. Poor Rose. We don't hear from Rose, though. She never talked to us. She only listened.

Before and

The Drowned Mermaid

ON THE MORNING AFTER THE storm the body of a drowned mermaid was washed ashore. She was curled in an almost S shape, her arms thrown over her head as if to block out the glare of the sun. Her skin was pale, rubbery and white. The kind of pale that comes from living either beneath the earth or beneath the sea. Her black hair was twisted with ropes of seaweed, and a bruise, golden brown and purple, stained the skin of her right cheek.

Helena found her. She had woken that morning from another dream of her daughter Jordan, from another night of terror and mystery in which she played the lead role. She'd been in a casino this time, after receiving instructions on how to win Jordan back: "Go to the roulette table, place your bet on black thirty-one, walk away from the wheel without collecting your winnings, and believe me," a disembodied voice told her, "you'll win. Walk toward the nearest restroom, but don't go in. A man in a dark suit will meet you by the door. Take his arm. He'll bring you to me."

She'd done as instructed, but as usual, never found her daughter. Never won her, never opened the locked safe without tripping the alarm. Or in another situation, she might be fooled into thinking Jordan was behind a certain door. But upon opening it, she would find nothing but a dark, empty room. As in the shell game, Helena could never pick the one under which the con man had hidden the ping-pong ball.

So she had come down to the beach after waking, leaving Paul asleep in bed. The sun had just risen, dappling the waves with light, and gulls screed in the air, circling and diving over the water.

From a distance the mermaid's body looked like driftwood, smooth and round, silhouetted by the morning light. It was only when Helena came closer that she noticed the scales glinting in the light; the thickly muscled tail; and after moving one of the mermaid's arms off of her face, the bulbous eyes, black and damp as olives.

She knelt beside the body and rested her ear against the chilled skin. A sluggish pulse still pumped through those emerald veins: a slow, locomotive beat. Unconscious then, Helena decided. She stood again, turning her head one way, then the other, scanning the beach to see if anyone else had ventured down this way yet. There was no one around at this hour. But that would change soon enough. It was the end of summer. Within an hour the beach would be strewn with bodies laid out for the sun to take. A ritual sacrifice.

Working quickly, she lifted the mermaid's arms and shoulders from underneath and started to drag her. She pulled her away from the hissing waves that collapsed under their own weight, turning to foam as they reached the shore. She dragged, then paused to catch her breath, then picked the mermaid up once more to go a little farther. And all the while the mermaid's head lolled on the stalk of her neck as if it had been broken.

It was a long, exhausting journey. But in this way, they reached home soon enough.

HOME WAS A HOUSE PERCHED forty feet above the beach on the edge of a cliff in southern California. Sleek and modern, it was filled with furniture that had been fashionable two decades before and had again come into style. There was a deck in back of the house, braced against the cliffside, and when high tide rolled in it would begin to resemble a pier, the pilings of the deck's foundation partly submerged in water. The side of the cliff was buried beneath a lumpy shell of boulders, an ad hoc seawall that served to deter any further erosion that might undermine the house's foundation. Helena and Paul had lived there for fifteen years, since he took the position teaching history at the university. Before the seawall was built, they had seen whole houses fold in on themselves.

The only problem to emerge since moving here, to a sleepy village by the sea, was that sometimes, often in the summer, homeless people or drifters would hole up beneath their deck. They'd stay for a day or a week,

Before and

making homes, fleeting as dreams, among the boulders. Then they'd vanish and never be seen again.

Helena and Paul never instinctively disliked or feared these people. But as Helena once articulated the problem, "It's that you can *hear* them down there, whispering, right below your feet." It would have been easy to have the drifters removed, but they never called the police. As Helena once pointed out to Paul, who stood with phone in hand, ready to dial 911, "What if it was Jordan down there? What if she just needed a place to stay the night?"

Paul had placed the phone back on its cradle, but not without saying, "If she needed a place to stay, why wouldn't she call? Why wouldn't she come home?"

In the past Helena would have supplied him with reasonable answers to these questions—it had once been a specialty of hers—but most questions that had anything to do with Jordan had become unreasonable. As well as inexplicable.

BY THE TIME HELENA REACHED the stairs leading up to the back deck, people had started to arrive. They came with surf boards lashed to the tops of their cars, or with children, lathered in sunblock, trudging wearily across the sand.

Helena climbed one step at a time, planting her feet securely before pulling the mermaid up to the next step. It took a long time. Sweat beaded on her forehead, then dribbled down into her eyes. She could hear her own breathing, sharp intakes of breath followed by exhausted sighs.

She wished she were younger, not slowed down by midlife. If I only had more energy, she thought several times a day, I could *do* more. As it was, she spent most of her days barely able to keep up with the house. Every time she turned around, there was a loose tile in the linoleum, or a burned-out bulb that needed to be replaced. Even caring for these small tasks drained her easily. She spent all of her energy in her dreams, overnight, looking for Jordan. By morning, she would wake exhausted, as though she hadn't slept.

Finally she reached the deck, forty steps high, where she sat down for a few minutes to catch her breath, arranging the mermaid's head on her lap. A few strands of hair trailed over the mermaid's face and Helena snatched at them, brushing them out of those dark, fishy eyes. And those eyes, a person could lose themselves in them, could dive down into their cold black waters and drown.

She slid the back door open, then pulled the mermaid into the house. Her tail bounced up and down as it rolled over the sliding door track.

Helena took her into the bathroom, heaved her tail up and over the lip of the tub, and followed with the upper half. The mermaid's skin squeaked against the porcelain. She ran cold water from the faucet until it splashed over the sides.

It was enough. She'd done enough. She leaned against the tub and sighed, satisfied.

Now for Paul. She would have to find a way to explain this to him as reasonably as she could. This was possible. This was reasonable. She had done something. She stroked her fingertips across the mermaid's bruised cheek and decided that that in and of itself, this purple and gold blossom, would win any argument with Paul.

But before she could wake him, there he was. He walked into the bathroom still wearing his pajamas, grinding the sleep out of his eyes. "Why all the racket?" he asked, yawning.

And when he removed his hands from his bleary eyes, Helena smiled up at him weakly and said, "Surprise."

PAUL WAS UNCOOPERATIVE, ANGRY, AND later he realized, a little unkind. Upon seeing his wife sprawled on the bathroom floor with that creature— he immediately thought of it as *that creature*—lounging in the tub behind her, he began to shout. "What have you done? Where did that creature come from? You must be insane, Helena. Completely mad! Get it out. Get it out right now."

She pleaded with him—he knew she'd plead with him, it was like Helena these days—and practically begged him on her knees. "You don't understand, Paul. She's hurt. She needs help. I found her on the beach. Just look at her face, the poor thing's skull has been battered. Please, you must. You have to. You must let her stay."

An awkward pause followed during which Helena looked longingly into his eyes and spoke to him like that, with her eyes. It was a trick she'd always been able to pull on him, and each time she did he was helpless. Flustered, he fled the bathroom and went to change out of his thin blue pajamas. He wanted real clothes covering his skin. The nightclothes made him feel caught off guard, vulnerable.

THEY PASSED THE DAY IN a series of short, sharp spats, nearly all of which originated with Paul sliding around the corner to stand uselessly in the doorway of the bathroom. He'd stare at Helena pouring handfuls of water along the puckering gills of the mermaid's throat, the thin little slits opening and closing, drinking the air out of the water. Or he would comment derisively on finding her stroking the mermaid's hair, humming a wordless tune to soothe her, something she once did for their daughter when she was a little girl. And then Helena would stop whatever she was doing and say, "What? What are you looking at? Go away!"

He told her he was going to take the mermaid himself and throw her back to the sea. He said, "There are proper channels for dealing with these things, and you, my dear, have followed none of them."

It was true. If she had notified the police, they would have said to leave the mermaid on the beach. They would have come and blocked the area off with sawhorses and yellow tape that had "Do Not Cross" printed on it in bold black. They had dealt with merfolk before, years ago. The proper thing to do would be to wait for high tide to roll in, and allow it to take her home.

They decided to make a pact. Helena explained that she couldn't allow the mermaid to go back with the tide in this condition. She's unconscious, she argued. Defenseless. In this state, a shark or some other scavenging creature could pick at her. Paul agreed easily enough to that. He said, "Till she's well enough, then." And Helena nodded, accepting this proposal. Although, Paul thought, it was a reluctant nod.

"Till she's well enough, then," Helena agreed.

Paul rolled his eyes at this childish bargaining and retreated to his study, hiding amongst his books, waiting for the moment he could get that creature out of his home. She was eerie. She floated in the tub like a corpse.

He spent the next two days hunched over his desk, busying himself with preparations for the coming semester, creating his syllabi and course summaries, until he heard the squeals and screams in the bathroom, announcing she had awoken.

AFTER SOMETHING SPECIAL OF ONE'S own disappears, a person should learn to be prepared for unexpected events. After Jordan disappeared, Helena came to feel, paradoxically, both ready to handle anything that might come her way, as well as on the verge of disintegrating into tears whenever she saw anything remotely reminiscent of her daughter. Because of these conflicting emotions, she found herself both willful and in tears as she struggled over a bra, black and frilled with lace—one Jordan had left behind—when the mermaid woke.

"You mustn't struggle so," she told the mermaid, who was attempting to tear the bra from her chest. Helena had covered her with it out of consideration for Paul. But the bra was too large for the mermaid, whose breasts were smaller, firmer than Jordan's, probably from all of that swimming she did. "But it will do," Helena said. She grabbed hold of the straining straps and pulled the bra back on, tightening it like a wicked stepmother. "It will do."

"Having trouble?" Paul asked. He stood in the doorway, still holding a book from his study in one hand.

Helena ignored him. The mermaid bared her teeth, two crooked rows of pearls, and hissed at them. Her bulbous black eyes seemed even more bulbous now that she was awake. And darker as well, like two black moons. They were set far apart in her head, but turned inward a little, so that they seemed to be communicating to each other some deeply private, mysterious secret.

"I'm sorry," Helena said, waggling a finger in the mermaid's face. "But there are rules in this house, young lady. We don't go traipsing around naked. Now it's time for some dinner and then you'll go straight to sleep. Consider yourself grounded. And don't ask for how long either. You've been worrying me sick."

The mermaid's body was so long that her tail hung over the lip of the tub, drooping down towards the tiled floor. She still had ropes of seaweed tangled in her black hair, and sand speckled her skin, as though she'd been dipped in glitter. Helena reached out a tentative hand to stroke the mermaid's hair, but snatched it back when the mermaid suddenly opened her mouth in a wide O and began to scream.

The scream spilled out at such a high piercing pitch, the bathroom mirror shattered. It burst apart in a rain of jagged silver, clattering into the sink, onto the tiled floor. Pieces lay at Helena's feet, each one reflecting an individual eye, a patch of green scales, or a mouth, unhinged and opened so wide you could see the red wet skin inside.

Even after the mirror flew apart, the screaming failed to stop. Helena clapped her hands over her ears and looked over at Paul, who had done the same. "Stop it!" she shouted as loud as possible. "Stop it this instant!" Her eardrums tightened and vibrated, thrumming. They were ready to burst as well. The mermaid gripped the sides of the tub, though, and threw her head back into a higher octave.

Hesitantly, Helena lifted her hand and slapped her across the face. Then the screaming choked off. "That's enough out of you, young lady," said Helena. She looked at her hand, pink from the slap, then back at the mermaid, who clutched at her cheek. It was the same cheek, already bruised and swollen with dead black blood from whatever accident had knocked her out and washed her ashore two days before. Helena could tell it hurt enough as it was. Now she knew it hurt even more.

Embarrassed, she stood and pushed her way past Paul, out of the room. Past Paul, who told the mermaid, "That's a fine way to act, now isn't it?"

Before and

HELENA TRIED FINDING THINGS FOR the mermaid to eat. She experimented with seafood first, offering up a plate of lemon-pepper whitefish on a bed of rice. But the mermaid wrinkled her nose and pushed the plate aside. When Helena brought her fried calamari, she hid her face underwater, and when presented with a bowl of fruit she pinched her nose between her finger and thumb. Paul chuckled when informed of this last reaction. "She finds the scent of apples repulsive?" he asked. And Helena shrugged, throwing her hands in the air.

"She has to eat, Paul," said Helena. She lay on the white leather couch in the living room, her head on the armrest, her feet elevated on pillows, exhausted. She'd been bustling around for the past two days with more energy than Paul had seen in her for the past year. Whenever she wasn't in the bathroom with the mermaid, she was fixing up the house. Patching cracks in the walls, polishing furniture, upending reclining chairs to sweep beneath them. There was so much to be done, she murmured as she went. She had let it all go, it had all gone astray.

"Let me have a try," Paul offered. Helena had been staring at the ceiling, at a brown spider-shaped waterstain she wanted to erase, but she turned her head toward him when he spoke.

"*You?*" She squinted at him.

"Yes, *me*," Paul said. "I'll take care of it." Then he rose from his chair, grabbed his jacket from the hall closet, and left the house.

PAUL SINCERELY WANTED TO HELP. Even though he was still angry with Helena, he couldn't stand to see her banging her head against walls over that creature. He'd been hoping she'd stop playing these games with herself. Over a month ago, he'd found a journal she'd been keeping secretly, in which she wrote long florid letters to their daughter. Or in which she wrote down detailed memories she wanted to capture before forgetting. He had found an entry that read: "My memories flash over my mind, like lightning briefly illuminating a dark landscape." He hadn't known his wife was a poet. He still didn't know if she was a good one or not. And he had found: "Dearest Jordan, I miss you so. When are you coming home? I found a coffee stain the other day and thought of you. Perhaps you made it, before you left? I'm not mad, though. We'll get new carpet! It'll be an excuse."

She collected old newspaper clippings, stories from over two decades before, now yellowed with age. Articles detailing the resurfacing of the merfolk. They had come with a message, although it took months for translations to occur. They didn't use words but spoke with squeals and clicks, like whales and dolphins. They were sad, they said. So sad to see us still walking on land. It looked painful and exhausting. And why, they wondered, did we continue to put ourselves through this self-imposed exile? It tortured them to see us torturing ourselves. Come home, they said. You've proven your point. All is forgiven.

They had disappeared soon after arriving, had only stay a few months. And soon after, people began disappearing as well. Or so it was said. Paul knew that Helena considered this to be a possibility with Jordan: that she'd gone down beneath the waves to join them. "Others have," Helena said. "A girl who lived down the street from me did. Martha. Martha Pechanski."

But Paul didn't believe Jordan chose that route. A year ago now—the last time he saw her—she'd been living with a group of squatters in an abandoned tenement in LA. A friend of Jordan's had phoned him, or someone who had once been a friend, and said she no longer attended classes at UCLA. That she'd hooked into a group, a bad group, the friend said. And that this is where you will find her.

Paul went one day, without Helena, and found Jordan in a dreary room, wearing stained jeans (stained with what, he couldn't tell) and a threadbare T-shirt with the word *Billabong* fading on its front. She'd been a surfer, and still had her board with her even then. Her hair was matted into dull and frizzy coils, almost dreadlocks. He shivered, seeing her like this. "Why?" he had asked. And she had replied, stroking the board that lay across her lap, "Because it's all a lie." He asked what she was talking about, he wanted her to tell him what it was that was all a lie, but Jordan would not elaborate. She only stroked her board like a cat.

She was high on meth, he discovered. He went home and told Helena, who shouted and screamed and immediately made him drive her to the place. By then, though, Jordan was gone again. "Why didn't you bring me with you?" Helena had demanded. "Why didn't you let *me* talk to her?" Paul had no answers for her then. He still didn't.

He stopped at an Asian grocery a few blocks from their house, where he bought food and drove home between the roadside corridors of palm trees. At home he unpacked the items in his experiment while Helena scrutinized everything. All of it was Japanese food, she pointed out. "I know," Paul said. "Take this to her." He held out a clear plastic package filled with sheets of greenish-black, papyrus-like material, which Helena sniffed at doubtfully.

"What is it?" she asked.

"Roasted seaweed," Paul told her.

MARTHA. MARTHA PECHANSKI. THE GIRL with the green eyes and blonde hair, the blonde hair that reached down to the small of her back.

Before and

And those legs—those legs that turned anyone's head. Twenty-three when Helena was seventeen, the girl who lived down the street, the girl who married into the sea. There were two stories about Martha Pechanski and Helena knew them both.

One story said Martha drowned herself in the ocean. She had tied plastic grocery bags filled with rocks around her belt loops and walked out and out, into the waves, until they covered her head like a veil. She was a sad girl, some said, cut quite a tragic figure. Had problems that no one else knew about. A person would say this while twirling a finger beside an ear. But Helena never liked those who insinuated Martha was crazy.

The other story said Martha Pechanski had fallen in love with a merman she met while surfing one day. She'd been out early in the morning, her legs straddling the board, waiting for a wave, when his head burst out of the water. Like a dolphin or a seal. Some said it was her legs he had noticed from beneath, dangling in the water.

The merman's eyes were like two black glass beads and his hair was moss green. His skin was ivory and his muscles moved beneath his skin like light rippling on water. If you kiss me forever, he told Martha, I can breathe for us both beneath the sea. And so she went, clasped in his arms, mouth on his cold mouth, his strong tail pushing them down deep, deeper, until they reached home. There she developed gills and a tail of her own and soon she forgot her former life. It was only in dreams, sometimes, that Martha possessed those head-turning legs once again. And in those dreams, her legs took her step by step back down to the water.

A sea gift, Helena thought. What the sea takes, it gives back in return. She leaned over the edge of the tub and watched the mermaid devour sheet after sheet of the seaweed paper. "You like that, don't you?" she said. That and the raw shrimp Paul bought, and the tuna and the salmon eggs. She was a luxurious girl, this one. This mermaid here, now she was a fussy one.

Over the past few days she had eaten her fill of the groceries Paul bought; she had calmed down a bit. With her stomach full, she'd given Helena this gift of proximity. She was allowed to be closer now, although the food had to keep coming. They fed her raw oysters, popping them into her mouth like grapes. The days were good, filled with peace and harmony once again. The only cloud obstructing their place in the sun was that several homeless people were sleeping under the deck again. Helena found them. Or rather, heard them, whispering beneath the deck. Let them stay, she told herself. A sea gift, she thought. A gift from the sea.

That and a neighbor had phoned to tell Paul he was bringing someone over to inspect his house; it seemed its foundation had been undermined over the past few years, and the seawall hadn't helped as much as they had hoped. Paul mentioned the call to Helena, but she didn't hear him. "We should get ours looked at as well," Paul said. "And soon. I start fall classes in less than a month."

"Do it then," Helena said. She didn't have time for that. She'd given up on the house to devote herself to the well being of this girl, this beautiful girl in the bathtub.

She ran a comb through the mermaid's dark, tangled hair. It was a silver comb, an heirloom handed down for generations in Helena's family. The mermaid seemed to enjoy it. She looked at the comb as though she might lick it. She seemed very partial to beautiful combs, Helena thought. Perhaps she lost her own in the accident?

The mermaid grinned at Helena, showing those crooked pearls for teeth. She wagged her tail happily at the other end of the tub. She had accidentally knocked a vial of lavender bath salts off of a shelf at the far end of the tub the day before and when they fell in they had clouded through the water, turning it a light purple, perfuming the air. They had been Jordan's. And now she smelled quite like Jordan used to, Helena thought. A little briny from all of that surfing, and a little lavender as well. Something above and something below.

The night before, Helena had had another dream. This time she'd been invited to a talk show, by an uplifting, sentimental host—a woman who was soft and fleshy and obstinately maternal. The show was about people who had disappeared and the loved ones left behind. Paul refused to come, but Helena told the motherly host everything, her whole story, in front of a studio audience. The audience cried at all the sad parts, which made her happy. Somehow, she thought, she'd told Jordan's story right.

When Helena had finished, the host waggled her eyebrows teasingly and said, "We've searched long and hard, far and deep, and we've found someone we think you'd like to see, Helena." A door opened on the set then, and out walked Jordan, young and beautiful, eager to be in Helena's arms. Tears were shed by all. The audience applauded and applauded again. And when all had quieted down, Helena asked, "Why, honey?"

But Jordan didn't answer. Helena smelled something fishy. She held her daughter out at arm's length. There was seaweed braided through her hair. The talk show host commented on how fashionable it looked. She asked, "Where did you have it done, dear?" Jordan opened her mouth to answer, but a scream spilled out instead. The scream spilled out and flooded the studio set, washed over the audience, and shattered the camera lenses. This broadcast was at an end. When Helena woke, her head was filled with static from a dead television channel.

Christopher Barzak   Before and

Helena began to hum a wordless tune, thankful that the dream hadn't been as futile as the ones that came before it. This one had a bit of hope. The mermaid now had finished off the seaweed sheets and was lounging extravagantly with her head nestled on the lip of the tub while Helena combed through her hair, freeing it of sea substances. Soon it would no longer be encumbered by kelp. A sea gift, Helena thought again. But now, thinking that, something made her afraid.

What if she had gotten it all wrong? she wondered. She remembered the articles about the merfolk resurfacing. They had said, "You came from the sea and to the sea you shall return."

But she'd been thinking of this process the other way around. Jordan had gone into the sea and returned. Certainly a little changed, but returned nonetheless. What if—and she cringed at this thought—what if this beautiful girl in the tub would have to go back? She had come from the sea. Would she have to go back? Helena couldn't bear that. She'd lost too much already.

The mermaid had fallen asleep. A mucousy film slid down over her black eyes, clouding them, making her look blind. "I need something from you," Helena whispered. "Not much. Just something to remember you by, in case you have to go."

She stood and padded out of the bathroom, returning a few moments later with a pair of orange-handled scissors. Kneeling beside the tub, she plucked a long tress of black hair away from the mermaid's face, lifting it to get at its roots. It smelled of lavender and of something dark and underwater. Sliding it between the mouth of the scissors, she gently squeezed them closed.

PAUL WAS ON THE BACK deck drinking a glass of bourbon when he heard the screams. At first he thought it might be another of the mermaid's fits, but soon he realized someone was in pain. He flew through the house until he came to the bathroom and grabbed hold of the doorframe to stop from running any further.

Helena sat on the floor with her legs folded beneath her, holding a pair of scissors in one hand and a hank of hair in the other. The mermaid writhed in the tub, throwing her tail back and forth, cracking it against the wall. Paint flaked off, and plaster had begun to fall away as well. Green blood pulsed out of her scalp, pouring over her face. "Shh, please, shh," Helena pleaded. "I'm sorry, I didn't mean, I only meant." She reached out to touch the mermaid reassuringly, but was rejected with bloody hands.

The mermaid squealed like a child. She screeched like a gull. She stuttered an annoying patter of clicks and stops, then moaned a deep mournful song that climbed steeply into a howl. "What have you done, Helena?" Paul asked. But Helena only shook her head, as if nothing was wrong. Nothing at all.

"That's enough," Paul said. He plunged his hands into the bath water and pulled the mermaid out. His back strained and he nearly buckled over. Her scales scraped at his flesh and a pink rash, the color of a fresh burn, bloomed on the insides of his arms. "It's no good," he told Helena. "I'm sending her home."

As soon as he made it to the back deck, Helena was up on her feet and behind him. "Wait, Paul, don't do this. You don't understand. You don't understand." But he didn't listen. He stepped down and down until his feet reached sand, and then he headed off in the direction of the nearest pier. He could see its lights in the distance, like strange pearls floating in midair.

"NO, PAUL," HELENA SHOUTED AS he stalked away, down the beach. But he didn't listen to her, only kept walking. She balled her hands into fists and hit the deck railing in front of her, then sat down in a chair and wept. "What's happened?" she thought. "What's happened? And why all of that blood?" Her thoughts raced in circles. She struggled to catch one. If she could only sort this out, she could stop things from progressing, she knew.

But her thoughts stopped abruptly, interrupted by what sounded like voices. Beneath her feet. Beneath the deck. "Go away," Helena murmured, but they continued to chatter beneath her anyway. "Go away, I said." She raised her voice. She stamped her foot on the floorboard beneath her. "Get out!" she screamed. "Get out of here!" She stood from her chair and began jumping up and down on the deck. The boards twittered beneath her. "Get the hell out of here!"

Beneath the deck, beneath her feet, they could see light from overhead, filling the cracks between the floorboards. Dust and sand sifted down between the cracks each time the woman jumped. "Get the hell out of here!" she screamed. And so they gathered up their sleeping bags and scrabbled down the boulders.

Helena watched them go. They scurried away like beach squirrels or rats. She yelled at them once more, for good measure. Then they disappeared, swallowed by the night.

"Where was I?" she thought. "Green blood," she reminded herself. "Start there. Find the thread and go back." What had happened?

But before she could begin again, the house moved beneath her, disturbed by its dreams. It shifted and trembled, as if an earthquake were occurring. The windows rattled in their frames. Pictures fell from their walls. The cracks Helena had patched days ago reappeared. She stood in the doorway between the deck and the house and waited to see what would happen.

FOR THE ENTIRE LENGTH OF the pier, Paul carried the mermaid in his arms like a bride. He staggered with her past fishermen with buckets full of sand sharks, past a cigarette stand closed for the night, past rollerbladers executing stunts on steps and benches. He walked all the way to the end of the pier, where a restaurant had been built as a tourist trap. People came here and went home to their friends and told them, "I ate over the ocean." As Paul passed by its plate glass windows, the people inside pointed out at him, or pressed their faces against the tinted glass to stare.

At the end of the pier, he lifted the mermaid over the rails and said, "Goodbye." For a moment, as he looked into her eyes, her face melted like hot wax and reformed itself into his daughter's face. He released her then, and she spiraled down to the black ocean like a green ribbon snatched from someone's hand by the wind. There was a splash, and then when he leaned over the rails to search for signs of her, he found nothing but the reflected yellow light from the pier lamps striping the black water.

BACK AT THE HOUSE, THE house that now swayed and creaked like a storm-tossed ship, Helena had fallen into bed. Furniture scraped across the floors. Wine glasses dropped from their racks in the kitchen to shatter like icicles against the linoleum floor. The house was crumbling, sliding slowly down the cliffside. With each bump and unexpected movement, Helena was tossed around on her bed. The tide was sweeping in, hissing up to meet the house on the beach. Soon it would be high tide and the house would no longer be a house. It would be a boat. A house boat. It would drift, unmoored, out to sea. By sunrise Helena expects she and the house will have already traveled some distance, but not so far out she'll be unable to step onto the back deck and wave to Paul, who will be on the beach. A tiny black speck scratching his head, wondering what was happening. She will wave to him with both arms, big enough for him to see. And then—because it's obvious now this house is unsound, its cracks appearing everywhere, certainly not a seaworthy vessel—she will abandon ship. She will wait till sunset, when the sun floats over the waves, and then she'll jump so that Paul and any other spectators will see her as a silhouette against it. A red disc spread out on the white sky, like Japan's flag, and inside it, a graceful woman diving into the sea.

Afterlives

The Drowned Mermaid

She will take with her only the mermaid's tress of hair, tied around her neck like a choker. And perhaps it will gift her with powers. Perhaps it will enable her to breathe water. Then she will swim down, like the Pechanski girl, like Martha, that crazy in love girl from her youth, and she will search the coral kingdoms for Jordan.

Perhaps one day she will wash ashore, a naked woman covered with nothing but her own bruises, who has been to the ends of the earth, to history, and back. And maybe someone will find her there and drag her home.

Helena rocks on the waves of her bed. The house rocks on the waves of the ocean. She understands that going under with only a lock of hair in her possession is not the sanest plan.

Still, she brings the hair to her face and inhales its salty lavender scent once more. She tells herself, "It will do."

Dead Boy Found

ALL THIS STARTED WHEN MY father told my mother she was a waste. He said, "You are such a waste, Linda," and she said, "Oh, yeah? You think so? We'll see about that." Then she got into her car and pulled out of our driveway, throwing gravel in every direction. She was going to Abel's, or so she said, where she could have a beer and find herself a real man.

Halfway there, though, she was in a head-on collision with a drunk woman named Lucy, who was on her way home, it happened, from Abel's. They were both driving around that blind curve on Highway 88, Lucy swerving a little, my mother smoking cigarette after cigarette, not even caring where the ashes fell. When they leaned their cars into the curve, Lucy crossed into my mother's lane. Bam! Just like that. My mother's car rolled three times into the ditch and Lucy's car careened into a guardrail. It was Lucy who called the ambulance on her cellular phone, saying, over and over, "My God, I've killed Linda McCormick, I've killed that poor girl."

At that same moment, Gracie Highsmith was becoming famous. While out searching for new additions to her rock collection, she had found the missing boy's body buried beneath the defunct railroad tracks just a couple of miles from my house. The missing boy had been missing for two weeks. He disappeared on his way home from a Boy Scout meeting. He and Gracie were both in my class. I never really talked to either of them much, but they were all right. You know, quiet types. Weird, some might say. But I'm not the judgmental sort. I keep my own counsel. I go my own way. If Gracie Highsmith wanted to collect rocks and if the missing boy wanted to be a Boy Scout, more power to them.

WE WAITED SEVERAL HOURS AT the hospital before they let us see my mother. Me, my brother Andy, and my father sat in the lobby reading magazines and drinking coffee. A nurse finally came and got us. She took us up to the seventh floor. She pointed to room number 727 and said we could go on in.

My mother lay in the hospital bed with tubes coming out of her nose. One of her eyes had swelled shut and was already black and shining. She breathed with her mouth open, a wheezing noise like snoring. There were bloodstains on her teeth. Also several of her teeth were missing. When she woke, blinking her good eye rapidly, she saw me and said, "Baby, come here and give me a hug."

I wasn't a baby, I was fifteen, but I didn't correct her. I figured she'd been through enough already. A doctor came in and asked my mother how she was feeling. She said she couldn't feel her legs. He said that he thought that might be a problem, but that it would probably work itself out over time. There was swelling around her spinal cord. "It should be fine after a few weeks," he told us.

My father started talking right away, saying things like, "We all have to pull together. We'll get through this. Don't worry." Eventually his fast talking added up to mean something. When we brought my mother home, he put her in my bed so she could rest properly, and I had to bunk with Andy. For the next few weeks, he kept saying things like, "Don't you worry, honey. It's time for the men to take over." I started doing the dishes and Andy vacuumed. My father took out the trash on Tuesdays. He brought home pizza or cold cuts for dinner.

I WASN'T ANGRY ABOUT ANYTHING. I want to make that clear right off. I mean, stupid stuff like this just happens. It happens all the time. One day you're just an average fifteen year old with stupid parents and a brother who takes out his aggressions on you because he's idiotic and his friends think it's cool to see him belittle you in public, and suddenly something happens to make things worse. Believe me, morbidity is not my specialty. Bad things just happen all at once. My grandma said bad things come in threes. Two bad things had happened: My mother was paralyzed and Gracie Highsmith found the missing boy's body. If my grandma was still alive, she'd be trying to guess what would happen next.

I mentioned this to my mother while I spooned soup up to her trembling lips. She could feed herself all right, but she seemed to like the at-

Before and

tention. "Bad things come in threes," I said. "Remember Grandma always said that?"

She said, "You're grandma was uneducated."

I said, "What is that supposed to mean?"

She said, "She didn't even get past eighth grade, Adam."

I said, "I knew that already."

"Well I'm just reminding you."

"Okay," I said, and she took another spoonful of chicken broth.

At school everyone talked about the missing boy. "Did you hear about Jamie Marks?" they all said. "Did you hear about Gracie High-smith?"

I pretended like I hadn't, even though I'd watched the news all weekend and considered myself an informed viewer. I wanted to hear what other people would say. A lot of rumors circulated already. Our school being so small made that easy. Seventh through twelfth grade all crammed into the same building, elbow to elbow, breathing each other's breath.

They said Gracie saw one of his fingers poking out of the gravel, like a zombie trying to crawl out of its grave. They said that after she removed a few stones, one of his blue eyes stared back at her, and that she screamed and threw the gravel back at his eye and ran home. They said, sure enough, when the police came later, they found the railroad ties loose, with the bolts broken off of them. So they removed them, dug up the gravel, shoveling for several minutes, and found Jamie Marks. Someone said a cop walked away to puke.

I sat through Algebra and Biology and History, thinking about cops puking, thinking about the missing boy's body. I couldn't stop thinking about those two things. I liked the idea of seeing one of those cops who set up speed traps behind bushes puking out his guts, holding his stomach. I wasn't sure what I thought about Jamie's dead body rotting beneath railroad ties. And what a piece of work, to have gone to all that trouble to hide the kid in such a place! It didn't help that at the start of each class all the teachers said they understood if we were disturbed, or anxious, and that we should talk if needed, or else they could recommend a good psychologist to our parents.

I sat at my desk with my chin propped in my hands, chewing an eraser, imagining Jamie Marks under the rails staring at the undersides of trains as they rumbled over him. Those tracks weren't used anymore, not since the big smash up with a school bus back in the 80's, but I imagined trains on them anyway. Jamie inhaled each time a glimpse of sky appeared between boxcars and exhaled when they covered him over. He dreamed when there were no trains rolling over him, when there was no metallic scream on the rails. When he dreamed, he dreamed of trains again, blue sparks flying off the iron railing, and he gasped for breath in his sleep. A ceiling of trains covered him. He almost suffocated, there were so many.

AFTER SCHOOL, MY BROTHER ANDY said, "We're going to the place, a bunch of us. Do you want to come?" Andy's friends were all seniors and they harassed me a lot, so I shook my head and said no. "I have to see a friend and collect five dollars he owes me," I said, even though I hadn't loaned out money to anyone in weeks.

I went home and looked through school yearbooks and found Jamie Marks smiling from his square in row two. I cut his photo out with my father's exacto knife and stared at it for a while, then turned it over. On the other side was a picture of me. I swallowed and swallowed until my throat hurt. I didn't like that picture of me anyway, I told myself. It was a bad picture. I had baby fat when it was taken, and looked more like a little kid. I flipped the photo over and over, like a coin, and wondered, If it had been me, would I have escaped? I decided it must have been too difficult to get away from them—I couldn't help thinking there had to be more than one murderer—and probably I would have died just the same.

I took the picture outside and buried it in my mother's garden between the rows of sticks that had, just weeks before, marked off the sections of vegetables, keeping carrots carrots and radishes radishes. I patted the dirt softly, inhaled its crisp dirt smell, and whispered, "Don't you worry. Everything will be all right."

WHEN MY MOTHER STARTED USING a wheelchair, she was hopeful, even though the doctors had changed their minds and said she'd never walk again. She told us not to worry. She enjoyed not always having to be on her feet. She figured out how to pop wheelies, and would show off in front of guests. "What a burden legs can be!" she told us. Even so, I sometimes found her wheeled into dark corners, her head in her hands, saying, "No, no, no," sobbing.

That woman, Lucy, kept calling and asking my mother to forgive her, but my mother told us to say she wasn't home and that she was contacting lawyers and that they'd have Lucy so broke within seconds, they'd make her pay real good. I told Lucy, "She isn't home," and Lucy said, "My God, tell that poor woman I'm so sorry. Ask her to please forgive me."

I told my mother Lucy was sorry, and the next time Lucy called, my mother decided to hear her out. Their conversation sounded like when my mom talks to her sister, my Aunt Beth, who lives in California near the

Before and

ocean, a place I've never visited. My mother kept shouting, "No way! You too?! I can't believe it! Can you believe it?! Oh Lucy, this is too much."

Two hours later, Lucy pulled into our driveway, blaring her horn. My mother wheeled herself outside, smiling and laughing. Lucy was tall and wore red lipstick, and her hair was permed real tight. She wore plastic bracelets and hoop earrings, and stretchy hot pink pants. She bent down and hugged my mother, then helped her into the car. They drove off together, laughing, and when they came home several hours later, I smelled smoke and whiskey on their breath.

"What's most remarkable," my mother kept slurring, "is that I was on my way to the bar, sober, and Lucy was driving home, drunk." They'd both had arguments with their husbands that day; they'd both run out to make their husbands jealous. Learning all this, my mother and Lucy felt destiny had brought them together. "A virtual Big Bang," said my mother.

Lucy said, "A collision of souls."

The only thing to regret was that their meeting had been so painful. "But great things are born out of pain," my mother told me, nodding in a knowing way. "If I had to be in an accident with someone," she said, patting Lucy's hand, which rested on one of my mother's wheels, "I'm glad that someone was Lucy."

AFTER I BURIED JAMIE'S AND my photo, I walked around for a few days bumping into things. Walls, lockers, people. It didn't matter what, I walked into it. I hadn't known Jamie all that well, even though we were in the same class. We had different friends. Jamie liked computers; I ran track. Not because I like competition, but because I'm a really good runner, and I like to run, even though my mom always freaks because I was born premature, with undersized lungs. But I remembered Jamie: a small kid with stringy, mouse-colored hair and pale skin. He wore very round glasses and kids sometimes called him Moony. He was supposed to be smart, but I didn't know about that. I asked a few people at lunch, when the topic was still hot, "What kind of grades did he get? Was he an honors student?" But no one answered. All they did was stare like I'd stepped out of a spaceship.

MY BROTHER ANDY AND HIS friends enjoyed a period of extreme popularity. After they went to where Jamie had been hidden, everyone thought they were crazy but somehow brave. Girls asked Andy to take them there, to be their protector, and he'd pick out the pretty ones who wore makeup and tight little skirts. "You should go, Adam," Andy told me. "You could appreciate it."

"It's too much of a spectacle," I said, as if I were above all that.

Andy narrowed his eyes. He spit at my feet. He said I didn't know what I was talking about, that it wasn't offensive at all, people were just curious, nothing sick or twisted. He asked if I was implying that his going to see the place was sick or twisted. "Cause if that's what you're implying, you are dead wrong."

"No," I said, "that's not what I'm implying. I'm not implying anything at all."

I didn't stick around to listen to the story of his adventure. There were too many stories filling my head as it was. At any moment Andy would burst into a monologue of detail, one he'd been rehearsing since seeing the place where they'd hidden Jamie, so I turned to go to my room and—bam—walked right into a wall. I put my hand over my aching face and couldn't stop blinking. Andy snorted and called me a freak. He pushed my shoulder and told me to watch where I'm going, or else one day I'd kill myself. I kept leaving, and Andy said, "Hey! Where are you going? I didn't get to tell you what it was like."

OUR TOWN WAS BIG ON ghost stories, and within weeks people started seeing Jamie Marks. He waited at the railroad crossing on Sodom-Hutchins road, pointing farther down the tracks, toward where he'd been hidden. He walked in tight circles outside of Gracie Highsmith's house with his hands clasped behind his back and his head hanging low and serious. In these stories he was always a transparent figure. Things passed through him. Rain was one example; another was leaves falling off the trees, drifting through his body. Kids in school said, "I saw him!" the same eager way they did when they went out to Hatchet Man Road to see the ghost of that killer from the '70s, who actually never used hatchets, but a hunting knife.

Gracie Highsmith hadn't returned to school yet, and everyone said she'd gone psycho, so no one could verify the story of Jamie's ghost standing outside her house. The stories grew anyway, without her approval, which just seemed wrong. I thought if Jamie's ghost was walking outside Gracie's house, then no one should tell that story but Gracie. It was hers, and anyone else who told it was a thief.

ONE DAY I FINALLY WENT to the cemetery to visit him. I'd wanted to go to the funeral, just to stand in the back where no one would notice, but the newspaper said it was family only. If I *was* angry about anything at all, it was this. I mean, how could they just shut everyone out? The whole town had helped in the search parties, had taken over food to Jamie's

Before and

family during the time when he was missing. And then no one but family was allowed to be at the funeral? It just felt a little selfish.

I hardly ever went to the cemetery. Only once or twice before, and that was when my Grandma died, and my dad and Andy and I had to be pall bearers. We went once after my mom came home in her wheelchair. She said she needed to talk to my grandma, so we drove her there on a surprisingly warm autumn day, when the leaves were still swinging on their branches. She sat in front of the headstone, and we backed off to give her some private time. She cried and sniffed, you could hear that. The sunlight reflected on the chrome of her wheelchair. When she was done we loaded her back into the van, and she said, "All right, who wants to rent some videos?"

Now the cemetery looked desolate, as if ready to be filmed for some Halloween movie. Headstones leaned toward one another. Moss grew green over the walls of family mausoleums. I walked along the driveway, gravel crunching beneath my shoes, and looked from side to side at the stone angels and pillars and plain flat slabs decorating the dead, marking out their spaces. I knew a lot of names, or had heard of them, whether they'd been relatives or friends, or friends of relatives, or ancestral family enemies. When you live in a town where you can fit everyone into four churches—two Catholic, two Methodist—you know everyone. Even the dead.

I searched the headstones until I found where Jamie Marks was buried. His grave was still freshly turned earth. No grass had had time to grow there. But people had left little trinkets, tokens or reminders, on the grave, pieces of themselves. A hand print. A piece of rose-colored glass. Two cigarettes standing up like fence posts. A baby rattle. Someone had scrawled a name across the bottom edge of the grave: Gracie Highsmith. A moment later I heard footsteps, and there she was in the flesh, coming toward me.

I was perturbed, but not angry. Besides his family, I thought I'd be the only one to come visit. But here she was, this girl, who'd drawn her name in the dirt with her finger. Her letters looked soft; they curled into each other gently, with little flourishes for decoration. Did she think it mattered if she spelled her name pretty?

I planted my hands on my hips as she approached and said, "Hey, what are you doing here?"

Gracie blinked as if she'd never seen me before in her life. I could tell she wanted to say, "Excuse me? Who are you?" But what she did say was, "Visiting. I'm visiting. What are *you* doing here?"

Afterlives

Dead Boy Found

The wind picked up and blew hair across her face. She tucked it back behind her ears real neatly. I dropped my hands from my hips and nudged the ground with my shoe, not knowing how to answer. Gracie turned back to Jamie's tombstone.

"Visiting," I said finally, crossing my arms over my chest, annoyed I couldn't come up with anything but the same answer she'd given.

Gracie nodded without looking at me. She kept her eyes trained on Jamie's grave, and I started to think maybe she was going to steal it. The headstone, that is. I mean, the girl collected rocks. A headstone would complete any collection. I wondered if I should call the police, tell them, Get yourselves to the cemetery, you've got a burglary in progress. I imagined them taking Gracie out in handcuffs, making her duck her head as they tucked her into the back seat of the patrol car. I pinched myself to stop daydreaming, and when I woke back up, I found Gracie sobbing over the grave.

I didn't know how long she'd been crying, but she was going full force. I mean, this girl didn't care if anyone was around to hear her. She bawled and screamed. I didn't know what to do, but I thought maybe I should say something to calm her. I finally shouted, "Hey! Don't do that!"

But Gracie kept crying. She beat her fist in the dirt near her name.

"Hey!" I repeated. "Didn't you hear me? I said, Don't do that!"

But she still didn't listen.

So I started to dance. It was the first idea that came to me.

I kicked my heels in the air and did a two-step. I hummed a tune to keep time. I clasped my hands together behind my back and did a jig, or an imitation of one, and when still none of my clowning distracted her, I started to sing the Hokey Pokey.

I belted it out and kept on dancing. I sung each line like it was poetry. "You put your left foot in/You take your left foot out/You put your left foot in/And you shake it all about/You do the Hokey Pokey and you turn yourself around/That's what it's all about! Yeehaw!"

As I sang and danced, I moved toward a freshly dug grave just a few plots down from Jamie's. The headstone was already up, but there hadn't been a funeral yet. The grave was waiting for Lola Peterson to fill it, but instead, as I shouted out the next verse, I stumbled in.

I fell in the grave singing, "You put your whole self in—" and about choked on my own tongue when I landed. Even though it was still light out, it was dark in the grave, and muddy. My shoes sunk, and when I tried to pull them out, they made sucking noises. The air smelled stiff and leafy. I started to worry that I'd be stuck in Lola Peterson's grave all night,

Before and

because the walls around me were muddy too; I couldn't get my footing. Finally, though, Gracie's head appeared over the lip of the grave.

"Are you okay?" she asked.

Her hair fell down toward me like coils of rope.

Gracie helped me out by getting a ladder from the cemetery tool shed. She told me I was a fool, but she laughed when she said it. Her eyes were red from crying, and her cheeks looked wind-chapped. I thanked her for helping me out.

I got her talking after that. She talked a little about Jamie and how she found him, but she didn't say too much. Really, she only seemed to want to talk about rocks. "So you really do collect rocks?" I asked, and Gracie bobbed her head.

"You should see them," she told me. "Why don't you come over to my place tomorrow? My parents will be at marriage counseling. Come around five."

"Sure," I said. "That'd be great."

Gracie dipped her head and looked up at me through brown bangs. She turned to go, then stopped a moment later and waved. I waved back.

I waited for her to leave before me. I waited until I heard the squeal and clang of the wrought-iron front gates. Then I knelt down beside Jamie's grave and wiped Gracie's name out of the dirt. I wrote my name in place of it, etching into the dirt deeply.

My letters were straight and fierce.

I WENT HOME TO FIND I'd missed dinner. My father was already in the living room, watching TV, the Weather Channel. He could watch the weather report for hours listening to the muzak play over and over. He watched it every night for a couple of hours before Andy and I would start groaning for a channel switch. He'd change the channel but never acknowledge us. Usually he never had much to say anyway.

When I got home, though, he wanted to talk. It took him only a few minutes after I sat down with a plate of meatloaf before he changed the channel, and I about choked. There was a news brief on about the search for Jamie's murderers. I wondered why the anchorman called them "Jamie's murderers", the same way you might say, "Jamie's dogs" or "Jamie's Boy Scout honors". My dad stretched out on his reclining chair and started muttering about what he'd do with the killers if it had been his boy. His face was red and splotchy.

I stopped eating, set my fork down on my plate.

"What would you do?" I asked. "What would you do if it had been me?"

My dad looked at me and said, "I'd tie a rope around those bastard's armpits and lower them inch by inch into a vat of piranhas, slowly, to let the little suckers have at their flesh."

He looked back at the TV.

"But what if the police got them first?" I said. "What would you do then?"

Dad looked at me again and said, "I'd smuggle a gun into the courtroom, and when they had those bastards up there on the stand, I'd jump out of my seat and shoot their God-damned heads off." He jumped out of his recliner and made his hands into a gun shape, pointing it at me. He pulled the fake trigger once, twice, a third time. Bam! Bam! Bam!

I nodded with approval. I felt really loved, like I was my dad's favorite. I ate up all this great attention and kept asking, "What if?" again and again, making up different situations. He was so cool, the best dad in the world. I wanted to buy him a hat: Best Dad in the World! printed on it. We were really close, I felt, for the first time in a long time.

GRACIE HIGHSMITH'S HOUSE WAS NESTLED in a bend of the railroad tracks where she found Jamie. She'd been out walking the tracks looking for odd pieces of coal and nickel when she found him. All of this she told me in her bedroom, on the second floor of her house. She held out a fist-sized rock that was brown with black speckles embedded in it. The brown parts felt like sandpaper, but the black specks were smooth as glass. Gracie said she'd found it in the streambed at the bottom of Marrow's Ravine. I said, "It's something special all right," and she beamed like someone's mother.

"That's nothing," she said. "Wait till you see the rest."

She showed me a chunk of clear quartz and a piece of hardened blue clay; a broken-open geode filled with pyramids of pink crystal; a seashell that she found, mysteriously, in the woods behind her house, nowhere near water; and a flat rock with a skeletal fish fossil imprinted on it. I was excited to see them all. I hadn't realized how beautiful rocks could be. It made me want to collect rocks too, but it was already Gracie's territory. I'd have to find something of my own.

We sat on her bed and listened to music by some group from Cleveland that I'd never heard of, but who Gracie loved because she set the CD player to replay the same song over and over. It sounded real punk. They sang about growing up angry and how they would take over the world and make people pay for being stupid idiots. Gracie nodded and gritted her teeth as she listened.

I liked being alone in the house with her, listening to music and looking at rocks. I felt eccentric and mature. I told Gracie this, and she knew what I meant. "They all think we're children," she said. "They don't know a God-damned thing, do they?"

We talked about growing old for a while, imagining ourselves in college, then in mid-life careers, then we were so old we couldn't walk without a walker. Pretty soon we were so old we both clutched our chests like we were having heart attacks, fell back on the bed, and choked on our own laughter.

"What sort of funeral will you have?" she wondered.

"I don't know, what about you? Aren't they all the same?"

"Funerals are all different," she said. "For instance, Mexican cemeteries have all these bright, beautifully colored decorations for their dead; they're not all serious like ours." I asked her where she had learned that. She said, "Social Studies. Last year."

"Social Studies?" I asked. "Last year?" I repeated. "I don't remember reading about funerals or cemeteries last year in Social Studies." Last year I hadn't cared about funerals. I was fourteen and watched TV and played video games a lot. What else had I missed while lost in the fog of sitcoms and fantasy adventures?

I bet Mexicans never would have had a private funeral. Too bad Jamie wasn't Mexican.

"I see graves all the time now," Gracie told me. She lay flat on her back, head on her pillow, and stared at the ceiling. "They're everywhere," Gracie said. "Ever since—"

She stopped and sighed, as if it was some huge confession she'd just told me. I worried that she might expect something in return, a confession of my own. I murmured a little noise I hoped sounded supportive.

"They're everywhere," she repeated. "The town cemetery, the Wilkinson family plot, that old place out by the ravine, where Fuck-You Francis is supposed to be buried. And now the railroad tracks. I mean, where does it end?"

I said, "Beds are like graves, too," and she turned to me with this puzzled look. "No," I said, "really." And I told her about the time when my grandmother came to live with us, after my grandfather's death. And how, one morning my mother sent me into her room to wake her for breakfast—I remember, because I smelled bacon frying when I woke up—and so I went into my grandma's room and told her to wake up. She didn't, so I repeated myself. But she still didn't wake up. Finally I shook her shoulders, and her head lolled on her neck. I grabbed one of her hands, and it was cold to the touch.

"Oh," said Gracie. "I see what you mean." She stared at me hard, her eyes glistening. Gracie rolled on top of me, pinning her knees on both sides of my hips. Her hair fell around my face, and the room grew dimmer as her hair brushed over my eyes, shutting out the light.

She kissed me on my lips, and she kissed me on my neck. She started rocking against my penis, so I rocked back. The coils in her bed creaked. "You're so cold, Adam," Gracie whispered, over and over. "You're so cold, you're so cold." She smelled like clay and dust. As she rocked on me, she looked up at the ceiling and bared the hollow of her throat. After a while, she let out several little gasps, then collapsed on my chest. I kept rubbing against her, but stopped when I realized she wasn't going to get back into it.

Gracie slid off me. She knelt in front of her window, looking out at something.

"Are you angry?" I asked.

"No, Adam. I'm not angry. Why would I be angry?"

"Just asking," I said. "What are you doing now?" I said.

"He's down there again," she whispered. I heard the tears in her voice already and went to her. I didn't look out the window. I wrapped my arms around her, my hands meeting under her breasts, and hugged her. I didn't look out the window.

"Why won't he go away?" she said. "I found him, yeah. So fucking what. He doesn't need to fucking follow me around forever."

"Tell him to leave," I told her.

She didn't respond.

"Tell him you don't want to see him anymore," I told her.

She moved my hands off her and turned her face to mine. She leaned in and kissed me, her tongue searching out mine. When she pulled back, she said, "I can't. I hate him, but I love him, too. He seems to, I don't know, understand me, maybe. We're on the same wavelength, you know? As much as he annoys me, I love him. He should have been loved, you know. He never got that. Not how everyone deserves."

"Just give him up," I said.

Gracie wrinkled her nose. She stood and paced to her doorway, opened it, said, "I think you should go now. My parents will be home soon."

I craned my neck to glance out the window, but her voice cracked like a whip.

"Leave, Adam."

I shrugged into my coat and elbowed past her.

"You don't deserve him," I said on my way out.

Before and

I walked home through wind, and soon rain started up. It landed on my face cold and trickled down my cheeks into my collar. Jamie hadn't been outside when I left Gracie's house, and I began to suspect she'd been making him up, like the rest of them, to make me jealous. Bitch, I thought. I thought she was different.

At home I walked in through the kitchen, and my mother was waiting by the doorway. She said, "Where have you been? Two nights in a row. You're acting all secretive. Where have you been, Adam?"

Lucy sat at the dinner table, smoking a cigarette. When I looked at her, she looked away. Smoke curled up into the lamp above her.

"What is this?" I said. "An inquisition?"

"We're just worried, is all," said my mother.

"Don't worry."

"I can't help it."

"Your mother loves you very much," said Lucy.

"Stay out of this, paralyzer."

Both of them gasped.

"Adam!" My mother sounded shocked. "That's not nice. You know Lucy didn't mean that to happen. Apologize right now."

I mumbled an apology.

My mother started wheeling around the kitchen. She reached up to cupboards and pulled out cans of tomatoes and kidney beans. She opened the freezer and pulled out ground beef. "Chili," she said, just that. "It's chilly outside, so you need some warm chili for your stomach. Chili will warm you up." She sounded like a commercial.

Then she started in again. "My miracle child," she said, pretending to talk to herself. "My baby boy, my gift. Did you know, Lucy, that Adam was born premature, with underdeveloped lungs and a murmur in his heart?"

"No, dear," said Lucy. "How terrible!"

"He was a fighter, though," said my mother. "He always fought. He wanted to live so much. Oh, Adam," she said. "Why don't you tell me where you've been? Your running coach said you've been missing practice a lot."

"I haven't been anywhere," I said. "Give it a rest."

"It's everything happening at once, isn't it?" Lucy asked. "Poor kid. You should send him to see Dr. Phelps, Linda. Stuff like what happened to the Marks boy is hard on kids."

"That's an idea," said my mother.

"Would you stop talking about me in front of me?" I said. "God, you two are ridiculous. You don't have a God-damned clue about anything."

My father came into the kitchen and said, "What's all the racket?"

I said, "Why don't you just go kill someone!" and ran outside again.

Afterlives *Dead Boy Found*

At first I didn't know where I was going, but by the time I reached the edge of the woods, I figured it out. The rain still fell steadily, and the wind crooned through the branches of trees. Leaves shook and fell around me. It was dusk, and I pushed my way through the brambles and roots back to the old railroad tracks.

His breath was on my neck before I even reached the spot, though. I knew he was behind me before he even said a thing. I felt his breath on my neck, and then he placed his arms around my stomach, just like I had with Gracie. "Keep going," he said. And I did. He held onto me, and I carried him on my back all the way to the place where Gracie found him.

That section of the railroad had been marked out in yellow police tape. But something was wrong. Something didn't match up with what I expected. The railroad ties—they hadn't been pulled up. And the hole where Jamie had been buried—it was there all right, but *next* to the railroad tracks. He'd never been under those railroad tracks, I realized. Something dropped in my stomach. A pang of disappointment.

Stories change. They change too easily and too often.

"What are you waiting for?" Jamie asked, sliding off my back. I stood at the edge of the hole and he said, "Go on. Try it on."

I turned around and there he was, naked, with mud smudged on his pale white skin. His hair was all messed up, and one lens of his glasses was shattered. He smiled. His teeth were filled with grit.

I stepped backward into the hole. It wasn't very deep, not like Lola Peterson's grave in the cemetery. Just a few feet down. I stood at eye level with Jamie's crotch. He reached down and touched himself.

"Take off your clothes," he told me.

I took them off.

"Lay down," he told me.

I lay down.

He climbed in on top of me, and he was so cold, so cold. He said there was room for two of us in here and that I should call him Moony.

I said, "I never liked that name."

He said, "Neither did I."

"Then I won't call you that."

"Thank you," he said, and hugged me. I let him. He said she never let him hug her. She didn't understand him. I told him I knew. She was being selfish.

I said, "Don't worry. I've found you now. You don't have to worry. I understand. I found you."

"I found *you*," he said. "Remember?"

"Let's not argue," I said.

Before and

He rested his cheek against my chest, and the rain washed over us. After a while I heard voices, faraway but growing closer. I stood up and saw the swathes of light from their flashlights getting bigger. My dad and Andy and Lucy. All of them moved toward me. I imagined my mother wheeling in worried circles back in the kitchen.

"Adam!" my father shouted through the rain.

I didn't move. Not even when they came right up to me, their faces white and pale as Jamie's dead body. Andy said, "I told you he'd be here. The little freak."

Lucy said, "My Lord, your poor mother," and her hand flew to her mouth.

My father said, "Adam, come out of there. Come out of that place right now."

He held his hand out to me, curling his fingers for me to take it.

"Come on, boy," he said. "Get on out of there now." He flexed his fingers for emphasis.

I grabbed hold of his hand, and he hauled me out onto the gravel around the hole and I lay there, naked, like a newborn. They stood around me, staring. My father took off his coat and put it on me. He told me to come on, to just come on back to the house. He put his arm around me, and we started walking down the tracks.

I decided right then I wasn't a freak, not really. I took his hand, sure, but not because of anything remotely like defeat. I hadn't "come to my senses." I hadn't "realized I needed help." I took it to make them feel better about themselves and to get them off my back.

What I was thinking as they walked me home was: You silly people, I'm already finished. I'm already dead and gone. All you have is some mess of a zombie shambling through your kitchens and your living rooms, turning on your showers and kissing you goodnight. All you have is a dead boy, only it's hard to tell, because I won't rot. I'll be like one of those bodies that people in South America pry out of old coffins, the ones whose hair and fingernails continue to grow in death. The ones who smell of rose petals, whose skin remains smooth and lily white. They call those corpses saints, but I won't aspire to anything so heavenly. I'll wash the dishes and do my homework and wheel my mother around in her chair. I'll do all of these things, and no one will notice there's no light behind my eyes and no heat in my step. They'll clothe me and feed me and tell me what good grades I get. They'll give me things to make me happy, when all I'll be wanting is a cold grave to step into. I'll grow up and go to college, marry a beautiful woman and have three kids. I'll make a lot of money and age gracefully, no pot belly. I'll look youthful when I'm fifty-eight.

What I knew right then was that everyone I'd ever know from here on out would talk about me and say, He's so lucky. He has everything a person could want.

A Mad Tea Party

ALL THROUGH THE REST OF the house, it is quiet and still.

Inside the dining room, the woman has decided to turn over the china cabinet. With labored breathing, she heaves it away from the wall, felling it in one strained motion like a lumberjack. Glazed plates with cornflower blue rings painted around their rims slide off their shelves and spin through the air like flying saucers. A matching set of teacups with miniature portraits of the house itself painted on their bottoms clatter and crash to the hardwood floor. After a moment where she pauses to catch her breath and run her fingers through her hair—a job well done—a cloud of dust stirred up by the fallen cabinet begins to settle. The woman peers around the room with her eyes darting around in their sockets, angle to angle, perspectives shifting, in search of her next victim.

Aha, she breathes, and walks determined and directly to the side table where the tea service has been set out for all to see, art objects of her mother's. The teapot is large and round, a swollen empty stomach. The woman picks it up by the handle and, spinning in a circle like a discus thrower, hurls it through the window over the sink that looks out onto the creek, where once she sat on a checked blanket and held mock tea parties with her older sister in the summers.

The teapot shatters the glass. The window is left smashed in the shape of an awkward star, with one shard of glass still dangling. It drops and clatters into the sink. The teapot is outside the house now, landing and rolling to who knows where.

The woman is the daughter of the woman who died in the house the night before. Just an hour after her mother died, she received a phone call from her older sister, and was told in the practiced tone of disdain her sister reserves for her, the tone that forces her to imagine scenes of arctic bleakness, "Mother's dead. The funeral is in two days. You can come or not." Then the phone went dead as well and she wondered why dead is an uninterrupted buzzing sound that issues from phones and heart monitors. Flies, too, but they can be stunned into silence with a swat of the hand. She wondered was her mother now buzzing endlessly, wherever her body had been laid out? Was she humming her own death?

Shelves with dolls and porcelain figurines of cats lined upon them—here are the new targets. She lumbers across the room, awkward and unruly, until she reaches the wall where the dolls and cats all smile down at her from their higher vantages. With one stroke she sweeps them from their perches and tramples each and every one. Here lies a doll's head with its eyes still clicking open and shut. There, in the corner, lay the porcelain scraps of a red Persian.

The Persian's face remains intact. Its mouth turns up at the corners. Bold and bodiless, it smiles.

A door opens unexpectedly in the house, and in rushes an autumn wind, chilling the air quickly. Goosebumps rise on her flesh, and she rubs her arms repeatedly. She turns from her task of destruction and peers wearily into the front room. There, in the doorway, stands her older sister, a silhouette backlit by the day.

"What have you done?" her sister says, shocked and gesturing at the mess the house has become. She moves across the room and surveys the domestic rubble, repeating the words, "What have you done, Alice? Just what have you done?"

Alice—for now that her sister has reminded her of who she is, she remembers—stands stock still in the heart of the disaster zone. She does not move, not even an inch. She wants to thank her sister, though, because she almost lost herself for a moment there. If Maureen hadn't swept in and named her so abruptly, she might have fallen down that dark, alien tunnel forever.

How did it happen? she wonders. How did she come to be here again? One moment she was answering the phone and hearing her sister's voice tell her, Mother's dead; and the next, she was boarding a plane that lifted her into thick darkness. She remembers a flight attendant nudging her awake in the middle of her flight—he had very white teeth and spoke with a French accent—and he said, "It's time, Cherie." He held a gold pocket watch close to her face, and it swung on its chain like a pendulum. Then

Before and

he led her down the narrow aisle—past disheveled passengers sleeping in their seats or paging through magazines—till they reached the emergency exit, which he popped open. Wind rushed in, so fast and heavy it felt like hands groping her all over her body. "Go ahead," the attendant said, nodding toward the black, curdling clouds outside. "Au revoir," Alice told him. And she jumped out, into the dark void.

Falling, falling.

"MOTHER'S DEAD," HER SISTER SAYS. It seems as though these are the only words in Maureen's vocabulary. Like a stroke victim left with partial aphasia, with two words she can use to respond to any question put to her.

Q: How are you today, Maureen?

A: Mother's dead.

Q: Would you like to go out for a breath of fresh air?

A: Mother's dead.

Q: Do you need to use the bathroom, dear?

(Her face seems to strain at this one. Her lips rise like curtains to reveal the empty stage of her mouth).

A: Mother's dead.

"Mother's dead, Alice," she says. "What is wrong with you?"

Alice doesn't know how to answer. It's the same question her mother and Maureen have asked since she was a little girl. She doesn't know what's wrong with her. She just does things that make them angry. Mostly because *she's* angry. She looks around in a sudden panic, searching the ruins of the dining room for some clue that will explain everything. The shards of cups and saucers lie strewn about her feet; the doll's bodies lie with their arms flopped out at their sides, as though they've been lined up and shot. She chews her bottom lip. The evidence is stacked against her.

"You're mad," Maureen says. She bends down at her knees and scoops up random pieces of porcelain. "Mother's *teacups*," she says, her voice straining. She holds the pieces in her cupped hands and rattles them at Alice. The porcelain scraps scrape against one another. "They were supposed to be left for me! You know how much Mother loved these. How *could* you, Alice? How *could* you?"

"I'm sorry," Alice says, her voice weak and milky. She scuffs one foot against the floor and looks over her shoulder to avoid Maureen's scrutiny.

"You're *sorry*?" Maureen says. "You're *sorry*? You're a mad woman is what you are. A mad woman! Get out of this house right now."

Afterlives   *A Mad Tea Party*

"No," Alice answers. "I won't leave. You get out." She will not be made into a stranger in this house again. She will not allow herself to be treated as she once had, when she'd run away from this home to find another, one that opened its doors for her and sealed behind her, shutting out the light. In that place, in that other house, she used to sit on a braided rug all day, watching the legs of other people walk around her. She'd put any powder or pill or needle into her body. Whatever anyone gave her, she put it inside her. It was always very dark in that house. The blinds were always closed. But one day, for no reason she could think of, she stepped out onto the porch, blinking in the warm sunlight, and saw palm trees tossing their heads by the roadside. She didn't know where she was, and stepped down off the porch. She called her mother's home from a pay phone on the street corner, and was received with the words, "You are not my daughter."

She picks up a sliver of plate, and holds it in her hand like a knife.

"Put that down, Alice," her sister warns, holding out her hands like a traffic cop. "Put that down right now. I'll call the police, I swear." But Alice swings the broken plate in the air, missing her sister with it purposefully.

Maureen screams and runs out the front door, leaving it swinging ajar behind her. Mother would not be happy with her, Alice thinks. Maureen knows better than to leave a door open behind her. It isn't proper. She was right though. I *am* mad. I'm a mad woman. This is a mad tea party and there is only room at the table for one.

THERE IS THE SOUND OF Maureen's engine turning over, then its revving, and Alice knows she has gone. The shard of plate she's holding slips from her grasp and falls to the floor. It clatters against the remnants of the other china, and Alice bends down to pick up the pieces. Now that she has nothing left to say to this room, she begins to clean it up. To pull it together again, back to a semblance of normality. All but one of the teacups is left in an irreversible condition, though, and even the sole survivor has been damaged. It has a long crack running through it. At any time it will split in two and then this particular species of teacup will be extinct.

"They were completely original," her mother says. "There was not a set of teacups like them on this side of the Atlantic. How could you, Alice? You were always a difficult girl."

Faint sobbing in the next room.

Alice gathers the pieces to her, holding them in her shirt as a peasant girl might gather apples in her apron, then pours them into the dustbin. Once she sets the china cabinet back on its feet (which is much harder than it was to topple it), she places the last teacup in the center of one of

Before and

its shelves. Behind the glass of the cabinet doors, the teacup looks like a relic. It looks as though it should be a museum exhibit, squared off by a velvet rope.

She hears a monologue run of its own accord in her head: This here is Alice's mother's last teacup. It was brought here in the late twentieth century, after Alice herself destroyed the rest. You can tell by the details of the portrait of the house at the bottom of the cup that the artist had a steady hand and, in fact, was Alice's father. Legend has it that he disappeared one night when Alice was a little girl, and that the circumstances surrounding his disappearance are vague. Alice's mother maintained that he was a sickly man, and had to go away for medical attention. But Alice's sister once told her he was a bastard and that she heard him one night on the phone, talking to a woman who was not their mother, and that she was glad he'd gone, and that she hoped he wouldn't ever come back. *Not ever!*

Are there any questions? Good. Then let's move on.

SHE IS TIRED. ALTHOUGH SHE'S the one who's been dealing out the blows, her body feels battered and old. A second hand coat. She pulls herself up the staircase, clinging to the banister in case her legs give way beneath her. When she reaches her room, her childhood room, she lays herself out on the bed with the lavender comforter and presses her face into a pillow.

She can't believe her mother's dead; it doesn't seem possible. This cannot be the woman she's wished dead so many times in the past, the woman who survived each death wished upon her. She was supposed to be invulnerable. She was supposed to live forever.

This is when she wants to scream and begin destroying the house all over again. This is when the air suddenly sticks in her throat, and she gasps over and over, suffocating. This is when the inside of her body aches hollow and empty, as if a fire's been burning her up from the inside out. If she opened her mouth to scream, black smoke would come billowing out. This is when she wants to cry so much, the rims of her eyes prick with pain and tremble.

But she refuses to do that. She's promised herself over and over again that she won't cry. That a dead mother won't defeat her like the living one did. That she won't feel anything. Nothing. Not a thing.

SHE PASSES THE NIGHT IN a constant state of waking. It is mere minutes that pass each time she closes her eyes before they flutter open again, and she stares blindly in the dark of the room to find the numbers on the alarm clock glowering at her. "Alice," she says, softly, every so often. "Alice, are you there?"

She nods in answer to herself. It is a system devised years ago, when she lived in the other house, the dark one. She based it off the game she and Maureen used to play in the swimming pool. "Marco!" she would shout with her eyes closed tight and her hands searching blindly through the water around her. "Polo!" Maureen would shout back, from a distance that was nearly incalculable.

In the morning, she dresses for the funeral. She still can't believe that her mother's dead and she has an incredible craving for a cup of tea. Sweet mint tea, like her mother always made for her whenever she was sad or sick or upset at something. She goes downstairs to make herself a cup and then remembers that she threw the teapot through the window, and that her mother was in the habit of storing her tea in that pot. She'd given up serving from it years ago, deciding to leave it out for show instead.

Alice convinces herself to do without it. She knows how to do without a lot.

At the funeral, Maureen stares coldly from beneath her black lace veil. Alice stands on one side of the grave, and Maureen stands on the other. Their mother is between them. Steven, the insurance agent, has his arm laced around Maureen's waist and looks briefly at Alice every few minutes. Each time he looks away, he fiddles with his tie. Probably he is remembering the time he kissed her and got slapped. The time he tried to sell life insurance to her and the girls in her dormitory. "Hey, Alice, let's write you up a policy. Let's make sure you're safe and insured."

They bent over the paperwork together, almost touching heads. And then he turned to her and, smack, he kissed her. And then, smack, she kissed him back with her hand. She never told Maureen about that, and by the time Steven did, it had become Alice who kissed him. Now that her Mother's dead, she supposes Maureen and Steven are rich. He has this great way of selling people insurance—he can convince almost anyone that they'll die someday.

Her mother is lowered into the ground and Maureen throws a handful of dirt ceremoniously onto the casket. Alice bends down and scoops up some dirt, too. She knows this is expected of her, that it's time to bury her mother. But her hand won't budge when she holds it over the grave. All she can think is, I want a cup of tea. I could really use a cup of tea right now. Tea would be good.

Her hand is shaking. A few clumps of dirt fall over the sides of her palms, dribbling against the casket lid. But those don't count! Those were dropped by chance, Alice thinks. Chance, I tell you! She clenches the dirt

Before and

in her hand, shakes her head, and walks away from the mourners, the dirt locked tight in her fist.

ALICE DOESN'T GO TO THE after-funeral party at Maureen's house. Besides, Maureen would probably chase her out anyway. Instead she walks all the way home from the cemetery, which is only a few miles away, along the banks of the creek, which is gurgling over smooth stones and carrying orange and yellow leaves along its current. She carries her high heels in her hands and ruins her stockings.

When she reaches her backyard, she rushes into the house because she still wants a cup of tea, mother's famous tea, with lots of milk like the English use, and honey to sweeten it up. She still has the dirt from the grave in her hand; by now she's molded it round and smooth and sweaty. If she held it in the hot palm of her hand and squeezed it for a long enough time, it might turn into a stone. A burial stone, in which she could drill a hole and thread it on a leather thong. She could strap it around her neck to wear forever.

But once she reaches the kitchen, she remembers again. The teapot—she threw it out the window, with all of the tea inside it too. She laughs out loud. This reminds her of something her mother used to say. "Don't throw the baby out with the bath water!" And how she never knew what that meant. She runs outside again and searches in some nearby shrubbery until she finds the teapot, exhumes it, only to discover it broken open and all of the loose black tea spilled out.

It blends in with the damp mulch so well.

She wants to scream again. All she wants is some tea. Is that so much to ask? She goes back into the house and pounds walls and tables, surfaces, with her open palm, the one without the dirt, until it reddens with pain. The house starts to shake again. She plays it for all it's worth, pounding on the dining room table, slamming her hand against the wall, stamping her feet on the hardwood floor. She curses. Is it so much to ask for some tea?

She sits down at the dining room table, lays her arms on the cold polished wood, then rests her head in her arms. Last night's tears and screams boil up inside her. They're in her throat, foaming. But she won't, she won't, she won't. She's promised herself that she won't. Her body shudders under the pressure.

"Alice!" her mother scolds. "Stop this right now. It's unattractive! Not like a lady at all."

Now her mother's hand is on her back, rubbing it. This feels really good. Alice lifts her head to find the teacup, the last of the teacups, sitting in front of her, empty.

"Cry into it, dear," her mother coos into her ear. "Your tears are hot enough."

She nods and nods, like a good girl, and she does. They slip out fast and hot down her cheeks and drop—drop one or two at a time—until the cup is full and the hand-painted house at the bottom is drowned beneath them. Enough tears to flood the entire house. Chairs and picture frames float down the hallways, and the walls collapse like a deck of cards. When she opens her mouth to breathe, a tiny squeal rushes out. Her cheeks and eyes are left streaked with mascara-tinted snail tracks.

"Drink," her mother tells her. Now she's kneading her shoulders. Alice looks into the cup to find a darkness appearing inside, spreading through her tears like octopus ink.

"Drink, love," her mother urges.

So she does. She drinks it. She almost chokes on the first sip, though. It is hot and bitter, not sweet at all. But she swallows and swallows, until every last drop is gone.

Before and

Born on the Edge of an Adjective

"I WAS BORN ON THE edge of an adjective," Neil tells me from San Francisco. He's calling on his new cell phone. He bought it because he thought it would add a little something to his image, but now he's not so sure. "Everywhere I look, people have these stupid things," he says. "I didn't realize till I had one of my own."

"You were what?" I ask.

"I was born on the edge of an adjective," he tells me. "That's for you," he says, and pauses to drag on his cigarette. "For your next song. At least a line, if not the title."

Neil's calling from a bar called the Shamrock, which he's frequented since leaving Youngstown behind. In the background of his voice, the crack of pool and the sound of eighties music. I can almost smell the smoke, see the haze. Neil hates eighties music, so I'm wondering why he's there. I'm wondering why he isn't here with me.

"That's a great line," I say. I don't tell him that I don't write songs anymore. That when he left, the music went with him, that I haven't written since. "You should write it," I tell him, and light a cigarette for myself.

"That's your thing, Marco," he says, and it still sends a thrill through my body to hear that name, instead of just Marc or Marcus. Only Neil calls me something different from everyone else.

"So when are you coming back?" I ask, then immediately revise my question. "When are you going to visit?"

"You know I can't, Marco," he says. "I can't come back, at least not for a while. I have to find out who I am. Ohio only obscures it. We've gone over all this before. Besides, I'm unboyfriendable. You need someone better than me. Someone solid."

I nod in agreement, even though Neil can't see. He went a thousand miles away to find himself, which sounds lame as a talk show conversation, but he did it, and I still can't help but ask when this self-imposed exile is going to end. Neil might not know himself, but I could tell him. I know who he is, he's just not listening. But when do any of us listen to what others have to say? I don't write music anymore. I only listen. If Neil asked me, I could sing him his song.

"I have to get going," Neil says impatiently. There's the click of his lighter and the exhale of smoke. "I have a date with this woman. I need to meet her on the other side of town."

"A woman?" I ask.

"She's cool," Neil says. "A dancer, real light on her feet. It's like gravity has no effect on her."

"So she floats? That's pretty amazing," I say.

"Seriously, Marco, she made me practice lifting her for her next recital. It was like picking up a teacup. An empty teacup. You would like her. Don't be a cynic. She's our type."

"That's great," I say. I tell him, "Call me soon," and put the phone down on its cradle. I turn up the radio, thinking she is not our type, not mine at least, and I wouldn't like her. I already hate this woman, Neil, and she's probably a bad dancer. Her legs are skinny like a flamingo's, and her hair is most likely blonde. Also, she floats. People who float aren't people. It's like a law or something. No floating for humans.

Neil likes his men different from his women. He prefers his men quietly smoldering, with dark eyes and thick hair. He likes his women blonde and loud as ambulances, with legs up to their chins. He used to read books with grand plots and lifeless characters. Now he reads books without plots that have grand characters, who think a lot throughout most of the book.

Take my hand, I want to tell him. Let me lead you through the hall of mirrors. I know your way. If I were alone, I'd be lost myself. But with you, I see the way clearly.

He wonders who he is, what it means to live in this world, how he's supposed to be. I've seen him clap his hands over his ears, as if the world grew too loud suddenly, and he sank down on my bed and curled into a fetal position. He wants to know what he's like, where he's going, where

Before and

he's been. He's a blank slate, he tells me, a *tabula rasa*. But this is not true. A more accurate description is possible.

He was like a book left behind by some weary traveler, in a country where no one knows how to read.

Take my hand, I want to tell him. Even though I'm blind on my own, I can see your path clearly.

WHERE ARE YOU GOING? WHERE have you been? These questions were our constant conversation. The first time we met, we were both at The Blue Note, one of the bars where the band I wrote songs for sometimes played. They still have an ongoing gig there, but I don't stop very often. They leave messages, various members of Winterlong, the lead singer, the bass guitarist, the piano player, Harry, who always says they're going downhill and need an injection of something new and different. "Give me a call, Marcus," he says. "Let's get together on something."

Neil was standing at the bar, in front of an empty stool, drinking from a pony-necked bottle. I sat three stools down. Finally, after the band took a break, he walked over, sat beside me, and, without looking at me, said, "The songs are good, but they need a new singer." I laughed involuntarily, almost spitting out a mouthful of beer.

"Really?" I said, grinning.

"Most definitely."

"And the songs? What makes them more deserving?"

"They're full of raw emotion. The lead singer doesn't know how to get that across."

It was something I'd heard other people say about someone else's music. Something you might read in a review, or hear on a college campus amongst earnest but not so humble students. But Neil was flattering. This quality is a necessary attractor. I was attracted, I cannot lie.

We went home that night together, after the band stopped playing, after closing down the Blue Note, and when we woke in the morning, him lying on his stomach, me flat on my back, his arm flung over my chest, I told him that I was the song writer.

"I knew that," he said.

"Why didn't you tell me?"

"Because you knew I knew. Really, don't act so innocent."

NEIL WORKS IRREGULARLY, ODD JOBS, temp work when he's desperate, and sometimes he'll tend bar. He did university for a few years, but he quit a semester before graduating. "It wasn't fun anymore," he explained. He'd been a Psychology major, a Philosophy major, an English major, as well

Afterlives   *Born on the Edge of an Adjective* as dabbling in Anthropology until it became too concrete, too biological, for his tastes. He switched majors every few semesters, and would then travel through the previous departments again, a phantom of academia.

"I've an insatiable mind," he told me, after we'd been seeing each other regularly for several weeks.

"I believe that," I said. And I did believe it. I believed him as much as is possible when you're beginning to know someone. It's a sweet period of discovery, and you can only take what the other person says as reality. Or not. Skepticism is possible. But then, why would you be there, listening, taking in another person, only to disbelieve them?

"You're a fool if you believe me, Marco," he said.

"I've been called worse."

"I'm sure," he said. "But isn't being called a fool somehow more hurtful?"

"Hmm." I thought for a moment. We were eating dinner at my apartment, drinking merlot and lapping up spaghetti. I wiped a napkin against my mouth, then looked at him and said, "It depends."

"On what?"

"On who calls you a fool."

He grinned, then frowned quickly, looking down into his glass of wine.

"What's the matter?" I asked, concerned, ready to soothe him. I was very ready to do that then. I still want to do that sometimes, soothe him, but I refrain from doing so. I might expect something in return. I might think Neil letting me care for him means something.

"Nothing's the matter," he said. "That's the problem. Nothing is the matter. With me. There's no me to have a matter about."

"That's not true," I said, swallowing the last of my wine.

"It is, Marco." He scraped his chair back, stood up and removed our plates, the glasses, to start the washing up.

I stood and went to him by the sink and put my arms around his waist, rested my chin on his shoulder. The heat of him, the scent of him, something a little like salt and a little like honey, the unbelievable solidity of his body was amplified by Neil's claim of not-being.

"You're here," I said. "And I may be a fool, but I definitely see someone where you're standing."

"Don't be ridiculous. I don't mean physically. I mean inside. Inside my head." He tapped two fingers against his skull.

"That's naïve nihilism," I answered, slowly removing my arms from his waist. I turned to leave him to the dishes, his forearms submerged in soapy water, and then he asked what I saw in him. Right then, at that moment.

"What do you see?"

What did I see? I didn't know if I'd be able to tell him, but he was calling my bluff. Had I really been paying attention? He stood before me with a plate in one hand and a dish rag in the other, waiting for my answer, which I found was ready on the tip of my tongue. Sometimes I surprise myself.

I told him he was outlandish, a loner, a hothouse flower who would wither if removed from his greenhouse. "This city," I said, "is your center. From here the sun can reach you. You rely on its depression, its darkness, its anonymity to the rest of the world. People don't even know this place exists. Some of those people live here. I've made up a slogan for Youngstown," I told him. "Youngstown: Why fix it if it isn't broken?"

But it was broken, is broken. No money, no jobs. This is what you call an economic depression. An economic depression means there's no money, and people are depressed about it. Buildings haven't been updated since the seventies, since the steel mills closed down. Sidewalks buckle, graffiti looms, vacant lots appear daily, filled with patches of yellow-brown grass and shattered beer bottles, and still the city will not change. Here, entropy is the golden rule. For some people that's attractive.

Neil didn't say anything. He continued washing up, sulking silently, his back bent over the sink, his head lowered, his entire body a question mark.

How to tally, to compose, to bring together answers? And what to do with them once they've been found?

"Are you working?" I ask when he calls me.

"I'm doing some carpentry for the dancer," he says.

"Is she paying you?"

"Of course she's paying me, Marco. I'm not a fool."

"I didn't say that."

"You implied."

"Forget it."

"I will."

"Good."

They've been seeing each other for two weeks now, maybe more, Neil and the flamingo. Her name, he's informed me, is Margaret Stanbottom. Not quite what I'd imagined for a dancer, but I can never predict who Neil will drag home. Or in this case, who he'll follow home.

They're living together, in her half of a Victorian house on Valencia. She's very wealthy, according to Neil, and she keeps him in clothes and well-fed, amongst other luxuries. She bought him the cell phone, which now has a message that goes something like: "I'm not here, but nothing changes. Leave me a message. That helps a lot."

Helps who? Helps Neil feel real, although not anyone would understand that. It's code, like mandarin poetry, like Tori Amos lyrics. It's Neil giving his callers an emotional update. I don't leave messages. The cell phone will list my number as having called him. That's enough to tell him I care.

He and Margaret are living life simply, he tells me. Their lives have become slightly hermetic. Excepting her dance recitals and his weekend pool league at the Shamrock, they spend most of their time at home. Margaret's dancing and Neil's pool league are the last remains of their social beings. They've agreed that each of them should keep hold of something outside of their relationship.

The Shamrock, house of eighties music that it is, is Neil's choice for keeping contact with the world. The thing about the Shamrock, though, is that more than half of its patrons are from Youngstown or Cleveland.

"It's a kind of halfway house for transplanted Northeastern Ohioans," Neil jokes.

"You're kidding me, right?" I asked when he first mentioned this.

"Not at all," said Neil. "After I got off my train in Monterey, I was hanging out at the wharf and I ran into this sweet couple who live in Berkeley. They were down for a weekend holiday, and it turned out they had moved from Youngstown to the Bay Area five years ago. They told me to go to the Shamrock when I rolled into San Francisco, that a lot of people from Ohio hang together there."

So Neil went first thing after his bus reached the city, and of course this couple hadn't been lying. The bartender, the waitresses, everyone in the Shamrock had originally grown up in Ohio, nine out of ten from Cleveland or Youngstown. The rest were from Akron or Kent. Sandy, the bartender, helped Neil find a room to rent in a boarding house run by a Pakistani family. "I could smell curry morning, evening and night," Neil said.

"Don't you think it's strange?" I asked. "Isn't it bizarre to find a sort of regional subculture centered in a particular bar?"

"Not really," Neil said. "I mean, maybe a little at first, but after a while, it just felt natural. I met Margaret at the Shamrock, too."

"Margaret's from Ohio?"

Neil laughed. I imagined him shaking his head and grinning at my stupidity.

"Margaret," said Neil, "cannot be categorized into any sort of region or geography. I'd say she's a citizen of the world, but even that doesn't describe her correctly. A citizen of the universe, is Margaret."

Before and

"She's from Mars then," I said, getting in a little gibe on the flamingo. "That would explain her talent for floating. Doesn't Mars have more gravity? Of course she'd float on this planet."

"No," Neil said. "Actually, we don't have the capability to pronounce her world's name."

For every bit of information, for every detail of his life he gives me, with which to build a model of his world away from me, another gap opens in the gulf between us. When the world was still new and undiscovered, not fully charted, the old map-makers used to close off the edges of their maps with the words "There Be Dragons". When I think of Neil and the Shamrock, of Margaret, I imagine myself in a tiny boat rocked in a sea carved with raucous waves. I reach the edge of the ocean, where Margaret Stanbottom resides, queen dragon of the depths, her scales glittering under the water, her breath foul, her rows of teeth sharp and eager, and my tiny boat slides off the edge of the world into darkness and cold points of light.

How to tally, to compose, to bring together answers? And what to do with them once they've been found?

We used to spend our weekends lying around my apartment, listening to music, or sometimes we'd walk into the city park, which is surprisingly beautiful and ranges for miles. The oasis in the desert of post-industry. Our favorite spot was Lanterman's Mill, where we'd stand on the back platform, leaning against the guard rail, where we could almost reach out to the waterfall and touch it as it crashed beneath our feet, where it once turned the wheel of the mill. A covered bridge spanned the air above the waterfall, and once, on a warm spring morning, we stood below and watched a couple above us being married. Their families crossed from either side of the bridge as part of the ritual of joining. Neil felt it was over-wrought. I said it was nice. A nice thing. I felt that. I still do.

We went home from the park that day and made love only moments after returning. Neil's T-shirt, hanging limply from the lampshade. My jeans, straddling the back of a chair. His lips moved over my body, eager, more eager than I could ever remember. I was quite taken with him like this, but also a bit suspicious. Why was he acting so determinedly passionate? Not that I minded. But my brain was saying, Something is wrong.

Afterwards, we lay exhausted on the rumpled bed sheets, staring at the ceiling. Actually how it happened was, I stared at the ceiling. Then I looked over and saw Neil staring up as well. It was a good feeling, a kind of synchronicity. I started to wonder what else we did at the same time.

I listened to our breathing. We breathed in time together. I put my ear to his chest and listened to the hum and gurgle of his inner workings. I imagined mine sounding the same.

"What are you doing?" he asked.

"Listening."

"Anything interesting?"

"Definitely. You have an orchestra in there."

"An orchestra? Ha!" He threw his head back and launched into a fit of laughter. "It's all music to you, isn't it, Marco?"

I nodded and smiled.

"And does your passion for music rub off on those old ladies and spoiled children you tutor?"

"I hope," I said. I taught piano, and it brought in decent money. The only downside was having to drive out of the city into the suburbs, where everyone I tutored lived.

"Do they listen to you, Marco?" he asked. "Do you speak to them like you do me?"

"I don't speak differently to different people," I told him.

"But you do," he said. "You do, and you don't have any control over it."

"How so?"

He turned his face to me, but stared somewhere down towards the end of the bed. "It's not you, or anyone's fault, Marco," he whispered. "People just do it. They change how you talk. They hear what they want to, hear it how they want it to sound, so much that if you spoke angrily to someone who didn't want to be hurt by you, they'd hear you differently. Or likewise, if you spoke lovingly to someone who didn't want to be loved by you, they'd turn your tone into something vile. It's a defensive strategy. It must be hardwired. People will never truly understand each other."

"And how do you know this?" I asked. I took his theories seriously, even though I didn't believe half of them. It was a conscious decision, to take anything he said seriously, if not literally. I thought it a respectable thing to do, and so I asked him, "Why do you think this is true?"

"I've gathered data," he said, turning his face away from me, staring back at the ceiling again. He twirled his index finger in the hair around his navel for a moment, then lifted it to rub his eye. "Firsthand experience, Marco," he continued. "Empirical evidence abounds."

It was the first time I began to distrust him. Had he pulled my strings at one time or another, to see how I'd react to the crazy things he said? Played a game to confirm his theories? I stood up from the bed, slid my jeans on, and walked out of the room, scratching the back of my neck. A nervous habit.

Neil followed me. When I went into the living room and sat in front of the television, he stood in my way. When I moved into the kitchen and sat at the dinner table with a book, he stood behind me, his chin on my shoulder, breathing hotly, reading along with me, a pet peeve of mine. I snapped the television off with the remote, snapped the book closed, and finally shouted, "What do you want?"

"A true answer," he said.

"An answer about who you are?" I asked. "You still want *me* to answer that question?"

"Yes," he said. Then he knelt beside me and put his finger on the space between my eye and the bridge of my nose. I have a birthmark there: small, round and impossibly brown. He touched it lightly, then ran his fingertip across it in whirls. When I was a teenager, I hated it, wanted to be rid of it in the worst way imaginable. I even tried to cover it with my mother's pancake makeup, but I'd still been able to see it even then. Finally I grew accustomed to it, learned to ignore it. Here he was, reminding me of it again.

"I've always loved this birthmark," Neil said, his fingertips lingering. He was shirtless, pantless, naked anyway you looked at him.

"I used to hate it," I said.

"Why?" he asked, a tone of sympathy in his voice, as if I were pathetic, a poor soul to whom he would bring solace.

"Because it made me look odd. Different."

"But that's good," he said. "I'd never have spoken to you at the Blue Note if I hadn't seen this birthmark. I don't have any, unfortunately."

"Liar," I said. "Everyone has birthmarks."

"I don't," he said, and so I searched him. I ranged over his body, exploring, covering his every inch only to find that he was being truthful. Completely bare of any markings, his skin was white and unblemished. When I looked up, he was crying without making a sound.

"Do you know what they call the places on maps that haven't been charted yet?" I asked.

He shook his head, blinking tears away.

"Sleeping beauties."

NEIL MET MARGARET STANBOTTOM WHILE he was pool sharking one night at the Shamrock. He'd made a few dollars, eighty to be exact, and was ready to spend the rest of the evening at the bar, drinking and telling Youngstown stories to Sandy or any of the other Ohioans crowding the bar that evening. He'd bought his first beer and taken a sip when Margaret walked in wearing a purple leotard, carrying a satchel over her shoulder, looking lost. She peered around the dim bar for a moment, looked both left and right, waved smoke away from her face, then turned and walked back out the door.

Neil didn't know why, but he felt an irresistible urge to follow her. As if a string ran from his body and connected to hers, he followed. Good dog. When he stumbled out onto the street, he saw her blonde mane turning a corner. He dashed after her, his mouth presciently filled with her name.

"Margaret," he shouted behind her, but she continued walking, all the way to Valencia, where she stopped in front of her two story Victorian, the bay window in her half, and turned to face him. Neil was wheezing from the fast pace he'd had to walk to keep up with her. Margaret, however, didn't seem phased. She looked him up, and looked him down, as if assessing his value, another piece of antique furniture, a plate of blue china from the Far East, and said, "Welcome home, Neil."

She held her hand out, palm up, and curled her fingers inward. *Come here.* Neil went to her, placed his hand in hers, and she closed her fingers over his. His hands were sweaty. Hers were cold and dry. Neil's palms sweat when he's nervous. His left eye twitches. Sometimes, when he can't think of anything to say in a social situation, he'll pretend to cough and look away.

Neil coughed.

"You don't have to be nervous, darling," she said. Can you believe it? *Darling.* As if he were a fifteen year old adolescent about to have sex for the first time. A regular Mrs. Robinson. "I know all about you," she said, and began to lead him up the steps of the front porch. A wind chime hung over the entryway. The wind blew faintly. The chimes swayed without making any sound.

Margaret opened the door to her half of the Victorian and led Neil into the foyer. She took off his leather jacket; she unbuttoned his collar; she made him a gin and tonic, his favorite. Then they sat in her living room: hardwood floors, buffed and polished; wicker furniture, creaking under their weight. The smell, Neil told me, reminded him of craft stores, a little dried-up floral potpourri mixed with furniture polish.

"Listen, Neil," she told him, "because I'm only going to tell you this once. You've been chosen. By me, of course. And what I'm about to offer is the chance of a lifetime. Of your lifetime, I mean. A human being's lifetime, that is."

Margaret proceeded to tell him about her alien status. She wasn't from Mexico, though, as Neil immediately thought. Margaret hadn't crossed any river; she hadn't hidden herself away in some truck full of oranges. She had crossed the galaxy, and she and her people, she told him, had

Before and

chosen humans to observe. People who could tell them something about humanity.

Neil was Margaret's baby. He'd made quite a splash with the others. Margaret extended an invitation for Neil to accompany her back to her home.

She was flattering. This is a necessary attractor. Neil was flattered, although this is something I've concluded on my own.

What was Neil thinking? I ask him, and he says, "Marco, I was thinking, what an opportunity. What an amazing woman. She could read my mind."

"She can read your mind?"

"It was how she knew my name, how I knew hers."

"So you can read her mind, too?"

"No, no, no," Neil says, frustrated. "She can project her thoughts *on* me, as well. She *gave* me her name, before we even spoke."

"Hmm." I decide not to say anything.

Finally, Neil says, "I know you don't believe me, but that's so like you, Marco."

"I never said I didn't believe you."

"I can tell you don't."

"What?" I say. "Are Margaret's powers rubbing off on you? You can read my mind all the way from San Francisco? You could get rich that way, Neil."

"I called you to say goodbye," he says.

"Goodbye? Why?"

"Because we're leaving. In a few days. I won't see you again. Ever. It won't be possible. If they fly me back, you and everyone else I know will be dead. The paradox of faster than light travel, you know. I wanted to tell you I love you, and goodbye. And to remember that line I gave you, which actually Margaret thought up."

"What line?"

"I was born on the edge of an adjective, Neil. God, don't you ever listen? Margaret told me that the other night. That's who I am. I think it's who you are, too. It's who we are."

"I love you too," I say. And when I start to tell him that he's crazy—that he should leave this crazy woman who has put this craziness into him, who tells him cryptic riddles that sound more like horoscope readings, that he should come back from San Francisco immediately, that I will pay for a bus ticket, a train ticket, a plane ticket, even a boat, whatever mode of travel he finds necessary to bring him home—he hangs up on me. A few moments of silence, then the phone disconnects.

AFTER I HANG UP I think, I should be worried. I should bite my nails, or pace the hallway. I should do something to make myself feel like I'm adequately caring, not numb to the situation. But I can't. I make a TV dinner. I eat it watching TV. I sit in my armchair with my legs over one arm of it, and my head lolling off the other, and stare at the ceiling for a while, wondering if Neil is staring at his ceiling in San Francisco, too. I drink a bottle of Cabernet. I spill a spot of it on my carpet. But all I can manage in the way of worry for Neil is that I'll soon see him on CNN making a fool of himself, connected with a cult happening. I hope they aren't the sort of cult that take their own lives. I can deal with Neil making a fool of himself, but not with him being dead.

The phone rings the next morning, and when I answer, Harry, the pianist for Winterlong, tells me, "Well, hello, stranger. Why haven't you returned my calls?"

"Sorry," I say, and launch into reasons for my own self-imposed exile. "I've been sick a little. I've been working a lot," I tell Harry.

"Excuses, excuses," Harry says.

We make a date to get together. Do I have any new material? No, I don't. I haven't been writing.

"It doesn't matter," Harry tells me. "Just let's get together. It's been too long."

"Any word on Neil?" he asks before we hang up.

"No," I say. "None." And afterwards I'm thinking, there never was.

I SIT AND WAIT IN the kitchen, staring at the phone. I lie on my bed with my head turned towards the nightstand, and stare at the phone. I stop on sidewalks, near phone booths, and wait for them to ring, but they never do. Or when they do ring, it's the wrong number, or it's Harry, or whoever. It isn't Neil.

I worry after a few days pass without hearing from him, so I pick up the phone and dial Neil's cell phone. A pre-recorded message tells me the number is no longer in service. So I dial Margaret's number, as Neil had called me collect from her house a few times and it's on my phone bill. But again, a recorded message.

"This number has been disconnected."

ANOTHER MOTTO FOR YOUNGSTOWN: IF you can be happy here, you can be happy anywhere.

HOW TO TALLY, TO COMPOSE, to bring together answers? And what to do with them once they've been found? I could throw Neil into the air

Before and

and disperse him, no more than stardust or pollen, a creature of light and lightness, not something with weight or gravity, to keep him down, to keep him here, with me. I could try to name him, define him, but for all my little words, something of him would still escape me.

"Let me lead you through the hall of mirrors," I whisper in a café downtown, even though there's no one near enough to hear me. I drink my coffee and begin to hum a new tune.

I imagine Margaret's Victorian, light pouring through the bay window at this moment. It's a beautiful morning in San Francisco. Her house is quiet. It smells like potpourri and furniture polish. Outside, a wind chime chimes, barely audible.

But inside, no one is home.

Christopher Barzak

Before and

The Other Angelas

SHE DECIDES TO KILL HERSELF. She decides she doesn't want to live any-more. She decides she's tired of finding her husband with other women, women who couldn't possibly be as loyal and charming and sexy for a woman of certain age as she is. She is tired of him returning after he is through with each one. She is tired of cleaning up his messes, handling his phone calls, telling his boss he isn't home or that he is sick. She is tired of excuses, of the constant mantra in her mind that goes, "He's having a rough time, middle age and all, he'll settle down again." She is tired. This, then, decides her. She will lay down and allow herself to cease existing. She will close her eyes and imagine her body's systems shutting down one by one, the lights in a building stuttering off floor by floor. Closing time.

In the morning she finds she is not alone. She rolls over into soft warmth. Didn't I die? She is puzzled. She opens her eyes to find another pair of eyes looking back. A pair of the same eyes in the same face with the same blonde hair, tangled and frizzy from sleep. What cracks in her lips! She raises her hand to her cheek, her cheek that is beginning to sag with age, and the other woman raises her hand to the cheek opposite. "Who are you?" they ask each other.

"I'm Angela," they both answer.

"*I'm* Angela," they counter.

"No, *I'm* Angela," they say. Their voices begin to harmonize.

"Is this going to be a problem?" asks Angela.

"It doesn't have to be, I suppose," says the other Angela.

THE OTHER ANGELA SELECTS AN outfit from the closet. The old Angela doesn't mind. "Take what you want," she says, so the other Angela does. She picks out a skirt that will flow around her legs, sheer and spring-like, and a white blouse. Nothing in here seems to match, so she will have to make do. This Angela would rather have new clothes. Wearing the old Angela's clothes makes her feel as if she is wearing the clothes of a dead woman. She doesn't like dead women. This is one of the first things the other Angela decides.

She goes out for the day, leaving the old Angela in bed, the house a mess behind her. "You should get up and get fresh air," she tells Angela before she goes, but the old Angela just waves her hand and says, "Go on, you go."

She goes, then, to the mall. She has the old Angela's credit cards. She buys a new outfit, a skirt and blouse that match and have more color. She buys a bracelet and matching necklace. She buys perfume. She comes home later and Angela is still in bed, but Angela's husband is sitting in the recliner. "Well who do we have here?" he says, a sly grin climbing up his face, very sexy she thinks instinctively.

They fuck on the floor, a fast fire, but within five minutes he is done and it is over. She decides sex isn't so special. She thought it would be better. She has vague memories—memories left over from the Angela in bed—of sex being incredible, spicy and full of musk and time stretching out like taffy. But that Angela is lying in bed like a sack of nothing, so what would she know?

Angela's husband buttons up his pants and asks what's for dinner. She says she doesn't know. "What do you mean?" he asks. "You always have dinner ready." She shrugs and tells him to get it somewhere else.

He looks upset and, in a threatening voice, says, "I guess I will. I guess I *will* get it somewhere else!"

He grabs his jacket and slams the door. She decides she doesn't like doors. They open and close far too much, and the sounds they make—some creaking, some slamming, some slipping closed with only a slight gust of air—all of these sounds she decides are unnerving. She will close all the doors, she decides, and lock them. She will have the locks changed, then he will never be able to open them again.

IN THE MORNING, SHE WAKES next to the old Angela, and on her other side another Angela has spent the night. The three wake up together at dawn, yawning, stretching their arms above their heads, sighing together. They make coffee. Even the old Angela gets out of bed. "I'm feeling better,"

Before and

she says. "I'm feeling like a million bucks." She thanks the other Angela for dealing with her husband.

"The locksmith is coming this afternoon," says the other Angela, and the new Angela says, "Oh good, I was wondering if you remembered."

They nod at each other, lifting their mugs to their lips and sipping.

In the afternoon the new Angela decides she wants a hairdo, a manicure, a pedicure, and maybe she would like to borrow that perfume. "Why?" says the other Angela. The new Angela shrugs.

"No reason."

She spritzes the perfume on her neck and shoulders, drives to the spa and has her nails done, her hair done, and smiles a lot at Gregorio, the man who gives her a back massage and touches her in places where he shouldn't. Well, she likes it, so it's okay, she's thinking, but really she never gave any indication that this was wanted. His skin is tan and his smile is straight and white. She decides she likes this, a white smile in a tan face. "What do you think about the beach, Gregorio?" she asks.

He purses his lips and thinks for a moment. "I like the beach," he says. "It's warm there. The sand is soft and hot. The waves are rhythmic, like lovemaking, no?"

"That's what I think too," she says. "Let's go."

They go to the beach and she fucks him behind a sand dune. He holds her tight and she can't help but keep from looking around, above her head, off to the side, to see if anyone can see them. No one does. The sand is soft and hot, like he said, but it's also itchy. He doesn't smile when he fucks her, he grits his teeth. He grunts a lot. She doesn't like this part of him, she decides. She says, "Smile!" as if she is taking his picture, and he does. A moment later, he goes back to grunting and gritting.

She comes home with sand clinging to her legs and takes a shower. That was interesting, she thinks. Now I know what that feels like. She doesn't understand the attraction. Is this what her husband does that keeps him so occupied with other women? There is a spark, she admits, but it isn't anything to keep her going.

She decides Gregorio was a decent lover, but nothing special. Not like his smile and his massage. His penis was much smaller than she imagined also. This is so often the case: Nothing in her imagination meets reality often enough. She decides the world isn't nearly as interesting as it is in her head.

THE FOUR OF THEM BEGIN cleaning up the house. The old Angela and the other Angela, the new Angela and the even newer Angela who arrived that very morning. One sweeps, one dusts, one scrubs, one packs their husband's bags. He has so many things that by the time she has him packed, over half the house is bare. She thought she had more things, but she doesn't. She is left with kitchenware, a bedroom suit, and several shells from a beach where they honeymooned. She is left with two chairs and a table, she is left with her grandmother's quilts and several almost full photo albums. She is left with the remains of his life outside her: people calling for her to tell them he is gone. She is left with only herself to rely on. She decides this is a good thing.

She sits down in one of the two chairs at the table. The other Angelas put away feather dusters and vacuums, then gather round, smiling, laughing at semi-funny jokes. The newest one elbows her to join in on the fun.

So she does. She smiles. She decides she can do that too.

Christopher Barzak   Before and

A Resurrection Artist

LYING HERE IN THIS ABANDONED hotel, I have done it once again. Once every year or so, depending on my finances, I allow myself to die. It's a way of life, a means to an end, or an end to life as a way of surviving. Any way you look at it, my body is a miracle.

Now comes the burning sensation of re-entry, a tingling that grows to feel like fire. As I find myself returning to my body, every cell expands, flooding with electricity. Then my eyes blink over and over, making adjustments to reality and to the grade of light. I gasp for a first breath, then howl like a newborn. After this I can begin to see the people who killed me hovering over my body, their oval faces peering down, curious, amazed.

This audience has been the eighth group to kill me. It was a thrill for them, I'm sure, even though some have already seen me do this. I'm developing a following. Times are rough, Jan constantly tells me. People need something to believe in. Jan is my manager. She's my sister, too. Improvisation, spins on old ideas, variations on a theme, she advises, is what's needed to keep this act alive.

This act can't die, though, even if I tried. Like the cat, I have nine lives. More than nine most likely, but in matters like this there's always the unpredictable to take into account. So far, though, Jan and I haven't figured out how to mess up death.

A young man wearing a dark suit says, "This can't be happening." I cough and spit up blood in my hands. There's a golden ring on one of my fingers that wasn't there when I died. This must be what I brought back this time.

Christopher Barzak

how they killed me, but can only remember in pieces: a burn ribs where a knife slid in, the jolt of a gunshot splitting my chest, my eyes flooding with blood after the blow of a hammer.

Believe," says Jan. I follow her voice to find her standing beside me. She waves her hand over my body, from head to toe. "You did it yourselves," she tells them. "Ladies and gentlemen, this is his body, his arms, his legs, his head and torso. You've kept vigil beside him since the moment of death. I hope the experience has been satisfying."

There's an old lady whose eyes have slowly narrowed to slits. "I'm not so sure," she says. "I mean, I *know* he died. We saw the heart monitor, the flat line. But now that he's alive again, it just doesn't seem fair."

A typical reaction, really. Some people are confused about what they truly want. She didn't pay for a resurrection; she only wanted the death.

But we have their money, ten thousand dollars a head, and there are eight of them. We kept this group small since outings like this—a killing instead of a suicide—are illegal. Hence the abandoned hotel, once known as The Flamingo. The carpet, the striped wallpaper, the floor of the drained pool, everything here is pink.

"Mrs. Bertrand," Jan says, "you've just witnessed a miracle. My little brother, barely twenty-three years old, allowed you to kill him so he could return to us from death. How can you possibly be disappointed?"

Mrs. Bertrand sniffles. "Oh yes," she says. "I know. I wasn't really complaining. Don't mind me."

Jan smiles. Mrs. Bertrand smiles. The rest of the killers smile. I try, but only manage a weak sneer.

"Well," Jan says later, "that was almost profitable." She's sitting at a table in the corner of the room. Calculator and laptop out, spreadsheet of our budget glowing onscreen. The killers have left, have said their goodbyes, their goodnights, have given me their best regards. I'm still half-naked and bloody, although the blood dried hours ago, while I was dead.

"Why *almost* profitable?" I ask. "Eighty thousand. That's a good haul."

"It will keep our heads above water," says Jan. She grimaces, taps her teeth with a long red fingernail. "Aiden," she says, looking at me in her serious way. "You can't go so long between exhibitions anymore. It's been almost two years since the last one. People forget about you if you don't give them what they want. Eighty thousand won't get us through the next two years. And besides, we shouldn't be so lazy. Dad raised us to work hard. We should honor his memory better."

Goosebumps begin to pop up on my legs. I look down and find something very like a beetle crawling across the hairs on my thigh. It has a red

V-shaped mark on its black-shelled back. I position my fingers next to it and flick it across the room, where it lands beside Jan's foot and waves its legs in the air desperately.

"Gross," says Jan. "Why don't you take a shower?"

"There's no water in this place."

"Well, put some clothes on and find some. You're a goddamned mess."

I'm a goddamned mess, I'm a goddamned mess. God damned, maybe; a mess, definitely. Jan has no tact, no consideration with words. She thinks they are so innocent, something you can take for granted, so she uses them without thinking. She's comfortable with clichés. I, on the other hand, am a little more than wary. Too often I find myself victimized by an over-used phrase. *You're a goddamned mess.* I'm certain Jan didn't think out the alternative meanings of that one.

First a stop at a gas station bathroom to wash the blood from my face so I'm suitable in public. Then a shower at the local Y, long and steam-heavy. There's nothing like it to make me feel fresh and new again. As I wash off the second skin of dried blood I think, this must be like afterbirth, how a nurse wipes it off of a newborn's skin.

"Jesus, what happened to you?" a man says beside me. He's soaping up his hairy chest, staring over at me like he's either disgusted or frightened. He walked in minutes after me and, though I've already washed off all the blood, a few fresh scars remain. Those will take a week or so to heal.

"Car accident," I tell him. "Head-on, couple of years ago."

"No kidding," he says, lathering his underarms.

"I was lucky," I say. "I wasn't even wearing a safety belt."

"Shit," he says. "You *are* lucky, buddy."

I nod in this way that makes me look like I feel really lucky. Someone like him would appreciate a nod like that, I think. You can't ever be sure what someone else wants, but I can't help but try to anticipate.

This time I've anticipated correctly. The guy gives me a sympathetic shake of his head, an I-feel-for-you-buddy face, but it only manages to disturb me.

I look away, tip my head back, and fill my mouth with hot water.

IT WASN'T ALWAYS SUCH A bother, really. Resurrection, I mean. For quite some time it was a necessary, meaningful part of my life. If I couldn't resurrect, I wondered, who would I be? Most likely I would have had a wallet with pictures of a wife and children inside it, credit cards, a driver's license, and a decent amount of money. These articles, then, would have defined my one, singular life. But I have to stop this line of thinking. I can't allow myself the fantasy of banality. It's been years since I first resurrected, but the quotidian can still drive me wild with envy and fear.

The first time I died, I was fifteen. We'd just buried my father two months earlier. I was having trouble learning how to live without him. I'd been crying a lot, and sleeping. Often I'd chew my nails down to the quick. Then one day I hung myself from our staircase banister. My mother found me later and, I'm sure you can imagine, a certain amount of hysteria followed from there.

She got me down, though, with Jan's help. Jan was going to college at the time, majoring in business management, but I'd had the decency to hang myself at Christmas, when I knew she'd be home to help my mother unhinge me.

My neck was broken. I can remember the snap, the grind of bone, and the awful copper taste that filled my throat. Then I fainted. Then I stopped breathing. Mom and Jan had gone out shopping. When they returned, arms strung with department store bags, I'd already been dead for several hours.

If they hadn't been so overwhelmed, if they hadn't wailed in confusion, they might have called an ambulance, and I might have resurrected under the blare of sirens. But instead my mother sobbed over my broken body while Jan tried to comfort her. They found a thick, leather-bound book in my hands, my fingers curled stiff around the spine. The pages were blank, so they didn't know what to make of it. Shouldn't it have held the reasons for my dying? Instead of being the period to punctuate the end of my life, though, it was blank, a beginning. When I opened my eyes and sat up a few minutes later, the first thing I did was ask if the stores had been crowded.

Jan slapped me. Jan slaps hard. She was so angry at first. Then after my mother came around from her faint and cheered up a bit, Jan had one of her big ideas. Those loans of hers, my mother's debts, my dead father's unpaid hospital bills. If I could do it again, this death trick, we could make a pretty penny. At the time I thought that could be a good benefit. But really the thing I was feeling was that, for the first time in my life, I'd found something a little like myself.

My mother refused. She shook her head and said no flat out. This was a miracle, she insisted, not a talent. Things like this happen for a reason, not over and over like sitcom reruns.

Jan nodded and said my mother was right. Of course it was a bad idea. But later, after our mother went to sleep, she came to stand in my bedroom doorway and said, "We're going to get to the bottom of this."

She led me to the bathroom, where she filled the tub with warm water and told me to get in. "What for?" I asked. I folded my arms across my chest, suddenly chilly.

Jan frowned. Tears started to fill her eyes. "Do this for me, Aiden," she said. She looked down at the tiled floor and wiped her eyes with the back of her hand.

I got into the tub and the water soaked through my jeans and t-shirt. Jan knelt on the floor beside me. She took my wrists, one after the other, and slid a razor up them gently. I winced, crying a little as the cuts she made separated. Blood pulsed out, but the tub caught it. It caught all of my blood for the rest of the night.

"I HAVE AN IDEA," JAN says. She's cleaned up the hotel room, destroyed the evidence. Not that the proprietors of the Flamingo will be returning. She's standing next to a sliding glass door that opens onto a balcony. You don't have to open it—the glass is shattered—so you can step right through. She points a finger in the air beside her ear, like a light bulb lighting, wagging it a little.

"What?" I say. I can't stand when she does this.

"We go global," Jan says. "I've built you that web page, but I don't think we've been using it to its full potential."

"Which would be?"

"Something big," says Jan. She paces back and forth in a square of sunlight falling through the shattered door. The web page she built has what I've named a "Diery" on it, a journal that chronicles my deaths. I write my entries in the leather-bound book I brought back the first time I died, then Jan transfers them to the web. The entries are the only thing I have to do with the site. Jan does all the rest. She says I have a way with words, but that I should let her take care of business.

"How big is big?" I ask.

"We advertise for a grand finale," says Jan. "We say it's your last appearance. Then the appointments pour in. It'll be like when some painter dies and his paintings suddenly become worth something. I'm a genius, I know, you don't have to say so."

"But that would be lying," I say. "You know I'll just come back."

"Oh Jesus, Aiden, no one will give a damn if we give them a good enough ending. Lighten up."

I WRITE:

Dear Diery,

There is only one other sensation like death available: orgasm. The French call it *la petite mort*, the little death. It's that brief moment during climax when everything is burned away from consciousness and a person feels a part of their self break off, snap in half, shatter into a thousand pieces.

Resurrection, like everything else, can be a form of art. I do my best to keep my dying pure, to make it something special. It's a high-wire act without a net, it's skating on melting ice. You fall through, you drown in that dark place. It's the ascension, when you resurface, when your head breaks the water, when you gasp for air again, that elevates the fall to something grander. Somehow you've survived.

It sounds as though it's done for audiences alone, but this is not true. It's the flare of recognition, the shock of being seen in such a vulnerable state, it's the cries of believers and unbelievers when I come round that thrills me back into my bones and blood. "A miracle!" they all shout, even though they've murdered me as best as they know how.

I TRY TO WRITE:

This was the first time I allowed myself to be murdered by strangers; it was also the last. Not having control of the situation, not being the one to take my own life is too horrible to repeat.

Resurrection isn't New Age or mystical. It's not something connected with people who migrate to be near the UFO infested desert skies of New Mexico. No aliens, no chakras, no spells, no crystals or runes will be found upon my person.

Resurrection is an art, not a movement. It's not something anyone can decide to do. And what I must be clear about is that I'm not someone that requires faith or belief. I'm no messiah, nor do my travels between death and life mean much beyond that event in and of itself. My deaths and rebirths remind others of their own forgotten lives. We all die, but we do not all resurrect. Herein lies a profound difference.

BUT JAN DELETES THIS SECTION. She says she will only publish entries that carry positive messages. "This stuff about being murdered," she says, "it's just too bleak. And as for the rest, talking negatively about certain groups of people, i.e. New Age followers and UFO cults, you just can't do that, Aiden. Don't alienate part of your audience."

"I was trying to explain," I say. "What I experience. What I know."

"Don't worry about things like that," says Jan. "That's not something anyone wants to hear anyway."

JAN IS ALL SECRETS AND mystery. She's rented me a room at an upscale hotel. She sends me an allowance every week. "You deserve it, baby brother," she says. "Live it up for a while, hear?"

"Thanks, Jan," I say, even though I'm bursting with suspicion.

She calls every day to make sure I'm having fun, eating well, seeing the sights. She emphasizes my having fun a lot, then her conversations shrivel. "You only live once," she says without thinking, and all I can do is nod.

Jan's very busy, she tells me, planning the big day. I think about how *the big day* is a phrase used by women concerning someone else's wedding. I wonder if Jan has managed to meet someone she desperately loves, who she intends to marry. I look at the gold ring I brought back when I died at the Flamingo. She could use it for the wedding. She could have it fitted.

"How are preparations?" I ask. I'm sitting on my bed watching a show with many ambulances and police car chases. Outside, framed by my window, a palm tree sways in a breeze.

"Fine," says Jan. "Don't worry about a thing."

I say okay but decide to push for details. "What *are* the plans this time?"

"Mother's going to visit soon," says Jan. Then she tells me she has calls to make, people to see. The phone clicks, then the tone of disconnection floods the line. I slowly put the phone back on its cradle.

On the television, sirens are blaring.

KNOCK, KNOCK.

"Who's there?" I ask, fitting my eye to the peephole.

It's Mother. She's standing in the hallway wearing a lemon yellow power suit as if she were a thirty year old businesswoman instead of fifty and happily out of work. I pull the door open and she thrusts a package at me. "Here, my love," she says. I take the package and set it on the nightstand to open later.

"So what brings you here, Mom?" I ask. It's not often that I see her. Soon after we discovered my talent, Jan rigged it so Mom took out a large insurance policy. Then I stepped off a curb and was smashed by a bus. There was a dead body, so the insurance company had to pay up. I lost my legal identity, but we were able to give Mom lots of money. Now she spends most of her time in the air, flying from the Caribbean to Europe to Asia.

She took care of my father before he died—stomach cancer—so we felt she deserved a rest.

"I need an excuse to visit my boy?" she says. "Is that what you're saying?"

"No, Mom," I laugh. I stuff my hands in my pockets and stare at my bare feet. The carpet here is almond, not pink like the Flamingo, which pleases me.

She hugs me but doesn't have time to chat. She has a plane to catch. "I hear you and Jan are planning a last performance?"

"Jan's planning it," I correct her. "I'm sitting here wondering what she's planning."

"Well, dear, Jan is very good at these things. Just let her take care of it. You should get out while you're here, have some fun. Live a little."

I look up when she says this. For a moment I think she's Jan.

"What?" she says. "Why are you looking at me like that?! Oh, Aiden, you're too flighty. Take a pill."

I don't mention that I once took a lot of pills, or that that exhibition paid off my father's hospital bills. I don't say anything because only one person is allowed to be a martyr, the same way no two objects can occupy the same space at the same time. I abdicate to my mother whenever possible; if I didn't, she'd steal the role. She has a story she tells about my father's funeral. At the dinner afterwards, at the church, she looked up from her plate of food and saw herself in a mirror across the room. She was sitting in the middle of a long table, Jan on one side, me on the other, a flock of relatives stretched out beside us. Her head was tilted to one side and she saw how she looked unimaginably hurt. "Betrayed," is how she puts it, and knew right then how it must have been for Jesus at the Last Supper. "That poor man," she says, "always trying to help others, and what did he get? He should have learned. I have."

After she's flown away, I open her gift. It's a glass globe and inside it is a miniature island village, palm trees staked at each corner of the island. It looks like it would be hot there. A hot place. I shake it and snow falls over the village. Snowflakes pile up on the palm leaves. There's a card, too, with an inscription: "Saw this and thought of you, dear. Had to buy it. Hope your grand finale goes off well. Alas, I won't be attending. Those things are so gruesome. Hugs, Mom."

I sit on the end of the bed and put my head in my hands and try not move or to make any sounds. If I can do that, I can do anything. It takes a few minutes, but I finally begin to not feel my own body. Then I can't hear. Then I can't see either. It's a difficult task, but it helps to burn through the hours of waiting.

Before and

"It's time," says Jan. She's arrived wearing a black leather outfit and too much perfume. Already the room's begun to smell like a Chanel factory and I can't stop thinking there's a cat burglar going through my closet instead of my sister.

"Time?" I say. "Time?"

"To go," Jan says. "The limo's waiting."

"A *limo*?"

"A limo," says Jan. "Can't you respond with anything but questions? Saying 'hi' never occurred to you? We have to go."

So we go. As we leave Jan stops and pays the bill, tells the desk clerk we won't be returning. She tips him twenty dollars and he says it's been a pleasure. Come back soon.

The limo is long and sleek, a black bullet waiting by the curbside. Evening light flickers over it. Inside it's cool and air-conditioned, a relief from the heat. I sit on one seat and Jan sits opposite. She mixes a drink. Then pulls a cigarette pack from her purse and shuffles one out, lights it, inhales as though she's drinking water. I watch the column of her throat move and imagine the smoke traveling down into her lungs, the nicotine sifting into her blood, calming her.

"Since when do you smoke?"

"I've been under a lot of stress lately, okay?" She runs her fingers through her hair. "It wasn't easy, arranging things for tonight."

"So what *are* the plans for tonight?"

Jan smiles, satisfied with herself. She lifts the whiskey to her lips.

"Tonight," says Jan, "we are giving the greatest show on earth. Nothing can top this. But I'd rather not tell you what it is just yet. Your own surprise will heighten the audience's. They've paid quite a bit of money." Jan rubs her thumb and forefinger together. "Crème de la crème," she says.

"I don't know about this," I say. "I mean—"

"What?" Jan interrupts. "Just what do you mean, Aiden? What's not to know? This is it. You can't wimp out now."

I nod and nod. I know, Jan. I didn't mean anything by it, Jan. I tell her the usual things to smooth her over, then pour myself a whiskey and drink it in one swallow.

We arrive at dusk at an abandoned warehouse near the ocean. I can't see any water, but I hear waves collapsing on a beach. Salt scents the air. Jan and I make our way toward the little door that opens into the warehouse.

The parking lot is filled to capacity with automobiles, buses, taxis. On the horizon I glimpse a sliver of red lowering itself down to the other side of the world. Amber light darkens by the minute. Jan puts her hand on my back, guiding me toward the entrance. She whispers words of encouragement, and between her words and the amber light, a memory of my father surfaces.

It was when he was still healthy, before he was sick; or if he was already sick, he wasn't saying. The cancer was still a secret buried in his flesh. We were sitting outside, catching our breath after a jog together. The sun was bright in our eyes. Clouds passed over and the world would be covered in shadow, then this amber light would return. It went on like that, light then dark, light then dark, and finally my father told me that people don't always have a choice in the matter of things like light or dark, or living or dying. But they have to make decisions when choices can be made. He put my face in his hands and held me together. I almost cried at what he was saying. I knew. I knew right then what he was saying.

It was afterwards, after his suicide to stop the pain he and my family were going through, then after my own, that I forgot everything he told me.

Jan swings the door open and a blast of heat hits me. The inside is lit by hundreds of candles. Bleachers line the walls. And in the center of everything, something stands shrouded in a red velvet curtain. The curtain sways a little, as if something large is breathing behind it. As we enter, the audience cheers.

They are spectacularly beautiful tonight, wearing tuxedoes and gowns and jewels. A small, nut-brown woman with a red dot on her forehead brushes her hand against me as I pass her. A touch, just a touch, to feel my power. Maybe it will rub off, they think. And if it doesn't, let him die, he deserves it, keeping a talent like that to himself. Who does he think he is?

A good question. But already Jan's voice is filling the warehouse, interrupting my answer. She uses a microphone to introduce me. "Everyone, put your hands together to welcome my very own little brother, the one and only Resurrection Artist!" she shouts. "The only one known to be alive at this time," she adds a second later, then laughs at her attempt at humor. Some of the audience chuckles. They'll laugh to grease her, anything to get this show moving.

Two heavily-muscled men wearing tuxedoes stand on either side of the red velvet curtain, holding a braided gold rope in their hands. Jan turns to them and shouts, "Here is the medium of death!" and the men pull the rope until the shroud lifts to reveal a large kiln with a fire roaring inside it. One of the men swings the gate open, a gate large enough for a man to step inside. The fire lifts and enlarges.

Jan motions for me to approach, and I do. Each step is like walking through water though, that slow trudge, but finally I stand before it and think, Is this what I want? What about my body? If it burns, will I still come back? Do I need a body to return to? There's so much we don't know. I've always had one before, even if it was bloody and battered.

The audience rises to its feet. When they stand to cheer I feel as though I should be in the Coliseum, preparing to battle a lion. Or in the corner of a boxing ring, an announcer calling out the names and win-loss ratios of each opponent. I'm in one corner, but who is in the other?

I look into the kiln, that gold and red waiting for my body, and see Jan at first. Then it isn't Jan, but my mother standing in the fire. Then my dead father, his eyes sunken and hollow, his flesh white and mushroom rotten. Then I see the reflection of the audience cheering behind me. Then I don't see any of them, but myself. I walk out of the kiln, licks of flame rolling off my skin like drops of water. *Ding, ding, ding.* We stare and stare at each other, then move toward the center, fists ready.

I turn to find Jan running back and forth in front of the bleachers, waving her hands, stirring the crowd into a frenzy. She's good at that sort of thing. I wait until she turns to give me a brief moment of attention and shout, "Call it off."

Jan's eyes narrow. She taps a finger on her ear: *What did you say?*

I repeat myself slowly so she can read my lips, and when she begins to understand, a shadow spreads over her face. She marches over, puts an arm around my shoulder and says, "Aiden, what the hell are you doing? These people have already paid."

"Send them away," I say. "Tell them I'm not dying. Whatever it takes, you can handle it."

"You little—I ought to kill you myself." Jan removes her arm and points a finger in my face. "How could you? How else are you going to live?"

To live. Isn't that the question? How to live? I've never answered it. I only know how to die. How to wait until the next death.

"I don't know," I tell her. "But I want to find out."

Jan folds her arms across her chest and shakes her head, astonished. I don't flinch, although I want to. I walk away and step out into the night. The audience titters and whispers. "What is going on here?!" a woman shouts.

I shut the door behind me and walk to the back of the building, sit down among shattered beer bottles. My legs stretch out in front of me and I stare at them, thinking, Those are my legs. I find them more interesting than I should probably.

Within an hour, the crowd disperses. The car engines turn over, the tires peel, the annoyed voices grow fewer. Finally, Jan finds me around back.

"Are you proud of yourself?" she asks. I nod. "Well I hope you're happy. I am no longer your sister. And don't think Mother won't hear about this. What would Dad say?"

She walks away, but I'm not concerned any longer. Jan will forgive me if it's possible. And if it isn't possible, I'll learn to live without her.

Suddenly I see a figure lurching toward me from the next lot over. After a moment the figure becomes a man, and then he stops, his tennis shoes scraping the asphalt next to me.

"You see the resurrection?" he asks, scratching his face.

"There wasn't one," I tell him. "It didn't go off."

"That's too bad. I wanted to see it. Something like that, the power to come back to life—I wonder what it's like. But that chick I phoned for tickets was asking way too much."

He's grunged out, the knees of his jeans ripped, a bruise on one cheek, a cut on his forehead. "Why would you want to see that?" I ask. "It isn't the most pleasant thing, dying."

"It's the comeback," he says. "That's what's appealing." He coughs and lights a cigarette. The end glows red then orange in the dark.

The comeback, I think. Yes, that's it. Life, life. The beat of a heart, the break of a wave on the beach. What a plunge. What a lark to live for even one day.

"It isn't too late," I say. His face screws up, his nose wrinkling in confusion. I lead him to the warehouse where the candles have all been put out, the bleachers emptied of human breathing. The kiln still glows. "Here is your resurrection," I tell him, not your death. I move toward the kiln, fidgeting, wondering what kind of fate the flames hold for me. I imagine myself a skeleton that turns to ash, then to dust. A wind comes along and blows me across the cosmos. I open the gate and the fire breathes heavy, a welcoming kiss.

I tell myself when I return this time I will be a bird of fire, holding a rose in my burning talons. I will stand before him then, this audience of one, whose face glows from my flames, whose skin flushes from my heat. And maybe, just maybe he'll say it was terrible to see me burning like that, but also how it was a beautiful thing. Not a rush, but a moment of grace. I will bow to him then, and begin again. This time for keeps. I will lay the rose at his feet.

Before and

The Boy Who Was Born Wrapped in Barbed Wire

THERE WAS ONCE A BOY who was born wrapped in barbed wire. The defect was noticed immediately after his birth, when the doctor had to snip the boy's umbilical cord with wire cutters. But elsewhere, too, the wire curled out of the boy's flesh, circling his arms and legs, his tiny torso. They didn't cause him pain, these metal spikes that grew out of the round hills of his body, although due to the dangerous nature of his birth, his mother had lost a great amount of blood during labor. After delivery, the nurse laid the boy in his mother's arms, careful to show her the safe places to hold him. And before her last breath left her, she managed to tell her son these words: "Bumblebees fly anyway, my love."

They followed him, those words, for the rest of his life, skimming the rim of his ear, buzzing loud as the bees farmed by his father the beekeeper. He did not remember his mother saying those words, but he often imagined the scene as his father described it. "Your mother loved you very much," he told the boy, blinking, pursing his lips. The beekeeper wanted to pat his son's head, but was unable to touch him just there—on his crown—where a cowlick of barbs jutted out of the boy's brown curls.

The beekeeper and his son lived in a cabin in the middle of the woods. They only came out to go into town for supplies and groceries. The beekeeper took the boy with him whenever he trekked through the woods to his hives. He showed the boy how to collect honey, how to not disturb the bees, how to avoid an unnecessary stinging. Sometimes the beekeeper wore a baggy white suit with a helmet and visor, which the bees clung to, crawling over the surface of his body. The boy envied the bees that land-scape. He imagined himself a bee in those moments. As a bee, his sting would never slip through his father's suit to strike the soft flesh hidden beneath it. His barbs, though, would find their way through nearly any barrier.

One day the beekeeper gave the boy a small honeycomb and told him to eat it. The comb dripped a sticky gold, and the boy wrinkled his nose. "It looks like wax," he told his father. But the beekeeper only said, "Eat," so the boy did.

The honeycomb filled his mouth with a sweetness that tasted of sun-light on water. Never before had something so beautiful sat on the tip of his tongue. Swallowing, he closed his eyes and thought of his mother. The way she held him in her arms before dying, the way she spoke before going away forever. The memory of his mother tasted like honey too, and he asked the beekeeper, "What did she mean? Bumblebees fly anyway?"

"Bumblebees shouldn't be able to fly," said the beekeeper, closing the lid on a hive. Honeybees crawled on the inside of the lid like a living carpet. "Their bodies are so large and their wings so small, they shouldn't be able to lift themselves into the air, but somehow they do. They fly."

WHEN THE BOY TURNED FIVE, the beekeeper sent him to school with the town's other children. At first the boy was excited, standing on the shoul-der of the highway where the trail that led back through the woods to the beekeeper's cabin ended. But soon the bus came and, as he stepped inside, he realized none of the other kids had been born wrapped in barbed wire. They were regular flesh children with soft hair any adult could run their fingers through. They looked at him, eyes wide, and said nothing. No one offered him a seat, so the boy sat behind the bus driver.

They all knew of the barbed wire boy, of course, from tales that had circulated since the day of his birth. But only a few had actually seen him. The one story the children lived on was told by a girl who had seen him in the fruit section of the grocery store late one night, shopping with his father. He had reached for a bunch of grapes, she said, but the grapes got tangled in the wire around his hand. His father bent down to remove them, carefully pulling the vines away, but several grapes remained stuck on his barbs, their juice sliding down the metal. "The manager made them buy that bunch," the girl said with an air of righteousness. After all, those grapes were ruined.

On his first day of class, no one talked to him except the teacher, Ms. Morrison, who told him where he could sit. She pointed to a desk in the back of the room, far away from the rows of desks that held the other chil-

Before and

dren. When he looked up at her, she could already see the question form-
ing on the cage of his face and said, "For their safety, dear. And for yours."

Ms. Morrison taught the boy how to read, how to write, and how to add
numbers. He already knew how to subtract. His father had taught him
that. So he was ahead of the class, or behind them, depending on your
view of subtraction.

This is how the barbed wire boy learned to subtract:

"How old am I?" he once asked the beekeeper.

"It's been four years since your mother died," the beekeeper replied.

"Four," said the barbed wire boy. "How much is four, Father?"

"Four is one less than five," said the beekeeper. "Three is one less than
four. And two is what your mother and I once were together."

It was only once Ms. Morrison took an apple and orange and put them
together that the boy realized things could grow in number.

The barbed wire boy kept to himself, but his solitude was not of his
own choosing. The town parents had warned their children. "You could
get hurt playing with that boy," they said. "You could get tangled up in his
barbed wire and then what would you do?"

The barbed wire boy understood their reluctance to engage him, but it
would be lying to say he did not long for a friend. For someone to at least
confide in. Day after day he sat on the teeter-totter during recess, waiting for someone to climb onto the side opposite, someone whose weight
would lift him high into the air.

It was not until years later, after the boy's limbs grew long and ropey,
after he nearly reached the same height as the beekeeper, after his body
began to fill up the coils of barbs around his body—the wire sinking into
the meat of his flesh—it was not until after he'd given up on the prospect
of communion that something just like that began to happen.

What happened was, a minister came to town holding a Bible in one
hand and his daughter's hand in the other. This minister had plans and
was telling everyone about them. He was going to re-open the abandoned
church that stood in the center of town where the two main streets in-
tersected.

For years the town had gone without a preacher, but although the
people had lacked a spiritual leader for several generations, you could
not say they were unspiritual. And this, the minister said that first Sunday,
was the reason why the Lord had led him to them. "You are a flock," he
told them, "without a shepherd. Come. Follow me to the Lord."

During services, the minister's daughter sat in the first pew, occasionally raising her hand to praise the Lord or her father. Sometimes it wasn't

apparent which one she lauded, but that didn't matter. To most people, and to the girl herself, the minister and God were one and the same. She was a righteous one, the minister's daughter. Everyone could see that from the start. When the minister asked the congregation to sing, "Shall We Gather at the River," she played the organ to accompany his strong, dark voice. When the minister asked the congregation to make a joyful noise, her voice curled up and over the others, rising up to reach the rafters.

Soon a great revival was in full swing and people began taking one another, friends and neighbors, to hear the minister. Several town mothers even gathered their courage to walk down the winding dirt road to the beekeeper's cabin in the forest. The beekeeper needed God as well, they all agreed. But when the beekeeper stood in his doorway and wouldn't hear of it, they implored him to at least let them bring the barbed wire boy to the Lord.

"He's never been baptized," said the mothers. "Since his life here on earth has been so mangled, you can at least secure the child a place in heaven." These same women had never before shown an interest in the condition of the barbed wire boy's soul, nor in their own children's, but now that the minister had spread the good news, they worried over this part of their existence, which previously they had never known to be lacking. "His soul!" they cried, as if it were an endangered species. "His soul!"

The beekeeper was not a religious man, but when he saw the look in his son's eyes at the sight of those mothers crowding the doorway, he decided to allow them to take the boy to church.

To say that a church is home to God and anyone who follows Him is to speak in sacred literality. Let us speak in metaphor then, because what the barbed wire boy saw after he crossed the threshold and sat in the last pew, listening to the hymns of his fellow townspeople, what he saw after one of the town mothers came over to give him a large Bible, apologizing for its age and thickness but saying she hoped he'd enjoy it "as a gift from the church", what he saw when he opened the book was nothing so much as the image of his own being. Upon the first crisp page he turned to, Christ hung on his cross. And although the blood seeping from his eyes reminded the boy of his own occasional bleeding, it was the crown of thorns upon the Lord's head that caught his eye. He licked his lips, wanting to cry, wanting to give a great shout or to fall on his knees. Never before had he felt so not alone in the world. Spread out before his very eyes was someone else who suffered the torments of body and spirit. Jesus hadn't been born wearing a crown of thorns, but metaphorically—and we have established that metaphorically is how we are speak-

Before and

ing—we could say that the Lord was born with that crown of thorns, for that crown was waiting for him since before his birthday.

It was during the preacher's sermon on Unity, how the town had fallen apart without God to bring them together, that the barbed wire boy was overcome with something he could only call holy. "Yes!" he shouted, mimicking the others. "Hallelujah!" he cried. Soon everyone's eyes were on him, as if he'd been saying hallelujah at an inappropriate moment, so he closed his mouth and sat down. As he took his seat, the wooden pew creaked in the silence, and in the front row the minister's daughter cocked her head to the side and smiled.

After the minister received the offering, everyone stood to leave. As they departed, the minister grabbed the hands of each member of his congregation. To shake the men's firmly. To hold and caress the women's palms, soft and noble as a knight. But when the barbed wire boy came to him, the minister only smiled, curious and wary. "Well now," he said with a squint in his eye. "I see we have a visitor."

"Not a visitor, sir," said the boy. "I plan to come every week." He almost reached out to take the minister's hand, to thank him for introducing him to Jesus, as if the minister's being in the Lord's favor would make the man immune to his barbs, but stopped halfway through the motion. Not even ministers, he figured, were immune to pain.

"That's a large cross you bear, son," said the minister, stern but fatherly. "You carry it well now, hear?"

The barbed wire boy beamed at hearing these words come out of the mouth of the very minister! He, too, saw the similarity then. Finally, thought the boy, finally I am home.

FOR THE NEXT FEW DAYS, the barbed wire boy talked about nothing but Jesus. He was Jesus this and Jesus that, and the beekeeper could only shake his head in annoyance. "What's all this about Jesus?" he said, and the boy blinked as if his father had asked the stupidest question in the world.

"Jesus is our Lord," said the boy. "He died to cleanse your sins."

The beekeeper shook his head, though, his eyes darkening with frustration. "You sound like your mother," he said, and turned to leave. But before he could make it out the door, the barbed wire boy grabbed hold of his father.

"How?" he asked, while at the same time a long barb sunk into the flesh between his father's neck and shoulder.

"Ow!" shouted the beekeeper. He pulled away from the boy's hand and blood welled in the spot where the barb had lodged, a fat apple. It burst a moment later and dripped down under the beekeeper's collar.

Afterlives   *The Boy Who Was Born Wrapped in Barbed Wire*

"How," said the boy. "How do I sound like her?"

The beekeeper took the boy up to the attic. He rummaged through boxes until he found what he wanted. "Aha," he said, and pulled out a dust-covered book. "This," he told the boy, "was hers."

It was a Bible, the pages tattered and yellow. "I hadn't known she was religious," said the barbed wire boy.

"She wasn't. But she often read it."

The barbed wire boy sat on the floor of the attic, paging through his mother's Bible. It did not have many pictures in it like the Bible the church mother gave to him. His mother's name had been written in pencil on a page recording the births in her family history. Below her name though, he found an empty space. There had been no time to enter him into her story.

He put aside his mother's Bible and took up the church mother's Bible, seeking out the picture he'd found earlier that week, after he'd returned from his first day of church. There it was, the one that made his heart swell, tightening the barbed wire coiled around it. The one of Lord Jesus with his mother, holding him in her arms, his side pierced, his forehead wet with blood. That embrace, the love in her eyes as she held her child, now a dead man, in her strong arms.

The beekeeper did not bother his son about church any further. He spent most of his time with his hives. The hum, the smell of honey, the flutter of light on wings—those were the beekeeper's religion. Some days he would do nothing but lick honey straight from their combs. The nectar of heaven, he called it. The only pure substance on earth. He seemed able to somehow get drunk off the sweetness. Sometimes he'd suit up and let the bees cover his entire body. He would hold his arms out, his face tilted toward the sky. And in those moments he'd think of his wife from the time before their son came through her. He would stare at the sun as bees covered his visor, eclipsing any visible light.

THE BARBED WIRE BOY REMAINED in the last pew for the next few weeks, learning when hallelujah was appropriate and when it wasn't. He learned the words to the hymns. He learned how to pray. Like most places he went, here people steered clear of him. But it didn't bother him as much since he was at church and Jesus felt closer.

One day, after the minister had preached a particularly vehement sermon on Job's burdens, the minister's daughter stood up to ask if anyone was sick. "I can feel it," she said. "Someone here needs healing. It's okay to raise your hand. Stand and let the Lord know your troubles, so He can take them away."

At first no one stood, so the girl continued. "Someone here is in pain," she said, closing her eyes, seeking out the shy, pain-ridden person with an inner sight. "Someone here is in a lot of pain," she kept saying.

She opened her eyes and stared past the pews of identical oval-shaped faces until she found the barbed wire boy with his spirals of wire making any sense of symmetry impossible. He stared back, lips slightly parted, knowing she wanted something. He nodded and she came to him then. Everyone turned to watch her walk to the back of the room, where she asked the barbed wire boy to stand. "Let God's touch heal you," she said. Then she placed the palms of her hands on his shoulders.

Closing her eyes in deep concentration, she muttered prayers while everyone looked on. The barbed wire boy himself couldn't understand why she was doing this, or even why he had nodded when she stared at him. He stood there, surprised as the others, and found his eyes full of tears. He could not remember the last time anyone had touched him.

When it was over, the minister's daughter pulled her hands away slowly. He could feel the suck of her flesh as it slipped off his barbs. She held her hands up then, showing them to the congregation. And there, in the middle of her palms, was the mark of the stigmata.

Someone shouted, someone fainted, someone praised the Lord. The minister himself said they had witnessed a miracle, though no one truly knew what the miracle had been. That the girl had been courageous enough to touch the boy's barbed wires? They weren't sure if that wasn't just plain foolishness.

"Let us celebrate this holy event by hosting a Feast of Love next Sunday," said the minister, but everyone stared back at him close-mouthed. "What is a Feast of Love?" they asked, and the minister took this opportunity to remind them of why he had been called to them. "Of course you haven't heard of the Feast of Love," he said. "That is why the Lord led me here." He went on to explain that the Feast of Love used to be a tradition of the church where everyone in the community gathered, rich and poor alike, and feasted at table together.

"Why was it abandoned?" one of the town mothers inquired, and the minister explained that the rich people had grown tired of eating with the beggars. And as it's not a command in the Bible to hold the feast, they agreed it would be in better taste to just cancel it.

The congregation thought this was a wonderful idea, and soon everyone was talking after services about the following Sunday's feast. "Now this is church! This is church!" one of the mothers shouted, and a hallelujah was sent up after her proclamation. In the bustle and excitement of planning the feast, the minister's daughter took the barbed wire boy by his hand and began to walk him home.

"You aren't afraid to touch me," the barbed wire boy said when they found themselves deep in his father's woods.

The minister's daughter shook her head.

"But everyone's afraid to touch me," said the boy. "Even my father."

The minister's daughter considered his question. "I liked the way they felt going in," she said, "coming out again." She smiled fiercely.

She stopped then, in the middle of the woods, and put her hands upon his face. Wincing, she stood on tiptoes to kiss him. As she lowered herself again, he saw that her mouth and chin were smeared with blood. "You're hurt," said the barbed wire boy. "I hurt you."

But the minister's daughter shook her head, wrapped her arms around his waist and rested her head on his chest. "I like it," she said, and they walked further into the woods, until they came to the place where the beekeeper's hives hummed in their boxes.

The barbed wire boy lifted a lid and gathered a swirl of honey on his fingertip. He turned to offer it to the minister's daughter and said, "My father says this is the true nectar of heaven."

"Eat of my flesh," said the minister's daughter, and lowered her mouth. Carefully she licked the honey from the tip of his finger and afterward pulled his mouth down to meet hers. She tasted tangy and sweet. She tasted of blood and honey.

She took the barbed wire boy by his hand and walked him away from the hives, off the path, to lie in a patch of daisies. With each touch the girl sucked in her breath, with each release she sighed. And later, while they lay among the shredded flowers, blood red on the white petals, it was the barbed wire boy who could do nothing but sigh and moan in exquisite pain.

HIS HEAD WAS FULL OF her then, every day for the next week. His thoughts ran to nothing but the minister's daughter. If the beekeeper asked him a question, the boy didn't hear. If dark clouds gathered over the forest and lightning cracked the sky open, the boy didn't notice. When he went with the beekeeper to check on the hives, he filled the bee boxes with enough smoke to knock the bees out for days. "What's wrong with you?" asked the beekeeper. "Is this something to do with Jesus?"

The barbed wire boy only smiled and said nothing, and the beekeeper suddenly felt something like a notion of worry over his son's well-being. He understood his boy's sadness, his boy's pain. These things defined living, thought the beekeeper. But when the barbed wire boy stumbled

Before and

along the forest floor with a stupid grin on his face, tripping happily, he suspected the worst. Love, thought the beekeeper. My boy's in love.

Though the beekeeper worried over the barbed wire boy's happiness like a town mother over the state of the boy's soul, it didn't matter. Parents worry over their children constantly. In the end they can do nothing to protect them. The barbed wire boy would have to learn his own lesson, thought the beekeeper. And he would do that. He would come to learn this the following Sunday, at the Feast of Love.

WHEN HE ARRIVED, THE CONGREGATION was already sitting at long stretches of picnic tables outside the church doors. The tables were heaped with a variety of dishes. Baskets full of fruit, roast of turkey, three-tiered cakes covered in creamy frosting and strawberries, lamb chops and mint jelly, bowls of pink and orange ambrosia. His mouth watered. He was about to comment on how perfect everything was when he turned from the food to find everyone staring, brows furrowed, eyes slanted. A town mother opened her mouth and said one word, "wicked," and fell silent again.

He searched for the face of the minister's daughter, that beacon, but she was nowhere to be found. He furrowed his brow then too, uncomprehending, until the minister himself came out the front doors of the church and stood on the top step to give a sermon.

"God has sent us many abominations to deal with these days," said the minister. "People are evil. They destroy buildings, fornicate before marriage, fornicate with their own gender, they want to take God out of our children's education. These are dark times indeed," he said regretfully. "It is a test. A test from God for His chosen. He is giving us these problems to sort out who is with Him and who is without. Why even in church abominations have crept inside to sit among us. Oh yes," said the minister, "do not think the Lord doesn't work mysteriously. You are not protected here in His house even. This is the testing ground, my friends."

The barbed wire boy swallowed, trying not to listen, for he realized the sermon was directed at him. When the minister said "abomination," he had looked at the boy. He felt stupid having come, not realizing the graveness of his error. Of course the minister would know what had happened between the barbed wire boy and his daughter. She would have gone home cut and bloody. She would have had no way to deny what they had done.

He turned to leave and though the minister continued his sermon, everyone watched the boy. He would not be able to return, he realized. He would not be able to sit and eat at their table. His leaving would only confirm their belief that God had sent him as an abomination, that the minister's words had caused him to leave. Perhaps I am an abomination, he thought as he walked through the woods back to his father's cabin.

He started to cry. Tears streamed down the barbed wire embedded in his cheeks, and soon he was running through the woods, faster and faster, pushing away branches, shredding leaves, until he came to his father's hives. Here the buzz of bees was loud in his ears. A hum, a mantra, a constant praying. He knew then why his father preferred his bees over anything.

Standing over the boxes, he watched them crawl inside, hundreds of them moving through the hexagonal caverns, their lion's bodies tight within the tunnels. And somewhere in that labyrinth, their queen.

He lifted the lid of a hive without smoking them and brushed his hand over their furry backs as if they were only animals in a petting zoo. The bees scurried though, frightened, fluttering their wings, lifting into the air until they were a cloud surrounding him, swarming. He closed his eyes as they landed and lit upon him, tilted his face toward the sun. Lift me up, he thought, into the blue air. But they were afraid of his disturbance and attacked instead.

He sucked in his breath as the bees began to sting him. He gasped like the minister's daughter had when his barbs slid into her. His flesh swelled, burning with poison. And there in the woods, with only the bees as witness, the barbed wire boy felt the nearness of God once more. The pain of his mother giving birth, the worry on his father's face at the first sign of happiness, the hurt that turns the world.

The stings. The stings of love.

Before and

Map of Seventeen

EVERYONE HAS SECRETS. EVEN ME. We carry them with us like contraband, always swaddled in some sort of camouflage we've concocted to hide the parts of ourselves the rest of the world is better off not knowing. I'd write what I'm thinking in a diary if I could believe others would stay out of those pages, but in a house like this there's no such thing as privacy. If you're going to keep secrets, you have to learn to write them down inside your own heart. And then be sure not to give that away to anyone either. At least not to just anyone at all.

Which is what bothers me about *him*, the guy my brother is apparently going to marry. Talk about secrets. Off Tommy goes to New York City for college, begging my parents to help him with money for four straight years, then after graduating at the top of his class—in studio art, of all things (not even a degree that will get him a job to help pay off the loans our parents took out for his education)—he comes home to tell us he's gay, and before we can say anything, good or bad, runs off again and won't return our calls. And when he did start talking to Mom and Dad again, it was just short phone conversations and emails, asking for help, for more money.

Five years of off and on silence and here he is, bringing home some guy named Tristan who plays the piano better than my mother and has never seen a cow except on TV. We're supposed to treat this casually and not bring up the fact that he ran away without letting us say anything at all four years ago, and to try not to embarrass him. That's Tommy Terlecki, my big brother, the gay surrealist Americana artist who got semi-famous not for the magical creatures and visions he paints, but for his horrifically exaggerated family portraits of us dressed up in ridiculous roles: *American Gothic*, dad holding a pitchfork, mom presenting her knitting needles and a ball of yarn to the viewer as if she's coaxing you to give them a try, me with my arms folded under my breasts, my face angry within the frame of my bonnet, scowling at Tommy, who's sitting on the ground beside my legs in the portrait, pulling off the Amish-like clothes. What I don't like about these paintings is that he's lied about us in them. The Tommy in the portrait is constrained by his family's way of life, but it's Tommy who's put us in those clothes to begin with. They're how he sees us, not the way we are, but he gets to dramatize a conflict with us in the paintings anyway, even though it's a conflict he himself has imagined.

Still, I could be practical and say the *American Gothic* series made Tommy's name, which is more than I can say for the new stuff he's working on: *The Sons of Melusine*. They're like his paintings of magical creatures, which the critic who picked his work out of his first group show found too precious in comparison to the "promise of the self-aware, absurdist family portraits this precocious young man from the wilderness of Ohio has also created." Thank you, Google, for keeping me informed on my brother's activities. *The Sons of Melusine* are all bare-chested men with curvy muscles who have serpentine tails and faces like Tristan's, all of them extremely attractive and extremely in pain: out of water mostly, gasping for air in the back alleys of cities, parched and bleeding on beaches, strung on fishermen's line, the hook caught in the flesh of a cheek. A new Christ, is how Tommy described them when he showed them to us, and Mom and Dad said, "Hmm, I see."

He wants to hang an *American Gothic* in the living room, he told us, after we'd been sitting around talking for a while, all of us together for the first time in years, his boyfriend Tristan smiling politely as we tried to catch up with Tommy's doings while trying to be polite and ask Tristan about himself as well. "My life is terribly boring, I'm afraid," Tristan said when I asked what he does in the city. "My family's well off, you see, so what I do is mostly whatever seems like fun at any particular moment."

Well off. Terribly boring. Whatever seems like fun at any particular moment. I couldn't believe my brother was dating this guy, let alone planning to marry him. This is Tommy, I reminded myself, and right then was when he said, "If it's okay with you, Mom and Dad, I'd like to hang one of the *American Gothic* paintings in here. Seeing how Tristan and I will be staying with you for a while, it'd be nice to add some touches of our own."

Christopher Barzak   Before and

Tommy smiled. Tristan smiled and gave Mom a little shrug of his shoulders. I glowered at them from across the room, arms folded across my chest on purpose. Tommy noticed and, with a concerned face, asked me if something was wrong. "Just letting life imitate art," I told him, but he only kept on looking puzzled. Faker, I thought. He knows exactly what I mean.

Halfway through that first evening, I realized this was how it was going to be as long as Tommy and Tristan were with us, while they waited for their own house to be built next to Mom and Dad's: Tommy conducting us all like the head of an orchestra, waving his magic wand. He had Mom and Tristan sit on the piano bench together and tap out some "Heart and Soul". He sang along behind them for a moment, before looking over his shoulder and waving Dad over to join in. When he tried to pull me in with that charming squinty-eyed devil grin that always gets anyone—our parents, teachers, the local police officers who used to catch him speeding down back roads—to do his bidding, I shook my head, said nothing, and left the room. "Meg?" he said behind me. Then the piano stopped and I could hear them whispering, wondering what had set me off this time.

I'm not known for being easy to live with. Between Tommy's flare for making people live life like a painting when he's around, and my stubborn, immovable will, I'm sure our parents must have thought at some time or other that their real children had been swapped in the night with changelings. It would explain the way Tommy could make anyone like him, even out in the country, where people don't always think well of gay people. It would explain the creatures he paints that people always look nervous about after viewing them, the half-animal beings that roam the streets of cities and back roads of villages in his first paintings. It would explain how I can look at any math problem or scientific equation my teachers put before me and figure them out without breaking a sweat. And my aforementioned will. My will, this thing that's so strong I sometimes feel like it's another person inside me.

Our mother is a mousy figure here in the Middle of Nowhere, Ohio. The central square is not even really a square but an intersection of two highways where town hall, a general store, beauty salon and Presbyterian church all face each other like lost old women casting glances over the asphalt, hoping one of the others knows where they are and where they're going, for surely why would anyone stop here? My mother works in the library, which used to be a one-room schoolhouse a hundred years ago, where they still use a stamp card to keep track of the books checked out. My father is one of the township trustees and he also runs our farm. We raise beef cattle, Herefords mostly, though a few Hereford and Angus mixes are in our herd, so you sometimes get black cows with polka-dotted white faces. I never liked the mixed calves, I'm not sure why, but Tommy always said they were his favorites. Mutts are always smarter than streamlined gene pools, he said. Me? I always thought they looked like heartbroken mimes with dark, dewy eyes.

From upstairs in my room I could hear the piano start again, this time a classical song. It had to be Tristan. Mom only knows songs like "Heart and Soul" and just about any song in a hymn book. They attend, I don't. Tommy and I gave up church ages ago. I still consider myself a Christian, just not the church-going kind. We're lucky to have parents who asked us why we didn't want to go, instead of forcing us like tyrants. When I told them I didn't feel I was learning what I needed to live in the world there, instead of getting mad, they just nodded and Mom said, "If that's the case, perhaps it's best that you walk your own way for a while, Meg."

They're so *good*. That's the problem with my parents. They're so good, it's like they're children or something, innocent and naïve. Definitely not stupid, but way too easy on other people. They never fuss with Tommy. They let him treat them like they're these horrible people who ruined his life and they never say a word. They hug him and calm him down instead, treat him like a child. I don't get it. Tommy's the oldest. Isn't he the one who's supposed to be mature and put together well?

I listened to Tristan's notes drift up through the ceiling from the living room below, and lay on my bed, staring at a tiny speck on the ceiling, a stain or odd flaw in the plaster that has served as my focal point for anger for many years. Since I can remember, whenever I got angry, I'd come up here and lie in this bed and stare at that speck, pouring all of my frustrations into it, as if it were a black hole that could suck up all the bad. I've given that speck so much of my worst self over the years, I'm surprised it hasn't grown darker and wider, big enough to cast a whole person into its depths. When I looked at it now, I found I didn't have as much anger to give it as I'd thought. But no, that wasn't it either. I realized all of my anger was floating around the room instead, buoyed up by the notes of the piano, by Tristan's playing. I thought I could even see those notes shimmer into being for a brief moment, electrified by my frustration. When I blinked, though, the air looked normal again, and Tristan had brought his melody to a close.

There was silence for a minute, some muffled voices, then Mom started up "Amazing Grace". I felt immediately better and breathed a sigh of relief.

Christopher Barzak

Before and

Then someone knocked on my door and it swung open a few inches, enough for Tommy to peek inside. "Hey, Sis. Can I come in?"

"It's a free country."

"Well," said Tommy. "Sort of."

We laughed. We could laugh about things we agreed on.

"Sooo," said Tommy, "what's a guy gotta do around here to get a hug from his little sister?"

"Aren't you a little old for hugs?"

"Ouch. I must have done something really bad this time."

"Not bad. Something. I don't know what."

"Want to talk about it?"

"Maybe."

Tommy sat down on the corner of my bed and craned his neck to scan the room. "What happened to all the unicorns and horses?"

"They died," I said. "Peacefully, in their sleep, in the middle of the night. Thank God."

He laughed, which made me smirk without wanting to. This was the other thing Tommy had always been able to do: make it hard for people to stay mad at him. "So you're graduating in another month?" he said. I nodded, turned my pillow over so I could brace it under my arm to hold me up more comfortably. "Are you scared?"

"About what?" I said. "Is there something I should be scared of?"

"You know. The future. The rest of your life. You won't be a little girl anymore."

"I haven't been a little girl for a while, Tommy."

"You know what I mean," he said, standing up, tucking his hands into his pockets like he does whenever he's being Big Brother. "You're going to have to begin making big choices," he said. "What you want out of life. You know it's not a diploma you receive when you cross the graduation stage. It's really a ceremony where your training wheels are taken off. The cap everyone wants to throw in the air is a symbol of what you've been so far in life: a student. That's right, everyone wants to cast it off so quickly, eager to get out into the world. Then they realize they've got only a couple of choices for what to do next. The armed service, college or working at a gas station. It's too bad we don't have a better way to recognize what the meaning of graduation really is. Right now, I think it leaves you kids a little clueless."

"Tommy," I said, "yes, you're eleven years older than me. You know more than I do. But really, you need to learn when to shut the hell up and stop sounding pompous."

We laughed again. I'm lucky that, no matter what makes me mad about my brother, we can laugh at ourselves together.

"So what are you upset about then?" he asked after we settled down.

"Them," I said, trying to get serious again. "Mom and Dad. Tommy, have you thought about what this is going to do to them?"

"What do you mean?"

"I mean, what the town's going to say? Tommy, do you know in their church newsletter they have a prayer list and our family is on it?"

"What for?" he asked, beginning to sound alarmed.

"Because you're gay!" I said. It didn't come out how I wanted, though. By the way his face, always alert and showing some kind of emotion, receded and locked its door behind it, I could tell I'd hurt his feelings. "It's not like that," I said. "They didn't ask to be put on the prayer list. Fern Baker put them on it."

"Fern Baker?" Tommy said. "What business has that woman got still being alive?"

"I'm serious, Tommy. I just want to know if you understand the position you've put them in."

He nodded. "I do," he said. "I talked with them about Tristan and me coming out here to live three months ago. They said what they'll always say to me or you when we want or need to come home."

"What's that?"

"Come home, darling. You and your Tristan have a home here too." When I looked down at my comforter and studied its threads for a while, Tommy added, "They'll say the come home part to you, of course. Not anything about bringing your Tristan with you. Oh, and if it's Dad, he might call you sweetie the way Mom calls me darling."

"Tommy," I said, "if there was a market for men who can make their sisters laugh, I'd say you're in the wrong field."

"Maybe we can make that a market."

"You need lots of people for that," I said.

"Mass culture. Hmm. Been there, done that. It's why I'm back. You should give it a try, though. It's an interesting experience. It might actually suit you, Meg. Have you thought about where you want to go to college?"

"It's already decided. Kent State in the fall."

"Kent, huh? That's a decent school. You wouldn't rather go to New York or Boston?"

"Tommy, even if you hadn't broken the bank around here already, I don't have patience for legions of people running up and down the streets of Manhattan or Cambridge like ants in a hive."

Before and

"And a major?"

"Psychology."

"Ah, I see, you must think there's something wrong with you and want to figure out how to fix it."

"No," I said. "I just want to be able to break people's brains open to understand why they act like such fools."

"That's pretty harsh," said Tommy.

"Well," I said, "I'm a pretty harsh girl."

AFTER TOMMY LEFT, I FELL asleep without even changing out of my clothes. In the morning when I woke, I was tangled up in a light blanket someone—Mom, probably—threw over me before going to bed the night before. I sat up and looked out the window. It was already late morning. I could tell by the way the light winked off the pond in the woods, which you can see a tiny sliver of, like a crescent moon, when the sun hits at just the right angle towards noon. Tommy and I used to spend our summers on the dock our father built out there. Reading books, swatting away flies, the soles of our dusty feet in the air behind us. He was so much older than me but never treated me like a little kid. The day he left for New York City, I hugged him on the front porch before Dad drove him to the airport, but burst out crying and ran around back of the house, beyond the fields, into the woods, until I reached the dock. I thought Tommy would follow, but he was the last person I wanted to see right then, so I thought out with my mind in the direction of the house, pushing him away. I turned him around in his tracks and made him tell our parents he couldn't find me. When he didn't come, I knew that I had used something inside me to stop him. Tommy wouldn't have ever let me run away crying like that without chasing after me if I'd let him make that choice on his own. I lay on the dock for an hour, looking at my reflection in the water, saying, "What are you? God damn it, you know the answer. Tell me. What *are* you?"

If Mom had come back and seen me like that, heard me speak in such a way, I think she probably would have had a breakdown. Mom can handle a gay son mostly. What I'm sure she couldn't handle would be if one of her kids talked to themselves like this at age seven. Worse would be if she knew why I asked myself that question. It was the first time my will had made something happen. And it had made Tommy go away without another word between us.

Sometimes I think the rest of my life is going to be a little more difficult every day.

When I was dressed and had a bowl of granola and bananas in me, I grabbed the novel I was reading off the kitchen counter and opened the back door to head back to the pond. Thinking of the summer days Tommy and I spent back there together made me think I should probably honor my childhood one last summer by keeping up tradition before I had to go away. I was halfway out the door, twisting around to close it, when Tristan came into the kitchen and said, "Good morning, Meg. Where are you off to?"

"The pond," I said.

"Oh the pond!" Tristan said, as if it were a tourist site he'd been wanting to visit. "Would you mind if I tagged along?"

"It's a free country," I said, thinking I should probably have been nicer, but I turned to carry on my way anyway.

"Well, sort of," Tristan said, which stopped me in my tracks.

I turned around and looked at him. He did that same little shrug he did the night before when Tommy asked Mom and Dad if he could hang the *American Gothic* portrait in the living room, then smiled, as if something couldn't be helped. "Are you just going to stand there, or are you coming?" I said.

Quickly Tristan followed me out, and then we were off through the back field and into the woods, until we came to the clearing where the pond reflected the sky, like an open blue eye staring up at God.

I made myself comfortable on the deck, spread out my towel and opened my book. I was halfway done. Someone's heart had already been broken and no amount of mixed CDs left in her mailbox and school locker were ever going to set things right. Why did I read these things? I should take the bike to the library and check out something Classic instead, I thought. Probably there's something I should be reading right now that everyone else in college will have read. I worried about things like that. Neither of our parents went to college. I remember Tommy used to worry the summer before he went to New York that he'd get there and never be able to fit in. "Growing up out here is going to be a black mark," he'd said. "I'm not going to know how to act around anyone there because of this place."

I find it ironic that it's this place—us—that helped Tommy start his career.

"This place is amazing," said Tristan. He stretched out on his stomach beside me, dangling the upper half of his torso over the edge so he could pull his fingers through the water just inches below us. "I can't believe you have all of this to yourself. You're so lucky."

"I guess," I said, pursing my lips. I still didn't know Tristan well enough to feel I could trust his motivations or be more than civil to him. Pretty. Harsh. Girl. I know.

Before and

"Wow," said Tristan, pulling his lower half back up onto the deck with me. He looked across the water, blinking. "You really don't like me," he said.

"That's not true," I said immediately, but even I knew that was mostly a lie. So I tried to revise. "I mean, it's not that I don't like you. I just don't know you so well, that's all."

"Don't trust me, eh?"

"Really," I said, "why should I?"

"Your brother's trust in me doesn't give you a reason?"

"Tommy's never been known around here for his good judgment," I said.

Tristan whistled. "Wow," he said again, this time elongating it. "You're tough as nails, aren't you?"

I shrugged. Tristan nodded. I thought this was a sign we'd come to an understanding, so I went back to reading. Not two minutes passed, though, before he interrupted again.

"What are you hiding, Meg?"

"What are you talking about?" I said, looking up from my book.

"Well obviously if you don't trust people to this extreme, you must have something to hide. That's what distrustful people often have. Something to hide. Either that or they've been hurt an awful lot by people they loved."

"You do know you guys can't get married in Ohio, right? The people decided in the election a couple of years ago."

"Ohhhh," said Tristan. "The people. The people the people the people. Oh, my dear, it's always the people! Always leaping to defend their own rights but always ready to deny someone else theirs. Wake up, baby. That's history. Did that stop other people from living how they wanted? Well, I suppose sometimes. Screw the people anyhow. Your brother and I will be married, whether or not the people make some silly law that prohibits it. The people, my dear, only matter if you let them."

"So you'll be married like I'm a Christian even though I don't go to church."

"Really, Meg, you do realize that even if you consider yourself a Christian, those other people don't, right?"

"What do you mean?"

Tristan turned over on his side so he could face me, and propped his head in his hand. His eyes are green. Tommy's are blue. If they could have children, they'd be so beautiful, like sea creatures or fairies. My eyes are blue too, but they're like Dad's, dull and flat, like a blind old woman's eyes rather than the shallow ocean with dancing lights on it blue that Mom and Tommy have. "I mean," said Tristan, "those people only believe you're a real Christian if you attend church. It's the body of Christ rule and all that. You *have* read the Bible, haven't you?"

"Parts," I said, squinting a little. "But anyway," I said, "it doesn't matter what they think of me. I know what's true in my heart."

"Well precisely," said Tristan.

I stopped squinting and held his stare. He didn't flinch, just kept staring back. "Okay," I said. "You've made your point."

Tristan stood and lifted his shirt above his head, kicked off his sandals, and dove into the pond. The blue rippled and rippled, the rings flowing out to the edges, then silence and stillness returned, but Tristan didn't. I waited a few moments, then stood halfway up on one knee. "Tristan?" I said, and waited a few moments more. "Tristan," I said, louder this time. But he still didn't come to the surface. "Tristan, stop it!" I shouted, and immediately his head burst out of the water at the center of the pond.

"Oh this is lovely," he said, shaking his wet, brown hair out of his eyes. "It's like having Central Park in your back yard!"

I picked my book up and left, furious with him for frightening me. What did he think? It was funny? I didn't stay to find out. I didn't turn around or say anything in response to Tristan either, when he began calling for me to come back.

TOMMY WAS IN THE KITCHEN making lunch for everyone when I burst through the back door and slammed it shut behind me like a small tornado had blown through. "What's wrong now?" he said, looking up from the tomato soup and grilled cheese sandwiches he was making. "Boy trouble?"

He laughed, but this time I didn't laugh with him. Tommy knew I wasn't much of a dater, that I didn't have a huge interest in going somewhere with a guy from school and watching a movie or eating fast food while they practiced on me to become better at making girls think they've found a guy who's incredible. I don't get that stuff, really. I mean, I like guys. I had a boyfriend once. I mean a real one, not the kind some girls call boyfriends but really aren't anything but the guy they dated that month. That's not a boyfriend. That's a candidate. Some people can't tell the difference. Anyway, I'm sure my parents have probably thought I'm the same way as Tommy, since I don't bring boys home, but I don't bring boys home because it all seems like something to save for later. Right now, I like just thinking about me, *my* future. I'm not so good at thinking in the first person plural yet.

I glared at Tommy before saying, "Your boyfriend sucks. He just tricked me into thinking he'd drowned."

Tommy grinned. "He's a bad boy, I know," he said. "But Meg, he didn't mean anything by it. You take life too seriously. You should really relax a little. Tristan is playful. That's part of his charm. He was trying to make you his friend, that's all."

"By freaking me out? Wonderful friendship maneuver. It amazes me how smart you and your city friends are. Did Tristan go to NYU, too?"

"No," Tommy said flatly. And on that one word, with that one shift of tone in his voice, I could tell I'd pushed him into the sort of self I wear most of the time: the armor, the defensive position. I'd crossed one of his lines and felt small and little and mean. "Tristan's family is wealthy," said Tommy. "He's a bit of the black sheep, though. They're not on good terms. He could have gone to college anywhere he wanted, but I think he's avoided doing that because it would make them proud of him for being more like them instead of himself. They're different people, even though they're from the same family. Like how you and I are different from Mom and Dad about church. Anyway, they threatened to cut him off if he didn't come home to let them groom him to be more like them."

"Heterosexual, married to a well-off woman from one of their circle and ruthless in a board room?" I offered.

"Well, no," said Tommy. "Actually they're quite okay with Tristan being gay. He's different from them in another way."

"What way?" I asked.

Tommy rolled his eyes a little, weighing whether or not he should tell me anymore. "I shouldn't talk about it," he said, sighing, exasperated.

"Tommy, tell me!" I said. "How bad could it be?"

"Not bad so much as strange. Maybe even unbelievable for you, Meg." I frowned, but he went on. "The ironic thing is, the thing they can't stand about Tristan is something they gave him. A curse, you would have called it years ago. Today I think the word we use is gene. In any case, it runs in Tristan's family, skipping generations mostly, but every once in a while one of the boys are born...well, different."

"Different but not in the gay way?" I said, confused.

"No, not in the gay way," said Tommy, smiling, shaking his head. "Different in the way that he has two lives, sort of. The one here on land with you and I, and another one in, well, in the water."

"He's a rebellious swimmer?"

Tommy laughed, bursting the air. "I guess you could say that," he said. "But no. Listen, if you want to know, I'll tell you, but you have to promise not to tell Mom and Dad. They think we're here because Tommy's family disowned him for being gay. I told them his parents were Pentecostal, so it all works out in their minds.

"Okay," I said. "I promise."

"What would you say," Tristan began, his eyes shifting up as if he were searching for the right words in the air above him. "What would you say, Meg, if I told you the real reason is because Tristan's not completely human. I mean, not in the sense that we understand it."

I narrowed my eyes, pursed my lips, and said, "Tommy, are you on drugs?"

"I wish!" he said. "God, those'll be harder to find around here," he laughed. "No, really, I'm telling the truth. Tristan is something…something else. A water person? You know, with a tail and all?" Tommy flapped his hand in the air when he said this. I smirked, waiting for the punch line. But when one didn't come, it hit me.

"This has something to do with *The Sons of Melusine*, doesn't it?"

Tommy nodded. "Yes, those paintings are inspired by Tristan."

"But Tommy," I said, "why are you going back to this type of painting? Sure it's an interesting gimmick, saying your boyfriend's a merman. But the critics didn't like your fantasy paintings. They liked the *American Gothic* stuff. Why would they change their minds now?"

"Two things," Tommy said, frustrated with me. "One: a good critic doesn't dismiss entire genres. They look at technique and composition of elements and the relationship the painting establishes with this world. Two: it's not a gimmick. It's the truth, Meg. Listen to me. I'm not laughing anymore. Tristan made his parents an offer. He said he'd move somewhere unimportant and out of the way, and they could make up whatever stories about him for their friends to explain his absence if they gave him part of his inheritance now. They accepted. It's why we're here."

I didn't know what to say, so I just stood there. Tommy ladled soup into bowls for the four of us. Dad would be coming in from the barn soon, Tristan back from the pond. Mom was still at the library and wouldn't be home till evening. This was a regular summer day. It made me feel safe, that regularity. I didn't want it to ever go away.

I saw Tristan then, trotting through the field out back, drying his hair with his pink shirt as he came. When I turned back to Tommy, he was looking out the window over the sink, watching Tristan too, his eyes watering. "You really love him, don't you?" I said.

Tommy nodded, wiping his tears away with the backs of his hands. "I do," he said. "He's so special, like something I used to see a long time ago. Something I forgot how to see for a while."

"Have you finished *The Sons of Melusine* series then?" I asked, trying to change the subject. I didn't feel sure of how to talk to Tommy right then.

"I haven't," said Tommy. "There's one more I want to do. I was waiting for the right setting. Now we have it."

"What do you mean?"

"I want to paint Tristan by the pond."

"Why the pond?"

"Because," said Tommy, returning to gaze out the window, "it's going to be a place he can be himself at totally now. He's never had that before."

"When will you paint him?"

"Soon," said Tommy. "But I'm going to have to ask you and Mom and Dad a favor."

"What?"

"Not to come down to the pond while we're working."

"Why?"

"He doesn't want anyone to know about him. I haven't told Mom and Dad. Just you. So you have to promise me two things. Don't come down to the pond, and don't tell Tristan I told you about him."

Tristan opened the back door then. He had his shirt back on and his hair was almost dry. Pearls of water still clung to his legs. I couldn't imagine those being a tail, his feet a flipper. Surely Tommy had gone insane. "Am I late for lunch?" Tristan asked, smiling at me.

Tommy turned and beamed him a smile back. "Right on time, love," he said, and I knew our conversation had come to an end.

I WENT DOWN THE LANE to the barn where Dad was working, taking his lunch with me when he didn't show up to eat with us. God, I wished I could tell him how weird Tommy was being, but I'd promised not to say anything, and even if my brother was going crazy, I wouldn't go back on my word. I found Dad coming out of the barn with a pitchfork of cow manure, which he threw onto the spreader parked outside the barn. He'd take that to the back field and spread it later probably, and then I'd have to watch where I stepped for a week whenever I cut through the field to go to the pond. When I gave him his soup and sandwich, he thanked me and asked what the boys were doing. I told him they were sitting in the living room under the *American Gothic* portrait fiercely making out. He almost spit out his sandwich, he laughed so hard. I like making my dad laugh because he doesn't do it nearly enough. Mom's too nice, which sometimes is what kills a sense of humor in people, and Tommy always was too testing of Dad to ever get to a joking relationship with him. Me, though, I can always figure out something to shock him into a laugh.

"You're bad, Meg," he said, after settling down. Then: "Were they really?"

I shook my head. "Nope. You were right the first time, Dad. That was a joke." I didn't want to tell him his son had gone mad, though.

"Well I thought so, but still," he said, taking a bite of his sandwich. "All sorts of new things to get used to these days."

I nodded. "Are you okay with that?" I asked.

"Can't not be," he said. "Not an option."

"Who says?"

"I need no authority figure on that," said Dad. "You have a child and, no matter what, you love them. That's just how it is."

"That's not how it is for everyone, Dad."

"Well thank the dear Lord I'm not everyone," he said. "Why would you want to live like that, with all those conditions on love?"

I didn't know what to say. He'd shocked me into silence the way I could always shock him into laughter. We had that effect on each other, like yin and yang. My dad's a good guy, likes the simpler life, seems pretty normal. He wears Allis Chalmers tractor hats and flannel shirts and jeans. He likes oatmeal and meatloaf and macaroni and cheese. Then he opens his mouth and turns into the Buddha. I swear to God, he'll do it when you're least expecting it. I don't know sometimes whether he's like me and Tommy, hiding something different about himself but just has all these years of experience to make himself blend in. Like maybe he's an angel beneath that sun-browned, beginning-to-wrinkle human skin. "Do you really feel that way?" I asked. "It's one thing to say that, but is it that easy to truly feel that way?"

"Well it's not what you'd call easy, Meg. But it's what's right. Most of the time doing what's right is more difficult than doing what's wrong."

He handed me his bowl and plate after he finished, and asked if I'd take a look at Buttercup. Apparently she'd been looking pretty down. So I set the dishes on the seat of the tractor and went into the barn to visit my old girl, my cow Buttercup, who I've had since I was a little girl. She was my present on my fourth birthday. I'd found her with her mother in a patch of buttercups and spent the summer with her, sleeping with her in the fields, playing with her, training her as if she were a dog. By the time she was a year old, she'd even let me ride her like a horse. We were the talk of the town, and Dad even had me ride her into the ring at the county fair's Best of Show. Normally she would have been butchered by now—no cow lasted as long as Buttercup had on Dad's farm—but I had saved her each time it ever came into Dad's head to let her go. He never had to say anything. I could see his thoughts as clear as if they were stones beneath a

Before and

clear stream of water, I could take them and break them or change them if I needed. The way I'd changed Tommy's mind the day he left for New York, making him turn back and leave me alone by the pond. It was a stupid thing, really, whatever it was, this thing I could do with my will. Here I could change people's minds, but I used it to make people I loved go away with hard feelings and to prolong the life of a cow.

Dad was right. She wasn't looking good, the old girl. She was thirteen and had had a calf every summer for a good ten years. I looked at her now and saw how selfish I'd been to make him keep her. She was down on the ground in her stall, legs folded under her, like a queen stretched out on a litter, her eyes half-closed, her lashes long and pretty as a woman's. "Old girl," I said. "How you doing?" She looked up at me, chewing her cud, and smiled. Yes, cows can smile. I can't stand it that people can't see this. Cats can smile, dogs can smile, cows can too. It just takes time and you have to really pay attention to notice. You can't look for a human smile; it's not the same. You have to be able to see an animal for itself before it'll let you see its smile. Buttercup's smile was warm, but fleeting. She looked exhausted from the effort of greeting me.

I patted her down and brushed her a bit and gave her some ground molasses to lick out of my hand. I liked the feel of the rough stubble on her tongue as it swept across my palm. Sometimes I thought if not psychology, maybe veterinary medicine would be the thing for me. I'd have to get used to death, though. I'd have to be okay with helping an animal die. Looking at Buttercup, I knew I didn't have that in me. If only I could use my will on myself as well as it worked on others.

When I left the barn, Dad was up on the seat of the tractor, holding his dishes, which he handed me again. "Off to spread this load," he said, starting the tractor after he spoke. He didn't have to say any more about Buttercup. He knew I'd seen what he meant. I'd have to let her go someday, I knew. I'd have to work on that, though. I just wasn't ready.

THE NEXT DAY I WENT back to the pond only to find Tristan and Tommy already there. Tommy had a radio playing classical music on the dock beside him while he sketched something in his notebook. Tristan swam towards him, then pulled his torso up and out by holding onto the dock so he could lean in and kiss Tommy before letting go and sinking back down. I tried to see if there were scales at his waistline, but he was too quick. "Hey!" Tommy shouted. "You dripped all over my sketch you wretched whale! What do you think this is? Sea World?"

I laughed, but Tommy and Tristan both looked over at me, eyes wide, mouths open, shocked to see me there. "Meg!" Tristan said from the pond, waving his hand. "How long have you been there? We didn't hear you."

"Only a minute," I said, stepping onto the dock, moving Tommy's radio over before spreading out my towel to lie next to him. "You should really know not to mess with him when he's working," I added. "Tommy is a perfectionist, you know."

"Which is why I do it," Tristan laughed. "Someone needs to keep him honest. Nothing can be perfect, right Tommy?"

"Close to perfect, though," Tommy said.

"What are you working on?" I asked, and immediately he flipped the page over and started sketching something new.

"Doesn't matter," he said, his pencil pulling gray and black lines into existence on the page. "Tristan ruined it."

"I *had* to kiss you," Tristan said, swimming closer to us.

"You always have to kiss me," Tommy said.

"Well, yes," said Tristan. "Can you blame me?"

I rolled my eyes and opened my book.

"Meg," Tommy said a few minutes later, after Tristan had swum away, disappearing into the depths of the pond and appearing on the other side, smiling brilliantly. "Remember how I said I'd need you and Mom and Dad to do me that favor?"

"Yeah."

"I'm going to start work tomorrow, so no more coming up on us without warning like that, okay?"

I put my book down and looked at him. He was serious. No joke was going to follow this gravely intoned request. "Okay," I said, feeling a little stung. I didn't like it when Tommy took that tone with me and meant it.

I finished my book within the hour and got up to leave. Tommy looked up as I bent to pick up my towel and I could see his mouth opening to say something, a reminder, or worse: a plea for me to believe what he'd said about Tristan the day before. So I locked eyes with him and took hold of that thought before it became speech. It wriggled fiercely, trying to escape the grasp of my will, flipping back and forth like a fish pulled out of its stream. But I won. I squeezed it between my will's fingers, and Tommy turned back to sketching without another word.

THE THINGS THAT ARE WRONG with me are many. I try not to let them be the things people see in me, though. I try to make them invisible, or to make them seem natural, or else I stuff them up in that dark spot on my ceiling and will them into non-existence. This doesn't usually work for very long. They come back, they always come back, whatever they are, if it's something really a part of me and not just a passing mood. No amount of willing can change those things. Like my inability to let go of Buttercup, my anger with the people of this town, my frustration with my parents' kindness to a world that doesn't deserve them, my annoyance with my brother's light-stepped movement through life. I hate that everything we love has to die, I despise narrow thinking, I resent the unfairness of the world and the unfairness that I can't feel at home in it like it seems others can. All I have is my will, this sharp piece of material inside me, stronger than metal, that everything I encounter breaks itself upon.

Mom once told me it was my gift, not to discount it. I'd had a fit of anger with the school board and the town that day. They'd fired one of my teachers for not teaching creationism alongside evolution, and somehow thought this was completely legal. And no one seemed outraged but me. I wrote a letter to the newspaper declaring the whole affair an obstruction to teacher's freedoms, but it seemed that everyone—kids at school and their parents—just accepted it until a year later the courts told us it was unacceptable.

I cried and tore apart my room one day that year. I hated being in school after they did that to Mr. Turney. When Mom heard me tearing my posters off the walls, smashing my unicorns and horses, she burst into my room and threw her arms around me and held me until my will quieted again. Later, when we were sitting on my bed, me leaning against her while she combed her fingers through my hair, she said, "Meg, don't be afraid of what you can do. That letter you wrote, it was wonderful. Don't feel bad because no one else said anything. You made a strong statement. People were talking about it at church last week. They think people can't hear, or perhaps they mean for them to hear. Anyway, I'm proud of you for speaking out against what your heart tells you isn't right. That's your gift, sweetie. If you hadn't noticed, not everyone is blessed with such a strong, beautiful will."

It made me feel a little better, hearing that, but I couldn't also tell her how I'd used it for wrong things too: to make Tommy leave for New York without knowing I was okay, to make Dad keep Buttercup beyond the time he should have, to keep people far away so I wouldn't have to like or love them. I'd used my will to keep the world at bay, and that was my secret: that I didn't really care for this life I'd been given, that I couldn't stop myself from being angry at the whole fact of it, life, that the more things I loved, the worse it would be because I'd lose all those things in the end. So Buttercup sits in the barn, her legs barely strong enough for her to stand on, because of me not being able to let go. So Tommy turned back and left because I couldn't bear to say goodbye. So I didn't have any close friends because I didn't want to have to lose any more than I already had to lose in my family.

My will was my gift, she said. So why did it feel like such a curse to me?

When Mom came home later that evening, I sat in the kitchen and had a cup of tea with her. She always wanted tea straight away after she came home. She said it calmed her, helped her ease out of her day at the library and back into life at home. "How are Tommy and Tristan adjusting?" she asked me after a few sips, and I shrugged.

"They seem to be doing fine, but Tommy's being weird and a little mean."

"How so?" Mom wanted to know.

"Just telling me to leave them alone while he works and he told me some weird things about Tristan and his family too. I don't know. It all seems so impossible."

"Don't underestimate people's ability to do harm to each other," Mom interrupted. "Even those that say they love you."

I knew she was making this reference based on the story Tommy had told her and Dad about Tristan's family disowning him because he was gay, so I shook my head. "I understand that, Mom," I said. "There's something else too." I didn't know how to tell her what Tommy had told me, though. I'd promised to keep it between him and me. So I settled for saying, "Tristan doesn't seem the type who would want to live out here away from all the things he could enjoy in the city."

"Perhaps that's all grown old for him," Mom said. "People change. Look at you, off to school in a month or so. Between the time you leave and the first time you come home again, you'll have become someone different, and I won't have had a chance to watch you change." She started tearing up. "All your changes all these years, the Lord's let me share them all with you and now I'm going to have to let you go and change into someone without me around to make sure you're safe."

"Oh Mom," I said. "Don't cry."

"No, no," she said. "I want to cry." She wiped her cheeks with the backs of her hands, smiling. "I just want to say, Meg, don't be so hard on other people. Or yourself. It's hard enough as it is, being in this world. Don't judge so harshly. Don't stop yourself from seeing other people's humanity because they don't fit into your scheme of the world."

I blinked a lot, then picked up my mug of tea and sipped it. I didn't know how to respond. Mom usually never says anything critical of us, and though she said it nicely, I knew she was worried for me. For her to say something like that, I knew I needed to put down my shield and sword and take a look around instead of fighting. But wasn't fighting the thing I was good at?

"I'm sorry, Mom," I said.

"Don't be sorry, dear. Be happy. Find the thing that makes you happy and enjoy it, like your brother is doing."

"You mean his painting?" I said.

"No," said Mom. "I mean Tristan."

ONE DAY TOWARDS THE END of my senior year, our English teacher Miss Portwood told us that many of our lives were about to become much wider. That we'd soon have to begin mapping a world for ourselves outside of the first seventeen years of our lives. It struck me, hearing her say that, comparing the years of our lives to a map of the world. If I had a map of seventeen, of the years I'd lived so far, it would be small and plain, outlining the contours of my town with a few landmarks on it like Marrow's Ravine and town square, the schools, the pond, our fields and the barn and the home we live in. It would be on crisp, fresh paper, because I haven't traveled very far, and stuck to the routes I know best. There would be nothing but waves and waves of ocean surrounding my map of my hometown. In the ocean I'd draw those sea beasts you find on old maps of the world, and above them I'd write the words "There Be Dragons".

What else is out there, beyond this edge of the world I live on? Who else is out there? Are there real reasons to be as afraid of the world as I've been?

I was thinking all this when I woke up the next morning and stared at the black spot on my ceiling. That could be a map of seventeen, too. Nothing but white around it, and nothing to show for hiding myself away. Mom was right. Though I was jealous of Tommy's ability to live life so freely, he was following a path all his own, a difficult one, and needed as many people who loved him to help him do it. I could help him and Tristan both probably just by being more friendly and supportive than suspicious and untrusting. I could start by putting aside Tommy's weirdness about Tristan being a cursed son of Melusine and do like Mom and Dad: just humor him. He's an artist after all.

So I got up and got dressed and left the house without even having breakfast. I didn't want to let another day go by and not make things okay with Tommy for going away all those years ago. Through the back field I went, into the woods, picking up speed as I went, as the urgency to see him took over me. By the time I reached the edge of the pond's clearing, I had a thousand things I wanted to say. When I stepped out of the woods and into the clearing, though, I froze in place, my mouth open but no words coming out because of what I saw there.

Tommy was on the dock with his easel and palette, sitting in a chair, painting Tristan. And Tristan—I don't know how to describe him, how to make his being something possible, but these words came into my mind: tail, scales, beast and beauty. At first I couldn't tell which he was, but I knew immediately that Tommy hadn't gone insane. Or else we both had.

Tristan lay on the dock in front of Tommy, his upper body strong and muscular and naked, his lower half long and sinuous as a snake. His tail swept back and forth, occasionally dipping into the water for a moment before returning to the position Tommy wanted. I almost screamed, but somehow willed myself not to. I hadn't left home yet, but a creature from the uncharted world had traveled onto my map where I'd lived the past seventeen years. How could this be?

I thought of that group show we'd all flown to New York to see, the one where Tommy had hung his first in the series of *American Gothic* alongside those odd, magical creatures he painted back when he was just graduated. The critic who'd picked him out of that group show said that Tommy had technique and talent, was by turns fascinating and annoying, but that he'd wait to see if Tommy would develop a more mature vision. I think when I read that back then, I had agreed.

I'd forgotten the favor I'd promised: not to come back while they were working. Tommy hadn't really lied when he told me moving here was for Tristan's benefit, to get away from his family and the people who wanted him to be something other than what he is. I wondered how long he'd been trying to hide this part of himself before he met Tommy, who was able to love him because of who and what he is. What a gift and curse that is, to be both of them, to be what Tristan is and for Tommy to see him so clearly. My problems were starting to shrivel the longer I looked at them. And the longer I looked, the more I realized the dangers they faced, how easily their lives and love could be shattered by the people in the world who would fire them from life the way the school board fired Mr. Turney for actually teaching us what we can know about the world.

I turned and quietly went back through the woods, but as I left the trail and came into the back field, I began running. I ran from the field and past the house, out into the dusty back road we live on, and stood there looking up and down the road at the horizon, where the borders of this town waited for me to cross them at the end of summer. Whether there were dragons waiting for me after I journeyed off the map of my first seventeen years didn't matter. I'd love them when it called for loving them, and I'd fight the ones that needed fighting. That was my gift, like Mom

Before and

had told me, what I could do with my will. Maybe instead of psychology I'd study law, learn how to defend it, how to make it better, so that someday Tommy and Tristan could have what everyone else has.

It's a free country after all. Well, sort of. And one day, if I had anything to say about it, that would no longer be a joke between Tommy and me.

Before and

Dead Letters

DEAR SARAH,

I have heard of your great misfortune to have gone and died so suddenly. Now I find myself writing after so many years have passed between us in the hopes that perhaps this news is not true. For a long time I believed I was dead too. Then one day someone called my name ("Alice. Do you remember her? Alice Likely. How she loved that girl.") and I opened my eyes in a dark place, like a fairy tale princess trapped in a coffin. Light appeared suddenly, a flash so sharp and blinding, it pricked my eyes and made them water. Anyone passing by might have thought I was crying. I must have looked so sad.

And someone did stop beside me. I was still trapped in that dark place, my body bagged in a sack of unbeing, but the flash of light had ripped a hole in the darkness. Through that opening, two hands reached in and gripped both sides of the fissure. The hands pulled the gap wider and wider until daylight surrounded me, and trees sprang up, row after row of them. Birds called out. Their notes pierced my eardrums like needles. I heard water, and then there it was too—a stone fountain next to the bench I lay upon, and the birds perched upon the fountain's ledge staring at me, their eyes black and serious.

Whoever freed me disappeared before I could pull myself together. A newspaper lay open across my chest, and another on my legs. I sat up and the paper on my legs slid to the ground, rattling. I held on to the section covering my chest and looked at it for a moment, only to see your

Afterlives   *Christopher Barzak*

name glaring up at me, as if your name had a life of its own, had your eyes and the looks you could give with them, and so your name glared at me in such a way that I could not help but notice it. It said you were dead. Twenty-eight years old. A promising local artist. Survived by her mother and father. Their names were listed as well, but it hurt to look at them. Particularly your mother's. She never liked me and I still don't know why. What did I ever do to her?

I am writing in the hopes that there may still be a chance for us to reconcile, to come together, to answer some of the questions that have burned inside me since you said goodbye. Why did you betray me? Whatever happened to our promise? And where have I been for so long, asleep and waiting for someone to wake me? Why didn't you do that? I don't even recognize my own body. My legs are long and my feet are large. When I peered into the fountain water, a face looked back that belonged to a stranger. Then the fountain turned on again, displacing the water, and the face broke apart into ripples.

Now I am writing this to you. Will you please talk to me? Can we forgive one another?

    Love,
    Alice

❧

I AM WRITING IN A notebook stolen from Rexall's drugstore, the sort of book Sarah and I used in school years ago, for doodling and note-taking. The cover of it looks like the black and white static on a dead television channel. "Snow," Sarah's father used to call that. "Nothing but snow here," he'd say, flipping the channel until something lively and entertaining appeared. He favored shows about policemen and vigilantes who saved the lives of people who could not save themselves from danger. He instructed the vigilantes and policemen on how to go about all of this saving-of-lives business, spouting advice from his reclining chair, waving the remote control like a scepter. Sometimes the vigilantes listened to him, sometimes they didn't. But they always saved the helpless victims in the end.

The pharmacist and his wife didn't recognize me. But I didn't recognize them at first either. They are old and gray now. Mrs. Hopkinsey's face sags. Her teeth are not her teeth any longer. I know this because I remember they were yellow and crooked and now they are white and bright and not so narrow; they line up in her mouth like good soldiers. She smiled at me. "Can I help you, dear?"

Such a nice woman, just as I remember. I told her I was browsing, and she nodded and turned back to shuffling cigarette packs into the storage bin over the checkout counter.

I walked the aisles slowly, touching candy bars, tubes of lipstick, barrettes in the shape of butterflies. I spun the comic book rack and paged through magazines, but the women inside were strange and alien, their faces harsh, skin like plastic or velvet. Too smooth. Their outlines blurred into the backgrounds. I found that a familiar feeling, though, and felt a stab of pity for the cover girl's blurry faces.

The greeting cards stood on the same shelves that they always had; I picked through them. One said, "I feel so lonely with you not here." On the cover was a picture of a little girl looking up at the moon, holding a doll at her side. Inside it read, "But we'll always be friends, no matter what the distance." I found myself crying, and stuffed the card under the waistband of my pants, covering it up with my sweater. I looked to see if anyone had seen me take it, but Mrs. Hopkinsey still restocked cigarettes and Mr. Hopkinsey stood behind the medicine counter, measuring out pills for a customer.

If Sarah had been there, she would have been the one to take the card. I would have been the lookout. Those had been our positions when we were children. I felt a little guilty changing places with her, like borrowing a friend's sweater and not returning it, even though you know how they love it so.

I found the notebook in the next aisle over. I hadn't known I was going to take it either. I needed things without knowing what I needed, so I let my hands think for me. They reached out and took things: the greeting card, several envelopes, the notebook, pens, a bar of chocolate, a ten dollar bill crumpled up on the black and white checkered floor. I used the money to buy a soda and a bag of potato chips, so as not to be suspicious. Mrs. Hopkinsey rang me up with her new smile still flashing, and when she handed me my change, I thought, *I am home.*

DEAR SARAH,

I refuse to believe you are dead. I myself am not dead, so it goes to figure that you are alive and well. The obituary I read must have been mistaken. Or else another Sarah Hartford exists and it is this other Sarah Hartford who has died. Not you.

I have seen the Hopkinsey's, those dear old people, and they have changed enormously. Do you remember how we'd steal candy and perfume samplers from them when we were girls? We were ridiculous, weren't we? And the Hopkinsey's are such good people, I feel ashamed to have stolen from them. Why didn't we ever shoplift at the Hoffman's grocery store instead? The Hoffman's were snobs. Missy Hoffman always thinking she was better than everyone because her DADDY owned the only grocery store in Kinsman, so she had "the whole town's money". How I wanted to punch that girl. Luckily I had you to restrain me, to whisper, "Calm down, Alice, just ignore her. She'll get hers some day." You were the one with your head about you, calm and collected, shoelaces tied, hair in place. No one could ruffle you. Not even Missy.

But what happened to change you? In the newspaper I read that you were murdered by your boyfriend. Tom or Don or Ron. Someone with a name like a mantra. Is this a true description? Did his name repeat in your head, again and again, like Chinese water torture? *Don, Don, Don. Tom, Tom, Tom. Ron, Ron, Ron.* What an awful rhythm to be ruled by.

You were obsessed with Ron, I'm guessing, because you were always obsessive, with your paintings and sketches, with your neatness, the constant smoothing-over of your clothes with the flats of your hands, erasing imaginary wrinkles. The way the part in your hair had to be perfect. The way you avoided cracks in sidewalks because of that nursery rhyme about mothers. I figure you became obsessed with this man in a similar manner.

Don abused you, the papers reported. In the past you had called the police on him. The two of you were noted for dramatic gestures. Did I read this correctly? You burned Tom on the neck with a curling iron? Or was it Tom that burned you? You hit him over the head with a Mason jar that you filled with brushes? Or did Don do that to you? Someone had to have fifteen stitches. Someone called 911 to report an intruder. By the time the police arrived, though, said intruder had vanished into thin air. In the end you and Tom reconciled. You smoothed out the wrinkles. Then he killed you six months later and smashed up all of your paintings. All the frames broken, the canvases torn with a hunting knife. Such a violent imagination. It is evidence like this that proves to me that the dead Sarah Hartford in the newspaper is not the same Sarah Hartford I once knew. She must be your double.

I am glad to know you continued painting. You had vision, I remember, even as a child. But even so, with all that vision, how could you have not seen this coming? To me it sounds as though you stood in the middle of a railroad crossing, not moving when the yellow eye of the train appeared in the night, nor when it whistled a warning. I don't mean to say you allowed Tom or Ron or Don to kill you. I mean to say, how could you allow yourself to be with such a person after the first time it happened?

Before and

If I'd been around, I would have been the one with my head about me, with my shoelaces tied and my hair in place. I would have led you by your ear out of Ron's reach, even if you struggled against me. This is a testament of my loyalty to our friendship. This is the reason why we need one another. For times like this, when we're not reasoning correctly.

Love,
Alice
P.S. You are NOT dead.

⤷⤶

"Promise," Sarah told me. "Promise, Alice." And so I did.

"We'll always be best friends, and here is proof of it." I touched my fingertip to Sarah's. They were both bloody from pricking the skin with a needle a minute earlier. We rubbed our blood together until it mingled and Sarah sighed, satisfied that the act was completed.

"Now no one will ever separate us," she said. "It's final."

A thrill sped up the length of my spine when Sarah said that. She was the only friend I can remember having. When we pledged our undying love for one another, I believed it in every part of my being. "I'm so happy you're my friend, Alice Likely," she said, smiling. I beamed.

But her mother came in a moment later. "What are you doing now?" she complained. Her voice sounded like knitting needles, clicking over and over. I didn't say anything. Sarah had warned me not to speak back to her mother. I was to keep my mouth closed, or else we'd never be allowed to see one another.

"I was just playing, Mom," Sarah answered.

"In the middle of your room? What's that, then? Give me your hand. You're bleeding, Sarah! How did you manage that?"

Sarah's mother led her into the bathroom to clean up her finger, all the while chastising. "What's wrong with you, Sarah? What am I going to do with you? You must go out. You must make friends. You're going to be thirteen next month. A big girl!"

"I do have friends," Sarah protested.

"Other friends," Mrs. Hartford muttered. "You mustn't hide yourself away only for the benefit of your dear Alice."

"I'm not hiding, Mother." Sarah's voice, harsher now, rising.

"Well, you certainly aren't making yourself much of a presence. Now help me hang the laundry. Make yourself useful."

Useful. One of Mrs. Hartford's favorite words. "What does it do?" she was always asking. "What use is it?" When the neighbor boy, Jimmy, started college as a Philosophy major, Sarah's mother asked, "And what will you do with that?"

Jimmy had stared at her for a moment, then shrugged and changed the subject to the weather. What a storm that was the other night, he told her. "Yes, a whopper," Sarah's mother agreed, without pressing him any further about the Philosophy major. "I expect it will help the corn, though," she said.

The weather. An awful part of my current circumstances. Though it is summer, it rained last night, and I was forced to seek shelter. My park bench provided no protection from the raindrops, warm as they were and welcome, as I've started to stink without a proper place to bathe. I finally stumbled into one of the baseball field dugouts, the home team side, and fell asleep on the cold concrete bench in there, with the sound of the rain pattering above me, and the smell of dirt from the baseball diamond turning into a thick, rich mud.

I dreamed of Sarah. She stepped down into the baseball dugout, kneeled beside me, and placed her cheek upon my stomach. I stroked her hair. How soft it was beneath my fingers. I almost believed I was awake and Sarah had finally come to me. When the sun broke through the night, though, and morning woke me, I felt a wave of sadness. I shivered, rubbing tears out of my eyes, for I had lost her again. Like the fog that hangs over the fields of the park, she had dissipated.

Dear Sarah,

I am very angry. Why will you not speak to me? Do you believe yourself above me for some reason? I'm not certain if you even read my letters. What should I do? Stop writing you? I will stop writing if only you would say so. Why don't you say so?

When I stroll through Kinsman, I often stop stock still in my tracks for strange reasons. Here I see you everywhere. In the school yard, the grocery store, or at the Rexall's. Leaning over a water fountain, pulling your hair from your face. Running through town square, to the park, where you left me that horrible day, so long ago. Yes, I remember. Did you think I would forget the pain you caused me, or how it was inflicted? I was attempting to be the bigger person, but now I see you have changed indeed, and I no longer know you. The Sarah Hartford who was my best friend would never have answered my letters with silence.

I suppose your mother finally got to you. When I say your mother, I mean this town. When I say this town, I mean this town with its one miserable Main Street and its overabundance of churches. No more than three thousand people live here and yet there are fifteen churches that

Before and

come to mind readily. What I mean to say is this town has you believing in its one screen drive-in movie theater, its Dairy Oasis, its Wildwood Café with the admittedly fantastic coffee, its park that consists of a water fountain, trees, a baseball diamond, and cemeteries. Granted, the cemeteries are well-groomed, and in autumn the trees light up with brilliant colors. But this town is not where you imagined yourself forever.

What happened to New York City? What happened to San Francisco? What about Europe? You said you'd die if you never made it to Paris. Now that I'm back, I discover that the only time you ever left this place was for a year and a half of college in Columbus. You never even left Ohio. Then Tom asked you to move in and you went to him. You went to him blindly, your arms outstretched, eyelids lowering. A sleepwalker.

That day in the park, it must have been fifteen years ago, you said you had something to tell me. You asked me to sit beside you on the bench near the water fountain. There were birds perched on the ledge of the fountain, dipping into the water for a drink, turning to stare at us, heads cocked at quizzical angles. Robins, I think, though I saw at least one blue jay among them, arguing. You said you loved me, but there was something you had to tell me. You said—

You said—

Damn you. Now I am crying. I can't even finish this letter. My hands are shaking so badly I want to hurt you. To hell with you, Sarah Hartford. Who needs you anyway? You are cruel, mean-spirited. Also thankless.

Signed,
Alice Likely (Or have you erased this name from memory?)

I'VE TAKEN A JOB AND found a bed to sleep in. I sell corn by the roadside. For every bag I sell, I can keep a dollar. I pick the corn every morning, while Mr. and Mrs. Carroll feed their livestock, fill up the water trough, milk the cows who have calves that won't suck, and attend to the children. They are a busy family, the Carrolls, too busy to check references, although I provided them. I am passing through on my way to California, where friends await me. Or so I have told them. How strange and liberating, this easiness in making up an identity. The Carrolls see me as a free spirit, a gypsy, someone from the 1960's, "new-agey", according to Mrs. Carroll, who has a friend who reads tarot cards and burns incense, and knows about these things.

"How long do you need work?" asked Mrs. Carroll when I came into her yard. She was beating a rug on her porch steps. Dust spun in the air

Afterlives

around her like tiny galaxies. She smacked the throw rug, then looked back at me for an answer.

"A few weeks," I said. "I just need to make some money and have a place to sleep for a while."

"Do you have references?" She lifted her chin a little, assessing. I said that I did, and handed her a list of names, phone numbers, addresses in New York City. I made up the zip codes and phone numbers. What does a New York City zip code look like? I am no better than Sarah.

Now I have meals with the Carrolls at noon and six o'clock in the evening. They have three children: Betsy, Peter Jr., and Bennie. Betsy is seventeen and last year's Corn Queen. Peter Jr. is fifteen and a 4-H member. Bennie, ten, continually asks me what it's like to be a girl. He's curious and Betsy will not tell him.

It is a strange dynamic, this being with other people. When Sarah and I were friends, we had no desire for contact with anyone but each other. Now I speak to twenty or thirty strangers each day, by the roadside, while I bag up a dozen ears of corn. They say hello, thank you, do I know you, how have things been going, that top is very flattering, how are the Carrolls treating you? The men call me blue eyes, sweetie pie, honeyface, miss, little miss, blondie. The women call me dear, dearie, sugar, they do not refer to my body.

I saw Sarah's mother two days ago, in Hoffman's grocery store, picking through the green peppers. I was shopping for the Carrolls, but as soon as I saw Mrs. Hartford I dashed into the soup aisle. I watched her shop for an hour, following behind so she wouldn't see me, ignoring my own shopping, so that I had to go back and finish after she'd gone. I couldn't bear to face her. How that woman hated me, though at first she'd thought me sweet and cute, would ask if I wanted anything, a cup of tea, some Kool-aid. Then she went cold. I still don't know what I did to deserve such treatment. Sarah used to say it's because I didn't come from a good family. I said, "What? How could she think that? My mother—"

I stopped talking. I didn't know what to say, only that I wanted to defend myself. Sarah patted my shoulder to comfort me.

"Your mother is a sweet lady," said Sarah. She looked up at the ceiling, and her eyes rolled up as if she were thinking deeply. Finally she said, "She works at the factory, like my father. She loves you but is not home very often. My mother believes a woman should be at home with her children. Also, your father left when you were just a baby. He was a drinker. But I think you're better off without him."

Before and

"I *am* better off without him," I shouted. "And my mother works her fingers to the bones! Who does your mother think she is? Not everyone has the luxury to stay at home with her children."

"I know, Alice," Sarah said. She leaned in and hugged me. "I know. She doesn't matter. It's just you and me, ok?"

I've mailed Sarah the card I stole at Rexall's. I realized I'd never mentioned where she could find me. Did I feel stupid? Yes, indeed, I did. So I sent the card and wrote for her to meet me in the park in two days. I will give her another chance, and if she still chooses to not see me, then maybe I *will* set out for California. Somewhere in the West, the Southwest even, where there is more space. Space enough to make a life out of nothing. I will be a pioneer of space, living off my wits and my good fortune. I will sit by the roadside and sell beaded necklaces while my skin turns tan and leathery. I will read people's fortunes in the palms of their hands for twenty dollars. People believe in things that aren't particularly believable. They wait all their lives for strangeness, for miracles.

I eagerly await our reunion.

SARAH,

I hope this card finds you well. Saw it and thought of you immediately. I have been hopelessly sending you letters, asking you to reply, and yet I never provided an address. I am red with embarrassment. Please meet me in the park, by the fountain, you remember, at noon tomorrow. I miss you dearly.

Always,
Alice

NO WORD FROM SARAH. NEITHER did she show up at the park yesterday. Although I did see two police officers, strolling in the general area. I nodded and smiled when they looked at me, then sat on the park bench and took out a book that Betsy lent me.

The policemen approached. They took off their caps and asked what I was doing. Reading, I told them. They nodded. "Are you waiting for anyone?" they asked. I said that I was indeed waiting for someone. "Who would that be?" asked the taller officer. I was immediately suspicious, so I told them I was waiting for Betsy, that I worked for her family. They said, "In that case, we'll need you to wait for her outside the park, Miss."

"What do you mean?"

"Nothing to concern yourself with. But you'd be doing us a favor if you read your book elsewhere." They put their hats back on and smiled. They waited for a while, badges glinting. Finally I stood to leave.

Why did she not meet me? My face is burning. I am so angry that I screamed at Bennie to leave me alone when I arrived back at the Carroll farm and he began pelting me with questions. I'll apologize later. For now I can only sit on my bed and cry. I wish my mother were still alive. Where is our house though? I can't even remember what road we lived on. Was our front door blue or green?

DEAR SARAH,
You said, "Alice, I have something to tell you." Do you remember? Does it hurt to be reminded? "You are not real, Alice," you said. "You are not real. Do you hear me? I made you up, Alice. You are not a real person."

I hate you, Sarah Hartford. How could you be so filled with cruelty? But don't worry. I've given up on you. You won't hear from me again. I wish you only the best for the future. Give Ron my regards.

Sincerely,
Alice Likely

I WRITE THIS HASTILY, AS I'm preparing to leave this town for good. It is home to me no longer. But now I wonder if it ever was. It was Sarah who I came home to in the morning, in the evening, and in the night. Now I know that she is in fact not receiving my letters. They have come between us in a way in which I never would have imagined them capable.

Yesterday, after the incident in the park with the police officers, I was lying in bed, crying, because I couldn't think of anything else more appropriate, when I became angry enough to write Sarah a hateful letter, a last letter. I was ready to give up, but only if I had a chance to give her a piece of my mind. This time I decided to do things differently. I planned on delivering my letter in person, and walked across town to the Hartford house on my own. I was through with dodging her mother, through with waiting. I had waited for so long in the darkness before someone called out my name, before the light came and freed me. Uncountable days, miserable, curled up in a fetal position. A fairy tale princess, like the ones in the stories Sarah used to read me. Waiting for someone to free them, their hands pressed against the lid of a glass coffin, struggling. Not again, I decided, and opened the front gate of the Hartford house and

Before and

climbed the front porch steps and knocked on the door. Three sharp raps, and it opened.

It was her that answered. Mrs. Hartford. She stood there in a floral print housecoat with an apron tied around her waist. How small she was. I looked down on her. Looked down on her gray hair, stringy and unbound, spreading over her shoulders. Gray sacs of flesh sagged under her eyes. She wore no makeup. She wore no pearls. She looked up at me, not smiling, and said, "Can I help you?"

"I'm h-here—" I said, stuttering. As small as she was, she still frightened me. Her panty hose had rolled halfway down her legs, just below her kneecaps. I wanted to bend down, pull them up for her. Brush her hair into something respectable.

She chuckled. "You certainly are," said Mrs. Hartford. "What do you need, dear?"

"I'm here for her," I said. "I've come for Sarah. Where is she? Sarah!" I shouted beyond Mrs. Hartford's head, hoping she'd hear. "Sarah, where are you?"

"*You,*" Mrs. Hartford whispered. Her mouth twitched wordlessly. "*You,*" she said again, and then Mr. Hartford was behind her, his face a map of wrinkles, his hair salt and pepper. What had happened to that vigilante? The man who would save others who could not save themselves? Where was he now? He could not save anyone, could not save Sarah.

"What's going on here?" asked Mr. Hartford, his blue eyes moving back and forth between us, piercing. Mrs. Hartford reached up and slapped me. My cheek burned and then she was hitting me on my shoulders, my arms, my chest, her hands lashing out randomly. I pushed out, away from her, and she followed me down the porch steps.

Mr. Hartford grabbed hold of her shoulders and turned her around to face him. She buried her face in his chest, sobbing. Her chest heaved. He looked over her shoulder at me and shook his head as if I was his own child. As if I was his own, disappointing child. Is this how he sometimes looked at Sarah? Is this how they made her feel when she said she wanted to leave her husband?

"Please leave," said Mr. Hartford. "Or I'll call the police, Miss, and have you arrested. Don't come back, and stop writing those horrible letters. Go on, get out." He nodded towards the front gate.

I stepped backwards slowly. Before I turned to go, I looked up at Sarah's old bedroom window. The lace curtains blew in the breeze. And behind them, I saw a face, the idea of a face, looking down at me.

I closed the gate behind me and ran away from the house, away from the sobbing.

Now I am writing this. It's early morning. I've gathered my clothes and some food from Mrs. Carroll. Before I left the kitchen she paid me for picking and selling the corn. She slipped me two fifty dollar bills along with what she owed, and told me to be safe. Her hands closed around mine and they felt scratchy and worn. I kissed her cheek.

I am off now, to space, to somewhere where there is more room for me. Somewhere in the West, or the Southwest even. I will sit in the desert below the blue bowl of sky until I become a part of that landscape. But not forever. I will move on, I will go further. I will do the things for which she never had the courage to leave.

✲

DEAR SARAH,

I realize now that my words will not reach you. This is a dead letter. You will never receive it.

Still, I cannot help but write in the hopes that somewhere my words are finding you. And maybe wherever you are, you are writing me too. Long letters, beautiful letters. Letters that one day I will find and read with great pleasure. Perhaps you are having adventures elsewhere, now that you're not here. Perhaps you've moved on to a place that I will only understand as being better at some later juncture in this life, this life you gave me. But still, at some intersection, my hope is for our words to cross each other, so that we will feel, if only for a moment, infinitely loved and happy. It is the least anyone deserves.

Love,
Alice

Before and

Plenty

ALTHOUGH I HADN'T SEEN MY friend Gerith in years, I wasn't surprised
to receive a letter from him, asking me to come home. Gerith had been
sending me these requests every year or so after I left Youngstown, most
of them chronicling the misfortunes of the old neighborhood where we
grew up. From his descriptions, it seemed not much had changed for the
better. Each day the city disintegrated a little further. People who had
once been important to us disappeared without warning. Often he'd ask
about my life now that I no longer lived there. *Are you okay?* he wondered.
Are you happy? And each time I answered: *I have a secure job, I live in a
great city, I have a girlfriend who loves me more than I love myself. I have
plenty.*

No matter how I answered them though, Gerith's letters filled me with
a sense of guilt. Whenever one arrived in the mail, I'd put it in the pocket
of my jacket for a while and forget about it. Then, after I'd get up the
nerve, I'd read it and end up laughing or crying, overwhelmed with nostalgia for the old neighborhood. Even though I'd spent most of my life
waiting to escape Youngstown, the place was still my home. Gerith's letters reminded me of that.

This time, as always, I hoped Gerith would allow me to finally make a
clean escape. I wanted him to tell me that the South Side had received
funding for re-beautification, that the shelter where he worked had
enough food and beds, and that life in general was an eternal flame of
mercy and generosity. But instead, his news left me reeling.

"Mrs. Burroway has died, David. The funeral is this Saturday. I hope you'll come home for it."

Immediately I had a vision of houses, stripped and gutted, left behind by the dead.

I'd already made plans for the weekend, so I spent a few minutes un-making them. There was the financiers' dinner on Friday, and on Saturday I'd promised my girlfriend we'd stay in and do nothing together all day. I called her answering machine and canceled our Saturday, then phoned the office and explained that an old friend had died. The boss was generous, asked no questions, only said to be careful if I planned on driving back. Then I packed a bag and left Chicago for Youngstown.

There was another reason for going home as well. I'd been keeping a secret for far too long, and now I needed to share it before it was too late. The secret involved a small amount of magic though, and these days magic is not something in which everyone can afford to believe. There is a suspicious absence of miracles. But sometimes impossible things happen when no one is looking.

IT HAPPENED IN YOUNGSTOWN, DURING my last year of college. Fall arrived early that year and spattered the few trees on our street rust red and wax yellow, cinnamon brown and orange. The leaves were a welcome relief from the sight of our crumbling surroundings: boarded-up warehouses, empty storefronts with cardboard covering the windows, and walls tattooed with strange but banal graffiti. I remember the Market Street Bridge in particular, and the words YOU HAVE CROSSED THE LINE scrawled on both sides of it in black spray paint. I passed under that banner each day, as I walked to and from school. It bothered me to no end. I wanted to know what line. And who, exactly, had power over the geography of my life?

Gerith and I bought a house together that year. We'd finally decided to cut the umbilical cords that tied us to our parents. Both of us had grown up in that post-industrial shell of a former steel town, a place steeped in a depression that no one knew how to relieve. Most people affected indifference to the situation. No one in our town wanted to be re-educated for alternative careers, but they'd spend their unemployment checks on the lottery and whiskey. We felt the world owed us some obscure inheritance. This strange psychology had been passed down by our parents and grandparents, who actually did lose their jobs during the seventies and eighties. We were children of the dispossessed who wanted to be the dispossessed.

Before and

The house we bought was an old Victorian on Chalmers Street, and it cost us only six thousand dollars. Houses were cheap in Youngstown because most of the city was a ghetto. The only profitable business was the university, which we thought would be our way out of town one day. Our house had two floors, a basement, an attic, and a front porch spread wide and deep as a cave. Between the turret that rose out of one corner of the roof and the newel posts on the stairwell, we felt like we'd bought our very own castle.

After using what money we'd saved to buy the place, Gerith and I were broke. We'd both won grants and taken out loans to pay for college, which left us with a little extra cash each semester, but that money never seemed to arrive at the right times. So for the first few months in our new house we had electricity and water but no telephone or heat. And when the autumn chill grew strong and wind began to rattle our windows, we wrapped ourselves in the afghans our mothers had crocheted for us before we left.

Whatever other luxuries we did without, the one that hurt most was food. We ate peanut butter sandwiches for lunch, ramen for dinner, and drank tap water that tasted of chlorine. On our kitchen table we kept a wooden fruit bowl that was always empty. After a few months of living like this, it felt like my taste buds had begun to deteriorate.

We didn't know much about our neighbors. Only that a black family lived on one side—a mother with two teenaged girls, one who had a son of her own—and on the other side was a Puerto Rican couple, Rosa and Manuel, who screamed at each other in Spanish until four in the morning most nights. Across the street in a Victorian like ours was Mrs. Burroway, a little, white-haired old lady who walked hunched over and carried a black cane with a silver horse head for a handle.

She seemed ancient to me even then, bone-thin, her skin hanging loose on her frame. She wore a pair of thick black-rimmed glasses that exaggerated her cloudy cataracts and the blue of her eyes. Almost every day she sat on her porch alone with her cane laid across her lap, watching the traffic go by at the end of the street. Sometimes when I was leaving for school, I'd see her heading to a neighbor's house carrying brown bags, overfull with groceries, which she'd place on their porch, ring the doorbell, then scurry home again, her horse-headed cane trotting in front of her like a guide. And it was in that way, actually, while she was delivering her mysterious goods, that we finally met.

One morning, as I gathered my schoolbooks, I heard a thump outside the front door. Then the doorbell rang repeatedly, loud and annoying, as it hadn't been replaced since the house was first built. I pulled my backpack over my shoulder already saying, "I heard you the first time," but when I opened the door there was no one on the porch.

A bird perched on the porch rail, cocking its head at me as I looked down to find a bag of groceries at my feet, a stalk of celery jutting out the top, a bag of bread and soup cans visible beneath. When I looked up again, I saw Mrs. Burroway crossing the street, hunched over as if several sacks of grain were piled on her back. "Wait a second!" I shouted, then picked up the bag and ran off the porch, finally catching her on the other side of the street. "I'm sorry," I said, "but why did you leave these groceries on my porch?"

She turned those blue, cloud-ridden eyes on me then, and licked her lips. "You boys are looking a bit slight," she said, uncovering her teeth with a smile.

"But surely you can't afford to buy us groceries." I smiled, holding the bag out for her to take back.

"No, no," she said, waving her hands as if the bag were cursed. "Those are yours now. Besides, I have plenty."

"Well," I said, and stood there for a moment, not knowing what else to say. "Well, thank you."

"My pleasure," she said. Then she turned around and continued on to her house.

GERITH AND I SPENT THAT day at home instead of school. We opened cans of soup, stripped bananas out of their skins, ate stalks of celery with cream cheese spread in the grooves. We drank a six-pack of grape soda I found at the bottom of the bag, and smoked marijuana, which Gerith supplied, wondering aloud at what we'd missed in our classes. By evening, most of the food was gone. One banana lay curled on its side in the fruit bowl and two cans of clam chowder stocked our pantry shelves.

"So," said Gerith, as we sat cross-legged on the braided rug in the living room. "Do you think Mrs. Burroway is crazy, or just very generous?"

I took a hit off the pipe and passed it back, holding the smoke inside until my lungs began to hurt. "Very generous," I said, exhaling the smoke. "Though that doesn't exclude the possibility of a mental disorder."

"Wow." Gerith shook his head. "That's pretty amazing."

I nodded, chuckling a little at Gerith's astonishment.

"What?" he said. "Did I say something stupid?"

I told him it was nothing though, and waved away his question with a crazy, expansive gesture that made us both laugh until we'd forgotten what we'd been talking about.

Before and

WINTER IN OHIO THAT YEAR filled the streets with snow and ice. The city became a stage for the weather to play on—ice-slicked streets, temperatures far below zero, and snowdrifts so big children cut tunnels through them. Winter that semester, I had International Finance, Human Impacts on the Environment, and Ballroom Dancing. By the end I still couldn't write an essay on acid rain that made any sense, but I'd learned how to waltz. It didn't matter. The finance course was my priority. Doing the work for that class drained me, but I kept reminding myself it would all be worth it one day.

Gerith, on the other hand, dropped his courses midway through the semester. He said he could finish them in summer, started to volunteer at the shelter, and soon everything he did and everyone he knew revolved around that.

One night in December, while I sat at my desk and studied the effects of chemical treatments on water, Gerith appeared in my bedroom door, ringing a bell. He lazily clanged it back and forth, smiling in a way I knew meant he wanted something. "I'm going to collect money for the Salvation Army at the grocery store," he said. "You should come with me."

"I have a final in two days," I said, tapping the book spread out in front of me.

"Come on," he said. "What are you going to learn tonight that you can't cram in tomorrow?" He moved into my room and put his hand on my desk, tapping his fingers near the edge of the book.

"I can't cram, Gerith. You know that."

"Do something worthwhile for once," he said.

"I am," I said. "I'm trying to graduate."

He flipped my book closed and grabbed my jacket off the doorknob.

"No more arguing," he said. "You're coming and that's final. This will be food for your soul."

WE STOOD OUTSIDE THE GROCERY store fifteen minutes later, in a swirl of snow. Christmas lights lined the awning, filled the storefront window, blinking on and off in time to Christmas songs. The Salvation Army bucket stood propped between us, and Gerith rang his bell continuously, clanging it louder whenever anyone approached from the parking lot or whenever the electric doors behind us slid open. I had a bell, too, which I rang reluctantly, only putting out an effort when Gerith shot me looks.

"I should be studying," I said.

"You're going to do fine," Gerith assured me. "You can take that test without opening a book."

Afterlives

"Easy for you to say. You've dropped out, and I have a C going into the final."

The doors slid open behind us and a woman carrying two plastic bags of groceries exited. Gerith rang his bell in the air and looked intently at her. "Merry Christmas!" he said.

The woman nodded and returned the greeting. She moved one of her bags into her other hand and searched inside her purse. When she brought her hand out again, she had a small pile of copper and silver, which she threw in the bucket, then walked away.

"Thank you," Gerith called after her. "See," he said. "You just have to call attention to the cause."

"Yeah," I said. I looked at my watch. "How long do I have to do this?"

"Three more hours." He raised his bell and rang it a few times to accent his answer.

"I'm going now," I said. I set my bell down on the bucket, the tongue choking inside it, and started to leave.

"You can't go now," Gerith called after me. "David, I mean—"

I turned back around with my hands stuffed in my pockets and yelled, "What? Just what do you mean?"

He rolled his eyes and stamped his feet on the snow-packed ground, then pulled his hair away from his face. "I mean, God, why don't you just care about something for once in your life? Something outside of yourself."

"You've got a lot of nerve," I said. "You're just as selfish as I am. Don't think I buy into your Gerith-the-all-giving act. You do that for yourself as much as I study my ass off to graduate so I can get the hell out of here." I kicked at a drift of snow and a chunk broke off, bursting into powder.

The doors behind Gerith slid open then, and Mrs. Burroway came toddling out, holding a bag of groceries in her arms. She looked at me and smiled, then looked at Gerith and asked, "When did you boys start ringing the bell? It was a nice old man when I went in."

"We just started half an hour ago," Gerith told her.

"Just missed you then," said Mrs. Burroway. "Here, hold this for me." She handed Gerith her bag, opened her purse and took out a few bills. She stuffed them in the bucket, her hand shaking as she pushed them inside. "Were you leaving just now?" she asked me.

"Yes," I said, grateful for her distraction.

"Good. I have some food to send home with you. Can you carry my bag home for me?"

I nodded and told her of course. By now Gerith and I were accustomed to accepting food from Mrs. Burroway. She brought us a sack every week.

Before and

Sometimes two. We never knew how she could afford it. She did the same for all our neighbors, and Gerith mentioned that she brought food to the shelter several times a week as well. I'd always assumed she was a well-off widow who lived modestly, but Rosa next door said Mrs. Burroway was as poor as anyone else in our neighborhood. "That Miss Burroway," Rosa told me one day, "she's a good woman. A saint. But you won't catch me spending too much time on her porch." I asked her to elaborate but Rosa would only say, "No white woman can cook like that."

When I took hold of Mrs. Burroway's bag that night in December, I didn't notice any food inside. It was mostly just furniture polish and toiletries, soap and hair spray. But at the time that still didn't seem strange to me.

"Thank you, David," she said, swinging a scarf around her neck with a little flourish before she put her horse-head cane out in front of her feet to propel herself forward.

I didn't look back at Gerith as we left. I couldn't. If I did I might succumb to guilt. I had too much pride for that. I couldn't let him beat me down for wanting something for myself.

Mrs. Burroway chattered beside me about the winter cold she'd just gotten over, about how terrible the weather was this year. We walked the few blocks to our street, and as we walked and spoke in that lunar landscape, I thought I could hear Gerith, ringing his bell behind us.

GERITH AND I DIDN'T SPEAK much after that. We moved around our home like ghosts or shadows, slipping out of the peripheries of each others vision. I kept to my room, planted at my desk, and Gerith continued to work at the shelter. During the late hours of the night, he'd come home from working there and ease the front door closed as quietly as possible. The front door creaked no matter how much we oiled it though, so I always knew when he'd returned. I'd listened to him pace the hardwood floor outside my room and make myself believe he was getting on fine without me.

In early April I was notified about a job I'd applied for in Chicago. I could start immediately after graduation if I liked, they said. I was ecstatic. A real job. Real money for the first time in my life. With the salary I'd be earning, I could pay back my school loans within two years. I called my parents to share the news, to show them that my schooling had paid off.

I had two months to graduate and tie up loose strings. There were few problems, really. The only person in my life who could cause me grief at that point was Gerith. I couldn't tell him. All through April and halfway through May, I tried to gather the stubbornness I thought I'd need to counter his own. I knew he'd be angry with me for leaving, especially since half the house was mine.

The day I finally confronted him arrived in the last week of May, when I only had a few weeks left before I planned to leave. I waited for him on our porch, sitting on an old sofa we'd propped out there the summer before. A clay pot filled with dirt but no plant sat beside me. I wondered if we'd ever tried growing anything in it. Gerith had pulled an all-nighter the night before, so when I saw him turn onto our ragged little street with his overnight bag, walking sluggishly, I entertained the idea of not telling him at all. Just leave and forget about him, I told myself. Forget about Youngstown. The future was my destination.

He greeted me as he approached the house, a half salute that trailed off into a wave. His hair was bound behind his neck in a ponytail, the skin beneath his eyes was puffy and gray. "Hey there," he said, climbing the steps. "How are things going?"

I shrugged.

"Something wrong?"

"I'm leaving," I said suddenly, my chest tightening as I said it. There, I thought. It was finally out.

"Leaving?" Gerith arched his eyebrows and held one of his hands out, palm up. "What do you mean?"

"I have a job," I said. I looked over at the dirt-filled pot and stuffed my fingers in the soil. "It's in Chicago."

Gerith didn't say anything right off, and I kept playing with the dirt so I wouldn't have to look at him. Eventually, though, I looked up.

His head was lowered, his eyes fixed on the peeling floorboards. He'd let his overnight bag slip from under his arm, and clung to it by a strap. He looked bewildered, as if he'd just won an enormous amount of money or lost a loved one in a freak accident. "Well," he said, looking up again as he spoke. "Guess you'll want me to buy your half of the house."

"No," I said. "It's yours."

He nodded and stared and finally he said, "I hope you don't like it. That job, I mean. You belong here, David. You'll always have a place here."

"Thanks," I said, "but I don't think I'll be coming back."

"It'll be here," he repeated. Then he went into the house.

I sat outside and wondered why he'd let me off so easy. It wasn't like Gerith to not put up a fight. Maybe I'd caught him when he was too tired. Maybe he'd realized arguing about this would have been futile.

I didn't move from the sofa. The sun moved across the sky like a hand on a watch and a pale crescent moon rose up to replace it. I noticed the Puerto Rican couple's house next door was up for sale, even though the prospect of it selling was low. Rosa and Manuel had moved out two weeks before and, within a week of leaving, the neighborhood had picked their house clean. During the night, people had come—neighbors and others from nearby streets—to remove the aluminum siding, the copper pipes and brass doorknobs, the leftover chairs and sofas. Anything that could be turned over for money. The house sparkled in the twilight now, a house with silver insulation wrap exposed on all sides. It looked as though it had been covered in chewing gum wrappers. I'd seen this happen several other times over the year on Chalmers Street. Houses left behind were veins to be mined by the living.

Two days before I left, an ice storm hit Youngstown. It started as rain, but then the temperature dropped and soon the city was encased in ice. I watched the whole affair from my bedroom window until the storm glazed my view over with a sheet of corrugated ice and I turned back. My bags were packed; my room was empty. Anyone could have lived there, or no one.

The electricity shut off sometime during the evening, and I wandered through the house with a flashlight, sweeping through the dark with its swathe of light. The house creaked under the weight of the ice and I wanted to be in Chicago already, as if in Chicago there would never be any ice, as if any house I lived in there would be so sturdy it would never creak. Gerith was at the shelter. He'd called earlier to say he'd be spending the night.

It wasn't until later, after night gathered and the storm receded, that I thought to check on Mrs. Burroway. All alone in her ramshackle house, she could have fallen in the dark of the blackout. So I put on my jacket and broke a seal of ice off the front door as I pushed out only to slip and fall in a tangle of limbs on the ice-glazed porch as soon as I stepped out.

When I got up, I saw that all the front lawns, sidewalks and streetlights had been covered with ice. Tree limbs sagged under the weight, grazing the ground. The neighborhood sparkled under the white light of the moon and stars like a world made of blown glass.

I moved cautiously down the steps and across the yard and street to Mrs. Burroway's front porch. I couldn't see any light through her front door's windowpane though, no candles or lamps or flashlights. I knocked and ice slid away where my knuckles hit. No answer came, so I knocked again, but there was still no answer.

I stepped back down to the lawn. Grass crunched beneath my shoes as I circled around to the side of the house like a thief looking for an entrance.

I wiped ice away from one of the side windows so I could peer in between cupped hands, hoping I'd find Mrs. Burroway safe.

With my face pressed against the chill of the kitchen window, all I could see was darkness at first. Then suddenly light entered the room, a small candle flame that shuddered and winked in the dark, throwing out shards of light, breaking the shadows. Behind the light, Mrs. Burroway followed. The flame spun and guttered in her shaking hand and when she set it on her kitchen table I saw oranges shining like globes of gold, turkey that steamed, sweating glistening juice, pies with cherry gel bursting from brown crusts, round chocolate cakes, cans of soup, jugs of milk, boxes of cereal, jars of honey. A feast.

Mrs. Burroway moved away from the table and disappeared into the shadows. A moment later she crept back into the light with a stack of brown paper bags in her hands. She set the bags on a chair, unfolded one, and began to pack fruit, cans of soup, jars of peanut butter, and cartons of eggs into it. She sliced the turkey and slid generous cuts into baggies before putting those in as well. My mouth watered as I watched her pack bag after bag. And when she finally emptied the table, she set the bags on the floor around it and wiped it down with a towel. I realized then I'd become enchanted by her ritual and was about to knock on the window when I saw something I never told anyone about afterward.

After Mrs. Burroway wiped down her table, the air shimmered faintly above the table surface, and more food, other kinds of food, materialized in place of what had been taken. Soon an abundance of grapes, Cornish hens, bags of rice and jars of golden-brown honey filled the space.

I fogged the window with my breath and wiped it away. But as I wiped, my hand squeaked against the glass and Mrs. Burroway turned toward me. At first she looked frightened, her eyes wide and jaw slack. Then she recognized me, and slowly she lifted a gnarled finger to her pursed lips.

I nodded and her mouth bloomed into a smile. She waved then, a silent goodbye, and I turned and went back to my own house.

I LEFT YOUNGSTOWN IN POSSESSION of that secret image of the table and its feast. Now the thought of Mrs. Burroway's house being stripped bare reminded me of what I needed to do. The neighborhood would take from her house what they could, but I had to make sure the table survived her.

I spent the night before the funeral with my parents rather than going to the house on Chalmers Street. I needed a night to myself before I faced Gerith, and my parents were happy to have a night to catch up with my life. Later I called my answering machine in Chicago. There was a message from my girlfriend saying to call when I could and that she hoped everything was all right.

In the morning I woke and dressed for the funeral and drove to the cemetery in a downpour. I was early, but the caravan of mourners arrived soon after. I waited in my car until everyone got out and hurried under purses and umbrellas to the chapel. I saw Gerith, in the line of pallbearers, grab a handle on Mrs. Burroway's casket to lift it out of the hearse. His hair was combed back into a neat ponytail and he wore a black suit. It was the first time I'd ever seen him wear one.

After the priest delivered his sermon, we all left the chapel. Gerith stopped me at the door and put an arm around my shoulders. "It's good to see you," he said. I patted him on the back and nodded.

"I'm sorry," I said, as abruptly as I must have when I told him I was leaving. I'm sure he probably thought I was talking about Mrs. Burroway, but I wasn't. It was an apology for not visiting earlier, for leaving and not keeping in touch. For not telling him about the table. For that night in front of the grocery store.

"I found her," he said. "No one had seen her for a couple of days, so I went over. I'd been visiting her every so often for the past few years to make sure she was okay. She was on her kitchen floor. A stroke, the doctor says. There was all this food on her table. She'd been cooking enough for an army again."

Hearing that, I said, "I have to show you something," and led him to my car. "Trust me," I said. "It's important."

We drove back to Chalmers Street together. The old neighborhood had changed a little, but most things remained the same. Rosa and Manuel's house had been razed. An empty lot was all that was left. Our house though, Gerith's and my house, was still standing.

"It's in Mrs. Burroway's house," I told Gerith, and he furrowed his brow.

"What are you talking about, David?"

I opened the car door and ran through the rain to Mrs. Burroway's front porch. Luckily it seemed no one had touched her place yet. I imagined this hesitation might be out of some obscure loyalty to her, although how long that loyalty would last was uncertain.

Gerith followed, jingling keys in his hands. "What is it?" he asked as he opened her door. I brought him through the front rooms of her house, which smelled of medicine and dust, and into her kitchen. It was still there, the table, filled with a preserved feast. "This is it," I said. And finally I told Gerith what I'd witnessed.

We cleared the table of food and moved it at my insistence, bumping into walls and lamps as we did, across the street to our own house. After moving Gerith's wobbly table into a side room, we stood on either side of Mrs. Burroway's. There in the light, I saw it had been inlaid with a lighter wood that had tiny runes of some sort burned along its border. I held a damp towel and said, "Ok, here we go. Let's see what's what."

But as I wiped and wiped her shining table nothing happened. There was no shimmering in the air over the surface, no ghostly scents preceding the transported food. Gerith looked at me skeptically. "It's okay, David," he said. "It's still a nice table."

"But—" I said. "I know what I saw." Then I had an idea. I handed the damp towel over the table to him. "You try," I said.

He must have pitied me because he began to wipe down the table with a sigh. "We can't do this forever, David. People are coming here for the memorial."

But even as he spoke, it was working. "Look," I said, and he moved his hand away. Already the air danced with tiny blue sparks. Then the food began to take shape. First transparent as a film projection; then, suddenly solid. Roasts and fruits, boxes of cereal and cans of soup. Gerith laughed, a little surprised sound, and looked at me with unbelieving eyes.

"It's how she did it," I said. "All those years."

WE TALKED FOR THE REST of the day, about old times, about Chalmers Street and the shelter. Neighbors came later to share stories about Mrs. Burroway, but I kept mine a secret between her and me and Gerith. Gerith and I caught up in between visits from neighbors and friends. I told him about Chicago, about my girlfriend and the house I'd bought. How I have everything I need. And through all of this, while neighbors visited, while Gerith and I got reacquainted, we sat around the table and its feast.

It was enough, I told myself. I knew the table would be in the best of hands with Gerith, the kind of hands that were like Mrs. Burroway's. Open from the start.

I left for Chicago a few days later. On the way out of town, I passed under the Market Street Bridge once again. It still said, YOU HAVE CROSSED THE LINE.

Christopher Barzak

Before and

The Ghost Hunter's Beautiful Daughter

"*Syl-vie! Syl-vie! Syl-vie!*" her father calls through the hallways of the house. The ghost hunter's beautiful daughter sighs, wipes a tear from the corner of her eye, looks out the cobwebbed window of the attic. Sometimes it's the basement, sometimes the attic. Occasionally a house has a secret crawl space, and if she sensed it, she'd go there and wait with the creepy crawlies and spinning motes of dust. Through the false eyes of the portrait of a lady with her toy poodle sitting on her lap, she'd watch her father negotiate the living room, the swathe of his flashlight cutting through the dark. "*Syl*-vie! *Syl*-vie! *Syl*-vie!" he'll call—always call—until the ghost hunter's beautiful daughter finally says, "Here, Daddy. I'm in here."

"Sylvie," he'll ask, "my God, how do you do it? Tell me how to find you."

How *does* she do it? If only Sylvie knew, she would try to stop it from happening. The whispered calls, the bloody walls, the voice of a house, the way it told you how bad it was hurting. If she could turn it off, she'd gladly do it. She's had enough of houses, their complaints, their listing, the wreckage of their histories. If only she could be normal!

She peeked her head out the side of the false wall that time, waved, and he gasped. "Clever girl!" he exclaimed a moment later, his shock fading, replaced by a grin. He ambled over to put his arm around her and squeeze her affectionately while he admired the dark passage behind the deteriorating gaze of a two-hundred year old society woman and her once white poodle.

He calls now, too. His voice comes from the floor below her. Upstairs is where this house's ghost lives, in the attic. They are so dramatic, ghosts, thinks Sylvie. If only they'd settle down, give up on whatever keeps them lingering, maybe their lives would get a little better. No more moaning in pain, no more throwing things around in frustration. No more struggling to get someone to notice you. Give up, thinks the ghost hunter's beautiful daughter. Why don't you just give up already!

"Here," Sylvie whispers. When her father calls again, she speaks louder. "Here, Daddy!" she shouts. "I'm up here. In the attic."

His feet thud on the pull-down steps until his head rises over the square Sylvie climbed through half an hour ago. The ghost here hadn't tried to hide from her like some. She hates that, the way some shudder when they see her, wrinkle their noses, furrow their brows—the way they disdain her very presence, as if they are saying, *You're not who I was waiting for. You're not the one I want.* This ghost, though, had little expectations. It had few conditions or requirements. It was an old woman, and old women aren't as picky as lost children, spurned lovers, old men whose sins were never forgiven, people who cannot bury hatchets, people who cannot bear to leave even after life has left them.

"Sylvie!" her father gasps. "Oh my, Sylvie, what have you found?"

The ghost is barely holding itself together. At first Sylvie wasn't sure if it was even human. It might have been some strange sort of animal. She's seen those before, though they're rarer. Afterwards, they don't always know how to hold the shape they had in life. The old woman is gaseous; she probably doesn't even know what she's doing in this attic. Liquids are sorrowful, solids angry, throwing chairs and mirrors and lamps across rooms at their leisure. Gases, often confused, are usually waiting for some sort of answer. What is the question, though, Sylvie wonders. What don't you understand, old woman?

The ghost hunter nods at his daughter briefly when she doesn't answer, then goes directly to the old woman's figure in the corner. The old woman turns to look at him. Her face is misty. Wisps of moisture trail in the air behind her when she turns too quickly. She is like a finely composed hologram until she moves, revealing just how loosely she's held together. She looks past the ghost hunter, over his shoulder, to meet his daughter's gaze. Sylvie turns away from her to look back out the cobwebbed window. A long, wide park of a yard rolls out and away, trees growing in copses, with a driveway unspooling down the middle of everything, leading out through the wrought iron fence to the tree-lined road. This was her father's favorite sort of grounds to hunt, his favorite kinds of ghosts lived

Christopher Barzak

Before and

in places like this, usually. Sylvie can't bear to look back at the old woman. She knows what comes next.

There is the click, the sucking sound, the high moan of the old woman's ghost, and then the silence ringing in the dusty attic. Her father sniffs, coughs, clears his throat, and Sylvie knows it is okay to look now. She turns to find him fiddling with his old Polaroid camera, pulling the film out and waving it in the air until it begins to develop. "That's a good one," he says. "Not the best, but not the worst either." The old woman's ghost is gone. He looks up and sees Sylvie watching him. Blinks. Sylvie blinks back. "Thank you, sweetie," he says. Then: "Come on now. The Boardmans will be back shortly. We should get going."

THE ROAD IS GRAY, THE tree trunks are gray, the sky is gray above her. There are no discernible clouds, only drops of gray rain pattering down, speckling the windshield of her father's car as they pull away, and further away, from the haunted mansion. Sylvie remembers visiting the mansion once with her mother. In October. For Halloween. The mansion, one of many, sat in the historic district of one of those small Midwestern cities in one of those states with an Indian name. Each Halloween, members of the community theater hid among the mansions and family cemeteries of the historic district, buried themselves in orangey-red leaves, covered themselves in clothes from the previous century, adopted slightly archaic ways of speaking. They were ghosts for an evening, telling stories to small groups of people—parents and children, gaggles of high school boys and girls who chuckled and made fun of their dramatic renditions—who had come on the Ghost Walk through the park and along the river, where once the people whose ghosts they now played actually had walked, loved, hated, drowned themselves out of unreciprocated affection, hid amongst the tombstones from abusive husbands, hung themselves before the police came to arrest them. Her mother's hand holding hers, how large and soft it was, moist, how her mother's hand quickly squeezed hers whenever a ghost brought his or her story to a climax. "This is it, Sylvie!" said her mother's hand in that sudden squeeze. "Something wonderful or terrible is going to happen!" the hand told her.

Out of those park-like promenades of oak and maple lined streets they drove, back into the center of their shabby little city. Warren. Named after the man who surveyed the area for the Connecticut Land Company that pioneered the Western Reserve, Sylvie had learned in Ohio History class only a week ago. Before that, when someone said the name of the city, she had always thought of mazes and tunnels instead of a man who measured land. She misses picturing those mazes, those tunnels. Though the city is small, shrinking each year since steel left these valley people decades ago, it is tidy and neat, not maze-like at all. It's a city you could never get lost in.

Once past the downtown, on the other side of the city, the wrong side of the tracks but better than where they'd been living, her father likes to say, they stop at the Hot Dog Shoppe's drive-thru window, order fries and chili cheese dogs for both of their lunches, then continue on to the house Sylvie's father purchased several months ago. "An upgrade, Sylvie," he had said when he took her to the old brick Tudor with the ivy creeping up one of its walls. Much better than the falling-down house where they'd lived when her mother was alive. Sylvie still passed that house on her bus ride to and from school each day. That house could barely hold itself up when they'd moved out last spring. Now it really was falling down, leaning to one side unsteadily. The windows had all been broken by vandals and thieves now, people looking for leftover valuables. Not jewels or antique furniture. Copper piping, aluminum window frames and siding—anything they could turn in for money. They found nothing in that house, though. Sylvie's father had already stripped the place before others could get to it.

Inside he sits at the computer desk, as usual, one hand pressing the hot dog to his mouth, the other moving the mouse, clicking, opening e-mail. They'd had a lot of work in the past year, after word spread that her father could truly rid homes of lingering spirits, temper-tantrum poltergeists and troublesome ghosts. He'd built his own website after a while, and bought the new house. He was going to give her a better life, he told her. A better life than the one he'd had. Sylvie wondered why he spoke as if his life was already over. Her mother was dead. Her father was alive despite his deathly self-description. How could he not see the difference?

"Another one!" he shouts while chewing a bite of his chili dog. He grabs the napkins Sylvie has placed beside the mouse pad and wipes away the sauce that dribbled out while he spoke. "Listen to this, Sylvie."

> *Dear Mr. Applegate,*
> *My husband and I have recently read in the newspaper about your ability to exorcise spirits. Frankly, my husband thinks it is bullshit (his word) but for my sake he said he is willing to try anything. You see, we have a sort of problem ghost in our home. It was here before we were. It's the ghost of a child, a baby. It cries and cries, and nothing we do stops it except when I sing it lullabies in what must have been the baby's room at some point in this home's history. Sometimes we'll find little hand prints in something I might spill on the*

floor—apple sauce, cake batter I might have slopped over while I wasn't paying attention because I was on the phone with my mother or perhaps a friend. If it were only the hand prints, I don't think it would matter very much to us. But the crying just goes on and on and it's begun to drive a wedge between my husband and me. He seems to be—well, I'm not sure how to put it. He seems to be jealous of the baby ghost. Probably because I sing it lullabies quite often. At least four or five times a day. Sometimes I worry about it, too, when I'm out shopping or seeing a movie with a friend or my mother, and I'll think, How is that baby? I hope the baby is all right without me. I mean, it won't stop crying for my husband even if he was at home. The baby doesn't like him. And often he'll leave and go to the bar down the road when that happens until I come home and sing it back to sleep. We're not rich people, though, Mr. Applegate. And the prices I read on your website are a bit out of our range. Would we be able to bargain? I know it's a lot to ask, considering the task, but as of now we could afford to pay you eight hundred dollars. I wish it were more, but there it is. You're our only hope. Would you help us?
Yours sincerely,
Mary Caldwell

Her father laughs after finishing the e-mail. His smile grows long and wide. "Eight hundred dollars," he says, leaning over the keyboard. "Eight hundred dollars will be just fine."

"She sounds upset," Sylvie says. She sits on the couch in the living room where she can still see her father in the little cubby hole room he calls his office, and eats a French fry.

"She *is* upset, Sylvie!" her father says, turning around as his sentence comes to a close on her name. "And people who are upset are our bread and butter. Without them, we wouldn't have this fine new house, now would we?"

Sylvie looks up and around along with her father after he says this, taking in the rooms that they've both looked at a hundred times in just this way over the months since they moved in. Each time her father feels she doesn't understand how much he does for them, for her, for their better life, he'll talk about the fine new house and look up and around at the ceiling and walls of whatever room they're in, as if this is necessary to pay your respects dutifully.

"Well, I think it sounds sweet," says Sylvie.

"What does?" her father says. He turns back to the computer to begin a reply e-mail to Mary Caldwell.

Afterlives   *The Ghost Hunter's Beautiful Daughter*

"The baby," says Sylvie. "Why would they want to get rid of it?"

"It's not even *their* baby, honey. And even if it were, people just want to live a peaceful life. Ghosts make that impossible. Don't judge so harshly."

Sylvie drops her French fry on the plate. She stands up and excuses herself, and her father asks why she hasn't eaten all of her lunch. "I'm full," says Sylvie, and leaves the room, her chili dog half uneaten.

THE CRAZY MUMBLER, THE SILLY girl in pigtails, the annoying policeman who is always pointing his finger and shaking it, the rich woman in the fur coat and hat with the golden pin of a butterfly on one side, the confused dog who runs in circles after his own tail, the maid who is always offering tea or coffee, the old man dressed in a severe black suit with tails and top hat, his long white mustache drooping over the sides of his mouth and down his chin like spilled milk. Page after page, she turns through them until she comes to the new one, the one her father gave her before sitting down to eat his chili dog and open his e-mail. "Here," he'd said, holding the photo by one corner as if it were the tail of a dead mouse, and handed it to Sylvie. "For the scrapbook. Keep her safe."

The old lady looks up and around the frame of the photograph, as if it is a fine new house for her, looks out at Sylvie, furrows her brow, then says, "Child, why have you done this? I thought we were becoming friends."

"It wasn't me," Sylvie tells her.

"She's telling the truth, my dear lady," the old man in the suit says from his page directly across. "It's not our young Sylvie here who has done this. It's the girl's father. The ghost hunter."

"Ghost hunter?" the old lady says. "Is that who flashed that camera at me?"

Sylvie nods.

"Well, I never. What sort of man goes around scaring the living day-lights out of you like that? What did I ever do to him?"

"It's not you," Sylvie tells the old woman. "It was your son and his family. They moved into your place after you died two years ago. Remember?"

The old lady's face grows more pinched, more confused, her wrinkles deepening. "Why no, I don't remember that at all!" she says. Then: "Wait. Oh, yes. You're right. They *did* move in, didn't they? I *am* dead, aren't I?"

Sylvie nods again, trying to look sympathetic. She hates when ghosts realize they're ghosts.

"Give her some time, Sylvie," the old man with his milk-flow mustache says. "It would be better if you just let me talk to her."

Sylvie knows the old man is right, and turns the pages back and back and back again until she comes to the first one, the very first ghost her

Before and

father captured. The very first entry in Sylvie's album. "Hi," she says, her voice almost a whisper, smiling as soon as she sees her mother's smiling face.

"Hello, my big girl," says her mother.

THERE ARE, PERHAPS, A FEW things that should be mentioned about Sylvie's mother before we go any further. Her name was Anna Applegate, but she was born to the Warners, one of Warren's well to do families that had kept their ties to the city, even after the manufacturing industry fled to poorer nations. Most of the wealthy had gone with their corporations, or had never settled in the communities who worked for them to begin with, but the Warners had a particular flaw, a flaw that only revealed itself in the receding tide of money: the Warners sometimes showed that they had what some people called "heart" or "feelings"—both enemies of profit, and because they had kept their modest wealth invested in the city, and lived among the people who worked for them, over a period of several decades they eventually "came a cropper", as Anna's father liked to tell friends and colleagues at the university in the neighboring city of Youngstown. He was an art historian—a dreamer and a good for nothing, his own father had called him as they had begun to feel the burden of becoming people who were required to think about money in relationship to need for the first time in several generations. He was fond of sayings, phrases and aphorisms from the past. He had a difficult time caring about anything that distracted his gaze from beauty. His family had lost their wealth, but he had not lost the sorts of desires wealth had once afforded them.

Sylvie's mother had inherited the Warner flaw of heart, and because of this she married Sylvie's father, a young man whose careers had ranged from convenience store clerk to selling cemetery plots to working in a cabinet factory by the time he'd turned twenty. She had married for love, and love led her into a falling-down house with her new husband, already carrying a child. And though the Warner family had come down the ladder, they had not come down so far that they would approve of Anna marrying such a man. "What kind of life can he give you?" her father had asked in the front room of their family mansion that was always cold, even in summer.

Anna had said, "Why does it matter what he can give me? What can *I* give *him*? What can we give each other?"

Her father had pursed his lips, closed his eyes and sighed, knowing sense would not reach her. He turned, lifting his hands in resignation, and left Anna standing under the candelabra with the wide staircase curling up on either side of the room to the second floor. She shivered for a while in the cold draft that came through the hallways. Then she made a decision. A decision that would take her to Sylvie's father's family home, into the ramshackle section of unemployed laborers and their raucous families, where Sylvie would be born eight months later.

"Hello, my big girl," says Anna. Sylvie wishes she could hug her mother instead of just see her and talk to her in the photo. It's been so long since she felt her mother's arms around her. Her father's hugs are tight and hot, but her mother's felt like spring mornings, light coming under the window shade, the smell of growing things pushing their way up and out of the earth.

"Hi, Mom," says Sylvie, though she's not sure what else to say. How many times has she opened this book of dead people just to look at her mother? Just to say hello? It's hard to have a conversation now that her mother's dead. Sylvie keeps on changing, but her mother will always be who she was when that picture was taken. She will be like that forever.

"What did you do today?" Anna asks. "I thought I'd see you this morning, but it's already afternoon."

"Dad had a job. At the Boardman mansion. She's at the back of the book with Mr. Marlowe. He's explaining everything to her now."

Anna sighs and shakes her head, leaning against the border of the photograph. "Your father is doing well then?"

Sylvie nods. "He got another e-mail today too. A baby ghost. Guess it's crying too much for the woman's husband."

"I wish he would stop," says Anna.

"I wish he would too," says Sylvie.

"I wish he'd never found out what you can do," says Anna.

"I don't mind, I guess," says Sylvie. "I mean, I just wish he would stop. That's all."

"Did you do your homework?" her mother asks, trying not to appear too obvious in her switching of the subject. Sylvie nods, then shrugs and says no. "You better do that, honey," says her mother. "I know it's hard right now, but you have to keep studying."

"What good is it anyway?" says Sylvie. "You're smart. Where did it get you?"

"Don't say things like that, Sylvie."

"I'm sorry, Mom," Sylvie says. "I just wish you were here. I mean, really."

"So do I," says Anna. "But you need to be strong, okay? I need you to be my big, strong girl."

Before and

Sylvie nods, even though she is neither big, nor strong. She kisses her mother's picture before closing the album and putting it aside to do her Algebra homework. She's fourteen, neither big, nor strong, but she can at least do Algebra for her mother.

WHILE SYLVIE DOES HER HOMEWORK, while she watches a movie about rich warlocks taking over a town their great grandfathers founded long, long ago, while Sylvie showers and walks around with her hair wrapped up in a towel like a beehive, while she puts herself to bed and falls asleep, while she dreams she is trapped in one of those police department rooms where people can see in but you can't see out, the ghosts in the photograph album gossip, debate, inform the new ghost—the old woman, whose name is Mrs. Clara Boardman, formerly of *the* Boardmans of Warren, Ohio—about the general condition of her recently transformed existence. Mrs. Boardman is outraged to discover that Sylvie's father believes he has freed her from ghosthood, that she's now resting at peace in some place people imagine to be heaven. "Only Sylvie can see and hear us then?" she asks.

The other ghosts murmur or mumble their confirmations, but Mr. Marlowe adds, "Well, the people we were haunting too. They could see and hear us, of course."

"It's why the ghost hunter's business is doing so well," adds the annoying policeman, who only the crazy mumbler can see is angrily pointing and wagging his finger as he speaks.

The rich woman in the fur coat and hat with the golden pin of the butterfly on the side of it says, "They're no longer crazy once Sylvie sees the ghosts too. When she's nearby, she makes us visible."

"Hence the photos," says Mr. Marlowe.

"Hence this album," says Sylvie's mother. "I'm sorry, everyone," she says. "I'm afraid I'm the one who started all this."

"Not at all," says Mr. Marlowe.

"It's not your fault," the mumbler says.

"You didn't make him capture you, or any of us," says the police officer.

The little girl with pigtails jumping rope smiles across the page from Anna. The dog chasing his tail barks twice. Anna sighs despite their effort to buoy her spirits. "I don't know," she says. "If I'd never haunted Sylvie, she might never have been able to see the rest of you. That could be enough reason to lay blame."

"Pish posh," says the rich woman, tugging at the collar of her fur coat. "Don't be silly, dear girl. You could never be blamed for this. It's not as if you're a magician who's given away trade secrets. Ghosts have a right to haunt, now don't we?"

"Well said," says Mr. Marlowe, and the dog chasing his tail barks once again.

Their voices seep out of the album while the ghost hunter's beautiful daughter sleeps. All night long she hears their voices without comprehending them; they are like songs teenagers hear in the buds of their turned-down-low iPod earphones while they dream. They make sense to Sylvie while she is sleeping, but in the morning, when she wakes, they fall away from her memory like sand through spread fingers.

AT SCHOOL SYLVIE ENJOYS A sort of fame that she had never felt before her mother died. Since the journalist from the *Warren Tribune* interviewed her father, everyone knows he can get rid of ghosts. Sylvie had read the article like anyone else ten months ago, in the Sunday edition. At first she'd been confused. Why had her father allowed a reporter to interview him? But quickly she came to understand that it was money. Money was almost always the reason for anything her father did, probably because he had so little of it.

In the article, he is quoted as saying, "After seeing how much it upset my daughter, after all my family and friends told me I was delusional, I decided to buy the equipment necessary to help my wife on her way to the afterlife."

This is the part of the interview Sylvie hates most. How he lied about her being upset. And the end of the article announcing that he could do this for others, that it was a service he could provide.

When she arrived at school the next day, everyone was waiting with sad eyes and invitations to parties or sleepovers. They believed she'd been through hell and, though many of them had never been haunted, enough had and now they were talking, sharing secrets, surrounding Sylvie with their stories of grief and torment. She'd understand, they thought. She knew the horror.

But Sylvie hadn't been horrified. She had loved seeing her mother walk around the same rooms she'd walked in when she'd been living. It was almost as if she wasn't dead. True, she could no longer touch her mother, but she could see and hear her, and sometimes she thought she could smell her perfume, *Eternity*, but she realized that was just a lingering memory after she started to see other ghosts. Ghosts don't have a scent, she now knows. Not unless you can remember what they smelled like when they were living.

Before and

So it had only been Sylvie that saw her mother at first. Her father didn't tell the reporter that. And then one day he had come home from working at the cabinet factory early, a stomach ache, and found his beautiful daughter in her bedroom of their slanted, narrow house, talking to his dead wife.

Sylvie had kept it secret until that day, which was also the day she realized others could see her mother if she didn't take precautions: arrange for times when she and Anna could sit and chat like nothing had ever happened. When her father saw, though, he told everyone, and everyone had patted his back and consoled him while disbelieving. For months afterwards he complained to friends and relatives that his wife was haunting him and his daughter, and for months friends and relatives made sympathetic faces, nodded politely, placing a hand on his forearm or putting an arm around his shoulders as they walked through the park, saying things like, "My mother thought my father was haunting her for a while after he died. Don't worry. It's just a phase."

He had been outraged by their belief that he was just another ordinary mourner. He had seen his wife standing right in front of him, talking to his daughter. It was no intimation, no product of his imagination. He could see her, speak to her, when Sylvie was in the room. But his friends and family would only bat their lashes while they pondered polite responses, trying to consider how to help him through his grief. *How must Sylvie be handling this,* they wondered, *if this is how Richard grieves?*

And then, as he said in the article, he found his father's old Polaroid camera and took a picture of Anna. He'd prove what he saw. He hadn't realized that, when he snapped her picture, she would disappear. He received his proof in the photo that she had been there, but when he looked at it, she was still as stone and no longer talking. Sylvie had cried and cried, curled her fists into balls and beat his chest until he grabbed her wrists and stopped her. "You killed her!" Sylvie screamed.

"No, Sylvie," her father said, "the cancer did that."

Later, her father gave her the picture to keep, after having passed it around to friends and family to prove his sanity.

It wasn't until he gave the picture to Sylvie, after he was through with it, that Anna spoke again. "We can't let him know about me this time," said Anna. And Sylvie, who had been crying, nodded and said, "I'm sorry, Mom. I'll be careful this time. I won't let him know you're still with us."

In the newspaper interview, her father had done something that Sylvie's mother said was noble. He had lied about how it was Sylvie who made his wife visible. He didn't admit that he'd never been able to see her without Sylvie nearby. He said nothing about the camera. He had told the reporter he'd bought the usual ghost hunting equipment for the job: infra-red temperature gauges, negative ion detectors, Geiger counters, electro-magnetic field sensors. He owned a few of those things now, for props. He had protected Sylvie.

"Dislike what your father's done," Anna told Sylvie, "but don't hate him. His intentions were good."

Now Sylvie is popular. Previously she'd been just another poor white girl who hadn't learned how to fight, avoiding everyone, head down, watch-ing her feet pull her through the hallways of Western Reserve Middle School. When she gets off the bus now, there is always someone waiting to walk and talk with her in the hallways.

"Did your father catch any ghosts this weekend?" Ariel Hyland asks during lunch on Monday. Ariel is probably the darkest-skinned black girl in Warren Western Reserve Middle School. For years she and Sylvie have shared a bus seat, talked in a minimal way about each others families, but other than that, the girls barely know each other.

Sylvie nods. Tells Ariel about the Boardman mansion. The girls and boys that line up on the benches of her table lean in to listen closer. They are always waiting to hear about another ghost, another capture. Sylvie's father is famous. He's been the lead story for *Ghost Hunter Monthly*. He's been invited to Pittsburgh to rid a hotel of a spirit that's stalked the place for four decades. What he's waiting for is a call from Hollywood, asking him to do a show. Sylvie tells the other students enough to satisfy their curiosity. But it's never enough. Even after she finishes telling them about Mrs. Boardman, how she had offered Sylvie tea when she came upon her in the attic, how nice she had seemed about being found, even after it is clear Sylvie will tell no more and changes the subject to the Ghost Walk that's coming up next weekend and would anyone like to go, they eye her greedily. They have no interest in community theater actors who just pre-tend to be dead. Only real ghosts matter.

HAVING MADE PLANS TO ATTEND the Ghost Walk on Saturday night with Ariel and a few of the other lunch table crowd, Sylvie starts to worry. For months she's tried to pretend her new fame will disappear, that at some point she can go back to being nobody. She doesn't know how to tell who really wants to be her friend and who wants to hang around her because of her father's escapades. She likes knowing where she stands. There are girls who leave letters in her locker now, telling her about their own ghosts. There are boys who come up to her at her lunch table and offer her trinkets of misplaced affection: photographs of glowing lights in their back yards they've taken, DVDs of *Ghostbusters* or *Casper*, once a silver charm bracelet with tiny, ghostly faces dangling from it. Before, when her mother was still alive but sick and losing her hair and refusing to take money from her family for a better doctor, for better treatment—and even before that, when Anna refused to take money for a college education from her father the art historian, because he'd offered it like she was just another charity organization after marrying Richard, and she would rather live and die working at Wal-Mart, as her mother once said—Sylvie had had few friends. Ariel Hyland hadn't been what she considers a real friend. Ariel had talked to Sylvie, but had never befriended her in a way that made Sylvie feel *known*, the way a true friend knows you, the way Sylvie's mother knows her. But still, out everyone at Western Reserve Middle School, Ariel is the closest thing she has. She'll stick close to Ariel at the night of the Ghost Walk, she decides.

"That's a good idea," Anna says when Sylvie confides in her. Sylvie tries not to burden her mother with her own problems, but sometimes she can't help herself. She tries to be big, to be strong, but sometimes she just wants her mother. "It's good that you have friends, Sylvie," says Anna. "You can't hide from the world forever."

"It isn't hiding," says Sylvie.

"What is it then?" Anna asks from the front page of the photo album. In the background Sylvie's dresser is pressed up against the wall of her bedroom in their old falling-down house, her old mattress thrown down on box springs that have been thrown down on the scratched up hardwood floor. It's where Richard took her picture with the Polaroid months ago. Haunting Sylvie's bedroom, as usual.

"It's refusing," Sylvie says. "I'm not hiding from the world. I'm refusing it."

"But why, honey?" her mother asks. It's times like this that Sylvie finds herself annoyed with Anna, like most girls at school act annoyed with their mothers. Whenever Sylvie admits that she doesn't love the world or life as much as her mother loved it, Anna begins to nag like any mother. "There's so much out there for you, Sylvie," says Anna. "Don't refuse the world. Embrace it."

"Mom," Sylvie says, "whatever's out there isn't you. I love you, but can we drop it?"

THE CHURCH WHERE SYLVIE AND Ariel meet the others from their lunch table is on a corner of courthouse square, all lit up on this October evening, leaves tumbling end over end across lawns, scraping across the sidewalks like the severed hands of zombies. Sylvie has always been a fan of Halloween—her favorite movie is *The Nightmare Before Christmas*, her favorite candy are those little sugary pumpkins, her favorite colors: purple, orange and black—and now it all seems a little ironic to her as she stands in the front room of the First Presbyterian Church sipping cocoa with Ariel and five of their cafeteria friends whose parents have dropped them off or sent them on their bikes with enough money to buy a ticket to the realm of the dead for the evening, making them promise to be back by ten o'clock.

An older woman comes over to ask if they're all part of a group or willing to mix with other travelers along the River Styx this night. Everyone laughs or smiles; she's obviously excited to call the Mahoning River the River Styx and to use grammatical constructions like "this night" to her heart's content. No one answers her immediately, so Sylvie speaks up. "We're going together if possible."

"All righty," says the old woman, who smells exactly like the church smells, Sylvie notices, a little musty and a little like Avon perfume. "Then go ahead and wait outside on the front steps. Your guide for the evening will meet you shortly."

Ariel says she's getting a refill of cocoa—"The damn ticket for this cost so much," she says, "might as well get my money's worth."—and everyone agrees. Their Styrofoam cups steaming with cocoa again, they wander out to the steps, which are wide and steep and face the tree-lined road of mansions their guide will take them down. They wait, sipping, discussing the potential the Ghost Walk has for being incredibly cheesy. "Too bad your dad's not here, Sylvie," a boy named Aaron says. "I bet he could tell better stories."

"Ghosts are ghosts," says Sylvie, shrugging.

The clatter of hooves on pavement distracts them. A horse-drawn hearse lit up with lanterns on each of its corners is coming down the street. The driver is headless, they see, when he pulls the hearse to a stop. Ariel asks how he manages to drive the horse if his head is really stuck down in his shirt. "Probably see-through," says Aaron.

"Or maybe there are little holes they cut in the shirt," says another boy, Patrick.

"Or maybe," says Sylvie, "he's dead but able to see without a head." No one says anything at first. They all look at Sylvie as if she could be the anti-Christ. Sylvie laughs. Then they all laugh. She's surprised them by being funny. Now she seems a little more like them. She's not just the ghost hunter's beautiful daughter.

The headless horseman turns to them and waves his gloved hand to follow. He tells the two horses to walk along, and Ariel says, "I heard his voice down in the middle of his shirt. He's got a head in there all right."

Before and

They follow the headless horseman's hearse, and at the street corner they find a woman wearing a black cloak. The headless horseman turns the horses down the street to come back around to the church and lead another group to this same spot. The woman in the cloak tells them that she's their guide now. She's tall and willowy with red hair curling out from her hood. She smiles, looking at each of them for a moment. "Everyone ready?" she asks. Everyone nods. "Well then, let me warn you before we begin our journey, there are some pretty scary ghosts out tonight, so stay together." The boys laugh, the girls smile. The woman wearing the cloak rolls her eyes at them and grins. Then she turns and they begin following her down the tree and mansion-lined sidewalk.

Sylvie has already been in several of these mansions, has already found several ghosts in them for the families that own them. The families that still live in the historic district of Warren are some of her father's best customers. They're gone for the evening, so the Ghost Walk can be held without the living passing by windows to go to the bathroom or sitting down at the table to eat dinner while townspeople gather outside. Sylvie has heard some of the stories already. The mad doctor who built his mansion with a pit in the basement and a trap door on the front porch. One pull of a switch and you fell into his dungeon where he'd perform experiments on you and you'd never be heard from again. The wife whose husband beat her, so she ran away to live in a nearby cemetery because her husband feared the dead and wouldn't go there to get her. The lawyer who hung himself from his porch because he'd killed a man who came to collect a debt. The actors' faces are powdered white. Moonlight glows on their cheeks and foreheads. But their cloaks and old fashioned dresses and suits don't seem nearly old enough to look authentic. It's better than real ghosts, thinks Sylvie. Better than watching them disappear when her father takes their pictures.

At the Jacobs House, Ariel leans close to Sylvie and whispers, "Who's that guy?"

Sylvie looks at Ariel, who nods at a middle-aged man in an old black suit standing next to their circle, listening to the Jacobs ghost tell her story. Sylvie shakes her head. "I don't know," she says. "Another actor?"

The man turns and looks at Sylvie as the Jacobs ghost finishes her story of eternal love for a boy who died before he could marry her, of how she drowned herself in the Mahoning River to join him. The man in the black suit nods at Sylvie. He has a strange beard, like Mr. Marlowe in her album, pointy and black with two lines of gray down the center. Skunk stripes. Sylvie nods back. Then their guide ushers them on to the next house. Sylvie hangs back until everyone is slightly ahead, and the man in the black suit falls in step beside her.

"Lovely night," he says. Sylvie nods again. "Are you enjoying the Ghost Walk?" he asks her.

"It's fun," she says, noncommittal, looking ahead at the others.

"But you've seen ghosts before. Other ghosts. *Real* ghosts. This is nothing for you."

Sylvie stops and looks at the man, hard. "Who are you?" she asks.

"You don't know me, but I know you," the man says. His voice sounds gravelly and vaguely British. His face is lined with acne crevices, but she can tell he's not as old as his scarred skin and pointy beard make him look. "Your father is the ghost hunter, isn't he?"

"That's right," says Sylvie. "What about it?"

"I want you to give him a message," the man in the black suit says. "Tell him he's being watched. Tell him perhaps he should put that camera down before someone gets hurt. Perhaps himself. Or perhaps his daughter, for example. Tell him some of us can do more than haunt. And we would hate to see such a bright young girl like yourself fall down a staircase in one of these old mansions. I hear some of these places aren't as safe on the inside as they appear."

Sylvie narrows her eyes. The man smiles and performs something like a little bow, holding one hand against his chest. "You're lying," she says. "Ghosts can't touch." She knows this because if they could, she and her mother would have always been hugging.

He takes her hand in his and bends to kiss it. It's cold to the touch, and solid. Sylvie flinches and takes a step back toward the edge of the street.

"Sylvie!" Aaron calls from nearly a block away. "What's the hold up?"

"Nothing!" she shouts over her shoulder. "Coming!"

She's already decided she will ask the man in the black suit how he did it, how he touched her, if it's because, as she sometimes worries, she spends more time with ghosts than living people, if it's because her father keeps asking her to find them, to see them, to talk to them. But when she turns back to question him, he's gone. Nothing is there but the wind pushing leaves across the sidewalk.

AT HOME HER FATHER ASKS if she had a good time. "Good enough," says Sylvie. "But there was a man there. I think he was a ghost."

"What sort of man?" asks her father, spinning away from his computer on his desk chair to face her. "What sort of ghost?"

"It was weird. He could touch me. He took my hand and tried to kiss it."

Before and

"Sylvie," her father says, red flags waving in his voice, "did he hurt you in any way?"

"No, it wasn't like that. I pulled away from him and this kid Aaron yelled to ask why I was lagging behind. I turned to tell him I was coming, and when I turned back, the man was gone. He said he was a ghost, and that you'd better stop hunting them."

"Ghosts can't touch people, Sylvie. You know that."

"But he did," says Sylvie. "I can still feel the cold on my hand where he held it."

Her father stands and comes to inspect her hand, holding it in his own like something broken that needs to be fixed. When he touches her, Sylvie begins to feel warmth in her hand again, but her father says, "It's like ice."

"You should stop, Dad," says Sylvie. "He said something else. He said he'd hate to see your daughter fall down a staircase in one of those mansions."

"Sylvie, Sylvie, Sylvie," her father whispers, pulling her into a hug, holding her, his arms wrapped all the way around. "You're tired, that's all. Whoever this man is, he's not dead. The dead can't touch us. He's probably some wacko. We have to keep an eye out for people like that."

"You can do something else," she says into his fuzzy wool sweater. "You can get a different job and then they'll leave us alone."

"Honey!" her father says, pushing her out at arm's length to look at her. "This is the best we've ever been able to do. The best we've ever lived. There's no reason to be afraid of a ghost. Besides, if he comes around, we'll take his picture. See how he likes that."

"You shouldn't be doing this. Mom—"

"Maybe you shouldn't bring your mother into this, Sylvie. It's been over a year now. I think it's time to move on, don't you?"

Sylvie shakes her head and sniffs, realizing she's about to start crying. She pulls away from her father and folds her hands under her arms, nods, and walks upstairs to her bedroom where the ghosts in the photo album are mumbling, conversing, skipping rope and barking, gossiping and reasoning. Sylvie opens it to talk to her mother, but when she pulls the cover back she sees her mother is asleep on the mattress on the floor of her old bedroom, her breathing even, her chest rising and falling. She looks so peaceful. Sylvie could wake her, but she decides to get through this on her own. "Good night, Mom," she whispers. Then gently shuts the book.

"YOU'LL HAVE TO EXCUSE ME. I didn't expect you all this early," says Mary Caldwell when Sylvie and her father arrive at the Caldwells the next morning. It's ten A.M. and Mary Caldwell is in the side yard burning trash in a barrel when they pull up her long, gravel drive. Smoke rises into the air in long dark tendrils beside her. The Caldwells aren't usual customers. They live in an old farmhouse on land where there's no longer an actual farm, in a township called Mecca. Years ago it was sold off, piece by piece, Mary Caldwell tells them as she invites them in to sit in the living room for coffee, leaving the barrel burning behind them. So now the land that was once the farm has other houses on it. Mary Caldwell's husband has gone to a bar down the road, a place Sylvie noticed when they drove around the town circle. The Hole in the Wall. Mary Caldwell's husband is often there, she tells them. He's a friend of the owner, but mostly he's always down there because he can't stand being inside the house with the baby. "I mean the ghost," says Mary, blushing. "We don't have any children of our own."

"I understand," says Sylvie's father. "We'll take care of everything, rest assured. In fact, you should probably join your husband. It's better if we're left alone to take care of the matter."

So you can't see how we do it, thinks Sylvie. But she holds her tongue.

Mary Caldwell sits up straight in her chair, puts her hands on her thighs and breathes a long sigh, as if she's entered a yoga position. "Thank you," she says. "But please, it won't be painful for the poor thing, will it?"

"Of course not," says the ghost hunter. "Think of it as releasing a lost soul. I'm sure it's simply confused about the state of its being."

"Yeah, probably," says Mary Caldwell. Sylvie likes Mary Caldwell. She likes the man's flannel shirt she's wearing, the way she hasn't done much with her hair but it still looks real nice, wavy, and that she doesn't wear any makeup but somehow still looks soft and pretty. That was how her mother used to be. Mary Caldwell catches Sylvie staring and smiles. "Would you like to come with me, honey? We could drive on out to the mall. I'm sure the whole thing must terrify a young girl like yourself, doesn't it?"

"Actually, Sylvie is my assistant," says the ghost hunter. He turns to Sylvie and smiles. "And it's not so terrifying an experience, really. Sylvie has seen other ghosts, obviously. Does it scare you, Sylvie?"

"No," says Sylvie. "It's not scary. Just sad."

"What do you mean?" says Mary Caldwell, her brows furrowing in alarm now.

The ghost hunter takes over. "She means simply that it's sad to see ghosts stuck here, instead of where they should be."

"Oh," says Mary Caldwell. "Well, yes, I can see that's certainly a sad thing. I'm always thinking that way about the baby. Wanting to help it somehow. I hope this is the right thing."

Christopher Barzak

Before and

The ghost hunter assures her it is. He asks Sylvie to show her the photo album. Sylvie takes it out of her backpack and shows Mary Caldwell pictures of ghosts, flipping from page to page while Mary Caldwell nods and mmm-hmms. Her father says, "These are all ghosts we've been able to help on their way." Sylvie doesn't show Mary Caldwell her mother. She shows her Mr. Marlowe, who plays with his mustache and snickers, though only Sylvie sees and hears him. She shows her the little girl skipping rope and the dog chasing his tail.

"Well, then," says Mary Caldwell. "All of these folks seem happy, I suppose."

"That's right," says the ghost hunter. He inquires about the form of payment, and Mary Caldwell pulls a folded envelope from the back pocket of her jeans and hands it to Sylvie's father. The ghost hunter accepts it appreciatively and leads Mary Caldwell out her door to the porch, down the steps to her car, where he shuts the door for her and waits in the drive until she's backed out onto the road and is on her way to the Hole in the Wall to meet her husband. After she's gone, he returns to the living room and says, "Okay, Sylvie. Where can we find this baby?"

Sylvie begins walking through the house, looking around, picking up snow globes, which apparently Mary Caldwell collects. They are everywhere Sylvie looks, on shelves and tables, on the hutch in the dining room. She picks up one with the Statue of Liberty inside it and shakes the globe, stirring the snow. She wanders up the wooden steps of the farmhouse to the second floor, leaving her father in the living room below. She peeks in doorways as she passes by them, the master bedroom with the unmade bed, the guest bedroom where everything is neat and tidy, the sewing room, where everything is a bit disorderly, pieces of fabric, spools and thimbles and pin cushions tossed on a worktable and in baskets littered on the floor. When Sylvie is about to leave the sewing room to check out the bathroom, she hears the first cry.

Angry but tiny, it comes from behind her. She turns around, and the cry comes again, then again. The voice does not seem to come from any one place in the room, but from the room itself, as if from every nook and cranny. "Hello?" Sylvie says. "I know you're here. Why don't you come out? Let me see you."

The baby's cries grow louder and faster, as if it's throwing a tantrum or suffering from colic. Sylvie coos to it several times, coaxing, and finally, suddenly, it appears on the worktable next to the sewing machine. It's so tiny! It wears a cloth diaper that's actually pinned. It's face is red and squinched up, as if it's in pain, and she goes to it, picks it up and says, "Hey now, hey now. No need to cry, baby." The baby's cries stretch out like taffy, but a silence grows between them, longer and longer, until it gives up and looks up into her eyes and quiets for good. Sylvie smiles, then realizes she's actually holding it. "Oh my God," she says. "You're like him. The man in the black suit."

The baby blinks twice, then fades away, leaving Sylvie holding nothing but empty air.

It reappears on the worktable a minute later, crying again. She goes to it, picks it up and tries to sing it a lullaby. Slowly, surely, it quiets again. "You're playing with me," says Sylvie, and the baby giggles and makes a handful of sounds like vowels.

"Excellent, Sylvie," her father says behind her. She turns quickly, still holding the baby in her arms. "You weren't lying. I can't believe it. You can touch it."

"I told you," says Sylvie. "I told you what the man said. You've got to stop, Dad. I have to stop."

Her father lifts the Polaroid to his eye and Sylvie spins around as it flashes behind her.

"Sylvie!" her father says. "What's the matter with you?"

"You can't, Dad. It's just a baby. And they're not gone. You know that."

"This is nonsense, Sylvie," her father says, his camera arm going limp beside him in exasperation. But Sylvie won't turn around. She curls herself over the baby as if any bit of it is exposed, the Polaroid might snatch it from her. "Sylvie, show me that baby," her father demands.

"Hide," she whispers to the baby. "And don't come back. You've got to hide, ok?"

The baby begins to disappear just as Sylvie's father places a hand on her shoulder and spins her around. "Stop this," he says, and then, when he sees Sylvie isn't holding anything at all, says, "What did you do, Sylvie? Why are you being so stubborn?"

Just then the baby begins crying again. Sylvie looks over her shoulder at the worktable. There it is, plopped down next to the sewing machine. Her father lifts the camera and snaps the baby while its mouth is wide open, screaming. The scream is cut short, replaced by a hissing sound, air leaking out of a balloon. The ghost hunter retrieves the picture, waves it in the air, and with each flick of his wrist the baby wavers, fading on the worktable, until it disappears. When her father hands the photo to her after it's developed, the baby's in the picture. Still screaming. "Dad," she says. "I don't want to do this anymore."

"Sylvie, it's not a question of want. It's a question of need. You need to do this. I need you to do this. Just settle down and let's talk about it."

Before and

But even though he's saying let's talk about, Sylvie can see that her father the ghost hunter really means, let's get over it, let's you listen to what I have to say and do as your told, let's just follow my lead, ok? Sylvie wonders if this is how Anna's father the art historian made her feel about the choices she made. She shakes her head and steps past him, leaving the sewing room and him behind saying, "Sylvie? Hey. Where are you going?"

She trots down the steps and picks the photo album up from the coffee table in the living room on her way out the front door. Her father appears on the landing of the second floor. "Honey?" he says. "Sylvie, stop. Where are you going? What are you doing?"

Sylvie doesn't look up at him, doesn't say anything. She runs down the porch steps into the side yard to the burn barrel. The fire is lower now but still going, the smoke not as thick but still smoking. She opens the album and places the baby's photo beside her mother's. Her mother says, "Sylvie, what's going on? What's happening?"

"I'm going to help you, Mom," says Sylvie. "I love you."

She closes the book before her mother can get another word in, and holds it to her chest, closes her arms around it, hugging it as tight as she can. The ghost hunter appears on the steps of the farmhouse. "Sylvie!" he shouts. "What are you doing?"

She holds the book out, dangling it over the fire, as if it's suddenly too hot, too dangerous. Smoke poofs up in a cloud from the burn barrel, and Sylvie imagines the album landing in the flames, catching a moment later, the plastic sizzling on the pages, the cover slowly browning, crisping to a dark charcoal. She imagines a hissing sound escaping from the fire, slowly, slowly like it does when her father's camera captures a soul and out comes the picture, developing in mere minutes. She imagines the smoke pouring forth in dark tendrils, streaking the air above. A popping, then snapping, as the fire grows. Then from the flames they will come, riding the smoke up and into the pale October sky like kites that have been let go. The dog barking, the baby crying, the little girl skipping her rope up and up and up, the mumbler mumbling, the rich old woman and Mr. Marlowe and Mrs. Boardman all quite startled, the cop wagging his finger at her as he floats up behind them. Her mother, too, looking down at her, smiling. "I love you, Sylvie," she'll say, blowing a kiss with one hand as she holds out the other as if she's trying to reach her, to touch her one last time, and is gone the next instant. All of them. Gone, gone, gone.

"Stop!" The ghost hunter shouts as he runs down the porch steps, coming toward Sylvie where she's holding the photo album over the flames in the barrel. "You don't know what will happen if you burn those!" he says.

Is he right? Will what she hopes for not be the thing that happens? Will she have done the stupidest thing in the world if she drops the photos in the flames? The pictures burn, the end, finished. No smoky ghosts riding the wind to heaven. She'll never see her mother again. And for what?

Sylvie's crying. She realizes this only after her father puts his hand on her shoulder when he reaches her, his face turned up to the sky where a moment ago Sylvie had been looking, imagining them soaring off and away into nothing. "Sylvie," he says, his voice low and serious.

She shakes her head, though. "I won't help anymore," she tells him. "I don't want to be a ghost hunter's daughter."

"Don't be like that, Sylvie," he tells her. "Remember your mother—"

"This isn't about Mom," says Sylvie. "Or at least it's not *just* about her." Sylvie puts her hand out and takes hold of his, squeezing tightly. They're warm to the touch, both of them. She thinks she can feel his pulse beating just there, where her thumb presses against his wrist. The baby's cries still ring in her ears. Somewhere Mary Caldwell is sitting on a bar stool, crying into a beer she's ordered before the bar even opens, even though she usually doesn't drink, while her husband watches a football game on the TV in the corner over the cash register. Somewhere someone is reading a magazine article about her father, about her father's ability to rid people and places of ghosts. Somewhere a pointy bearded man wearing a black suit is stalking the leaf-strewn sidewalks of Warren, Ohio. Sylvie hopes he won't hurt her father, now that she's made a decision for both of them. If she stops finding ghosts, he won't be able to capture them. She laughs and cries, happy and mad all at once. She's not sure which to feel, or if it's all right to feel both. But she takes the album away from the fire and holds it to her chest. "This is about us," she says, before squeezing her father's hand so tight no wind could ever take him from her.

Before and

Caryatids

I'M LEANING AGAINST A WALL in the Miro District when the Doctor comes by to say he wants me as a girl. I tell him there are plenty of girls, just look around, and I point to a few girls who sit in the center of the square on the edge of the stone fountain. The women gather there, safety in numbers. The Doctor says, "No, not a girl. I don't want a girl. I want *you* as a girl." He holds a needle up that's filled with a green liquid. Looks like a fungus cocktail, but I know better. With the doctor it's never so simple. It's one of *those* jobs.

I lift my chin and say, "What's this one?"

"Nanomites," he says. The sort that will rewrite my genes and reconstruct my body. I know queens who would near die for a shot of that stuff. It's too expensive, unless you're someone like the doctor. Then you have all the money you want and you can wave stuff like this under our noses, make our mouths water. I'm not interested in being a woman though. I tell him, "Talk to Petra. She's been saving for one of these modifications forever. Might as well help you and help herself at the same time." Petra is one mean-looking queen. Doesn't look much like a girl. Shaves her face each morning but it's covered with a shadow come evening. Has legs with more muscle than most. She's ripped, but she thinks she looks all sweet and dainty.

"I don't want Petra," the Doctor growls. He grinds his teeth together. In the Miro District, I'm the boy voted most willing to try anything once. We've done business before, and the Doctor always has some fantasy to enact. Last time he grew wings out of my back. They were useless; I couldn't fly. But they were beautiful, the way they unfurled and I could move them like arms or legs and the feathers smelled like earth mornings.

It's been years since I smelled earth. This place, Beroke, especially this city, Melas, it stinks like sewage. The whole planet is covered with phosphorescent fungus, except where they've got nanotechs terraforming. They've done that before, though, the terraforming. It lasts for a decade maybe, but the fungus just comes back. You can't get rid of it. Only thing it's good for is the juice sac inside its flesh, the main ingredient of a fungus cocktail. The Doctor is a fungus-head. He says he can understand this place when he takes it. He can hear the voice inside the planet. Each time he's rented me, he's ended up sprawled out on the floor unconscious or else dreaming awake, too tweaked to actually use me.

I shake my head. "Nah, Doc, I'm not up for that, unless you have another that'll change me back." Like I said, I'm not interested in being a girl. It's hard enough being a boy in this world. Why make things more difficult?

The Doctor reaches inside his jacket and pulls out another needle.

"This will take care of everything, Lucius," he says, and slides both needles back into his pockets. I can't help but feel a little resentment. Like what is ever going to satisfy him? Wings? A boy inside a girl's body?

But I nod anyway. He pays more than anyone. Already he's slipping into my wrist node, smooth and sweetly. The transfer fibers stretch forward from his index finger and find their way inside me, transferring enough credit into my account to live on for two months. His hand remains on my hand afterwards. A slight electrical afterglow still lingers. The others hate it that the Doctor always comes for me. But I have a pretty face for a boy. Even after a few nasty encounters, it's still damned pretty.

THE DOCTOR DOESN'T WASTE HIS money this time. Soon as we walk through the city, over the stone bridge that leads to his building, we hurry into the elevator and he has my hands pinned over my head and makes these snuffling noises, like a pig searching for a truffle, licking my Adam's apple. He likes me to act like myself, a real boy's boy, but pliable. Before the elevator lifts us to his floor—I know, *his floor*, he owns a whole level—he takes out a needle and slips it under my skin. Then he pulls it out, no pain, just a pinch. A drop of blood beads up where he punctured me and inside I can't feel the nanomites swarming, but they are doing just that already. The doctor gives me an affectionate peck on the cheek. Rubs his face against mine, the stubble on his face bristling against me. Then the elevator doors open onto marbled floors and a hall filled with pillars

Before and

sculpted to look like women. Their arms hold up the ceiling. Caryatids, he calls them. They look tired, but pretty.

"Rest now," he says. "The process will take a while."

He shows me to his bedroom and I strip off my clothes and slide under his sheets. He doesn't follow. Within a few minutes my eyelids flutter under their own weight.

When I wake again, it's some other night. Who knows how much time has passed. There are four moons framed in the window.

"Good, good," the Doctor says. The room comes into focus. I sit up, feeling strangely out of proportion. The Doctor sits down on the edge of the bed and strokes my breasts. I look down and there they are—my breasts—and the nipples stiffening under his fingers. It all feels, well, I don't know. Different. I'll just commit to "different."

He leans in and kisses me. His tongue finds its way into my mouth quickly. The Doctor is a good looking man. He has brown hair and green eyes and his nose is sexy. Not too big and not pug or beak-like. He has full lips and his breath usually smells good, even though he takes too much fungus extract. He takes care of himself. Probably his body teems with nanomites that keep him looking young and healthy. I could do a worse trick. Sometimes I even let myself imagine he's someone who loves me. But only for a little while. I'm not stupid.

We lay back in bed and explore my new body. My hips are round and my skin is soft as a baby. I have this long black hair that Petra would fucking die for. Maybe I'll cut it off and save it for her before I become a boy again. And down there—something is suspiciously absent. Or maybe not absent, but present in a way I've never experienced. I reach down with one finger and feel the new space inside me. Moist and warm. My body shivers. All of it.

The Doctor shimmies out of his pants and his dick is hard already. It stands up proud like a good soldier. He doesn't waste any time; he's probably been hard like that for hours. He gets right on top and puts it in me. It hurts at first, but then things get smoother. His body crashes into me over and over. I think this must be what erosion feels like, a slow effacement, waves slapping against land, taking a little bit of earth with it each time it pulls away again.

The Doctor's face floats above me, his eyes wincing, his teeth gritted. Sweat beads on his forehead. I pull his face down and kiss him while he moves inside me. His dick throbs inside me, swelling, pushing my cunt apart as it grows even bigger, moving blindly, searching, trying to find me, the me he's hidden. But the Doctor won't find him under all this woman. Even though his body presses against me more desperately, even though he bites at my shoulder and squeezes my left breast hard enough to hurt, I feel protected. I'm usually the one who does the fucking. But here I am, on the bottom, raising my hips to meet his thrusting.

In the end I even cry out, "Oh God," as I'm coming. I haven't said that word in years. God, I mean. And I notice now my voice has changed. I've heard my voice played back to me before, and it never sounded like the voice I heard inside my head, my secret voice, the one no one but I ever heard. It's like that, but even more different. I *sound* like a girl, all soft and cottony.

"Hello," I say to the air. "Nice to meet you, dear."

The Doctor is asleep beside me, his chest rising and falling, his lips parted for breathing. I'm ready to go again, but he looks worn out already. I stick the tip of my index finger between his lips, just barely, and tap his two front teeth. He doesn't wake up.

I put my hands to my throat and—guess what—no Adam's apple.

WE SPEND SEVERAL DAYS HAVING sex and dozing. At one point I climb on top of him, knees straddling his waist, and lower myself onto him, taking him in slowly. Oh, what luck, what incredible luck this is. I put my hands on his chest and grind into him. He says, "I can see you in there, little boy blue. I know you're in there." He calls me little boy blue because of my eyes and the usual state of my emotions. He reaches up to clasp a hand around my mouth and chin, but I push his hand away. I ignore him. My hair falls over his face.

I don't even see him any longer. I'm concentrating on this body, how it feels and how it's working. I'd grown so used to the old one, and the positions with which it was familiar. I feel like I'm alone here. The Doctor is just another piece of furniture. Or it's more like it's me and this body, this fabulous woman around me. The two of us are figuring things out together, laughing a little, because sex is funny when you think about it. Too many people, like the Doctor, think sex is embarrassing. They pay people like me to do the things they're ashamed to ask of their lovers.

I STAY FOR A WEEK before he grows bored with this fantasy and tells me, "All right. You can go now." He jacks into my wrist node once more to tip me, but there aren't any fingers lingering on mine afterwards. There isn't any moment or shock of recognition. One week of work and I'm set for months. No worries. As he escorts me out, he gives me the other needle.

"I suppose next time we meet, you'll be a pretty boy again, Lucius." He pats my back like a friend—like a father—and ushers me into the elevator. He wants me gone because he's starting to feel guilty and he probably has a patient waiting to see him and he can't concentrate on this patient or even himself when he's feeling guilty. He'll come for me again when he's forgotten that feeling.

Before the doors close, I take one long look at the women holding up the ceiling, their hair curling around their shoulders. Caryatids, he calls them. Tired but pretty. I don't think I could carry all that weight by myself either.

I walk down the avenue towards the Miro District. I'm wearing a silver evening gown that'll make Petra salivate. High heels that match even. When I reach the square and see the girls gathered around the stone fountain, a few notice me. They look up and wave me over, so welcoming and they don't even recognize me. I move towards them. I open my purse to make sure the needle is in there, is real and not imagined. Then I snap the purse shut and join the girls. For a while, at least. You know, safety in numbers.

Before and

A Beginner's Guide to Survival Before, During, and After the Apocalypse

FIRST, REMEMBER WHAT IT MEANS to be human. Even when your country has turned against you, even when some other part of the world has been decimated (by bomb, by terrorist cells, by forcible entry and removal of dissidents to dark and forgotten chambers, by hurricane or tornado or tsunami), even then remember that you can retain your humanity if you continue to be humane.

Despite that, you will have certain struggles, like finding work when you're not the right sort (too young, too old, too female, too ethnic, too queer), or like that time you went to the grocery store and the cashier refused to touch your money because you were one of them: one of those Other People. Stay calm. If you are not a part of a normalized group, your chances of being strung up for giving the wrong look or replying with the wrong tone might be more than enough reason for a society gone wrong to cast you out even further, or perhaps kill you. Instead, say "Thank you." Say, "I'm sorry, that's not what I meant." Say, "You're absolutely right, I'm sorry. I wasn't thinking. I'm sorry." Say it again: "I'm sorry. I'm sorry. I'm sorry."

Wear the requisite uniform. Brush the dust off your shoulders and polish your shoes. Look like you mean this pose you're taking. You love this country more than you love life itself. Practice these phrases: "I am a patriot of the first order," and, "God has shown me the light," and, maybe the most important one, "If you don't like it here, go somewhere else."

Afterlives   *Christopher Barzak*

This last one is most effective in proving your loyalty. Do not hesitate to degrade your fellow man if it means your life or his is at stake.

Go to underground meetings in the back rooms of bars and coffee shops. It will not be like the 1960s. There is no free love, just fear, fear, fear. Despair reigns over these conversations, and occasionally you find yourself trying to annihilate your desperation by taking other meeting-goers to bed after too many drinks. Say, "Do you think this is it?" And when they ask, "This what?" say, "The end of the world. Do you think this is it?"

They'll say, "If it isn't the end of the world, I don't want to know what is."

They will cry after you make love to them. They will tell you secrets. Secrets about the child they aborted ten years ago, when that was still legal, before they began to arrest women post-facto. That was what they called it in the Reformation Papers: post-facto. After the fact. Retrospective retribution. They will tell you secrets about the last lover they had, before their lover was outed during the Reclamation Period, when all of the homos and queers were given the choice: normalize or die. It was fairly simple. Most chose life. It is one of the most unfortunate aspects of being human, this drive to survive no matter what the cost. Their last lover will have been called Jason, and you'll wonder what sort of person Jason was, what kind of lover. Do you remind this person with whom you've chosen to abandon reality of Jason? Do you have the same eyes? The same smile? The same voice? The same scent? Are you Jason-esque?

Take drugs. They will keep you not-feeling. Numbness is important when the world is coming apart. Refuse the hallucinogens. Accept the dampeners. You need to see the world as it is. You cannot afford to see it as it isn't.

Remember. This is one of the verbs they will try to remove from your brain. Remember. If you cannot remember, they can tell you anything about the past—your own or the world's—and you will not be able to know if they are telling the truth. Sit in the library, that most taboo of places, and read as many books as they still allow to be kept on the shelves. Download illegal information. Use false service provider addresses. Move around. If you stay still, you're certain to be caught.

When the first of the bombs go off, go into hiding. When you are safe, grieve. Sit in your cave, the one in the hills that used to belong to your family, and grieve the loss of so many lives. Lives you never knew personally. Imagine their faces. Imagine the faces of those you knew and loved. Imagine the mushroom clouds and the clouds of viruses. Imagine the way skin crackles and crisps, the way the body can turn against itself in

Before and

mere minutes or hours when exposed to the right amount of radiation or illness.

Stay where you are. Keep silent. When you hear others pass by your carefully obscured cave entrance, bite your bottom lip and pray. Pray, even if you don't believe in a god. It may help you to keep silent if you are speaking the language of angels, which can never be heard by human ears. It is the language of thought, plucked like rays of light from the sky and carried off to some other place, where you hope some higher power may hear you.

At night, build a small fire out of moss and straw and twigs. Do not risk the luxury of true warmth and light. It will reach the eyes and ears and noses of those who would take what little luxury you have planned for: a six month supply of canned meats and vegetables, a mattress and a pile of blankets, a lantern and gobs of oil to burn. Soap. A creek you can wash yourself in at night, even though it chills you to the bone.

Be vigilant during the daytime. Erase the tracks you make between your regular routes from the cave to the nearby river where you sometimes try to fish but rarely catch anything worth starting a fire over. Gather berries and nuts from different bushes and trees, so that no one can see them disappearing so obviously from one place. Notice the curl of blue smoke coming over the hillside. Walk toward it until you see the farm from which it comes. It is a four-mile walk to this place. Not far. Remember that they can see anything you might smoke just as you saw theirs.

Ignore the human howls of pain and starvation that pierce the early morning air. Ignore the disappearance of the animals that had occasionally blundered into your cave in those first few months after the bombs went off. Surely this is bad news. But what can you expect? This is the end of the world you're trying to live through. Animals may disappear. It is your job not to let yourself disappear with them.

Learn how to swim, strong and hard. Don't trust old women who live in shacks in the woods. If someone pulls out a dagger, even in an innocuous manner, run. Hide in disgusting places, because no one will want to look there, even if they know they should.

When the world grows quiet, remember what it used to be like before the apocalypse, remember what it felt like to live in a town with streets on a grid, a tree growing strong and proud in front of each house. Remember the scent of your mother's rosebushes, and how she called them her babies. Remember how your father picked you up when you fell off your bicycle and the asphalt of the street ate a chunk of the palm of your hand. Remember how he said, "Shh, shh, it's okay, baby," and try not to make any noise when you feel the tears falling down your cheeks. There are bandits moving around outside. If they hear, everything you've managed to accomplish—constructing this semblance of existence after the world has ended—is finished.

Start talking to your shadow. It sits on the wall of your cave each night like an angry imp. Arms folded. Chin tucked into its chest like a sulking child. Tell it to cheer up. Tell it to stop whining. Tell your shadow it needs to buck the hell up or get lost. You don't have time for stragglers in this screwed-up world. You can't wait around while it sorts out its feelings. Ask it, "Are you a man or a shadow?" When it remains silent, say, "I thought so."

Stare at the sky over the hillside for a number of days and notice how the ribbon of smoke that occasionally found its way over the farm behind that hill has stopped appearing. Don't do anything right away. Just count the days. One. Two. Three. Four. Like that, until you get to ten full days with no smoke dawning on the horizon. Walk over the hill to the farm. Creep around its perimeter. Wait for an hour or two, just watching, to make sure there are no signs of life. Peer into the kitchen window. Dirty dishes are stacked and scattered everywhere. The body of an old woman lies at an odd angle beside a table overflowing with old newspapers, plastic grocery bags and rubber bands. Enter the house quietly, and make your rounds until you're sure no one living remains. Then raid the kitchen, take the food stored in the basement, the guns in the living room, the newspapers and boxes of matches for starting fires more easily, then—

Stop. Why are you taking everything when you can move what you have to the house instead?

Bury the old woman. Lie in her bed each night staring up at a foreign ceiling, but remember how familiar it is to do this, unable to sleep, a ceiling above you. Not the cold walls of a cave. You are still a bit human, then. You can remember creature comforts, luxuries. You didn't completely devolve.

And here you have a house! And a river nearby, and a garden, and a barn where six chickens and a rooster all sit on their nests like the little members of royal families, clucking their way through the dead days of the apocalypse. They lay eggs, and you fry them in a pan on an antique stove. The old woman was a collector. Everything in this house is old, old, old.

Sit down in the old woman's old rocking chair. Push yourself back and forth on the balls of your feet like you are her. Grip your fingertips over the arms of the chair. Smile as you turn your face to look out the nearest window, where the sun falls through in a long golden shaft, and dust motes spin like stars inside it. Beyond it, though, take notice of the smoke curling up and into the sky above the hillside. Someone has taken your old cave.

Be cautious, but not illogical. Whoever it is up there, they're just another person trying to eke out an existence under ridiculous circumstances, just like you. Watch the perimeter of your property, though. Pay attention to all of the places you yourself used to hide when you were spying on the old woman. Take notice that you think of the old woman's land as your property now. No one owns the world any longer. It is all yours.

On a cool evening, drift through the purple gloaming that hovers beneath the trees around your property and climb the hillside from a secret angle. When you see the person living in your cave, wince in confusion. They are so familiar. Those eyes, that hair, the curl of the lips, the set of the shoulders. It's you, actually, after all. To be precise, it's your shadow. It never left the cave when you moved into the old woman's house. It had stayed behind in the surroundings to which it had grown accustomed. It can never forget what it went through. It can never move with you into the old woman's house. If it did, it would forget everything that happened to it, and in the moment of its total forgetting, it would cease to exist.

Leave your shadow be. Let it continue on as it wishes. Go back to the old woman's house and make yourself dinner. A nice salad. Some eggs, hardboiled. Sigh when you're all finished. It's hard to get the image of your shadow out of your memory. The food doesn't distract you. The warm water of the bath you boil up with plenty of kettles an hour later can't either. So you sit in the dented copper basin in the pantry like some kind of pioneer days person, knobby knees sticking out of the sudsy water, and weep. Weep for everyone you used to know. Many names can be included on this list that you conjure, including your own.

There is such a thing as survivor's guilt, even at the end of the world, even after the end of the world is over. But don't worry. Like everything else, this too shall pass.

Christopher Barzak

Before and

Smoke City

ONE NIGHT, I WOKE TO the sound of my mother's voice, as I did when I was a child. The words were familiar to my ear, they matched the voice that formed them, but it was not until I had opened my eyes to the dark of my room and my husband's snoring that I remembered the words were calling me away from my warm bed and the steady breathing of my children, both asleep in their own rooms across the hall. "Because I could not stop for death," my mother used to tell me, "he kindly stopped for me." They were Dickinson's words, of course, not my mother's, but she said them as if they were hers, and because of that, they were hers, and because of that, they are now mine, passed down with every other object my mother gave me before I left for what I hoped would be a better world. "Here, take this candy dish." Her hands pushing the red knobbed glass into my hands. "Here, take this sweater." Her hands folding it, a made thing, pulled together by her hands, so that I could lift it and lay it on the seat as my car pulled me away. Her hand lifted into the air above her cloud of white hair behind me. The smoke of that other city enveloping her, putting it behind me, trying to put it behind me, until I had the words in my mouth again, like a bit, and then the way opened up beneath me, a fissure through which I slipped, down through the bed sheets, no matter how I grasped at them, down through the mattress, down through the floorboards, down, down, down, through the mud and earth and gravel, leaving my snoring husband and my steadily breathing children above, in that better place, until I was floating, once more, along the swiftly flowing current of the Fourth River.

When I rose up, gasping for air, and blinked the water from my eyes, I saw the familiar cavern lit by lanterns that lined the walls, orange fires burning behind smoked glass. And, not far downstream, his shadow stood along the water's edge, a lantern held out over the slug and tow of the current, waiting, as he was always waiting for me, there, in that place beneath the three rivers, there in the Fourth River's tunnel that leads to Smoke City.

It was time again, I understood, to attend to my obligations.

HISTORY ALWAYS EXACTS A PRICE from those who have climbed out to live in the world above. There is never a way to fully outrun our beginnings. And here was mine, and he was mine here. I smiled, happy to see him again, the sharp bones of his face gold-leafed by the light of his lantern.

He put out his hand to fish me from the river, and pulled me up to stand beside him. "It is good to see you again, wife," he said, and I wrapped my arms around him.

"It is good to smell you again, husband," I said, my face pressed against his thick chest. They are large down here, the men of Smoke City. Their labor makes them into giants.

We walked along the Fourth River's edge, our hands linked between us, until we came to the mouth of the tunnel, where the city tipped into sight below, cupped as it is within the hands of a valley, strung together by the many bridges crossing the rivers that wind round its perimeter. The smoke obscured all but the dark mirrored glass of city towers, which gleamed by the light of the mill-fired skies down in the financial district, where the captains sit around long, polished tables throughout the hours and commit their business.

It did not take the fumes long to find me, the scent of the mills and the sweaty, grease-faced laborers, so that when my husband pulled me toward the carriage at the top of the Incline Passage, a moment passed in which my heart flickered like the flame climbing the wick of his lantern. I inhaled sharply, trying to catch my breath. Already what nostalgia for home I possessed had begun to evaporate as I began to remember, to piece together what I had worked so hard to obscure.

I hesitated at the door of the Incline carriage, looking back at the cavern opening, where the Fourth River spilled over the edge, down into the valley, but my husband placed two fingers on my chin and turned my face back up to his. "We must go now," he said, and I nodded at his eyes like

Before and

chips of coal, his mustached upper lip, the sweat on his brow, as if he were working, even now, as in the mill, among the glowing rolls of steel.

The Incline rattled into gear, and soon we were creaking down the valley wall, rickety-click, the chains lowering us to the bottom, slowly, slowly. I watched out the window as the city grew close and the smoke began to thicken, holding a hand over my mouth and nose. An Incline car on the track opposite passed us, taking a man and a woman up to the Fourth River overlook. She, like me, peered out her window, a hand covering her mouth and nose as they ascended the tracks. We stared at each other, but it was she who first broke our gaze to look up at the opening to the cavern with great expectations, almost a panicked smile on her face, teeth gritted, willing herself upward. She was on her return journey, I could tell. I had worn that face myself. She had spent a long year here, and was glad to be leaving.

They are long here, the years in Smoke City, even though they are finished within the passing of a night.

At the bottom, my husband handed me down from the Incline car, then up again into our carriage, which was waiting by the curb, the horses nickering and snorting in the dark. Then off he sent us, jostling down the cobbled lane, with one flick of his wrist and a strong word.

Down many wide and narrow streets we rode, some mud, some brick, some stone, passing through the long rows of narrow workers' houses, all lined up and lean like soldiers, until we arrived at our own, in the Lost Neighborhood, down in Junction Hollow, where Eliza, the furnace, blocks the view of the river with her black bulk and her belching smoke. They are all female, always. They have unassuming names like Jeanette, Edith, Carrie. All night long, every night, they fill the sky with their fires.

Outside, on the front stoop of our narrow house, my children from the last time were waiting, arms folded over their skinny chests or hanging limply at their sides. When I stepped down from the carriage onto the street, they ran down the stairs, their arms thrown wide, the word "Mother!" spilling from their eager mouths.

They had grown since I'd last seen them. They had grown so much that none of them had retained the names I'd given them at birth. Shauna, the youngest, had become Anis. Alexander was Shoeshine. Paul, the oldest, said to simply call him Ayu. "Quite lovely," I said to Anis. "Very good then," I told Shoeshine. And to Ayu, I said nothing, only nodded, showing the respect due an imagination that had turned so particularly into itself during my absence. He had a glint in his eyes. He reminded me of myself a little, willing to cast off anything we'd been told.

When we went through the door, the scent of boiled cabbage and potatoes filled the front room. They had cooked dinner for me, and quite proudly Anis and Shoeshine took hold of either elbow and led me to the scratched and corner-worn table, where we sat and shared their offering, not saying anything when our eyes met one another's. It was not from shame, our silence, but from an understanding that to express too much joy at my homecoming would be absurd. We knew that soon they would have no names at all, and I would never again see them.

We sipped our potato soup and finely chewed our noodles and cabbage.

Later, after the children had gone to bed, my husband led me up the creaking stairs to our own room, where we made love, fitting into one another on the gritty, soot-stained sheets. Old friends, always. Afterward, his arms wrapped around my sweaty stomach, holding me to him from behind, he said, "I die a little more each time you are away."

I did not reply immediately, but stared out the grimy window at the rooftops across the street. A crow had perched on the sill of the window opposite, casting about for the glint of something, anything, in the dark streets below. It cawed at me, as if it had noticed me staring, and ruffled its feathers. Finally, without turning to my husband, I said, "We all die," and closed my eyes to the night.

THE DAYS IN THE CITY of my birth are differentiated from the nights by small degrees of shade and color. The streetlamps continue burning during the day, since the sun cannot reach beyond the smoke that moves through the valley like a storm that will never abate. So it always appears to be night, and you can only tell it is day by the sound of shift whistles and church bells ringing the hours, announcing when it is time to return to work or to kneel and pray.

No growing things grew in Smoke City, due to the lack of sunlight. On no stoops or windowsills did a fern or a flower add their shapes and colors to the square and rectangular stone backdrops of the workers' houses. Only fine dusty coatings of soot, in which children drew pictures with the tips of their fingers, and upon which adults would occasionally scrawl strange messages:

Do Not Believe Anything They Tell You.

Your Rewards Await You In Heaven.

It Is Better That Others Possess What I Need But Do Not Understand.

I walked my children down the road, past these cryptic depictions of stick men and women on the sides of houses and words whose meanings

Before and

I could not fathom, until we came to the gates of the furnace Eliza, whose stacks sent thick plumes of smoke into the air. There, holding the hands of my two youngest, I knelt down in the street to meet their faces. "You must do what you are told," I instructed them, my heart squeezing even as I said the words. "You must work very hard, and never be of trouble to anyone, understand?"

The little ones, Anis and Shoeshine, nodded. They had all been prepared for this day over the short years of their lives. But Ayu, my oldest, narrowed his eyes to a squint and folded his arms over his chest, as if he understood more than I was saying. Those eyes were mine looking back at me, calling me a liar. "Do you understand, Ayu?" I asked him directly, to stop him from making that look. When he refused to answer, I asked, "Paul, do you understand me?" and he looked down at his feet, the head of a flower wilting.

I stood again, took up their small hands again, and led them to Eliza's gates, the top of which was decorated with a flourish of coiled barbed wire. A small, square window in the door opened as we stood waiting, and a man's eye looked out at us. "Are they ready?" he said.

I nodded.

The window snapped shut, then the gate doors began to separate, widening as they opened. Inside, we could see many people working, sparks flying, carts of coal going back and forth, the rumble of the mill distorting the voices of the workers. The man who had opened the gate window came from around the corner to greet us. He was small, stocky, with oily skin and a round face. He smiled, but I could not manage to be anything but straight-faced and stoic. He held his hands out to the little ones, who went to him, giving him their hands as they'd been instructed, and my heart filled my mouth, suffocating me, so that I fell to my knees and buried my face in my hands.

"Stupid cow," the gateman said, and as soon as I took my hands away to look up, I saw Ayu running away, his feet kicking up dust behind him. "See what you've done?" *Do not look back,* I told Ayu with my mind, hoping he could somehow hear me. *Do not look back or you will be detained here forever.*

Then the gates shut with a metallic bang, and my small ones were gone from me, gone to Eliza.

THE FIRST MONTH OF MY year in the city of my birth passed slowly, painfully, like the after effects of a night of drunkenness. For a while I had wondered if Ayu would return to the house at some point, to gather what few possessions he had made or acquired over his short lifetime, but he stayed away, smartly. My husband would have only taken him back to Eliza if he found him. That is the way, what is proper, and my husband here was nothing if not proper.

We made love every night, after he returned from the mill, his arms heavy around my waist, around my shoulders. But something had occurred on the day I'd given up the last ones: my womb had withered, and now refused to take our love and make something from its materials.

Still, we tried. Or I should say, my husband tried. Perhaps that was the reason for my body's reluctance. Whenever his breath fell against my neck, or his mouth on my breasts, I would look out the window and see Eliza's fires scouring the sky across the mountaintops, and what children we may have made, the idea of them, would burn to cinders.

"You do not love me anymore," my husband said one night, in my second month in the city; and though I wanted to, badly, I could not deny this.

I tried to explain. "It is not you, it is not me, it is this place," I told him. "Why don't you come with me, why don't we leave here together?"

"You forget so easily," my husband said, looking down into his mug of cold coffee.

"What?" I said. "What do I forget?"

"You have people there, in the place you would take me."

I looked down into my own mug and did not nod.

"It is what allows you to forget me, to forget our children, our life," said my husband.

"What is?" I asked, looking up again. Rarely did my husband tell me things about myself.

"Your bad memory," said my husband. "It is your blessing."

IF MY MEMORY WERE TRULY as bad as my husband thought, I would not have been returned to the city of my birth. He was incorrect in his judgment. What he should have said was, *Your memory is too strong to accomplish what you desire,* for I would not have been able to dismiss that. It is true, I wanted nothing more than to eradicate, to be born into a new world without the shackles of longing, and the guilt that embitters longing fulfilled.

But he had said his truth, flawed as it was, and because he had spoken this truth we could no longer look at each other without it hovering between us, a ghost of every child we had ever had together, every child I had taken, as a proper wife and mother, to the gates. They stared at me for him, and I would turn away to cook, clean, mend, to keep the walls of the house together.

Before and

Another month passed in this way, and then another. I washed my husband's clothes each day in a tub of scalding water. The skin on my hands began to redden, then to peel away. I began to avoid mirrors. My hair had gone lank and hung about my face like coils of old rope, no matter how I tried to arrange it. I could no longer see my own pupils, for there was no white left in the corners. My eyes had turned dark with coal dust and smoke.

One day a knock at the front door pulled me away from the dinner I was making for my husband's return from another sixteen-hour shift. When I opened the door, a man from the mill, a manager I vaguely recognized, was standing on my stoop. He held a hat against his protruding stomach, as if he had taken it off to recite a pledge or a piece of poetry. "Excuse me," he said, "for interrupting your day. But I come with sad news."

Before he could finish, I knew what he would say. Few reasons exist for a mill manager to visit a worker's wife.

"Your husband," he said, and I could not hear the rest of his words, only saw the images they carried within them: my husband, a slab of meat on the floor of the mill, burned by Eliza. My husband, a slab of meat on the floor of the mill, dragged away to be replaced by another body, another man, so that Eliza could continue her labors.

"You will need time to rest, of course," the manager said. "I'm sure it is quite a shock, but these things happen."

I nodded, dumbly, and stood there, waiting for something.

"We will be in touch, of course," said the manager as he stepped off my stoop back onto the cobbled street.

If I would have had any sense left in me, I would have done what Ayu had done, I would have run away as fast as possible, I would have done what I had done before, a long time ago, when I'd left the first time, with my mother's hand raised in the air above her cloud of white hair, waving behind me.

Instead, I sank down into my husband's chair in the front room and wept. For him, for our children, wept selfishly for myself. What would I do without him? I could feel him all around me, his big body having pressed its shape into the armchair, holding me in its embrace.

WITHIN A WEEK, A MASS of suitors arranged themselves in a queue outside my door. They knocked. I answered. One was always waiting to speak to me, big and hulking like my husband had been, a little younger in some cases, a little older in others. Used up men and men in the process of being used. They wanted me to cook, clean, and make love to them. I turned them away, all of them. "No thank you," I said to each knock, glancing over their shoulders to see if the line of suitors had shortened. It stretched down the street and around the corner, no matter how many men I turned away.

There was a shortage of women, one of the suitors finally informed me, trying to make his case as a rational man, to explain himself as suitable for someone like me. There were many men in need of a good wife.

"I am not a good wife," I told him. "You must go to another house of mourning," I told him. "You must find a different wife."

The suitors disappeared then. One by one they began to walk away from the queue they had formed, and for a while my front stoop was empty. I went back to sitting in my husband's chair, grieving.

My memory was bad, he had told me, but he was wrong. My memory kept him walking the halls and the staircase, my memory refused to let go of him completely, as it had refused to let go each time I left. *I die a little more each time you are away,* he had said the first night of my return to the city. Now he was dead, I thought, there would be no more dying. Upon realizing this, I stood up from his chair.

Before I could take a step in any direction of my own choosing, though, a knock arrived at the front door, pulling me toward it. How quickly we resume routine, how quickly we do what is expected: a child cries out, we run to it; something falls in another room, we turn corners to see what has fallen; a knock lands upon a door, we answer.

Outside stood three men, all in dark suits with the gold chains of pocket watches drooping from their pockets. They wore top hats, and long waxed mustaches. They wore round spectacles in thin wire frames. I recognized them for what they were immediately: captains of industry. But what could they be doing here, I wondered, on the front stoop of a widow at a forgettable address in the Lost Neighborhood, down in Junction Hollow.

"Forgive us for intruding," they said. "We do not mean to startle you."

They introduced themselves, each one tipping his hat as he delivered his name: A.W., H.C., R.B. All captains' names are initials. It is their badge of honor.

"We understand," they said, "that you have recently lost your husband."

I nodded, slow and stupid.

"And we understand that you have turned away all of the many suitors who have come requesting your hand in marriage," they continued.

I nodded again.

"We are here to inquire as to your plans, madame, for the future," they said, and took their pocket watches out to check the time, to see if the future had arrived yet. "Do you mean to marry again?" they asked. "Do you plan to provide us with more children?"

I shook my head this time, and opened my mouth to ask the purpose of their visit. But before I could form one word, they tapped at my chest with their white-gloved hands.

"Now, now," they said, slipping their watches back into their pockets. "No need for any of that."

Then they took hold of my arms and pushed me back into my house, closing the door behind them.

WITHIN THE PASSING OF A night I became sick with their children; within a week, the front of my housedress began to tighten; and within a month, I gave birth: three in all. One by one, their children ripped away from me and grew to the size of the children I had walked to the gates of Eliza.

I did not need to feed them. They grew from the nourishment of my tears and rages. They knew how to walk and talk instinctively, and began to make bargains with one another, trading clothes and toys and whole tracts of land.

Soon their fathers returned to claim them. "Thank you very much," said the captains, as they presented each child with a pocket watch, a pair of white gloves, a top hat. Then they looked at me. "In return for your troubles, we have built you a library."

They swept their arms in wide arcs to the opposite side of the street. Where once a row of houses stood shoulder to shoulder, now a three-story library parked its bulk along the sidewalk. "Where are my neighbors?" I asked. "Where are my friends?"

"We have moved them to another part of the city," said the captains. "Do not worry. We are in the midst of building them their own library at this very moment. We do not take, you see, without giving back."

Then they clapped their hands and curled their index fingers over and over, motioning for their top-hatted, white-gloved children to follow, checking the time on their new pocket watches as they walked toward the financial district.

A DARK RUMOR SOON BEGAN to circulate throughout the back rooms in pubs and in the common rooms of the libraries of Smoke City. The captains' children were growing faster than their fathers could manage, it was said. The captains themselves, it was said, were having difficulties with their wives, who remained in their stone mansions on top of the mountains ringing the city, above the strata of smoke. One wife had committed suicide and another had snuck out of her mansion in the middle of the night, grew wings, and flew across the ocean to her home country, where her captain had found her many years ago sitting by a river, strumming a stringed instrument and singing a ballad of lost love. Those of us who lived below their homes above the point where the wind blew smoke away from the captains' houses had never seen these women, but we knew they were aching with beauty.

I could see it all now, what lay behind that terrible evening, and the plans the captains' children had been making as they'd left with their fathers, opening the backs of their pocket watches to examine the gears clicking inside, taking them out to hold up to the non-existent light.

Indeed, the future spread out before me, a horizon appearing where the captains' sons were building machines out of the gears of their pocket watches, and more men lumbered away from the mills every day to sit on porches and frustrate their wives who did not know how to take care of them while they were in their presence.

A future will always reveal itself, even in places like Smoke City.

But smoke nor soot nor the teeth of gears as they turned what arms once turned, as they ground time to chafe and splinters, could not provide the future I desired. I had seen something else—a long time ago, it seemed now, or a long time to come—and though it came with the price of unshakable memory, I began the journey that would return me to it.

THROUGH THE STREETS I TRUDGED to the Incline platform, where I waited for my car wearing nothing but my worn-out housedress, my old shoes covered in mud and the stinking feces of horses. No one looked at me. I was not unnatural.

When the car arrived, I climbed in. And when the car began to lift, rickety-click, I breathed a small sigh. This time, though, as I turned to peer out the back window, my mother was not there, waving her hand in the air. Only the city. Only the city and its rooftops spread out behind me. This time, I was leaving without the cobwebs of the past clinging to me.

On the way up, a car went by in the opposite direction, carrying a woman with her man inside it. I stared at her for a moment, staring at me through her window, a frightened look on her face, before I broke our gaze to look up at the mouth of the Fourth River's cavern, and the water spilling from it.

When the car reached the top, I exited to wander through the lantern-lit cavern, the river beside me, until the walls were bare and no lanterns lit the way any longer, and the roar of the river was in my ears and the dark of the cave filled my eyes.

At some point, I felt the chill of rising water surround me. It trickled over my toes at first, then lifted me off my feet. I began to swim upward, pulling my arms through the current, kicking my legs furiously. Up and

Before and

up and up I swam, until I opened my eyes to sunlight, blue skies that hurt to look at, yellow bridges, vast hills of green, and somewhere on the other side of this city my husband in this place would be waking up to find I had left him in the middle of the night again. He would wake the children next, the children I would never give over, and together they would walk to the place where I found myself surfacing. They have come across me here before. My husband will take my hand, say, "Early riser," and I would bring his hand to my lips to kiss it.

I gasped, taking the blue air into my lungs, the light into my eyes. The city, the city of my refuge, spread out before me, the rivers on either side of me spangled with light, a fountain spraying into the air, the towers of downtown gleaming. The smoke of that other city was gone now, the fires in that other sky were nowhere on this horizon. The smoke and the fires were in some other world, and I found that I could only weep now, selfishly grateful that it was no longer mine.

Christopher Barzak   **Before and**

Vanishing Point

You asked me, sir, to tell you about my son's disappearance. I must admit that I did not know what to think when your first letter arrived. And when you phoned, I think I was a bit startled by all your attention. We don't get many phone calls here, you see. But since last week, when I told you an interview was out of the question, I've been unable to stop thinking about Nathan and how, as a mother, I have a duty. Others should know the truth. You wanted to know what life was like here, in my house, in my family, with Nathan and then, afterwards, without him. It's not as simple as that, though. A person isn't here one day, then gone the next. If I'm going to tell you anything, it won't be what you're expecting. It might not be what you want to hear. But, in any case, I'll tell you what I know. What I know is the truth.

From the beginning, his growing absence was oppressive. If I was not in the kitchen making supper for Sarah and myself, I was attending to my son in his room. We seemed to eat a lot during those days. An affliction of hunger consumed us that could not be satisfied. As Nathan disappeared, Sarah and I ate and ate. I made meals we'd never heard of, recipes out of foreign cookbooks, fancy dishes that required an orange peel or a sculptured radish rosette on the side. We were pretending to have money, even though we had no money. I do have money now, though. Now that Nathan is not so demanding. Yes, sir, Sarah and I are off the dole.

We ate exotic foods, Thai and Indian curries. We ground our own spices in the coffee grinder. Also we had a peculiar taste for Ethiopian, and Sarah and I would sometimes joke about this. You know, how starving those people are and how we craved their recipes. What a laugh! It was a laugh then, I tell you. I had my own boy starving. Starving for solidity. Sometimes he could barely move off of his bed.

Do you know those movies where a person suddenly acquires the ability to walk through walls? The ones where someone becomes transparent to the point that no one else can see them unless looked at very hard? *The Invisible Man*? Movies like that? Let me tell you, they're a pack of lies. Those people never seem to have problems. They move through life more easily in fact. Now they can walk through moving traffic and never have to wait for the light. Now they can strip off their clothes and sneak into shower rooms to watch people, bodies, drifting through steam, larger than life, without ever getting caught.

There were days when Nathan couldn't bring himself to go to the bathroom on his own. There were days when Sarah and I tried to help him into the shower, but he fell through our hands, through the hardwood floor, down into the living room. We'd find him lying under the coffee table, his arms threaded through the table legs. Or, once, splayed out in the middle of the broken plants and pottery he'd landed on. I was always frightened. Someday, I thought, he will fall and fall forever, and then where will he go? I remembered how, when we were little, we thought if a person dug a deep enough hole in the ground, they'd fall through to China. Our parents frightened us with thoughts like that. Why was it they wanted to frighten us?

Nathan never fell to China. Or if he did, he fell back in time for me not to notice. I don't think this is possible. I don't think this ever happened. Still, though, I'll leave it open. I have learned to leave things open, sir. Have you?

It was a Friday last September the school called me. The school nurse said, "I think you need to come down." I told her that I had to work, and she said, "I really think you should come down, Miss Livingston." She said my name real tough-like, like she was gritting her teeth.

"All right," I said. "All right. I'll come down."

Nathan was waiting for me in the nurse's office. He was lying on a table, like in a doctor's exam room, with the crackling paper rolled over its top. Only that paper didn't crackle. It didn't make any noise at all. Now being a doctor yourself, sir, you know you can't shut that paper up. Even though you are up there at the university studying "the social implications of phenomena", as you put it in your letter, and are in great need of "personal narratives" and "statistics" so that the research will be "pure", and are not

Before and

a real doctor, practicing medicine and such, I'm sure you have been on one of those tables before. Not even staying completely still, which is impossible if you ask me, will shut that paper up. I asked, "What's wrong? What's happened here?" And the nurse, a woman who was not as severe as I had expected, a woman who wore a fuzzy blue sweater and did not have her hair up in a bun but let it fall over her shoulders like dark cream, she said, "I'm so sorry."

I went over to Nathan and looked at his eyes. His eyes were open, but he didn't seem to see me. They were blue eyes, watery eyes, my father's eyes. When he was born, how happy I was to see those eyes! Not my husband's, who was a drunkard and a cheater, not his eyes. I said, "Nathan? Honey, what's wrong?" His lips trembled. I thought, What am I going to do? Already I knew without knowing what afflicted him that things were going to change.

The nurse put her arm around me and said, "Be calm." She unbuttoned Nathan's shirt, one button at a time, her fingers were so deft, and pulled back each side of his shirt like a curtain. If you could see what I saw that day. It was not always like that, I assure you. Nathan: his chest, only his chest, had gone translucent. I saw those lungs filling and expelling air, two brownish, soggy sacs going up and down, up and down. And his heart, it throbbed beneath them. The blood slid through his veins and I thought of blue rivers winding on a map. The nurse covered him over again and began buttoning his tiny buttons. And look here, I thought, even those buttons are clear.

Perhaps I am exaggerating this all a bit. I don't know. This is how I remember it: his lungs, his heart, the blood in his veins and arteries, the webbing of his nerves. Sir, I know you are a not a real doctor and all, but let me ask you something. Have you ever seen anything like this? Have you ever seen your own child like this? Sir, do you have children?

I took my son home and, while we drove in the car, neither of us said anything. Nathan looked out the window at the passing mills and factories, the ones that all closed down years ago. Their smokeless stacks loomed above us, gray against the gray sky. I live on the south side of town, not the best place to raise children, Lord knows, but I did the best I could.

The factories we passed were tattooed with graffiti. The gridwork of their windows was busted out. Kids used to come down to the mills to paint their names, to spray-paint their useless childhood loves, to mark down their childhood enemies as though they were making hit lists. They threw rocks, pieces of broken concrete, at the gridded windows high overhead. The glass would shatter and rain down at their feet, onto the factory floors, and oh, how we laughed and gripped each other's shoulders at these small victories. It felt good to bust up those places that broke first our parents' backs, and then, after shutting down, their spirits.

I think Nathan and his friends did this, too. To let out frustration. I don't know. I'm only guessing. It's something I've learned to do.

FOR THE FIRST FEW MONTHS, things were not so bad. Not as bad as some of the others I've heard of. Nathan was not quick to disperse and he did it quietly. He lingered, and Sarah and I began to eat.

I will say here that I do not blame Sarah for what she did. She was only sixteen. She was jealous of her little brother. Nathan had been popular at school. After he started to disappear, I think she expected that popularity to wane a little. Instead, six other students started to disappear as well. Several of them girls who I hear had crushes on Nathan. He was a good-looking boy. He could turn heads, just like a pretty girl.

I had phone calls, let me tell you. Muffled voices in the middle of the night, hoarse voices threatening to burn down my house, to cut my brake lines, to put a bomb in my mailbox. *Just keep your kid away from mine!* But we both know, sir, this disease is not catching. I'm glad to see the new commercials and ads informing people of this.

Sarah—well, she was unhappy. She sulked in her bedroom and listened to sulky music, and sometimes she'd come into whatever room I was in and she'd sulk there. I made her doughnuts to perk her up, fried them myself, and then she'd be a happy girl for several hours. It was worth it to see her smiling around a cinnamon doughnut, her favorite, even though she did gain an awful lot of weight. Acne, too. Little red bumps spread over her cheeks and on her chin, cranberry-colored. She always complained because they were the kind you couldn't pop, you had to wait until they decided to go away on their own, there were no white heads on them to pinch. They took so long to go away. I was sorry I couldn't afford a dermatologist for her then.

As I mentioned, I don't blame her for what she did.

One day I came home from shopping to find two women in my living room. They were dressed in elegant black dresses, wore black high heels, and one of them covered her face with a veil. My living room smelled of lilies, thick and sweet.

They were Mourners. I could tell that from the start. They had knocked on my door before, usually on Sundays, and Sarah and I had hid behind the curtains of the picture window, sneaking glances out, waiting for them to leave. I don't know how they knew about Nathan. I assume they

Before and

had an informant at the hospital, even though those records of Nathan's visits are supposed to be private.

Sarah sat in a chair opposite them on the couch. She'd set out a tray of sugar cookies on the coffee table between them. When I saw those cookies, the sugar glittering like grains of powdered glass on top, I almost ran over to snatch them away from those women. I said, "What's all this?" I still held the grocery bags in my hands.

One of the ladies stood up and extended her hand. She was the one without the veil. She said, "Hello, Mrs. Livingston. I'm Hilary Love. So pleased to meet you."

I looked at the hand for a moment. She wasn't taking it back. It floated there between us, so finally I set down my bags and shook it.

The other lady was a widow. Her name was Sally Parkinson. Her husband had disappeared last year. She said, "We've been having a wonderful talk with your daughter."

I said, "Go to your room, Sarah." I gave her a look and she didn't say anything, but went straight up the stairs, her feet thumping unpleasantly all the way up.

"Now Mrs. Livingston," said the Widow Parkinson. "There's no need to be angry with her. She's a delightful girl, full of *life*."

I said, "Don't talk to me of life." I asked, "Why are you here and what have you said to my daughter?"

"Nothing," they swore. "*Nothing*, Mrs. Livingston."

Now that's the last time I allowed that. I corrected them. "It's *Miss* Livingston, thank you very much," I said.

They said, "Oh, I'm so sorry."

"No need to be sorry," I said. "He was a worthless drunk. He used to hit me. I threw him out."

"We want to talk to you about Nathan," they explained. But I already knew that.

I told them, "Take your pamphlets and yourselves out of my house. He is not dead."

"Oh, but Miss Livingston," said the Widow Parkinson. "You don't realize it yet. You're in denial. You just wait, one day you will understand."

Hilary Love patted the widow's leg when she said this, then squeezed her knee. She left her hand there and her fingers spread over the widow's knee like the jointed legs of a spider. The widow, you see, she thought the same as me at first. She thought maybe her husband's not really dead, maybe he's not really disappearing. Maybe, she thought, he is simply shifting over to a different kind of life. I nodded. I agreed with that. She said, "Miss Livingston, I was wrong. He was dead from the day he started to vanish, and we are here to help you deal with that. You must understand, Nathan is gone and you are neglecting a very much alive daughter. Let us take what's left of him to a center, where he can continue this final process in private. You must get on with your life. It can take so long, such a long time for him to go. In fact, he is already gone. Only the body is remaining, such as it is."

That threw me, so I stood and asked them to leave. I waved my hand in the direction of the front door. They hesitated, blinking dumbly at each other, so I asked them not to make me call the police. They nodded. "Yes," they said. "Of course," they said. I escorted them to the door and left them out in the cold of that autumn day, with the wind blowing red and gold leaves onto the steps of my porch. Later, when I passed by the door, I found a pamphlet one of them had stuffed in the jamb. On the cover, in large letters, it said: LET THE DEAD BURY THE DEAD. I wrinkled my nose. What did they know about being dead anyway? I threw the pamphlet in the trash.

I didn't yell at Sarah. I didn't carry on and tell her how much she'd hurt me. We were supposed to be a team in this, and here she was, letting in the enemy. I grilled a steak and sautéed onions for her that night.

NATHAN—HE CONTINUED TO GROW IN his absence. Almost every day was different. Some days I'd find him quite substantial, with sweat beaded on his forehead. Sweat I could touch and wipe away, as though he were simply a fevered child. Believe me, though, this was not a regular event. Most days he was gone as much as a ghost. I could pass my hands right through him. His body would seal around my hands as if I had plunged them into water. Lord, I even expected him to wash away sometimes! But somehow he pulled himself together. He was a fighter—he always fought—up till the end.

IN THE MIDDLE OF ALL this I lost my job at the paper. I'd been inserting advertisements and coupons into the local newspaper for a little over minimum wage. You know, on the assembly line with several other women, catching the papers as they came down our row, folding the ads into them quick as you can. I came home with my fingers inked black. If I didn't wash my hands straight away, I'd leave prints all over the house. Cupboard doors, drinking glasses, the handle of the refrigerator. Ink smudges everywhere. You could always tell where I'd been.

I lost the job because I called off too much. I had to take care of Nathan, and some days I couldn't bear to leave him alone in that big old house, with only Sarah's sulky presence.

Before and

Some days he looked so frightened. I can't remember his eyes ever closing for more than a few hours at a time. And when he did close them,
it didn't matter. Those eyelids were clear, and I could see his blue eyes
behind them, as if I'd bent down to look through a keyhole, to find him
staring back at me from the other side.

One day, when he had enough strength to squeeze out a few words and
asked me to sit with him a while, I called my boss, Albert, and said, "My
boy's not doing well, Albert. I have to stay home."

"That boy's never doing well, Em," said Albert. "Doris Eliot's girl has the
same thing your boy has, and Doris makes it to work okay. I need you
here."

It was a Saturday night, so there were obviously a lot of inserts of ads
and coupons for the Sunday paper.

I said, "I can't. He spoke today, Al. I'm sorry, but I can't."

"I can't hold your job either, Em," said Al. He said, "I'm sorry, too."

So that's why I was on the dole for a while, sir. After Nathan's dilemma
ended, though, I immediately went back to work. I am not the sort to take
and take for no good reason.

I NEVER GAVE UP ON Nathan. Not like so many of these other families
of the Disappeared do. Let me tell you, I held firm in my convictions. He
was not dead, like the Mourners would have us believe. I know this. I have
proof. He's not dead still, and I will even tell you why.

AFTER NEARLY TWELVE MONTHS, NATHAN had almost completely disappeared. At the end, or what seems like it is the end for most people, I
would look in on him and could barely make him out. He was thin, unlike
Sarah and myself, and the blanket I'd covered him with barely moved as
he breathed. Once I held a mirror under his nose and it came back with
just a dusting of white steam. It made me happy to see even that. I drew a
heart in the condensation and showed it to Nathan. Look, I wanted to say,
here is proof. He smiled a thin smile back, his lips parting to reveal his
upper row of teeth. His teeth weren't white, though, and they appeared
unenameled. They winked briefly with light. I saw tendrils of roots, brown
nerves, suspended inside them. I didn't say anything, but his teeth looked
like glass.

He became completely clear at one point. Clear as those transparent
pages of the human body you will find in some encyclopedias. Like the
plastic models of the human body in biology classrooms, I saw everything
he held inside. The cage of his ribs; the lungs and heart moving blindly
as a cat under a blanket; the intestines, both upper and lower, twisted

together; the butterfly-shaped pelvis; and, of course, his skull, with his blue eyes looking jellyish in their sockets. There was so much of his life beyond me, so much I didn't know. Here he was, revealing his most private organs, and I still knew nothing at all. What were his favorite colors, his favorite music? Where did he like to spend his afternoons? Was he really as popular at school as I'd imagined? Why had he, for the past two years, taken to holing himself up in the attic on weekends, carrying along a supply of books, food, pillows and blankets, refusing to eat dinner in the kitchen with Sarah and me, saying angrily, "Can't I do anything without you knowing? Don't you know what privacy is?" Was it my fault I had no husband, or one that was worthless, and that I had to work afternoons and evenings to support the kids? I'm not asking for pity, sir. Lord knows I did the best I could.

I could say things about him. I could say he was a sad child. Next to him, Sarah's melancholy seemed like happiness. I could say he needed a father figure. He needed a school where he did not have to worry about being robbed or shot. He needed friends who did not give him drugs. I found them—I was not unaware. But what could I do? If I threw a fit, grounded him, said to get a job, snapped his cigarettes in half, brought out from the attic the other stuff, screamed, *Not In My House,* as loud as I could, stamped my feet, shook him by his narrow shoulders, hugged him and wept, said, *Please Don't Do This To Me, I Can't Bear It Any Longer*—what use would that have been? Would it have kept him in his body?

I could say he was not as strong as my daughter. He could not stand up to the pressure as Sarah has. She has my blood in her. He was weak like his father. Instead of the drink, he chose to disappear, so that no one could ever touch him—could ever hurt him—again. I could say for your benefit, sir, He was not made for this world. There are some people who just simply cannot thrive. Would that help your studies? There, I've said it. Consider it a gift.

BY THE FOLLOWING DECEMBER, NATHAN'S insides had disappeared as well. He was now entirely transparent, a plastic model of the human body without a view of the organs. I crawled into bed with him one day and lay there and hummed, in case he could still hear. I thought that might be a comfort. A year and a half he lay on that bed, flickering. How do you comfort that?

I went out into the blizzardy snow one evening and bought him a fish. I went to one of the top-notch places, one of the stores in the mall. I wanted him to have the best fish, the very best. When he was a little boy he wanted one, and I, foolishly, hadn't allowed it. Instead, I had tugged on his arm and hissed, "They're too expensive!"

I bought the whole set-up: the aquarium and the filters, the diver figurine that rested on the layer of blue stones at the bottom, the cave for him to explore. When I looked in one of the store's tanks, I found something called ghost fish swimming inside. You could almost miss seeing them, if you didn't look hard. The ghost fish were completely translucent, except for the tiny shadows of their skeletons cupped in their transparent flesh. They swam in hordes, back and forth across the tank, miniature fish skeletons rippling the water. The saleswoman helping me said, "Those are our best sellers."

"They won't do," I said. I didn't explain. I bought a Siamese fighting fish instead, with all those iridescent colors: blue and purple and red shining scales. The fins trailed around its body like silk scarves. I thought, How beautiful. I had forgotten such a thing could exist. It was so insistent on being seen.

The saleswoman helping me said, "Just don't put two of this type in the same tank or they'll fight. They're fighting fish." She explained how they puff up really large and all of their colors turn radioactive, how they tear into each other as though one tank isn't big enough for the both of them. I laughed and laughed. I had to hold my aching stomach. She made it sound like a Western movie.

I don't know if it was a comfort to Nathan, but it was to me. I needed something in his room. A fish that insists on being seen seemed right.

The night before Christmas, Sarah and I gathered around his bed to open presents. Nathan could not be moved. My hands swam through him if I tried to lift him, and Sarah had no better luck. We had wanted to take him down by the fireplace—with the stockings hanging on the mantel—down by the Christmas tree to see its winking lights. After running our hands through his body though—after that, we gave up. The fish tank gurgled on top of Nathan's scarred wooden desktop, casting bluish light over the room, rippling water shadows over the walls. The Siamese fighting fish floated in the water. It watched us seriously. Maybe it wished not to be separated by the plate of aquarium glass. I wanted to smack it, tell it to leave us alone, that this was a private moment. As glad as I was to have that fish in Nathan's room, it was starting to feel like competition.

I gave Sarah a new sweater and jeans, and the latest CD of her favorite sulky music. She hugged me and I almost cried to feel her arms tighten around my shoulders. I thought, Why haven't we been hugging all the time?

Afterlives

Nathan was barely present. His head was tilted towards Sarah and me, and I think I saw him smile once or twice. I don't know. I might have imagined it. But in my memory, he smiled.

The next day he was gone. I woke and wandered sleepily into his room to find his bed empty. The blanket lay across his bed in rumpled hills and valleys, but underneath, nothing stirred. I sucked my breath in hard, so hard it cut down the length of my throat like a knife. That first breath wasn't enough, though, and I kept gasping for air. Each time I did, the knife cut deeper.

I attacked the bed, scooped up armfuls of quilting and sheets. I think I howled a curse. I screamed, "Nathan! Nathan!" over and over. I threw off every blanket and then the mattress, the box springs. I would have ripped up the floorboards if I'd had the strength. I ran downstairs and looked in the living room, where sometimes he'd land after a fall in the past. He wasn't there. I ran down to the basement and searched through boxes full of discarded memories, but he was not there.

He was not there.

HE WAS NOT THERE. NOT anywhere in the house. Sarah finally found me in the kitchen, nibbling a Christmas cookie, one of those that have been cut into a shape. I was eating a Christmas tree trimmed with green frosting. She asked me what was the matter and I shook my head. She knelt beside me and said, "Mommy." I almost cried. She never called me that. It was always Mother. Never a sign of affection from that girl, but I am proud of her for that. In this way, she is protected.

I didn't know what to do, what the procedures were, so I took the bus to the hospital. I went to the ward where Nathan had had tests at one time. There was a nurse at the desk, scribbling on a pad. I said, "My son—"

"He's doing well," she told me. I blinked. "You're Mrs. Murphy, right?" I nodded, wanting to be Mrs. Murphy instead of Mrs. Livingston right then. "You can go in and see him now," the nurse said. She pointed to the door behind me. I went in. There he was—Mrs. Murphy's son—sitting in a chair next to his bed, staring out the window. I looked where he was looking, but the window was filled with light. Light so bright, no one could look at it without going blind. I turned to him again and saw the floral pattern of the wallpaper behind him. I saw it *through* him.

SARAH AND I DID NOT eat much after the memorial service. She lost a lot of weight and I got a new job, cleaning rooms at the Bakersfield Inn. I bought her a new wardrobe as soon as I could, and took her to a dermatologist. She was so happy. She practically danced through the front door after school each day. We tried to put Nathan behind us as best we could, but it was difficult. While we ate supper together one evening, Sarah put her fork down on her plate and said, "He's still here. I can feel him. He isn't gone, Mother."

We both looked up at the ceiling for some reason, but there was nothing there.

I should have known she was right, though. She is a smart girl, smarter than I'd ever guessed. She brings home straight A's. When she said he was still here, I should have believed her.

Several nights after Sarah and I looked up at the ceiling, I heard someone knocking at my front door. It was very late, after midnight. I immediately suspected trouble, but I gathered my robe around me and went down to see who was there.

The knocking grew more insistent as I went downstairs. At first it had been a rapping, but now it became forceful, and the door shook a little in its frame. I grabbed at the collar of my robe, as if that could protect me.

I went to the picture window first, and pulled back the curtain a little. It was snowing outside, the flakes drifting in piles along the windowsill, collecting on the steps of my porch. Under the florescent street lamps, the snow in the front yard, and in my neighbors' yards, seemed to glow purplish-white under the dark sky. The window was cold. It gave off coldness as a fire will give off heat.

There was no one on my porch, but I still heard the knocking. I pulled back from the window and looked at the door again. It shook in its frame.

I dropped the curtain and went to the door. I opened it just a little, in case someone was out there and I needed to close it quickly. It didn't matter, though. There was no one. I swung the door wide and stepped outside.

The knocking had stopped as soon as I opened the door. Now I looked around, turning my head quickly one way, then the other, trying to see if any prankster shadows ran off, scurrying down the street, choking on their own laughter. I saw nothing. I looked down, puzzled, and saw the snow piling up on my porch steps, drifting onto the porch itself.

There were no footprints.

I stepped back inside and slammed the door. I locked it. I pressed my back against the door, and again the knocking started. The door bucked at my back, lifting under the blows.

"Stop it, Nathan," I whispered. "Please stop it." Sarah was at a friend's house, spending the night, and I was thankful she was not here right then. The knocking continued.

I ran upstairs and went into his room. I had tried not to go there since that Christmas morning, only to feed the fish and that was all. The bed still lay on the floor in a jumble, mattress and box springs thrown against opposite walls. The fish tank gurgled, its small light glowing in the dark room. The Siamese fighting fish floated inside, fanning its fins. I closed my eyes, opened them. The knocking would not stop.

I went over to the fish tank and peered inside. I pressed so close my head bumped against the glass. The fish must have felt my bump against the aquarium was an attack, though, because suddenly it turned on me, a bloated red tumor, and swam at me, fins flying.

I don't know what came over me, sir, but I couldn't help myself. I grew angry too. I couldn't help it. Perhaps my own face grew bloated and red as well. As the fish charged, I grabbed hold of the edge of the tank and pushed it onto the floor. Glass shattered. Water poured out, and the fish with it. It flipped and flopped on the hardwood floor, next to the diver figurine that had landed nearby.

Sometime during all of this, the knocking had stopped.

HE IS NOT DEAD, AS I told you. I want you to say that in your book. That night was only the first in a series of visitations. Sarah has been here to witness several others since. He knocks on the door. He turns on the shower. Sometimes he will even cook us a meal. But his favorite is the knocking. He continues to return to that.

The Widow Parkinson had been right at one time. I suspect that, before she opened her door to the Mourners, her husband had been visiting her as well. But she's denied what I've come to know, down in my bones, deeper even. Sometimes you don't see things for what they are until they reach a vanishing point.

But that was the widow's choice. This is mine. Right now, no matter what anyone tells me, I know Nathan is here. He is here, sir, in this house, in these rooms, breathing along with us. He is entirely alive.

If you're very quiet, you may be able to hear him. It's him you should be talking to anyway.

Listen closely.

I think he has a lot to say.

Before and

The Language of Moths

1. Swallowing Bubbles

THE FOUR OF THEM HAD been traveling for what seemed like forever, the two in the front seat rattling maps like they did newspapers on Sunday mornings. They rode in the wagon, her favorite car, the one with the wood paneling on its doors. The wagon wound through the twisty back-roads of the mountains, leaving behind it clouds of dust through which sunlight passed, making the air shimmer like liquid gold. The girl wanted the wagon to stop so she could jump out and run through the golden light behind her. She climbed halfway over the back seat and pushed her face against the rear window, trying to get a better look.

The little old man beside her shouted, "No! No! No! Sit down, you're slobbering all over the glass. Sit down this instant!" He grabbed her around her waist and pulled her back into a sitting position. He pulled a strap across her chest, locking it with a decisive click. The little old man narrowed his eyes; he waved a finger in the girl's face. He said things at her. But as his words left his lips, they became bubbles. Large silver bubbles that shimmied and wobbled in the air. The bubbles filled the car in mere moments. So many words all at once! The girl laughed delightedly. She popped some of the bubbles between her fingers. Others she plucked from the air and swallowed like grapes. She let them sit sweetly on her tongue for a while, before taking them all the way in for good. When the bubbles reached her stomach, they burst into music. The sound of

Christopher Barzak

them echoed through her body, reverberating. She rang like a bell. One day, when she swallowed enough bubbles, she might understand what the little old man beside her was saying. All of the time, not just now and then. Maybe she'd even be able to say things back to him. She wondered if her own words would taste as sweet. Like honey, maybe. Or like flowers.

2. Being Selfish

ELIOT IS WATCHING HIS MOTHER hang bed sheets from a cord of clothesline she's tied off at two walls facing opposite of each other in their cabin. "To give us all a sense of personal space," she explains. Eliot tells his mother that this cabin is so small, hanging up bed sheets to section off rooms is a futile activity. "Where did you learn that word," his mother asks. "Futile. Who taught you that?"

"At school," Eliot says, paging through an *X-Men* comic book, not bothering to look up.

His mother makes a face that looks impressed. "Maybe public school isn't so bad after all," she says. "Your father was right, as usual."

Eliot doesn't know if his father is right, or even if his father is usually right, as his mother seems to imagine. After all, here they are in the Allegheny Mountains, in Pennsylvania, for God's sake, hundreds of miles away from home. Away from Boston. And for what? For a figment of his father's imagination. For a so-called undiscovered moth his father claims to have seen when he was Eliot's age, fourteen, camping right here in this very cabin. Eliot doesn't believe his father could remember anything that far back, and even if he could, his memory of the event could be completely fictional at this point, an indulgence in nostalgia for a time when his life still seemed open in all directions, flat as a map, unexplored and waiting for him.

Eliot's father is an entomologist. His specialty is lepidoptera, moths and butterflies and what Eliot thinks of as creepy-crawlies, things that spin cocoons around themselves when they're unhappy with their present circumstances and wait inside their shells until either they've changed or the world has, before coming out. Eliot's father is forty-three years old, a once-celebrated researcher on the mating habits of moths found in the Appalachian Mountains. He is also a liar. He lied to his grant committee at the college, telling them in his proposal that he required the funds for this expedition to research the habits of a certain species of moth with which they were all familiar. He didn't mention his undiscovered moth, the one that glowed orange and pink, as he once told Eliot during a reverie, with his eyes looking at something unimaginably distant while he spoke of

Before and

it. Maybe, Eliot thinks, an absurd adventure like this one is a scientist's version of a mid-life crisis. Instead of chasing after other women, Eliot's father is chasing after a moth that, let's face it, he probably imagined.

"There now, isn't that better?" Eliot's mother stands in the center of the cabin, which she has finished sectioning into four rooms. The cabin is a perfect square with clothesline bisecting the center in both directions, like a plus sign. Eliot owns one corner, and Dawn, his sister, has the one next to his: That makes up one half of the cabin. The other half has been divided into the kitchen and his parents' space. The sheet separating Eliot's corner from his sister's is patterned with blue flowers and tiny teacups. These sheets are Dawn's favorites, and secretly, Eliot's too.

Eliot's mother glances around, smiling vaguely, wiping sweat off of her brow. She's obviously happy with her achievement. After all, she's an academic, a philosopher, unaccustomed to cleaning house and rigging up clotheslines and bed linen. The maid back in Boston—back home, Eliot thinks—Marcy, she helps around the house with domestic things like that. Usually Eliot's mother uses her mind to speculate on how the mind works; not just her own mind—but *the* mind—the idea of what a mind is. Now she finds herself using her mental prowess to tidy up a ramshackle cabin. Who would have guessed she'd be so capable? So *practical*? Not Eliot. Certainly not herself.

The door to the cabin swings open, flooding the room with bright sunlight that makes Eliot squint. He shields his eyes with one hand, like an officer saluting, to witness the shadowy figure of his father's body filling the doorframe, and his sister Dawn trailing behind.

Dawn is more excited than usual, which has made this trip something less than a vacation. For Eliot's father, Dr. Carroll, it was never a vacation; that was a well-known fact. For Dr. Carroll, this was an expedition, possibly his last chance to inscribe his name in History. But the rest of the family was supposed to "take things easy and enjoy themselves." When Dr. Carroll said that, Eliot had snorted. Dr. Carroll had placed his hands on his hips and glowered. "Why the attitude, Eliot?" he'd asked.

"Take it *easy*?" Eliot repeated in a squeaky-scratchy voice that never failed to surface when he most needed to appear justified and righteous. "How can you expect us to do that with Dawn around?"

Dr. Carroll had stalked away, not answering, which didn't surprise Eliot at all. For most of his life, this is what Eliot has seen whenever he questions his father: his father's back, walking away, leaving a room full of silence.

Dawn pushes past Dr. Carroll and runs over to Eliot's cot. She jumps on the mattress, which squeals on old coils, and throws her arms across the moth-eaten pink quilt. The quilt smells of mold and mildew and something a little like mothballs, as if it had been stored in a cedar chest for a long time. Dawn turns to Eliot, her wide blue eyes set in a face as white and smooth as porcelain, and smiles at him, her blonde hair fanning out on the pillow. Eliot considers her over the top of his comic book, pretending not to have noticed her.

Dawn is autistic. She's seventeen years old, three years older than Eliot. But when she's around, Eliot feels as if he's already an old man, forced into an early maturity, responsible for things no fourteen year old boy should have to think about. He blames this all on his parents, who often encourage him when he pays attention to Dawn, who often scold him when he wants something for himself. "Being selfish," is what his mother calls that, leaving Eliot dashed to pieces on the rocks of guilt. He feels guilty even now, trying to read the last page of his comic book instead of paying attention to Dawn.

"I'm leaving," Dr. Carroll announces. He's wearing khaki pants with pockets all over them, and a wide-brimmed hat with mosquito netting pulled down over his face. A backpack and sleeping bag are slung on his back. He lifts the mosquito netting and kisses Eliot's mother on her cheek and calls her Dr. Carroll affectionately, then looks at Eliot and says, "You take care of Dawn while I'm away, Eliot. Stay out of trouble."

He walks outside, and all of them—Eliot, Dawn and their mother—move to the doorway. As if magnetized by Dr. Carroll's absence, they try to fill the space he's left. They watch him become smaller and smaller, a shadow, until he reaches the trail that will take him farther into the graying mountains, where his moth awaits.

"Good luck," Eliot's mother whispers, waving goodbye to his back, his nets and pockets. She closes her eyes and says, "Please," to something she cannot name, even though she no longer believes in higher powers, ghosts or gods of any sort.

3. First Words

IT WAS STRANGE FOR THE girl in this place; she hadn't been prepared for it. Suddenly the wagon had come to a stop and they all spilled out. The mother and the father, they seemed so excited. They smiled so hard, their faces split in half. The little old man kept scowling; he was so funny. She patted him on his shoulder and he opened his mouth to make room for one huge silver bubble to escape. She grabbed hold of its silky surface and almost left the ground as it floated upwards, towards the clouds. But it popped, and she rocked back on her heels, laughing. When the bubble popped, it shouted, "Get off!"

The father left soon after. The girl was a little frightened at first. Like maybe the father would never come back? Did the father still love her? These thoughts frightened her more than anything else. But then she watched the little old man chop wood for the fire, his skinny arms struggling each time he lifted the axe above his head, which made her laugh, sweeping the fear out of her like the mother sweeping dirt off the front porch. Swish! Goodbye, fear! Good riddance! She forgot the father because the little old man made her laugh so much.

There were so many trees here, the girl thought she'd break her neck from tilting her head back to see their swaying tops. Also, strange sounds burrowed into her skin, and she shivered a lot. Birds singing, crickets creeking. This little thing no bigger than the nail of her pinky—it had transparent wings and hovered by her ear, buzzing a nasty song. She swatted at it, but it kept returning. It followed her wherever she went. Finally the mother saw it and squashed it in a Kleenex. But as it died, it told the girl, "You've made a horrible mistake. I am not the enemy." Then it coughed, sputtered, and was dead.

The girl thought of the wagon. It was still one of her favorite things in the world. But now she was thinking she wasn't so sure. Maybe there were other things just as special as riding in the wagon with the mother, the father and the little old man. She wished the mother wouldn't have killed the winged creature so quick. She wanted it to tell her more things, but now it was dead and its last words still rang in her ears. When the winged creature spoke, no bubbles came out of its mouth. Words, pure and clear, like cold water, filled her up. The winged creature had more words for her, she just knew it. She knew this without knowing why, and she didn't care. She only cared that the bubbles didn't come between her and the words when the creature spoke to her. One drink of that and she wanted more.

4. The Scream

BEFORE ELIOT'S FATHER LEFT, HE placed him in charge of Dawn, and his mother seems more than willing to follow her husband's orders to the letter, leaving Eliot to look after Dawn while she sits on the front porch of the cabin, or in the kitchen, and writes. Eliot finds his mother's loyalty to his father's declarations an annoying trait, as if she had no say-so about anything when it comes to her children; she simply goes along with whatever his father says. He's watched Dawn every day since his father left, which has been for an entire week. He's taken her on the trails that are clearly marked; they've stared into the shallow depths of a creek where the water was as dark as tea, where red and blue crayfish skittered for cover under rocks. He's introduced Dawn to grasshoppers, which she loved immediately and, to Eliot's amazement, coaxed into a perfect line, making them leap in time together, like figure skaters. He was proud of Dawn for that, and could tell she was too; she looked up at him after the synchronized leap went off without a hitch and clapped her hands for a full minute.

Each day they pick wildflowers together, which, when they return in the late afternoons, hang tattered and limp in Dawn's grip. Still, their mother takes them from Dawn gratefully when they're offered. "Oh, they're beautiful," she says, and puts the ragged daisies and buttercups in empty Coke bottles, filling the cabin with their bittersweet scent.

Eliot never gives his mother flowers. He leaves that pleasure for Dawn. And anyway, he knows something Dawn doesn't: his mother doesn't even like flowers, and Dr. Carroll doesn't even give them to her for Valentine's day or for their wedding anniversary. Eliot has to admit that his mother's graciousness in the face of receiving a gift she doesn't like is a mark of her tact and love for Dawn. He couldn't ever be so nice. He watches his mother and Dawn find "just the right place" for the flowers and thinks, I am a bad person. He thinks this because he's imagined himself far away, not from his present location in the mountains, but far away from his family itself. He's imagined himself in a place of his own, with furniture and a TV set and his own books. In none of these fantasies does his mother or father appear, except for the occasional phone call. He never misses them and he wonders if this means he's a wrong person somehow. Shouldn't children love their parents enough to call every once in a while? Apparently in these fantasies, parents aren't that important.

Dawn isn't a part of these fantasies either. Eliot doesn't even imagine phone calls from her because, really, what would be the use? At most, Dawn might latch onto a phrase and ask him it over and over. She might say, like she once did at his twelfth birthday party, "How old is your cat?" sending all of his friends into fits of laughter.

Eliot doesn't have a cat.

Eliot's mother has begun a new essay, and during the day, she spends her time reading essays and books written by other philosophers and scientists who she thinks has something to say on the subject she's considering. "This one," she tells Eliot one morning, "will be a feminist revision of *Walden*. I think it has great potential."

She's packed her Thoreau, Eliot realizes, irritation suddenly tingling at the base of his neck. He's beginning to suspect that, this summer, he has become the victim of a conspiracy got up by his parents, a conspiracy that will leave him the sole caretaker of Dawn. Within the frame of a few seconds he's turned red and his skin has started to itch. He's close to yelling at his mother. He wants to accuse her of this conspiracy, to call her out, so to speak. To scold her for being selfish. I could do that, he thinks. Scold his parents. He's done it before and he'll do it again. He finds nothing wrong with that; sometimes they deserve to be reprimanded. Why does everyone think that because someone gives birth to you and is older, they inherently deserve your respect? Eliot decided a long time ago that he wouldn't respect his parents unless they respected him. Sometimes this becomes a problem.

Before he unleashes his penned-up tensions, though, his mother stops scribbling and lifts her face from her notebook. She smiles at Eliot and says, "Why don't you go into that village we passed on the way in and make some friends? You've been doing so well with your sister. You deserve a break."

She gives Eliot ten dollars from her purse, which he crumples into a wad in his front pocket. She's releasing him for the day, and though he's still fuming over the conspiracy, he runs at this window of chance. He grabs his bike and trots with it at his side for a minute, before leaping onto its sun-warmed seat. Then he peddles away, down the mountain.

When he thinks he's far enough away, Eliot screams at the top of his lungs, an indecipherable noise that echoes and echoes in this silent, wooded place. The scream hangs over the mountainside like a cloud of black smoke, a stain on the clear sky, following Eliot for the rest of the day. Like some homeless mutt he's been nice to without thinking about the consequences, the scream will follow him forever now, seeking more affection, wanting to be a permanent part of his life.

5. The Butterfly's Question

THE GIRL FOUND THE BUTTERFLIES by accident. They were swarming in a small green field splashed yellow and white and orange from their wings. She ran out to meet them, stretched out her fingertips to touch them, and they flitted onto her arms, dusted her face with pollen, kissed her forehead and said, "Child, where have you been?"

The butterfly that spoke to her was large, and its wings were a burnt orange color, spider-webbed with black veins. It floated unsteadily in front of her face, cocking its head back and forth as if examining her. No silver bubbles came out of its mouth when it spoke, just like the first winged creature, just like the grasshoppers who performed their leaps, their little tricks just for her pleasure.

"Well?" The butterfly circled her head once.

"I don't know," Dawn said. "It's hard to explain. But there are these people. They take care of me really nice."

"I would expect nothing less," said the butterfly, coming to rest on the back of her wrist. It stayed there for a while, its wings moving back and forth slowly, fanning itself. Finally, it crawled up the length of the girl's arm and came to rest on her shoulder. It whispered in her ear, "Why now? Why have they brought you too us now, so late in your life?"

The girl didn't know how to answer the butterfly. She simply looked down at her bare feet in the high grass and shrugged. "I don't know," she told the butterfly, and nearly started crying. But the butterfly brushed her cheek with its wings and said, "No, no. Don't cry, my love. Everything in its own time. Everything in its own time. Now isn't that right?"

6. Centipede

WHEN ELIOT RODE INTO THE village his first thought was: What a dump. When they passed through it a week ago, they had driven through without stopping, and he figured his father must have been speeding because he hadn't noticed how sad this so-called village is. It has one miserable main street running through the center, a general store called Mac's, a gas station that serves ice cream inside, and a bar called Murdock's Place. Other than that, the rest of the town is made up of family cemeteries and ramshackle farms. The Amish have a community just a few miles out of town, and the occasional horse-drawn buggy *clop-clops* it way down the main street, carrying inside its bonnet girls wearing dark blue dresses and men with bushy beards and straw hats.

Inside Mac's general store, Eliot is playing *Centipede*, an incredibly archaic arcade game from the 1980s. He has to play the game with an old trackball, which is virtually extinct in the arcade world, and it only has one button to push for laser beam attacks. Ridiculous, thinks Eliot. Uncivilized. This is the end of the world, he thinks, imagining the world to be flat, like the first explorers described it, where, in the furthest outposts of undiscovered country, the natives play *Centipede* and sell ice cream in gas stations, traveling from home to school in horse-drawn buggies. He misses his computer in Boston, which offers far more sophisticated diversions. Games where you actually have to think, he thinks.

Before and

The front screen door to Mac's squeals open then bangs shut. Mac, the man behind the counter with the brown wart on his nose and the receding hairline, couldn't have oiled the hinges for ages. Probably not since the place was first built. Eliot looks over his shoulder to catch a glimpse of the tall town boy who just entered, standing at the front counter, talking to Mac. He's pale as milk in the gloom of Mac's dusty store, and his hair looks almost colorless. More like fiber optics than hair, Eliot thinks, clear as plastic filaments. Mac calls the boy Roy, and rings up a tin of chewing tobacco on the cash register. Another piece of pre-history, Eliot thinks. This place doesn't even have price scanners, which have been around for how long? Like more than twenty years at least.

Eliot turns back to his game to find he's been killed because of his carelessness. That's okay, though, because he still has one life left to lose and, anyway, he doesn't have to feel like a failure because the game is so absurd that he doesn't even care anymore. He starts playing again anyway, spinning the trackball in its orbit, but suddenly he feels someone breathing on the back of his neck. He stops moving the trackball. He looks over his shoulder to find Roy standing behind him.

"Watch out!" Roy says, pointing a grease-stained finger at the video screen. Eliot turns back and saves himself by the skin of his teeth. "You almost bought it there," says Roy in a congratulatory manner, as if Eliot has passed some sort of manhood rite in which near-death experiences are a standard. Roy sends a stream of brown spit splashing against the back corner of the arcade game, and Eliot grins without knowing why. He's thinking this kid Roy is a real loser, trashy and yet somehow brave to spit on Mac's property when Mac is only a few steps away. Guys like this are enigmas to Eliot. They frighten him, piss him off for how easy-going they act, fire his imagination in ways that embarrass him. He abhors them; he wants to be more like them; he wants them to want to be more like him; he wants them to tell him they want to be more like him, so he can admit to his own desire for aspects of their own personalities. Shit, he thinks. What the hell is wrong with me? Why do I think these things?

After another minute, Eliot crashes yet another life, and the arcade game bleeps wearily, asking for another quarter for another chance. Eliot turns to Roy and asks, "You want a turn?"

Up close, he can see Roy's eyes are green, and his hair is brown, not colorless. In fact, Eliot decides, in the right light, Roy's hair may even be auburn, reddish-brown, like leaves in autumn.

Roy gives Eliot this dirty grin that makes him appear like he's onto Eliot about something. His lips curl back from his teeth. His nostrils flare, then retract. He's caught the scent of something. "No," he tells Eliot, still grinning. "Why don't we do something else instead?"

Eliot is already nodding. He doesn't know what he's agreed to, but he's willing to sign on the dotted line without reading the small print. It doesn't matter, he's thinking. He's only wondering what Roy's hair will look like outside, out of the dark of Mac's store, out in the sunlight.

7. Do You Understand Me?

THE MOTHER CAME OUT OF nowhere, and the girl looked frantically around the field for a place to hide, as if she'd been caught doing something bad, or was naked, like that man and woman in the garden with the snake. Sometimes, the grandma who babysitted for the mother and the father would tell the girl that story and say, "Dear, you are wiser than all of us. You did not bite that apple." The grandma would pet the girl's hair, as if she were a dog or a cat.

The mother said, "Dawn! What are you doing so far away? I've been looking for you everywhere! You know you're not supposed to wander." The mother was suddenly upon the girl then, and she grabbed hold of her wrist, tight. "Come on," said the mother. "Let's go back to the cabin. I've got work to do. You can't run off like this. Do you understand me? Dawn! Understand?"

The mother and father were always talking about work. The girl didn't know what work was, but she thought it was probably something like when she had to go to the special school, where the Mrs. Albert made her say, "B is for book, B. B is for bat, B. B is for butterfly, B. Buh, buh, buh." It was a little annoying. But the girl was given a piece of candy each time she repeated the Mrs. Albert correctly. The candy made the buh, buh, buhs worth saying.

The mother tugged on the girl's wrist and they left the field together. The girl struggled against her mother's grip, but could not break it. Behind her, the butterflies all waved their wings goodbye, winking in the high grass and yellow-white flowers like stars in the sky at night. The girl waved back with her free hand, and the butterflies started to fly towards her, as if she'd issued them a command. They ushered the mother and girl out of their field, flapping behind the girl like a banner.

When they reached the cabin, the girl saw that the little old man was back again. Something was funny about him now, but it wasn't the kind of funny that usually made her laugh. Something was different. He didn't look so old anymore maybe, as if all the adulthood had drained out of his normally pinched-looking face. He didn't even scold her when she

Before and

ran up to him and squealed at him, pointing out the difference to him, in case he hadn't noticed it himself. The little old man didn't seem to be bothered by anything now, not the girl, nor the mother. His eyes looked always somewhere else, far away, like the father's. Off in the distance. The mother asked the little old man, "How was your day?" and the little old man replied, "Great."

This was a shock for the girl. The little old man *never* sounded so happy. He went into the cabin to take a nap. The girl was curious, so she climbed onto the porch and peered through the window that looked down on the little old man's cot. He was lying on his back, arms crossed behind his head, staring at the ceiling. His face suddenly broke into a smile, and the girl cocked her head, wondering why he would ever do that. Then she realized: He'd found something like she had with the insects, and it made her happy for them both.

The little old man stopped staring at the ceiling. He stared at the girl, his eyes warning signals to keep her distance, but he didn't yell like he usually did. The girl nodded, then backed away from the window slowly. She didn't want to ruin his happiness.

8. Life in the Present Tense

ELIOT AND ROY ARE SITTING in the rusted-out shell of a 1969 Corvette, once painted red, now rotted away to the browns of rust. The corvette rests in the back of a scrap metal junkyard on the edge of town, which Roy's uncle owns. His uncle closes the place down every afternoon at five o'clock sharp. Now it's nine o'clock at night, and the only light available comes from the moon, and from the orange glow on the cherry of Roy's cigarette.

Eliot is holding a fifth of Jim Beam whiskey in his right hand. The bottle is half empty. He lifts it to his lips and drinks. The whiskey slides down his throat, warm and bitter, and explodes in his stomach, heating his body, flushing his skin bright red. He and Roy started drinking over an hour ago, taking shots, daring each other to take another, then another, until they were both good and drunk. It's the first time for Eliot.

"We need to find something to do," Roy says, exhaling a plume of smoke. "Jeez, this'd be better if we'd at least have a radio or something."

"It's all right," Eliot says, trying to calm Roy down before he works himself up. He and Roy have been hanging out together relentlessly for the past few weeks. Here's one thing Eliot's discovered about Roy: He gets angry over little things fast. Things that aren't really problems. Like not having music in the junkyard while they drink. Roy's never satisfied with what's available. His mind constantly seeks out what could make each moment better than it is, rather than focusing on the moment itself. Roy lives in the future imperfect, Eliot's realized, while Eliot mainly lives in the present tense.

"I hate this town," Roy says, taking the bottle from Eliot. He sips some of the whiskey, then takes a fast and hard gulp. "Ahh," he hisses. He turns to Eliot and smiles, all teeth. His smile is almost perfect, except for one of his front teeth is pushed out a little further than the other, slightly crooked. But it suits him somehow, Eliot thinks.

"I don't know," Eliot shrugs. "I kind of like it here. It's better than being up on that stupid mountain with my parents. They're enough to drive you up a wall."

"Or to drink," says Roy, lifting the bottle again, and they both laugh.

"Yeah," Eliot says, smiling back at Roy. He leans back to rest his head against the seat and looks up through the rusted-out roof of the Corvette, where the stars pour through, reeling and circling above them, as though some invisible force is stirring them up. "It's not like this in Boston," Eliot says. "Most of the time you can't even see the stars because of the city lights."

"In Boston," Roy mimics, his voice whiney and filled with a slight sneer. "All you talk about is Boston. You know, Boston isn't everything. It's not the only place in the world."

"I know," Eliot says. "I was just trying to say exactly that. You know, how I can't see the stars there like I can here?"

"Oh," Roy says, and looks down into his lap.

Eliot pats him on the shoulder and tells him not to get all sad. "We're having fun," Eliot says. "Everything's great."

Roy agrees and then Eliot goes back to staring at the stars above them. The night air feels cold on his whiskey-warmed skin, and he closes his eyes for a moment to feel the slight breeze on his face. Then he suddenly feels hands cupping his cheeks, the skin rough and grainy, and when Eliot opens his eyes, Roy's face floats before him, serious and intent. Roy leans in and they're lips meet briefly. Something electric uncoils through Eliot's body, like a live wire, dangerous and intense. He feels as if all the gaps and cracks in his being are stretching out to the horizon, filling up with light.

"Are you all right?" Roy asks, and Eliot realizes that he's shaking.

"Yes," Eliot says, so softly and quietly that the word evaporates before it can be heard. He nods instead and, before they kiss again, Roy brushes his thumb over Eliot's cheek and says, "Don't worry. We're friends. It's nothing to worry about, right?"

Eliot can't help but begin worrying, though. He already knows some of the things that will come to pass because of this. He will contemplate suicide, he will contemplate murder, he will hate himself for more reasons than usual—not just because he doesn't want to be away from his family, but because he has turned out to be the sort of boy who kisses other boys, and who wants a son like that? Everything seems like a dream right now, though, so sudden, and maybe it is a dream, nothing more than that. Eliot is prepared to continue sleepwalking.

He nods to answer again, his voice no longer functioning properly. Then Roy presses close again, his breath thick with whiskey and smoke. His body above Eliot blocks out the light from the stars.

9. Sad Alone

IN THE WOODS AT NIGHT, the girl danced to the songs of frogs throating, crickets chirring, wind snaking through leaves, the gurgle of the nearby creek. A happy marriage these sounds made, so the girl danced, surrounded by fireflies and moths.

She could still see the fire through the spaces between the trees, her family's campsite near the cabin, so she was safe. She wasn't doing anything wrong—she was following the rules—so the mother shouldn't come running to pull her back to the fire to sit with her and the father. He was back again, but he didn't seem to be there. Not *really* there, that is. He didn't look at the girl during dinner, only stared into the fire before him, slouching. He didn't open his mouth for any bubbles to come out.

Now that it was night, the little old man was back again. This had become a regular event. In the early evening, after dinner, the little old man would leave, promising to be back before sunset at nine-thirty, or else he'd spend the night with his new friend. This time, though, the little old man had come back with his new friend riding along on a bike beside him, saying, "This is Roy. He'll be spending the night."

The girl missed the little old man when he was gone now, but she didn't dwell on this too much. The little old man no longer glowered at her, no longer gripped her hand too tight like the mother did; he no longer looked angry all the time, so she forgave his absence. He was happy, the girl realized, and in realizing the little old man's happiness and the distance between them that went along with it, she realized her own happiness as well. She didn't miss him enough to be sad about his absence, unlike the father, who made the mother sad when he was gone, who made everyone miss him in a way that made them want to cry or shout in his face.

This moth, the girl thought, stopping her dance for the moment. If she could find this moth, the moth that the father was looking for, perhaps he would come back and be happy, and make the mother happy, and then everyone could be happy together, instead of sad alone. She smiled, proud of her idea, and turned to the fireflies and moths that surrounded her to ask the question:

"Can anyone help me?"

To which the insects all responded at once, their voices a chorus, asking, "What can we do? Are you all right? What? What?"

So the girl began to speak.

10. Each in their Own Place

DR. CARROLL IS SITTING BY the campfire, staring at his two booted feet. Eliot's mother is saying, "This week it will happen. You can't get down on yourself. It's only been a month. You have the rest of the summer still. Don't worry."

Eliot's mother is cooking barbecued beans in a pot over the campfire. The flames lick at the bottom of the pan. Dr. Carroll shakes his head, looking distraught. There are new wrinkles in his forehead, and also around his mouth.

This has been a regular event over the past few weeks, Eliot's father returning briefly for supplies and rest, looking depressed and slightly damaged, growing older-looking before Eliot's eyes. Eliot feels bad for his father, but he'd also like to say, I told you so. That's just too mean, though, he's decided. The Old Eliot would have said that, the New Eliot won't.

The New Eliot is a recent change he's been experiencing, and it's because of Roy. Roy's changed him somehow without trying, and probably without even wanting to make Eliot into someone new in the first place. Eliot supposes this is what happens when you meet a person with whom you can truly communicate. The New Eliot will always try to be nice and not so world-weary. He will not say mean things to his parents or sister. He will love them and think about their needs, because his no longer seem so bad off.

Roy says, "Is it always like this?" He and Eliot are sitting on the swing in the cabin's front porch. The swing's chains squeal above their heads as they rock. This is Roy's first visit to the place. Eliot's tried to keep him away from his family, because even though he's made the choice to be nice, he's still embarrassed by them a little. Also, he'd rather have Roy to himself.

That's another thing that's come between them. It happened a couple of weeks back. Roy and Eliot had been hanging out together, getting into minor trouble. They'd spray-painted their names on an overpass; egged Roy's neighbor's car; toilet-papered the high school Roy attends; drank whiskey until they've puked. It's been a crazy summer, the best Eliot can remember really, and he doesn't want it to ever stop. Usually he goes to computer camp or just sits in front of the TV playing video games until school starts back up. Besides the vandalism and the drunken bouts, Eliot thinks he has fallen in love. Something like that. He and Roy have become like a couple, without using those words, without telling anyone else.

"My father's like Sisyphus," Eliot says, and Roy gives him this puzzled look.

"What did you say?"

"Sisyphus," Eliot repeats. "He was this guy from myth who was doomed by the gods to roll a rock up a mountain, but it keeps rolling back down when he gets to the top, so he has to roll it up again, over and over. Camus says it's the definition of the human condition, that myth. My mother teaches a class on it."

"Oh." Roy shakes his head. "Well, whatever."

That *whatever* is another thing that's come between them. Lately Roy says it whenever he doesn't understand Eliot, and doesn't care to try. It makes Eliot want to punch Roy right in the face. Eliot has taken to saying it as well, to see if it pisses off Roy as much, but whenever he says, "Whatever," Roy doesn't seem to give a damn. He just keeps on talking without noticing Eliot's attempts to make him angry.

The fireflies have come out for the evening, glowing on and off in the night mist. Crickets chirp, rubbing their legs together. An owl calls out its own name in the distance. Dawn is running between trees, her figure a silhouette briefly illuminated by the green glow of the fireflies, a shadow in the woods. Eliot still hasn't introduced her to Roy, and Roy hasn't asked why she acts so strangely, which makes Eliot think maybe he should explain before Roy says something mean about her, not understanding her condition. Dawn irritates Eliot, but he still doesn't want other people saying nasty things about her.

"She's autistic," Eliot says all of a sudden, pre-empting Roy's remarks. He pushes against the porch floorboards to make them swing faster, so Roy can't get off this ride too quick.

Roy doesn't seem shocked, though, or even interested in Dawn's erratic behavior. And why should he be? Eliot thinks. Roy himself has told Eliot much weirder things about his family. He told Eliot that first day, over an ice cream at the gas station, that he lived with his grandparents because his mother was an alcoholic, and his father was who-knows-where. That his mother would fight anyone in town, even Roy when she was drunk. That his grandfather was a member of the Ku Klux Klan, that he had found the white robes and the pointy hood in his grandfather's closet. That his grandmother used to sit him down at night before bed and read to him for a half an hour out of the Bible, and that afterwards she'd tell him he was born in sin, and should pray for forgiveness. It frightens Eliot a little, and makes him shiver, thinking of what it must be like to be Roy. He only hopes Roy's secret-sharing doesn't require an admission of his own private weirdnesses. He's not ready for that.

"Let's go inside," Roy says, putting his feet down flat on the porch. The swing suddenly comes to a halt. Roy stands and Eliot follows him into the cabin, already knowing what's going to happen. It's a vice of Roy's, fooling around in places where they might get caught.

We won't get caught here, Eliot thinks. His parents are outside by the heat of the fire, involved in their own problems. They won't bother to come inside the cabin now. Roy leads Eliot to the pink-quilted cot and they lay down together, and begin to kiss.

Roy's lips are larger than Eliot's. Eliot feels like his lips aren't big enough. They're too thin and soft, like rose petals. Roy, he thinks, would probably like his lips bigger and rougher, chapped even. He can feel the cracks in Roy's lips, can taste Roy's cigarettes. Roy's stubble scratches Eliot's cheeks in this way that makes him crazy. Then Roy is pulling off Eliot's shirt, kissing Eliot's stomach, unbuttoning Eliot's shorts. Eliot closes his eyes. He mouths the words, *Someone is in love with me.* He is in the habit of mouthing sentences silently when he wants what he is saying to be true.

He feels his shorts being tugged down, then his breath catches in his throat, and he is off, off, off. Far away, his parents argue and his sister runs through the wilderness like a woodland creature, a nymph. Each of them in their private spaces, like the sections his mother made of the cabin when they first arrived. Each of them in their own place.

11. What the Firefly Said

"So," said the firefly, "you're looking for a moth."

The girl nodded. "Yes," she said. "Actually, it's for my father. He's been searching for over a month."

"And what does it look like?" the firefly said, floating in front of her face. "You know, a moth is a moth is a moth. But that's just my opinion."

"This one glows," she said. "An orangey-pink. It has brown and gold streaks on its back, and also it only comes out at night."

"Hmm," said the firefly. "I see. Wait here a moment."

The firefly flew off. The girl watched it for a while, then lost it among the other greenish blips. She sighed, sat down on the ground beneath a pine tree, picking up a few needles covered in sticky sap.

"I'm back," said the firefly, and the girl looked up. It had brought a friend, and they both landed on her lap.

"I know who you're looking for," the other firefly said.

The girl felt a rush of excitement churl in her stomach. Her face flushed with heat. "Really?" she said. "Oh, please, you must help me find it."

"This moth, though," the firefly said, "it's a bit of a loner. There are a few of them I know of, but they don't even talk amongst themselves. I don't understand them. You know, we fireflies, we like to have a good time. We like to party." It chuckled softly and nudged its friend.

"I'll do anything," the girl said. "Please, if only it would make my father happier. He looks paler and thinner each time he comes back."

"Well," the firefly said. "Let me see what I can make happen. I have a lot of connections. We'll see what turns up."

"Thank you," said the girl, "Oh, thank you, thank you."

The fireflies both floated off. She sat under the tree for a while longer, thinking everything would be good now. Her whole family would be happy for once.

Then the mother and the father were calling her name, loud, over and over. She saw them coming towards her, running. The mother pulled her up from the ground and said, "I was so worried, so worried." The father grunted and led them back to the cabin, where the little old man and his new friend were sitting by the campfire.

"I can't do this anymore," said the mother. "I can't keep her in one place. She's always wandering off."

"Just a little longer," said the father. "I can't go back without it. I've been teaching the same classes to an endless stream of students. I can't go back without this."

The mother nodded and rubbed her temples. "I know," she said. "I know."

Then the little old man told his friend, "This is my sister. Her name is Dawn. She doesn't talk much."

The little old man's friend stared at her for a moment. His eyes grew wide; he smiled at her. The little old man's friend said, "Your sister's beautiful," as if he couldn't believe it himself.

12. *Your Sister's Beautiful*

YOUR SISTER'S BEAUTIFUL.
  Your sister's beautiful.
  Your sister's beautiful.
  Lying on his cot, staring at the bare rafters of the cabin, imagining Roy hanging by his neck from one of the rafters, his face blue in death, Eliot cannot force Roy's words out of his mind. He's been hearing them over and over since Roy—stupid idiotic trashy no-good thoughtless bastard—said them three nights ago.
  Your sister's beautiful.
  And me? Eliot thinks. What about me? Why couldn't Roy have said the same thing about Eliot, with whom he's much more involved and supposedly loves enough to take to bed? Eliot is thinking, I should kill him. I should be like one of those people on talk shows, or in novels. I should commit a crime of passion that anyone could understand.
  Outside somewhere, Roy is hanging out with Dawn. He's been with Eliot for over a month and never once cared to come up to the cabin until Eliot brought him himself. Now he's come up everyday since that first night, and Eliot has been ignoring him defiantly, walking away when Roy starts to speak, finding opportunities to make Roy feel stupid, talking to his mother about high-minded philosophical things in front of Roy. Even if Eliot himself doesn't understand some of the things that comes out of his mother's mouth, he's been around her long enough to pretend like he knows what he's talking about; he knows enough catch-phrases to get by. Whatever works, he's thinking, to make that jerk go away or feel sorry.
  Eliot notices that everything is strangely quiet, both inside the cabin and out. He sits up in bed and looks out the window. The campfire is a pile of ashes, still glowing orange and red from last night. His mother is nowhere to be seen, and both Roy and Dawn aren't around either. His father, he thinks, is who-knows-where.
  Eliot goes outside and looks around back of the cabin. Nothing but weeds and a few scrub bushes and saplings grow here. He walks to the edge of the woods, to where the trails begin, and starts to worry. Dawn. He hasn't been in a state of mind to watch her, and his mother has proved ineffectual at the task. He mouths the words, *My sister is safe and around that tree there, playing with a caterpillar,* and then he goes to check.
  Dawn's not behind the tree, and there are no caterpillars in sight. Eliot suddenly clenches his teeth. He hears, somewhere close by, Roy's voice. He can't make out what Roy is saying, but he's talking to someone in that voice of his—the idiotic stupid no-good trashy bastard voice.

Before and

Eliot walks in the direction of the voice. He follows a trail until it narrows and dips down into a ravine. There's the creek where he and Dawn watched crayfish for hours. The way water moves, the way it sparkles under light, and reflects the things around it, the trees and Eliot's and Dawn's own faces, can entrance Dawn for hours. The creek holds the image of the world on its surface, the trees and clouds and a sun pinned like a jewel on its narrow, rippled neck. Beneath the creek, under the water, is another world, full of crayfish and snakes and fish no bigger than fingers. Eliot wonders if his mother has included something philosophical about the creek in her feminist revision of *Walden*. He wonders if she's noticed the same things that he notices.

Roy's voice fades, then reappears, like a trick or a prank, and soon Eliot sees him sitting under a tree with Dawn. Roy's talking to her real sweet. Eliot recognizes that voice. He's playing with Dawn's hand, which she keeps pulling away from him. Roy doesn't know Dawn hates to be touched. The only thing she can stand is a tight embrace, and then she won't ever let go. It's a symptom, her doctor has told the family, of her autism.

Now Roy is leaning into Dawn, trying to kiss her, and Dawn pulls her head back. She stands up and starts walking towards the creek. Eliot feels his hands clench, becoming fists. Roy stands up and follows Dawn. He walks in front of her and she squeals in his face. A high-pitched banshee squeal. The squeal, Eliot thinks, of death.

Eliot finds he is running towards them, his fists ready to pummel Roy. He wonders if he can actually do it, he hasn't ever used them before, not like this. Can I do it, he wonders, as Roy turns with a surprised expression on his face.

Yes, he can.

His first punch lands on Roy's cheekbone, right under Roy's eye. The second one glances blandly off of Roy's stomach, making Roy double up and expel a gasp of breath. Then Eliot is screaming at the top of his lungs, "Get out! Get the hell out! Get the hell out!" His voice turns hoarser each time he screams, but he keeps screaming anyway. Roy looks up at Eliot with a red mark on his face. It's already darkening into a bruise that Eliot wishes he could take a picture of and frame. He'd like to hang it on his wall and keep it forever. A reminder of his ignorance.

Roy says, "Whatever. Fucking faggot," and starts to walk away, back up the trail. When he reaches the top of the ravine and walks over it, he disappears from Eliot's sight, and from Eliot's life, forever.

Eliot is breathing heavily, ready to hit Roy again. He's a little surprised at how easy it was, that he has a space inside him that harbors violence.

At the same time, he's impressed with himself. He's not sure if he should feel afraid or proud of his actions. He's not sure if he has room for both.

Dawn stands beside him, looking into his face. She's quiet and still for once in her life. She smoothes down the wrinkles in her shorts with the flats of her hands, over and over. He's most likely disturbed her. Or Roy has. Or both of them did. Eliot says, "Come on, let's go back." He doesn't yell at her or yank her wrist. And Dawn follows him up the trail, out of the ravine, back to the cabin.

13. The Assignation

SOMETHING WOKE HER LATE IN the night. *Tap, tap, tap.* Something kept tapping, and so she sat up in bed and looked around her. The mother and father were asleep on their cots, the little old man slept on the other side of the sheet separating them. None of them were tapping.

Then she heard it again, and looked over her shoulder. In the window square, two fireflies hovered, blinking out a message. *Outside. Five minutes.*

The girl quietly got out of her cot and stepped into her sandals. She pulled a piece of hair out of her mouth. Peaking around the corner of the sheet, she watched the little old man for a while, his chest rising and falling in steady rhythms of sleep. Earlier that evening, she and the little old man had sat in their respective corners, on their respective cots, and by the light of a lantern, they had made shadow creatures appear on the sheet separating their rooms. Bats and butterflies, and even a dog's head that could open its mouth and bark. She loved the little old man, and wished she could tell him as much.

Then she tiptoed out of the cabin, closing the door behind her carefully. The two fireflies were waiting for her by the smoldering campfire.

"What's the matter?" the girl asked. "Has something happened?"

The fireflies nodded together. One of them said, "We've found your moth. The one you asked about. Orangey-pink glow, gold and brown streaks on its wings? We found him."

"Oh, thank you so much," she told them. "How can I repay you?"

"Wait," the fireflies both said. "He isn't here with us. You'll have to wait. He was busy. A real snob, if you want our opinions. But he said he would drop by tomorrow evening. He asked why you wanted to meet him. We said you were a new fixture here, and wanted to meet all the neighbors."

"That's wonderful," the girl said, liking the idea of her being a fixture here, of being a part of the natural surroundings.

She told the fireflies she would be waiting by the campfire the next evening, and that they could bring the moth to her there. "Won't my father
be surprised!" she told the fireflies, and they both shrugged, saying, "It's
just a moth, I mean really! What's so special about that?"

You have no idea, she wanted to tell them. But she simply told them
thank you, and crept back into the cabin to sleep.

14. Why Now?

WHEN DR. CARROLL RETURNED FROM his latest outing, he looked ready
to fold up and die on the spot. Eliot and Dawn hung back in the shadows
of the porch, swinging a little, while their mother sat at the campfire with
their father and tried her best to comfort him. There was still no moth, he
told her, and he was ready to face up to the possibility that this summer
has been a total waste, that his memory of something unique that no one
else had ever discovered was probably false.

Eliot decided to make himself and Dawn scarce, so he took her inside
the cabin and, lighting a lantern, entertained her with hand shadows
thrown against the sheet separating their cots. They fell asleep after a
while, and when Eliot wakes the next morning, he finds his mother and
father already outside, cooking breakfast over the fire.

"We're going to leave tomorrow," Eliot's father tells him, whisking eggs
in a stainless steel bowl.

"Good," says Eliot, rubbing sleep out of his eyes. He yawns, and takes
a glass of orange juice his mother offers him. She's been to town already,
and has brought back some fresh food and drinks from Mac's. He takes a
sip of the orange juice and holds it in his mouth for a moment, savoring
the taste.

"Well, I for one have got a lot of work to do when we get back," Eliot's
mother says. "A whole summer spent camping, and I haven't prepared
anything for my fall classes yet."

Eliot looks at Dawn, who sits on a log on the other side of the fire, eating
sausage links with her fingers. He smiles at her, and gives her a wink.
Dawn, to his surprise, smiles and winks back.

The day passes with all of them making preparations to leave the next
day. They pack the wagon full of their clothes and camping equipment,
and then retire at dusk to the fire, where their faces flush yellow and
orange from the flames. All four of them stare at each other, or stare at
the last pot of beans cooking on the fire. They're tired, all of them. Puffy
gray sacs of flesh hang under their eyes. They are a family, Eliot thinks, of

zombies. The walking dead. Faces gray, eyes distant, mouths closed. No one speaks.

Soon after they're finished eating, Dawn gets up from her seat and wanders away from the fire. But not so far that her mother and father can't see where she has gone. Finally, when the fireflies have come to life, filling the night air with an apple green glow, Eliot spots it, his father's moth, pinwheeling through the air around Dawn, surrounded by an orangey-pink halo.

"Dad," he says, "Dad, look." And Dr. Carroll turns to see where Eliot is pointing. A strange little noise comes out of his mouth. Almost a squeak. He heaves himself off the log he's crouched on, and stumbles towards Dawn and the moth.

There it is, thinks Eliot. Why now? Why has it decided to make an appearance after all this time, after all this pain? Why now? he wonders, wanting answers that perhaps don't exist. He suspects Dawn has something to do with it, the same way Dawn made the grasshoppers line up together and do synchronized leaps.

Dr. Carroll shouts, "Keep an eye on it, don't let it get away!" and he rushes to the car to dig through the back for a net or a box. He comes jogging back with a clear plastic box that has a screen fitted into the lid and vents on the sides. A few twigs and leafs wait inside of it. He opens the lid, scoops up the moth, and snaps the box shut.

But then Dawn is squealing. She runs over to her father and tries to pry the box out of his hands. What is she doing? Eliot can't understand why she'd do a thing like that. She's beating at her father's chest, saying—what?—saying, "No! No! No! You can't lock it up like that!"

What? Eliot's thinking. He's thinking, What's happening here?

His mother steps between Dawn and Dr. Carroll, grabbing Dawn around her shoulders to pull her in for a hug. Dawn is sobbing now, her shoulders heaving, and she leans into her mother for the hug, and doesn't let go for fifteen minutes at least. Eliot stays by the fire, afraid of what's going on in front of him. He doesn't know what to do or say.

Dr. Carroll says, "What's wrong with her? I can't believe she tried to do that."

Eliot's mother says, "Leave her alone. Just leave her alone, why don't you? Can't you see she's upset?"

Dr. Carroll walks away from them, holding his box with the moth inside it close to his chest. It glows still. The box lights up like a faery lantern. The smile on his father's face tells Eliot exactly what he is holding. This box, says Eliot's father's smile, contains my youth.

Before and

15. The Message

IT IS LATE NOW, so late that Eliot has fallen asleep for several hours and then, inexplicably, woke in the night. He doesn't have to pee, and he doesn't feel too hot, or sick. But something is wrong, and it makes him sit up and look around the cabin. His parents are asleep on their cots. The cabin is quiet except for their breathing. He gets out of bed, and once again, the coils of the cot squeal as he removes his weight from them. He pulls back a corner of the sheet separating his room from Dawn's and finds that she is not in her bed. She's not in the cabin at all.

Eliot runs out of the cabin in his bare feet. The grass is dewy, wetting his feet. He doesn't look behind the cabin, or by the fire, or in the nearby field. He runs down the trail to the ravine where he hit Roy, and finds Dawn there, standing by the creek. Mist and fog hover over the water. Dawn stands in the mist surrounded by a swarm of fireflies. She looks like a human Christmas tree with all of those lights blinking around her. She looks like a magic creature. Like a woodland spirit, Eliot thinks.

"Dawn," he says when he reaches her. But Dawn holds out her hand and raises one of her fingers. Wait, she is asking. One moment. Wait.

Eliot stands before her, and suddenly the fireflies drop from the air as if they have all had sudden heart attacks, their lights extinguished. They lay at his feet, crawling around in the grasses. Then, all at the same time, their lights flicker on again, and Eliot finds they have arranged themselves into letters. Spelled out in the grass, glowing green, are the words *Love You, Eliot.*

Eliot looks up to find Dawn's face shining with tears, and he feels his own eyes filling. He steps around the fireflies and hugs Dawn, and whispers that he loves her, too. They stay there for a while, hugging, until Eliot takes Dawn's hand and leads her back to the cabin before their parents wake up.

16. Now

WHEN THE CARROLLS RETURN HOME from Pennsylvania, they do their best to return to their lives as they once knew them. Eliot's father, uncanny specimen in hand, sets to work on his new research. His mother resumes classes in the Fall and publishes an essay called "Woman, Nature, Words" in a feminist philosophy journal.

On Mondays, Wednesdays and Fridays, Dawn attends school—she has learned how to say "My name is Dawn Carroll, I am seventeen years old, Thank you, You're Welcome, Goodbye, Goodbye, Goodbye." Goodbye is her favorite new word. She sometimes shouts it at the top of her lungs, and Goodbye floats up to the vaulted ceilings at home, spinning this direction and that, searching for an escape route, a way out of the confines of walls and floors and ceilings. Eventually it bursts, and bits of Goodbye, wet and soapy, fall back down onto her face.

Eliot returns to school as well, to high school, where he learns to slouch and to not look up from his feet, and how to evade talking to other people as much as possible. He begins to dress in black clothes and to listen to depressing music—"Is that what they mean by Gothic?" his mother asks him—but he doesn't dignify her question with an answer. His grades flag and falter. "Needs to work harder," his teachers report. Mr. and Mrs. Carroll send him to a psychologist, a Dr. Emery, who sits behind her desk and doesn't say much of anything. She waits in the long silences for Eliot to begin speaking, and once he starts talking, it's difficult to stop.

Eliot tells her everything that happened over the summer, and Dr. Emery nods a lot and continues to offer little in the way of conversation. Dr. Emery advises Eliot to tell his parents whatever he feels he needs to, and that she will try to help them understand. But Eliot isn't ready, not yet at least, and now that he's told someone else what happened, he wants to think about other things for a while. Video games, music, television, even his schoolwork. Things that are comforting and easy. For now it's enough to have Dr. Emery to talk to, someone safe and understanding. For now.

This is the first in a series of people that Eliot finds he can actually talk to. The others will come to him, friends and lovers, scattered throughout the rest of his life. In a few years he won't even be thinking that no one can understand him. He will be leaning back on his pillows and staring at the neon plastic stars he's pasted to his ceiling, in his own apartment a few blocks from where he attends college, and he will be thinking about that night in the ravine, by the creek. He'll remember Dawn lit up by fireflies, and how they arranged themselves into glowing green letters, like the constellation of glowing stars above him, like the stars he watched through the roof of the rusted-out corvette with Roy. He'll think about his sister and how she learned to speak the language of moths, the language of fireflies and crickets. How he had learned the language of love and betrayal, the language of self-hate and mistrust. How much more his sister knew, he realizes later, than he ever did.

When he thinks about Dawn's message, Eliot will be in love with someone who loves him back. This boy that he'll love will be asleep beside him while Eliot stays awake, staring at the stars above, thinking about Dawn's message.

Love You, Eliot, she had instructed the fireflies to spell out.

At the time, Eliot had interpreted Dawn's message to mean she loved him, and of course there's that, too. But when he thinks about it now, in the future, he's not so sure. The "I" of her message was mysteriously missing, but its absence might only have been an informal gesture on Dawn's part. He wonders now if Dawn was saying something entirely different that night. Has he misunderstood her message, or only understood half of it? Meaning is always lost, at least partially, in translation, he thinks.

Love You, Eliot, she had told him, the letters glowing like green embers in the grass.

Now, in the future, this future that he imagined so many years ago, the future in which he lived in his own apartment, with his own television and his own books, the future in which he goes to college and finds himself not as wrong or as weird as he once thought he was, in this future he wonders if Dawn was also giving him a piece of advice.

Love You, Eliot, she had told him.

And he does that. He knows how to do that.

Now.

Christopher Barzak

Before and

Publication History

"What We Know About the Lost Families of – House," *Interfictions*, 2007
"The Drowned Mermaid," *Realms of Fantasy*, 2003
"Dead Boy Found," *Trampoline*, 2003
"A Mad Tea Party," *Lady Churchill's Rosebud Wristlet*, 1999
"Born on the Edge of an Adjective," *Lady Churchill's Rosebud Wristlet*, 2002
"The Other Angelas," *Pindeldyboz*, 2004
"A Resurrection Artist," *The Third Alternative*, 2004
"The Boy Who Was Born Wrapped in Barbed Wire," *The Journal of Mythic Arts*, 2005
"Map of Seventeen," *The Beastly Bride*, 2010
"Dead Letters," *Realms of Fantasy*, 2006
"Plenty," *Strange Horizons*, 2001
"The Ghost Hunter's Beautiful Daughter," *Asimov's Science Fiction*, 2009
"Caryatids," *Nerve*, 2001
"A Beginner's Guide to Survival Before, During, and After the Apocalypse," original to the book
"Smoke City," *Asimov's Science Fiction*, 2011
"Vanishing Point," *Descant*, 2003
"The Language of Moths," *Realms of Fantasy*, 2005

Christopher Barzak   **Before and**

Acknowledgements

MY HEARTFELT THANKS GOES OUT to the editors who first brought many of these stories to readers of their magazines and anthologies: Delia Sherman, Theodora Goss, Kelly Link, Gavin Grant, Sheila Williams, Scott Westerfeld, Andy Cox, Ellen Datlow, Terri Windling, Susan Marie Groppi, Jed Hartman, Karen Meisner, Lynne Thomas, and Shawna McCarthy. Thank you also to Richard Bowes, Mary Rickert, Alan DeNiro, Kristin Livdahl, and Barth Anderson, who served as first readers for many of these stories. The publisher of this collection, Steve Berman, deserves more gratitude than words can possibly convey. And more than anyone, thank you, Tony Romandetti, for everything you do to help me keep telling stories.

CHRISTOPHER BARZAK grew up in rural Ohio, went to university in a decaying post-industrial city in Ohio, and has lived in a Southern California beach town, the capital of Michigan, and in the suburbs of Tokyo, Japan. His stories have appeared in a many venues, including *Nerve*, *The Year's Best Fantasy and Horror*, *Interfictions*, *Asimov's*, and *Lady Churchill's Rosebud Wristlet*. His first novel, *One for Sorrow*, won the Crawford Award. His second book, *The Love We Share Without Knowing*, is a novel-in-stories set in a magical realist modern Japan, and was a finalist for the Nebula Award for Best Novel and the James Tiptree Jr. Award. He is the co-editor of *Interfictions 2*, and has done Japanese-English translation on *Kant: For Eternal Peace*, a peace theory book published in Japan for Japanese teens. He is also the author of *Birds and Birthdays*, a triptych of short stories inspired by surrealist painters. Currently he lives in Youngstown, Ohio, where he teaches fiction writing in the Northeast Ohio MFA program at Youngstown State University.

CPSIA information can be obtained at www.ICGtesting.com
Printed in the USA
BVOW08s0126140715

408674BV00002B/48/P